I0526726

Spirit of the

Wolf

Edited by Carol Hightshoe

WolfSinger Publications ❭ Brackettville, Texas

Copyright © 2025 by WolfSinger Publications
All Stories Copyright by their authors

All rights reserved.
No part of this book may be used or reproduced in any manner
whatsoever without the written permission of the copyright owner.

For permission requests, please contact WolfSinger Publications at
editor@wolfsingerpubs.com

All characters and events in this book are fictitious.
Any resemblance to persons living or dead is strictly coincidental.

Cover Art © 2025 by Carol Hightshoe

ISBN 978-1-944637-78-1

Printed and bound in the United States of America

Table of Contents

Introduction

High in the mountains of southern Colorado, where wind whispers through the pines and stars burn brighter than city lights, there is a sanctuary built from compassion, perseverance, and the wild song of wolves. It is called Mission: Wolf—a place where the voices of wolves still echo across the ridges.

Mission: Wolf began with a promise. Its founders, Kent Weber and Tracy Ane Brooks, saw what happened when human fascination with wolves turned to possession—when wild spirits were born into cages, bred for novelty rather than respect. They created a refuge for those animals who could never again return to the wild, a home built in the mountains where wolves and wolf-dogs could live out their lives safely, with dignity and care.

The sanctuary runs on sunlight, hard work, and heart. Every fencepost and cabin has been raised by volunteers. Every howl that rises into the Colorado air is a reminder that even in captivity, the wild heart endures. Visitors who travel the long dirt road to the site often speak of the hush that falls when they first hear the pack call —a sound that humbles, a sound that reconnects them to something ancient and essential inside us all.

The people of Mission: Wolf do more than care for the animals in their charge. They teach respect—for wolves, for the wild, and for the delicate balance between humans and nature. Their work reminds us coexistence is possible, that understanding can replace fear, and that every act of kindness ripples outward.

This anthology was born from that same spirit. Within these pages are stories that celebrate wolves in all their forms—mythic and modern, fierce and gentle, real and imagined. They honor the guardians of the wilderness, the symbols of loyalty and freedom, and the echoes of the primal song that still stirs in our blood.

Every story shared here carries a piece of that song—and every book sold will help sustain the sanctuary that keeps it alive. Proceeds from this collection will be donated to Mission: Wolf, to aid their continued care, education, and advocacy for these magnificent creatures.

The Natural Order of Things

Michael La Ronn

My aunt and I were mushroom hunting in the woods when the deafening rifle crack rang out through the trees. Everyone on the globe heard it, from the pine forests of Oregon to the Tibetan plateau, including the yelp that followed, for it was the death of the wolf and the death of the world as we knew it.

They say the actual death occurred somewhere in the forests of Europe. I don't want to imagine the majestic animal lying on its side, drawing a final breath in the middle of a tragic light-soaked clearing. I don't want to imagine the hunters pushing aside sharp branches to behold their spoil.

My aunt and I felt the shift instantly. The sharp smell of pine resin in the air morphed into something dull, wet, and coppery. The pines shook down their cones in a furious rain and the earth trembled as the world's energy tilted violently on a supernatural axis.

We heard the shot, practically felt it. My aunt fell moaning into the wet dirt. I tossed aside my bag of morels and held her.

I live with my aunt in the woods on the Oregon coast. When I turned eighteen, my parents kicked me out of the house. They said it was time for me to find my own way through the woods of life, so to speak. Such a cruel way to treat a teenager. I wasn't ready. I was just a girl uncertain about her future. Getting thrown into the wilderness didn't help.

I spent every dollar I had to travel to Oregon. I stood on the doorstep of Aunt Raella's yurt in the middle of the woods during a torrential downpour. She took one look at my haggard, frightened face and she knew. She ushered me into her amber-lit yurt filled with half-painted canvases, made me a cup of tea, and she listened with the wood fire flickering in her brown eyes. When I think of her, I think of the warmth—not only in her eyes, but also in the Irish fisherman sweaters she was so fond of, and in the cozy cups of herbal tea whose leaves she grew in her garden.

Aunt Rae doesn't ask anything from me, and I don't ask anything from her. Sometimes we live in each other's presence for days without saying anything at all. Other times, we savor each other, like when we hunt mushrooms in the spring after rain.

She always warned me the day would come—that the world would kill the wolf and we'd have to be ready. But no warning could have lessened the shock.

The first news reports of the wolf's extinction aired the same night as the rifle crack. The gunshot still rang in our ears as the anchors of the world read a unified message.

Good evening. Tonight, we share somber news: the last known wolf has passed away, marking the extinction of an iconic species. Wolves, long celebrated for their majesty and importance to ecosystems, are now gone forever—a loss that has stunned the world.

Never again will a lone wolf's mournful howl echo under a silver moon, or will a pack move as one, weaving through the forest like shadows in pursuit of their prey. The world has grown quieter, the wilderness emptier, with their passing.

In response, many governments have declared a day of mourning. Vigils are taking place globally, offering communities a chance to grieve and honor the wolf's legacy. Attendees are encouraged to bring meaningful items, such as photos or memorabilia, symbolizing the wolf's spirit.

Stay with us for more on this developing story.

And develop it did.

Imagine candlelight vigils in every city. Crying men and women holding flickering candles in a grassy courtyard, or maybe a cordoned-off urban intersection, or the edge of a cornfield as stars began to wash across the night sky.

Now, imagine all those people with their wolf-related bric-a-brac that could decorate the gaudy flea markets of the world: frumpy t-shirts with wolves howling at the moon, angsty wolf posters, rugs, rings, shot glasses, necklaces, and more.

Can you hear the stereos playing "Hungry Like the Wolf" by Duran Duran and "The Wolf at the Door" by Radiohead?

Well, maybe you can imagine all of this, and maybe you can hear the music. But none of these things happened.

All traces of the wolf on the memorabilia of the world also faded away. They vanished into the night just before the candlelight vigils.

All those t-shirts turned blank. The wolves etched into the rings and woven into the rugs disappeared too. All known recordings of those famous songs could no longer be found. Even the phrases in common vernacular suddenly became difficult to recall. Lone wolf…raised by wolves…wolf in sheep's clothing. Suddenly, people had to use other words.

The world learned what the word "extinct" truly meant.

Aunt Raella and I knew this would happen. We didn't need to visit town to see the confusion that ensued.

We knew the conversations people would be having in the middle of the streets, scratching their heads as they tried to recall the wolf and the words to describe it. The words would skate to the tips of their tongues, only to vanish like a timber wolf in the pines.

We knew the shop owners who would be staring at their shelves, unable to believe all their products were suddenly blank and had no value. They would forfeit their products by the truckload. The landfills of the world would pile up as if humanity were throwing dead wolves on them.

We knew all the books, movies, and television shows rendered nonsensical now because every reference to the wolf would be removed. Try watching "Dances with Wolves" or reading a paranormal romance novel about wolf shifters…without wolves.

But Aunt Rae and I have a secret.

The wolf didn't die inside us. We can still see it and all its majesty: the piercing cabochon-like eyes, the furrowing snout, the razor-sharp teeth. We hold the wonderful creature in our mind's eyes. It lives there, and we feed it with our sympathy. Packs run wild across the slanted snowy fields of our minds. Somewhere, a lone wolf howls at a moon that shines between our world and the next.

We still know all the words, all the songs, all the references. We hold the wolf in our heads like precious water.

Aunt Rae is an artist. She paints watercolors and oils, mostly of landscapes both real and imagined. Her yurt brims with canvases, and we live in a labyrinth of artwork.

Sometimes we eat rubbing elbows against surreal forests dripping in autumn reds and golds. I sleep on the futon in the corner under the watchful eyes of the animal portraits Aunt Rae paints.

Ironically, she never painted a wolf as long as I lived with her. Once, I asked why not.

"One day, I'll paint enough wolves to last me forever," she said. "And so will you."

She taught me how to paint. Aside from a really cool portrait of an owl I painted once, I'm not very good. I can do landscapes okay, but I struggle with lighting. Aunt Rae once said the sunlight I painted looked like it was from another world. She meant it as a compliment, but it always hurt my feelings.

But now that the wolf is dead, I *must* paint. I don't have a choice.

On the night the wolf died, Aunt Rae and I returned home from mushroom hunting as quickly as we could.

The smell of the yurt's wooden lattice walls and drying canvas greeted us as we rushed inside. I put on a kettle and fished out all the extra paint from a storage cabinet. Aunt Rae brought in all the blank canvases from her storage shed.

We laid everything out on the fading rug in the middle of the room. We had enough to paint for a week nonstop. Only then would we have to drive into town.

Aunt Rae set up her first canvas on an easel and wheeled toward it on a stool with a palette in her fingers. I watched in wonder as she splotched the first blob of gray paint on white.

She worked at the canvas with the skill of a tearful virtuoso. Each stroke tortured her, and at one point I thought I would have to call an ambulance. I couldn't tell where Aunt Rae ended and the paint began. She became the painting—the portrait of a wolf in double exposure.

I watched her until the sun dropped into the trees. The night cast long shadows that started in the soft dome ceiling and swept gently down across our candlelit home.

The canine's head clarified into focus, followed by a furry neck that seemed to drip every Oregon pine and spruce onto the bottom of the canvas. Careful flecks of yellow completed the luminous eyes.

When my aunt feathered her brush across the animal's nose, a chill ran down my back.

We had taken that precious water in our heads and poured it onto the canvas.

We had so much more to pour.

A week passed. Aunt Rae painted her canvases, and I imitated her. I was convinced my amateur swirls didn't match hers. The moonlight didn't fall on my wolf packs as it did on hers. Her paintings were as if they were scrim-lit; mine looked like a high school art student's—awkward and otherworldly, like they belonged in a flea market.

I painted a geometric wolf stalking toward the viewer in a swirling, psychedelic aperture that seemed as if it were going to shutter any moment.

I painted a dreamcatcher whose netted curves met in the aquamarine eyes of an alpha. The colors bent like a reflection on a pond before rippling away.

I painted a mother suckling her pups in the shadows of a crepuscular cave. As I painted it, I wondered what kind of world awaited them outside.

I expected Aunt Rae to criticize my paintings. I craved her soft criticism to confirm for me that I had no talent. But she hardly spoke to me. We didn't need to speak.

Aunt Rae started her last piece. She used a dry brushing technique with a stiff bristle that made the paint rise off the canvas in gorgeous ridges. A pack of brown wolves walking together on a rocky outcrop, probably in the Himalayas somewhere. The pristine mountain sky swelled over them, endless, curved, and blue. Powdered mountains rose into the clouds, and on the horizon—just over there—a hawk tilted toward the sun.

The rough-textured scene struck me as the beginning of a story. An adventure underscored by a dramatic symphony as the camera panned over the valley, up the mountains, and toward a golden-lettered title slowly fading into view.

My aunt adorned the hawk's final wing and stepped back. She took my hand and asked me how beautiful it was. I told her it was her best work.

"Do you really think so?" she asked.

"It's the best, Aunt Rae. It's going to make such an impact."

"I…hope so."

She felt flush. I sat her down and made her a cup of basil tea. I helped her into bed and pulled a fleece blanket over her, kissed her on the forehead.

She watched me paint a canvas that represented a gray and black bicolor wolf's fur.

"Thoroughly esoteric," she said. "Thoroughly canine."

As I blended the fur, I wanted to know something.

"Aunt Rae, do you think the world will even care about what we're doing? I mean, they'll be curious that we have all this knowledge, but will it be enough? It has been such a long week, and you are tired. I am tired. I'm scared, Aunt Rae. Once we reveal ourselves, I don't know how we're going to navigate it all. We'll be famous. Ha ha, maybe we can upgrade to an extra-large yurt. Plant that Christmas tree farm you always wanted to have. Auntie?"

My aunt usually snored. She was silent.

She lay sleeping in the bed, the moonlight falling through the yurt's leaded casement windows into gentle pools on the fleece blanket.

But something felt wrong. I inched toward her, every hair on my body raising in an electric hum. My heart pounded. When I placed my hand on hers and sensed the fading warmth in her palms, I wept.

Aunt Rae was dead.

It was all up to me now.

I rented an art gallery in town—a small, brick-walled boutique space just big enough to house all of our pieces. It stood solitary in the joisted masonry town square, flanked by a law office and bank.

It took me seven trips from the farm to town in Aunt Rae's pickup truck to transport all the paintings.

I was so tired. My bones ached.

I barely remembered the phone calls to all the media outlets. At first, they dismissed me as a kook, but when I told them to high tail it to the gallery address and that I promised to show the world what it had recently forgotten…well, the journalists couldn't resist.

I wanted to sleep, but I couldn't. Daylight twisted into moonlight and moonlight softened into dawn. I stood in front of a dozen camera crews eager to glimpse behind the reveal curtains.

The photoflashes blinded me. The constant question shouting unnerved me. I checked my watch, waited for the second hand to crawl to twelve, announcing the top of the hour.

I inhaled, exhaled, then opened my mouth to speak.

But I didn't say anything.

My lips moved, but the collective voice of the wolf spoke through me.

"We are leaving," it said. "You didn't learn the lessons we taught you. We hoped you would rise, but we watched you falter. You took us for granted. We have left you these paintings as mementos of our time on this earth. Now you must learn to live without us. We will return someday, perhaps millennia from now. Do not be sad. Do not feel guilty. We are free, and we will prepare the next world for your coming. We wish to impart a final lesson upon you."

"What is it?" the journalists asked, lenses flashing.

I started to speak, but suddenly my legs wobbled. My eyes felt heavy. The gallery and all my paintings twirled around me slowly as if I were a spinning top on its final revolution.

I collapsed onto the floor and hit my head.

I woke to a gentle, warm hand on my face.

Aunt Rae. I sat up in her bed. The cool, pine-laced breeze of the forest streamed in from the open window behind me.

"You were wonderful," Aunt Rae said. A flickering fire lit her silvering hair in a fiery glow.

I glanced around. We were in her yurt—I was sure of that—but the moonlight didn't seem right. And, well, obviously, Aunt Rae was dead.

The yurt walls disconnected with a loud snap, letting in more of the cool air. Aunt Rae and I watched as the walls fluttered toward the sun, throwing a brilliant corona across the blue sky.

"Aunt Rae—"

My aunt put a finger to her lips and helped me out of bed.

The forest around us slid away, as if invisible hands grabbed the trees by the edges and spread them out. Then the hands bent the ground into a bowl-shaped valley. Mountains ratcheted up from the horizon.

A few hundred yards away, several shapes waved at us. I recognized them as my parents. They were smiling.

"I told you not to be too hard on them," Aunt Rae said. "You had to come to me for the good of the pack."

I squinted at her. "Pack?"

Aunt Rae began walking. Her tiny frame shrank until a black wolf loped across the rock.

Ahead, my parents had transformed into wolves. They began walking toward the mountains.

Suddenly, I knew what to do. As my skin morphed to wavering fur, excitement burned through my body.

But before I tell you what lay beyond, let me share our final message. The message I hope will transcend universes. Abide by it, and I will see you in the next world.

You may not be free, but live as if you are.

Life is understood in loneliness and reflection, but it is meant to be lived together.

I whispered those words again as I slipped into my final form and followed my aunt. Together, we crossed through a veiled curtain of light that hung over the rocks. As we passed, the curtain trembled and sighed with a final, mournful howl that circled the globe before dying somewhere in the pines.

~ *  * ~

Michael La Ronn has published over 100 science fiction & fantasy novels and self-help books for writers. He writes bold, imaginative science fiction & fantasy featuring underdogs, unusual heroes, and the power of found family. His fiction includes the urban fantasy Good Necromancer series, the dark fantasy Last Dragon Lord series, and the futuristic science fiction Android X series.

Michael devoted himself to the writing life in 2012 after a near-death experience, writing while juggling a demanding full-time job as an insurance executive, raising a family, and attending law school classes in the evenings. His productivity methods are so effective that his YouTube subscribers have accused him of being a cyborg in disguise (he pleads the fifth).

If you enjoyed "The Natural Order of Things," dive into more short fiction with Michael La Ronn's *Strange Stories* series—available in ebook, paperback, and audiobook formats at your favorite retailer. Explore his catalog at www.michaellaronn.com.

Love Song for the Moon

Janice Rider

My people love stories. The first story I ever heard as a pup was told to me by my mother. It explains how wolves came to be. I will tell this story to you so that you understand my people and their ancestors better.

In the days when the Earth was young, Sun was self-assured and bold. Sun was also generous and permitted plants to capture some of his energy and convert it into food for plant eaters, which in turn became food for flesh eaters. When the theropods, meat eating dinosaurs who walked on two feet, evolved into feathered creatures that could fly, Sun was impressed by their diversity and beauty. Most of these feathered ones worshiped the warmth and light of Sun. They celebrated the dawn of each new day with a chorus of bird songs and a flurry of feathers. This adulation went, over a period of time, to Sun's head. He thought to himself, "All of creation should praise me, for I am the most radiant star in the solar system."

Sun spoke to the creatures of the Earth, his bass voice booming, "I want all of you to worship me each morning. All of you must raise your voices to the sky at the first hint of dawn." There were many animals who grumbled and groused about this edict, but as Sun was integral to their life on the planet, the creatures of the Earth decided they would, indeed, raise their voices to the sky at the beginning of each new day. That is, all the creatures of the Earth agreed to capitulate to Sun's demand except for our early ancestors, animals called miacids. These ancestors of ours had long, elegant bodies, and lengthy tails. The miacids were also independent thinkers and carried themselves with dignity and grace as they went about their business, much of which consisted of catching small mammals and invertebrates to eat. Their prey wasn't large because miacids weren't big, powerful animals; in fact, they were little bigger than ground squirrels.

On the first day following Sun's proclamation, the clamor of sound coming from the Earth was tremendous. It was a positive cacophony. Amidst such a clamor, it would be logical to conclude Sun couldn't tell if the miacids were part of the tumult or not; however, Sun knew right away one group of animals was not saluting his morning rising ritual. He just didn't know who wasn't contributing to the racket.

As for Moon, who had been diligently reflecting Sun's rays all the previous night, the tremendous noise coming from the Earth made her feel quite queasy. Her habitual state of mind was calm and peaceful, but the discordant sounds sent ripples of rage through her body. It was her custom to rest throughout the day, while the sun sparkled and gleamed, but that day she couldn't rest as a result of her anger. When night fell, she refused to reflect Sun's light while he rested, and the Earth was plunged into such a deep state of darkness that even nocturnal creatures were forced to stay in their homes, and all animals quivered in fear under the night's intense embrace.

In the morning, when the animals of the Earth complained to Sun about the eerie and utter blackness of the night, he was furious. Moon needed a talking to, he decided, and he went to speak with her. "It is your job to reflect my light at night," he admonished. "Why weren't you doing your duty?"

Moon squinted as she gazed at Sun's brilliance. "Yesterday morning, there was such a ruckus from the Earth, I was unable to relax and rest. Therefore, when Darkness rolled her blanket over the planet, I wasn't up to the task of reflecting your light. I was still recovering. What was all that noise about, anyway?"

"It wasn't noise! It was a joyful greeting of my return to the sky!"

"Wasn't the dawn chorus of the birds enough?"

"Without me, there would be no life on Earth. Everyone should pay their respects to me. Absolutely everyone. And speaking of paying respects, one group of creatures neglected to raise their voices in praise of me."

Moon gave a sigh, but she was interested in this information. "Who omitted to welcome your arrival this morning?" she asked.

"I'm not sure, but I'm sure to find out."

"Whoever the creatures are, they should be applauded for pulling back from such a brouhaha."

"You are in an uncivil mood today, Sister!"

"As you would be if you were disturbed during your recuperation time, Brother. May I suggest that things go back to the way they were? After all, I don't expect to be serenaded for my part in helping out the Earth, and I am the keeper of the tides."

Sun flared, hot red splotches appearing on his cheeks. "The morning ritual shall continue!"

Moon did reflect Sun's light that night. She knew he had asked the creatures of the Earth to report any animal that didn't celebrate the dawn. Reflecting Sun's rays, she peered into crevices and crannies, under rocks and in caves, beneath trees and roots. It was amongst some roots that she spotted a group of miacids seated in a circle and talking earnestly. Listening in, she discovered they were the ones who'd neglected to demonstrate their appreciation of her brother's morning arrival.

"It is not good for Sun to be so full of himself," one of the lithe animals said. "He is liable to swell with importance and make the world a much hotter place."

"Yes," another miacid with an intelligent face replied, "you are quite right. It is one thing for Sun to receive appreciation, but quite another for him to dictate that we flatter him."

"Myself," a third individual said, "I prefer the pale light that Moon casts. Hunting in the cool, sweet hours of the early night under Moon's light is lovely. Besides, Moon doesn't flaunt herself the way Sun does."

The original speaker sighed. "What if one of the other creatures informs Sun about our lack of compliance?"

The group of miacids contemplated this question. As a rule, the animals of the Earth did not try to make trouble for one another. Yes, they had to eat according to the dictates of their bodies, but that was about survival.

At this point, Moon spoke. "Miacids, I congratulate you on your ability to think for yourselves and act in the interests of the community of creatures on this planet. I believe I can intercede on your behalf."

The miacids turned astonished faces with long snouts in her direction. Moon was able to see her own reflection in their dark eyes. Then, as if on an invisible cue, the miacids turned and vanished into the forest. Their bushy tails disappeared last.

The next day, when Sun came up, Moon rose, too. The two of

them stood together in the sky, Moon wearing a serene expression and Sun wearing a sullen, suspicious one. "What are you about, Sister?" Sun asked, speaking loudly to make himself heard above the uproar from beneath them.

"I am here to listen to the creatures of the Earth sing my praises!" Moon yelled.

"They are singing my praises, not yours!"

"Well, that's alright. I'll wait until they're finished honoring you with their pandemonium, and then they can begin to honor me with soft lullabies, so that I may rest."

Sun flushed crimson with vexation. "You have never required lullabies to soothe you before, why should you need them now?"

"You have never needed this commotion to welcome you as you rise from your bed before. Why is it necessary now?"

"You are impossible!"

"And you are incorrigible!"

The animals on the Earth became quiet. Then a miacid slid out from under the roots of a tree. The miacid folded her paws over her chest and began to sing. For such a tiny mammal, she had a powerful voice. She sang of the oceans from which all life came. She sang of the strange miracle of life, its mystery and its diversity. She sang of Sun's warmth and Moon's soft glow. She sang of the pull of tides and the need to embrace our true natures. Her baritone voice was magical.

As Sun listened to the miacid, his pride slipped away, lulled as he was by the music. As Moon listened, she felt every fiber of her being resonate. All the other animals were entranced by the haunting rise and fall of the melody. When the miacid finished, Sun inquired, "Who are you?"

"Ylva," the miacid said.

"Ylva, your music has brought me to my senses," Sun said. "I shall see to it Creator hears from me about you."

"I, too, shall mention you to Creator, Ylva," Moon told the miacid.

And so, from that time onward, the dawn chorus consisted of birdsong, and Moon was able to rest during the day. But Sun and Moon kept their promises and told Creator about the courageous miacid, Ylva, and her valiant people. As a result, Creator made some changes to the miacids. They grew bigger and more powerful over time. In recognition of their ability to work together, they were blessed with strong family bonds. They cooperated with one another to achieve what individuals could not. And every night, they sang love songs to the Moon. In short, our ancestors, the miacids, became wolves.

I stand on a bluff overlooking the meadow below. Moon is round and full in the evening sky, although faint wisps of cloud are drifting across her face like thin veils. In her light, it is easy to see a herd of bison resting in the meadow. Most of the herd are lying down, but there are sentries on duty. Two of these sentries are massive bulls. On the edge of the herd, I spot an animal that is injured. It is a bull, and this individual rests its nose on the ground and tips its head at an odd angle. It is the latter part of the summer, a time when bulls are in rut and fighting for the right to breed with cows. Perhaps this male was injured in a battle.

I raise my nose towards the night sky and fix my eyes on Moon before beginning to howl. It seems to me Moon shivers with pleasure, but it might be the clouds hanging around her moving enough to give the illusion Moon is vibrating. As my voice floats out on the air, I can see the fog of my breath. From beneath me, two other wolves, my mother, our pack leader, and my brother, Bardou, call back to me. From my left, just below the bluff I stand on, my sister, Lovette, howls. Her voice holds intimations of my mother's voice. Then my father calls from below the bluff on my right, his deep bass tones descending into dark depths. Each of us sings using a different pitch, which makes it easy to know who is calling. The vocalizations of my family are familiar and dear to me. They remind me of my connections, and my heart swells with love.

I notice the two bull sentries stiffen to attention. They swivel their enormous heads around, and look up in my direction. I descend to my family members, greeting each of them by wagging my tail and licking their muzzles. They respond in kind. Mother whines, "Did you see a bison that looks like a promising meal?"

"I did. A bull is lying at the edge of the herd. He is holding his head as if in pain."

"Then perhaps we shall eat," Father barks.

Each time we embark on a hunt, we are more likely to fail than succeed in bringing down prey. Animals like bison are formidable opponents, and should one of my family members get injured, their chance of survival is low. As a result, we prefer to wear our prey down before closing in for the kill. A dangerous animal like a bison is easier to subdue once it has expended much of its energy and we have less chance of a tired animal goring one of us with a horn or kicking one of us with a flailing hoof. Unlike cougars and other cats, who rely on stealth and a sudden burst of speed to catch prey, we wolves are built for distance running. Our legs are long, our muscles are lean, and our deep chests permit us to capture large amounts of air in our lungs. We have been known to chase prey for hours, and on rare occasions, days. It's a good thing we revel in running because we have to do a lot of it.

My family and I move down onto the meadow together, entreating Moon to grant us success. We pretend we have no particular target in mind, trotting along in a casual fashion, but the sleeping bison are alerted by the snorts of the sentries and scramble to their feet. Calves tuck in close to their mothers' flanks. Affecting nonchalance, we gaze up at Moon, honoring her with our eyes and noting her regal bearing in the sky. The bison grumble and rumble around us, a symphony of low voices. "Quit dissembling, Wolves! We know what you're about. When we arrived on this continent, you were already here. We learned about you quickly enough."

"Then you learned that we need to eat," Lovette says.

"Full wolves are happy wolves," Bardou yips.

Mother and Father hold their tongues. They don't see the point of bantering with bison. The bull on the edge of the herd rises to his feet with difficulty. Like all my kind, I am observant, and the bull's pain is as evident as if it were my own. As we thread our way amongst wary mothers and calves, he stands with his head hanging low to the ground. He is weary. Suddenly, on Mother's cue, a sharp snap of her head, we swivel ninety degrees and charge at the herd. This unexpected attack startles them into plunging away from us and pushes them away from the fatigued bull. We follow the herd for a ways and then reverse direction to sprint back to our target. He has backed himself up against a thick stand of cottonwoods and stands, waiting. We take turns attacking from first one side and then the other, drawing his attention right and then left. His vulnerable hindquarters are difficult to access. His mammoth head and its sharp, black horns swivel from side to side. We play the long game, coming in again and again. After three hours, the bull lowers his great bulk to the ground. He says to us, "I surrender to your need to eat. Soon, I shall run with those of my kind who have passed before me. Don't forget to give thanks for my life."

Wary of the bull's hooves, we plunge in where we are safest and finish the job we started. The bull has a wound in his right shoulder, where he was gored by another male. We can tell the wound is infected by its smell. His misfortune has benefited our pack on this night, and it feels good to fill our bellies. Once we have eaten, we pay our respects to the bull for his life and his death. He is part of us now, and we are grateful his strength has passed into our bodies. Next, we serenade Moon, our benefactress, our poignant voices rising up beyond the reach of the trees beyond the meadow.

Afterwards, we head back to our rendezvous site. Another sister of mine, Ulla, is babysitting there, watching over my parents' latest offspring, my youngest siblings, four pups almost four months old. Ulla and the pups greet us with enthusiasm, licking our muzzles repeatedly, urging us to regurgitate food for them, which we do. We speak of the hunt, then, describing it in detail as Ulla and the pups eat, not forgetting to mention Moon in our telling. Moon must always be honored. Then we find comfortable places to lay down and sleep. My brother, Bardou, and I curl up against one another, sharing our warmth and our friendship.

Under my front paws, I have a marten's long, bushy tail pinned down. The rest of the animal's slender body is curled towards me, and it is showing me a fine set of pointed teeth. Martens have short legs and sharp claws on their feet in order to move with ease through the trees after their favorite prey, squirrels. This one, though, came across the carcass of the bull bison my family and I killed and was greedily stuffing himself when I caught him unawares early this morning. "Looks like you're in a spot of trouble," I say.

The marten gazes up into my eyes with impudence. "You're Ylva, aren't you?"

"Yes."

"Named after your famous ancestor?"

"Correct."

"You won't hurt me."

"What makes you say that?"

"My mother told me your miacid ancestors resembled creatures like me. She said wolves won't kill animals that look like their ancestors."

"Your mother is correct," I tell him, removing my feet from his tail. "But my sense of satisfaction at having trodden on your tail is immense. Whom do I have the pleasure of addressing?"

"Sable."

"Well, Sable, you may eat as much of this bison as you wish. I dare say the ravens will soon join in the feast, too."

"Did you know Goliath has scented your kill?" Sable asks. "The bear is moving this way as we speak."

Goliath. The grizzly. He is an impenetrable mass of muscle and hair. What's more, he can really eat. I sigh. "Thanks for letting me know, Sable." Pointing my muzzle to the sky, I let my family know what's happening. They are with me when Goliath arrives, as are a number of ravens. Sable is ensconced in a tree at the meadow's edge, watching us all with bright eyes.

Goliath moves with gravity and dignity. He is an old bear, but he is powerful and well respected by other bears, as well as animals like ourselves. As he saunters our way, he growls at us, "Move, Wolves. It is my turn."

"We would be more amenable to your feasting if you ate less," I say.

"We're worried that once your turn is over, only scraps will be on offer," Bardou chimes in.

"If you get any bigger, you're liable to pop," Lovette teases.

My parents make a sudden rush at Goliath with bared teeth, but he sits his imposing bulk down beside the carcass without even glancing their way. "As far as I'm concerned," he chuckles, "you're still miacids. Look how skinny and fragile you all are in comparison to me." Goliath strips some meat from a bone, and I salivate.

"It's a curious thing," I remark. "Our ancestors resembled animals like martens and yours resembled animals like us."

"Your point?" Goliath asks.

"Well, it seems to me that, when all is said and done, we're all very much alike."

The grizzly shakes his head and scratches the top of it with the long claws of a massive paw. "Bears are not philosophers, Wolf. We do not sit and ponder the ways of the world or cogitate upon our beginnings. We are practical. We eat, eat, and eat, then we sleep before repeating the cycle."

My family and I lie down in the grass, watching in envy as Goliath gorges himself. Ravens help themselves to lots of scraps, and the bear is content to let them partake of the meal, too. Wise birds, the ravens. We wolves have a close relationship with these proud creatures. Often they lead us to kills, making our lives easier, and we show our gratitude by letting them dine with us. When Goliath finishes stuffing his belly, he waddles away and stretches out under some trees surrounding the meadow to sleep.

We join the ravens on the bull bison, eating until our own bellies are round again, then hang about to ensure some other predator, like a cougar, doesn't steal from the carcass. Bardou returns to the rendezvous site, though, to feed the pups and give Ulla a chance to join us at the kill. In the late afternoon, the rest of us return to the rendezvous site together.

Once all of us have congregated, our hunger satiated and our bodies rested, we romp with the puppies. They are brazen, these siblings of mine, pulling on tails, pouncing on our shoulders, and snarling with pretended ferocity. I love these family times. It is at times like these I feel most relaxed and content, most safe and secure. My parents' eyes shine with love and pride, and they too, are objects of the playful pranks of their children. Lovette encourages one of the pups to chase and wrestle her for a leg bone she brought back.

By the time Moon rises, we are sprawled in various postures upon the ground under the trees, but Moon's presence invites us to rise. We begin to sing. We sing of the oceans from which all life came. We sing of the strange miracle of life, its mystery and its diversity. We sing of Sun's warmth and Moon's soft glow. We sing of the pull of tides and the need to embrace our true natures. Our voices harmonize, rising and falling in unison like the rise and fall of tides, honoring life's fragility and its persistence.

~ * 🐺 * ~

Janice Rider (she/her) resides in Calgary, Alberta, Canada, close to the Rocky Mountains. She has a deep love of the outdoors, and this is reflected in her writing. Janice's background is in zoology, conservation, and education. Wolves have always fascinated Janice. Five of her short stories are in the following anthologies: the North American Jules Verne Society's *Extraordinary Visions*, Word Balloon Books' *Beware the Bugs*, Speculation Publications' *Beach Shorts*, and Critical Blast Publishing's *The Devil You Know Best* and *The Fables Next Door*. Janice directs *The Chameleon Drama Club* for children and youth. Three of her plays for youth have been published with Eldridge Plays and Musicals.

More information related to Janice may be found on LinkedIn.

The Unsatisfactory

Nature of Existence

Steven Lente

Wolf M182 was dead, at least that's what Clifton Stewart at the Minnesota Wolf Management Center in Ely presumed. Clifton had monitored M182 and his mate, M181, for over six years; their first catch-and-release radio collaring and physical exam suggested M182 was three years old then, which now made him about nine and over twice the average age of wolves in the wild.

Notification of a death typically comes after three days of non-movement when a tracking collar sends a separate code known as the 'mortality' signal. The biologists who actually go out to search for the one-and-a-half pound collars often hope to find them simply stuck on a low tree limb or a bush, but Clifton's long experience with observing this pack's semi-annual comings and goings between Canada and the United States suggested otherwise; he was not as optimistic, and he started making loose plans to locate the source of the signal and investigate its cause before winter set in. However, with the holidays approaching, the search would more likely get pushed out to mid-January.

The amount of data gathered on M181 and M182 also implied they had been together for an uncommon eight years and were the alpha leaders and mated pair who ran this current pack of four other subordinate adults and two yearlings. Pups would typically come in early May and the group's winter size could grow by adding them, merging with other packs, or allowing lone wolves to join. Conversely, the pack size would shrink as underlings left or member wolves died.

With the coming of snow the wolves habitually followed the deer south, and in early October the signals from M181 and M182 indicated the wolves had moved from the summer hunting grounds of Ontario's Quetico Provincial Wilderness and into Minnesota's

Superior National Forest. The pack was now bedding down in the tree lines overlooking a valley filled with empty summer campgrounds and plenty of prey. The wolves made their shelters by pawing out depressions in the snow, then turning around two or three times to tramp them flat. When curled up in these simple dens a wolf would be protected against the wind and loss of body heat.

What works well for humans can also be good for wolves: hunting together, rearing the young as a community, and uniting to defend against territorial threats. Biologists who study wolves tend to humanize any animals who exhibit unique personalities and naming them is common. Years ago Clifton Stewart was doing some late-night data processing and, while listening to the music of Billy Holiday, spontaneously named wolf M181 *Lady Day*.

For a while the name stuck, but the fly in the ointment showed up in the form of a bureaucratically minded financial supporter from Minneapolis who noted M181 was of the small number of adult wolves whose fur was still black and someone might wrongfully associate her color with that of the late Blues singer. After some back and forth discussion, the compromise was to identify the wolves with their species but skewed to the Canadian spelling, thus M181 became *Lady Grey* and her mate, *Lord Grey*.

Contrary, though, to any perceived showings of human characteristics, animals mostly respond by instinct to events related to their lives: when hungry, they eat; when tired, they sleep; they move with the seasons, and mate when there is a need for reproduction.

One thing, though, an animal doesn't do is measure time as a concept. Lady Grey could not understand lifespans, and she did not know days led to months and then to years; she knew nothing about numbers on calendars that note anniversaries or remembrances.

And, generally speaking, neither do animals understand cause and effect. While chasing deer two days ago Lord Grey slipped from a muddy trail and onto some rocks below causing severe internal injuries, and his eventual passing would change the dynamics of the pack.

Lady Grey woke at dawn and felt Lord Grey next to her. He used to be warm, but now he was not, and she sniffed at his muzzle only to find some bits of fresh blood but no breath. She stepped over his body and out from under the fallen trees of their makeshift den. She needed to give notice to her pack and started a low, throaty call to awaken the others.

The wolves gathered in a large, loose circle. They joined in the soft howling for a few minutes, then as the quiet returned, each wolf came forward to share in the ritual of sniffing and nuzzling Lord Grey's body.

Lady Grey, wolf M181, was now alone, and even though she and Lord Grey were responsible for this pack for a very long time, member loyalty would quickly gravitate to the next eldest and mated pair. Lady Grey walked away and her dark fur quickly blended with the shadowed forests of pine and aspen. She did not look back.

Caleb Malone stood when the doctor came into the room. "You may want to sit down," the doctor said, "this is not going to be good."

"Doc, I was a Marine, and then a cop. I've had my share of bumps and bruises, and even a couple of holes to remind me of the bad days. I'll take the news standing up if you don't mind."

In a tip-of-the-hat salute, the VA physician continued: "No, I don't mind, so here goes—early tests indicate you have pancreatic cancer, but the worst part is it looks like the cancer may already be spreading to nearby lymph nodes. I have to assume you have been feeling like crap for a while. Is that so?"

"Yes sir, but I do have a pretty high pain tolerance. My daughter talked me into coming to see you about my options. What is a normal plan for this?"

"We would do more tests to confirm—CTs, MRIs, laparoscopic procedures—but considering your symptoms of abdominal pain, weight loss, nausea and vomiting, the listlessness, and so on, I'm pretty confident in the diagnosis."

"What's the treatment?" Caleb asked.

"Well, it just might be too late to do anything about this, but normally surgery would be the first option, however that's really only effective if all the cancer is confined to the pancreas; next would be chemo, then radiation, or a combination of the two. None the less, it won't be pretty and there is no guarantee of success, especially if it's already in the lymph nodes."

"And, if I choose to let this take its own course?"

"With treatment, the five-year survival rate is about sixteen percent if it's only spread to the lymph nodes, but it lowers to about three percent once it hits the other organs. Without treatment…." The doctor paused. "Well, you get the picture, the percentages are even lower. Regardless, the last six months will be the worst. We would manage the pain with medication, and trust me, you'll want to do that," he said.

"Or," Caleb retorted, "treat it with fine whiskey because life's too short to drink bad liquor.

"Doc, the burn scars on my left leg were from an IED in Afghanistan that took out our HUMVEE, and two of the four of us didn't make it out."

Pointing to his right shoulder, Caleb continued: "This through-and-through in my right shoulder was from a bad guy who shot me when I cornered him in a liquor store robbery that went south.

"Those things happened so fast all we could really do was react, but this is different because now I have the time to think about it, if only for a couple of months."

"In that case," the doctor said holding out his right hand, "you're going into unexplored territory, and you'll be doing advanced recon for the rest of us."

"OORAH!" Caleb said as he shook the doctor's hand; he crisply turned, walked out the door, passed through the lobby, and stopped at the driver's side car door. Resting against the vehicle Caleb took a few minutes to calm the trembling in his hands before he could climb into the driver's seat, start the engine, and head home.

Although animals don't know about appointments, humans do, and it would be because of her father that Becky Walters would be late for the first time in years. Over one thousand miles away Becky fretted over her morning schedule and knew she would miss the start to a ten o'clock meeting. This made her anxious and maybe even a little angry because years of preaching by Old Mr. Marine Corps taught her if she wasn't fifteen to thirty minutes early, she was late. And ironically, it was her father's phone call that would cause this lateness.

"Becky, I'm sorry to bother you this early but I got my test results back yesterday. I didn't sleep at all last night worrying about this call." Caleb hesitated for a moment to catch his breath, and then he continued. "You should know I have pancreatic cancer."

Now it was Becky's turn to breathe. She inhaled then exhaled loudly before speaking. "Dad, what are our options?"

"Honey, I don't mean to be harsh, but there aren't any options. My clock is ticking, and I don't really know what time the bells will chime."

Becky always knew with the choices her dad made about his life there was the possibility the day would come when she got another gut-wrenching phone call; it was only two years ago her mother had succumbed to a heart attack.

"Dad, since you lost mom it almost seems like you've given up on living. Am I not worth fighting for? What about your grandchildren?"

"Sweetheart, most of us think we have control over our time on earth, but because of pre-destination, fate, God's will, or just plain bad luck, few really get to choose how they go. We all want to believe our lives had meaning, but it's really up to our survivors to determine what that meaning is.

"This form of cancer does not give us much to go with, so perhaps we should be talking about the quality of my remaining time instead of any lack of quantity."

"What are you going to do?" Becky asked.

"I don't know yet. I'll take a few days to think about it, but I know one thing for sure, this is not the way I envisioned it. How about I come out next month, before Thanksgiving, and we can talk about it some more. Maybe I'll have some ideas by then."

The bottle on the table was about a third empty and Caleb had fallen asleep in the easy chair in front of the television. A strange howling sound woke him.

"What was that?" he blurted out.

Caleb fumbled around the end table until he found the remote control, then he played the DVR back to a commercial for the Colorado Wolf Preserve. The ad was only a minute and it ended with the wolves howling at a full moon above the tree line. A hazy idea formed at that instant and Caleb copied down the Preserve's website and telephone number, turned off the TV, and pushed back into his chair.

The next day at about 5:00PM, Caleb drove up State Highway 24, through Divide and then to a county road that took him to the Preserve. He had a reservation for the night wolf show to include a one-on-one with a tour guide.

Caleb grilled his guide: "Where is the largest natural population of wolves in the U.S.?"

"Minnesota, about twenty-seven hundred wolves more or less," his guide answered.

"Do they always hunt in packs?"

"Usually, but there can be lone wolves, and they're not like the renegades you see in the movies killing all the sheep and the villagers. We call them dispersers, wolves who may have broken off for some reason, and they might even continue to hunt for their old pack, some could be accepted into another pack and find a mate, but about ten percent of them will die off within the year after separating."

"What is their normal prey?" Caleb asked.

"Depends on where the wolves reside. But basically any animal, large or small, that also lives in the area. In Yellowstone, it might be elk, bison are too big unless it's a sick or lame animal. In Minnesota it would likely be deer. Minnesota's deep snow is not an issue for running wolves as they have naturally large paws that spread open like unfolding fans; deer do not have that advantage. And they will also catch voles, mice, and rabbits if there are plenty around, anything they prefer."

"Prefer?" Caleb injected.

"Some studies theorize that wolves can develop a taste for specific foods, venison for instance, and might pass up other forms of prey to focus on the one they like. Some of our wolves here ignore the chicken parts we throw into their pens but will jump on a squirrel in a heartbeat. But again, these are just theories, it would be difficult to objectively prove any of this."

"Do they eat what they kill?"

"Yes; they will gorge themselves, however they typically dig out caches in the snow or dirt to hide what's left over. Unless scavengers find the remains, the wolves can return to the cache if they don't find an easier source of food later."

"And human prey?"

"There is little historical evidence to support the idea wolves actually eat humans. Internationally, there have only been two documented cases in the last twenty-five years of wolves even chasing down a human let alone hunting one for food."

And the questions went on, but before the evening was over, Caleb had his plan.

In mid-November, Caleb flew to Seattle. Becky picked him up at SeaTac International, and aside from hugs and a rudimentary conversation, the ride to Becky's house was quiet. Later, Caleb greeted the twins and Becky's husband Glen, settled into the spare bedroom, then he and Becky moved to the back deck for a private continuation of the October telephone call.

"Do you remember your sweet-sixteen birthday trip we took you on?" Caleb started.

"Yep! For a girl who wanted nothing more than to get her driving license, we went instead to Minnesota to run around on snow machines and dog sleds. So, why that memory?"

"Well, I'm going back there."

"What? Why?"

"Sweetheart, those who carry a gun maintain a level of silent violence deep inside which can sometimes be difficult to control, and the responsibility can wear a person down. When we were in the woods there, I felt very much at peace…I need to feel that way again, even if it's just for a short while.

"There's more, though. The guy who took us sledding kept saying 'Watch out for the wolves'! Well, we never saw a single wolf, remember? I want to see at least one in the wild. I went to a wolf preserve outside Colorado Springs, and it really inspired me to do this."

"When will you go?"

"In a few weeks, maybe a month, after the New Year at latest."

"Okay, dad, I get it, but I still don't like it. You should be taking the doctor's advice and starting your treatments by now."

"Beck, that's not the way I want to end it all! I've been a warrior my whole life, this has been my *Ikigai*, my reason for being; when I enter the land of shadows, I want to go in with my guns blazing and my boots on. You know what they say about a good death that honors a person's life."

"Jesus dad, you're being melodramatic; don't give me that *'fine day to die'* bullshit. You act like you know what will happen with the Titanic and yet you're booking a seat on her anyway. It may matter to you how you go, but there's no difference to us…you'll be just as gone either way. And Minnesota isn't Valhalla, you don't have to go there with a sword in your hand."

Caleb chuckled and put his arm around his daughter pulling her close. "How about my KA-BAR then?" he said. "You know I've had that knife since before you were born."

Becky accepted this conversation would lead nowhere other than where her father wanted it to go. She sighed deeply, hugged him tightly, and said: "Let's go inside; it's getting cold out here."

Becky stopped at the door and turned to her father. "I love you dad, I always will. No matter what choice you make."

The pack's new leader, the eldest son of Lord and Lady Grey, intuitively understood the value of letting his mother remain nearby. Lady Grey was still of much use, her expert senses undimmed by age, and although she now moved a bit slower she continued to track well.

Lady Grey followed the deer for miles to where they stopped in a field to dig in the snow for grass and other vegetation. The wolf howled to call in the rest of the pack, and although the deer were alerted, they could not pinpoint the source of the sound, and when the howling stopped the deer resettled into foraging.

It didn't take long for the pack to arrive and circle six of the herd, but the pack only needed three, and they singled out the ones who would eventually die anyway: weakest, oldest, infirm, or injured. The wolves had no difficulty in pulling the deer down.

Rhythmically, the pack members ate, then they dug their caches for the leftover pieces. Experience among the older wolves had planted memories of unpredictable winters in Minnesota that could thin out the deer herds, and the hidden food might be necessary for survival.

When done, the pack moved out of the clearing and followed their trails back to the dens leaving Lady Grey behind.

Caleb followed his map and ran the snowmobile to the end of the trail. He put on his snowshoes, gathered his pack, and started walking. Although the area was covered in snow, the way to a campground was easy to follow because forest service workers had previously cut a four-foot-wide path out of the trees and undergrowth. In spite of his health, it was an easy hike.

In the early morning Lady Grey could smell the man even before approaching the site. She sniffed at the abandoned snowmobile first, then followed the human's scent to where she spotted him huddling next to a tree in a makeshift shelter. There was no fire.

The wolf quietly circled the area a couple of times checking the buried caches of deer meat left from the last hunt; they were still there and undisturbed. The wolf crouched under the pines, the boughs hanging low because of the weight of the snow. She was about thirty feet away from the blanketed figure, and the man still did not see her.

Caleb was startled when the wolf howled. Keeping a blanket wrapped around his shoulders, he crawled out of his lean-to and stood up, then turned in a circle to see where the wolf might be. Not finding it, Caleb stumbled further out into the sunshine and sat down on a rock in the clearing.

Lady Grey slowly moved from the darkness of the tree line and sat down at the edge of the open space. The animal showed no hostility, and Caleb felt no fear. The wolf raised her head once more and howled. Within minutes, like echoes, distant howls came from the forest. Although Caleb felt the hairs on his neck twitch, he remained unafraid.

Caleb and Lady Grey continued to watch each other into the late afternoon. The winter sun was nearing the treetops, and as if on cue, the rest of the pack arrived and formed a circle around the man in the clearing. Caleb stood and removed the blanket from his shoulders and spread it on the ground. He took off and tossed aside his hat, gloves, and coat. Caleb laid himself on the blanket face up and watched the green glowing waves of the aurora borealis start their dance across the sky.

Lady Grey walked over to Caleb and looked into his face; she could sense the man was not frightened although he was shaking from the twenty-degree weather. With her two front paws, the wolf gently stepped onto Caleb's chest and shifted her ninety pounds of weight forward.

Caleb instinctively tried to adjust his body in order to breathe easier but the weight of the wolf restricted his efforts. His right hand reached for his fighting knife, the KA-BAR, and although Caleb pulled it from the scabbard he kept it by his side.

The lack of oxygen in Caleb's brain caused his vision to narrow sharply and focus on the golden color of Lady Grey's eyes. Caleb chuckled softly to himself and whispered, "In the movies, wolf eyes are blue."

Life has fleeting moments of perfect balance, a stillness of intent before being disrupted by the chaos of action; the wolves started their chorused howl, some higher pitched and others deeper throated. Caleb heard them all, and he smiled.

Then his shivering stopped.

"Sheriff's Department, is this an emergency?"

"No ma'am. My name is Clifton Stewart; I'm at one of the entrances to Voyagers National Park by the Rainy Lake trail, and I think we may have found an abandoned vehicle."

"What do you have there Mr. Stewart?"

"It's a Ford Explorer, and there's a single towing trailer attached, like one used for moving a snow machine around."

"Is there a license plate still on the SUV?"

"Yes, one-two-two GHY, Minnesota. The trailer has one too."

"That's okay, Mr. Stewart, give me a minute to run this plate." After a pause of a few moments, the dispatcher returned. "Yep, we have this SUV listed as missing and possibly stolen from a rental place in Minneapolis. I'll send a deputy out, but it will take about an hour for him to get there. Are you alone?"

"No. There are two of us. Jenna Lake and I are from the Wolf Management Center, and we have radio and cellular contact with our control room as well."

"Okay. You should stay in the parking lot, but don't confront anyone who might come back. If you feel threatened in the least, leave if you can."

"No problem. You have my phone number on your caller ID, don't you."

"Yes, sir. Deputy Clark is on his way. And thanks for reporting this."

When Deputy Clark arrived, he shook hands with Clifton and Jenna, and asked, "You two still alright?"

"Yes, no activity in the area at all. We stayed in the truck. What do you need us to do?"

"Well, I'm going to call for the cavalry first, and we'll need our own machines to get in there to see what's going on. Dispatch told me the car and the trailer are rentals, and we're assuming there was a snowmobile on the trailer. So there is at least one person out here somewhere and we don't know if there are weapons involved."

"Deputy, we came out here to track a couple of our wolves we collared years ago. One of those radios hasn't moved for over two months and we suspect that wolf may be dead, but there is still one signal moving out there and probably an active pack of nine or ten to go with it. We can go in with your team if you wish."

"The sheriff will make that call, but I imagine he will welcome your overwatch. If you two have thermoses, you'd better get them out, it might be a long day."

Lady Grey had not left the area for days and continued to watch from the trees. A few times she even hovered closer to Caleb's body whenever ravens or other scavengers tried to move in.

She heard the machines first in the distance, then nearer, and finally they arrived: by their scents five men and a woman, all looking over the area, some touching Caleb. Twice Lady Grey saw the woman and one of the men point in her direction, but they did not come close enough to worry her, nor did any of the humans get near the food caches.

At one point, Lady Grey watched as one of the men and the woman departed on a machine and went in the direction of wolf M182's resting place. It took most of the day for the remaining humans to finish their work and leave, towing Caleb's body on a sled.

Staying well behind, the wolf followed the humans to Caleb's abandoned snow machine which one man brought back to life. Then she tracked the whole group to the parking lot where she watched the humans load all the vehicles and drive away. Lady Grey turned north and made her way to her old bedding site. At the entrance of her former den she stopped and sniffed: one man and the woman had been there, and Lord Grey's remains were gone.

The caller ID on Becky's cellphone said "KOO CTY SHERIFF" and Becky answered on the third ring.

"Hello, Ms. Walters. I'm Robert Ives, Sheriff of Koochiching County in Minnesota. Do you have some time to talk?"

"I do, Sheriff, and I've been expecting a call like this for a month or so. Not from you personally, but from Minnesota at least. I suspect we're not going to talk about the weather there."

"No ma'am, I'm sorry to say we're not. You seem ready to hear this so I'll come to the point, and I hope I'm not being too blunt or inconsiderate of your feelings."

"No Sheriff, you are not. Press on."

"Do you know a Caleb Malone?"

"He's my father," Becky said as she dropped heavily into the chair by the kitchen window. She knew the direction this phone call was going to take, and she steeled her nerves to continue with it.

"We found some human remains in one of our forests that we think might be his. We could confirm it with a DNA match, but I'm pretty sure it's him."

"How did you decide to call me, and how do you figure it's my dad?"

"Well first, we have your telephone number. We found a cell phone in the pocket of a coat at the scene, the battery was dead, but when we charged it up, the lock screen was not on and the only number in the contact list was yours. Second: we also found a wallet with his driver's license and a credit card in his name, and we had the bank who issued the card run a list of purchases, which matched up with the items we found at the scene including a rental SUV, a snowmobile and its trailer. The keys to the SUV were in the coat pocket."

"What type of charges were there, other than the vehicles?"

"Nothing unusual. A cold weather sleeping bag and a couple of wool blankets from a sporting goods store in Ely, gas and some food purchases at roadside restaurants between here and Minneapolis."

"So, how did you narrow down to where he was?" Becky asked.

"We already had missing vehicle reports on file for the car, trailer, and snowmobile when they weren't returned on time. Later, a couple of concerned citizens found the same vehicles abandoned in a parking lot of a campground near International Falls. From that parking lot, we were able to follow the snowmobile tracks, and then those of a person to where we found the body."

Becky had to ask: "What was the cause of death, Sheriff? How did he die?"

"The coroner is initially ruling natural causes, specifically hypothermia; he likely froze to death."

"I presume," Becky continued, "his body is with the coroner right now? I can give you some details that will help confirm my dad's identification."

"What would those be, Ms. Walters?"

"Please, call me Becky. My dad had the standard USMC tattoo on his right forearm. Plus, there is an old bullet hole in his right shoulder. Last, there will be a burn scar on his left calf and thigh."

"Those wounds are a little unusual, Becky. But the coroner's report has them listed just as you say."

"My dad was a Marine in Afghanistan. He was the one who made it back alive. He was also a cop, which led to the shoulder. The bad guy who gave it to him was not so lucky."

"Whew, that's something. It's obvious you have great respect for him."

"Yes, sir, I do. So what is my next step?"

"Well, my guess is you are the official next of kin, since there was no indication of a wife in the contact list."

"Mom passed a couple of years ago, so yes, I'm it."

"Okay. Unfortunately, you will need to come to International Falls to positively identify him, and then we can release him to you. I suspect it will take you a few days to make travel and other arrangements. I'll text you with my direct phone number and some suggested places to stay, and I'll pick you up at the airport, no need for a car. So keep me posted, and I'll see you when you arrive. And please accept our sincere condolences."

"Thank you Sheriff. I'll get back to you soonest."

As Becky slumped in the chair, Glen and the twins came over to comfort her. "Well, that's two for two. I didn't get to say goodbye to either of my parents!" The tears started, and they did not stop for hours.

Becky Walters caught the earliest puddle jumper flight from Minneapolis/St Paul to International Falls, arriving at 10:15 in the morning. She spent the night before at a Holiday Inn near the airport after traveling all day from Seattle. She was out of sync with the time zone changes and did not sleep well at the hotel. None the less, when she got to International Falls, adrenalin and caffeine kicked in and by the time Sheriff Ives walked up to the baggage section, Becky was alert and ready to keep moving forward. After the introductions and cordialities, Becky got right to business.

"Can I see my father now?" Becky asked.

"Certainly, but don't expect too much of our facilities; we're a small county and our coroner is also the senior doctor at the hospital. That's where we're going."

The morgue was in the basement and Becky asked to use the stairs to stretch her tired legs. Ives introduced Becky to Doctor Albans, who took them to the cold storage area.

"You ready?" Albans asked as he pulled out the sliding drawer.

"I am," Becky replied. She took a deep breath, held it for a few seconds, then let it out slowly. Carefully, Dr. Albans folded the sheet down to Caleb's waist, and other than the standard autopsy sutures, there was no other damage to his body.

"It's him. And I'm a little surprised at how good of shape he's in," Becky blurted out.

"What were you expecting?" Sheriff Ives asked.

"Well, this may be an odd question, but were there any signs of wolves in the area?"

"As a matter of fact, there were plenty of tracks in and around your dad's camp. There were also tracks next to the snowmobile, and then some further out. We just happened to have with us a couple of wolf researchers from the Management Center in Ely. They were the ones who made the initial 'abandoned vehicle' call and then identified the wolf tracks. They stayed with us for a little bit before heading off on wolf business of their own.

"Oh, and one of my deputies thought he saw a lone wolf hanging around in the trees while we worked the scene, and the number of tracks in the camp led us to believe there might be more out there, but then we likely would not have seen them anyway. None bothered us at all, we didn't think much more about it. So, what's up?"

"Nothing, never mind," Becky replied.

Becky turned to Doctor Albans: "Dad had pancreatic cancer that was spreading to other parts of his body, but I guess the autopsy told you that."

"Well it did, but it wasn't relevant to my ruling on cause of death. Would I be wrong if I suggested he had only months to live?"

"No, sir, you would not."

The Sheriff interrupted cautiously: "But where were you going with your wolf question?"

"Dad wanted to have a warrior's death. I know this sounds a bit romantic, but did he have his knife out when you found him? Were there signs of a struggle or a fight?"

"As a matter of fact, yes, the knife was in his hand, and it's a hell of a big knife. But no blood, no bite marks, no violence at all." Ives stopped for a second before asking the next question.

"When I called you said you'd been expecting me. Are you suggesting your father committed suicide?"

"No, sir. What I do know is he wanted to control the terms of his parting, his transition, he used to call it. As a warrior he wanted to go out fighting although I have no idea why he didn't use that knife to defend himself. But, if I understand what you've just said, he wasn't attacked. He just went to sleep and crossed into Heaven or Elysium or whatever you want to call it.

"I didn't always understand dad's ways, but he did live a meaningful life. It seems he was at peace with his end, he was still mentally with it, and I suspect when I settle his estate, I'll find his finances are in order.

"But, Doctor, does what I've just said change your ruling in any way?"

"No, Ms. Walters, it doesn't. Even if a wolf had killed him it would still be natural causes, especially in the woods of Minnesota. At worst, I could modify the report to "accidental death" but the result to you would not change, so I see no reason to alter it."

"Becky," Sheriff Ives interjected, "unless you need more time here, why don't we get you some lunch and then to your room; I'm quite sure you've had an exhausting two days. We can discuss tomorrow how you want to handle your father's body; I can set up an appointment with our local mortuary."

"I've already thought this through." Becky looked at the doctor. "Unless you give me a reason otherwise, I want him cremated. I can stay here long enough to get that done, then I'll take him back to Colorado where he'll be with my mother's cremains.

"And you're right, I need something to eat, then I'm taking a long nap. Thanks so much to both of you, and to all who helped with this."

At the national cemetery near Colorado Springs, Becky and her family gathered before the white marble stone engraved with her father's name and rank, and below that was the name of her mother.

Becky had combined the ashes of her parents into one wooden box, and she dropped to her knees and cried softly as she lowered it into the bottom of the small square pit. From her coat pocket Becky pulled out her dad's knife and tossed the sheath into the grave.

"Good hunting, dad," Becky said gently as she reached down and pushed the KA-BAR up to the hilt into the soil next to the small casket.

The family stood at attention while the guns were fired and the folded flag presented. Glen Walters sprinkled a handful of dirt on top of the box, followed by each of the children, and as Becky took her turn she cited Kipling: "The strength of the pack is the wolf, and the strength of the wolf is the pack."

No offense to her husband, but it occurred to Becky that she was now her pack's leader.

Lady Grey remained at the den she had shared with Lord Grey. She looked over the valley and took occasional stretches in the sun to warm her frail body. She did not know age would catch up with her in a week, and three days after that her mortality signal would start pinging the same location to Clifton Stewart where he and Jenna found wolf M182.

To Lady Grey her remaining days were no different from those that came before because, after all, everyone knows animals have no concept of the passing of time.

~ *  * ~

Steven Lente is a retired USAF security forces veteran who carries an ASIS International certified protection professional lifetime rating. Steve has had several short stories published in anthologies released by <u>WolfSinger Publications</u> and <u>The Desert Writers Guild</u>. He and wife Brenda travel regularly with and without an RV from their home in Colorado.

Steve is a member of the Colorado Authors League. You can visit his website at www.stevenlente.com.

Appleseed

Marisca Pichette

There is a legend where I come from about bare feet and tin pots. A map full of footprints and cider, lines of branches and bark. Dogfennel obscures lands once called home, before that name was taken and replaced with Frontier.

The hills I left behind smell sour and old.

You've heard the story:

A child is walking through the woods, looking for a grandmother. The child wears red and carries something—a basket, a briefcase, a mush pot. The child is naive. The child should never have entered the woods alone. The child is destined to die.

But there is a man. The man has an ax, a rifle, or a blanket bathed in disease. The man is strong, and he is a hero because he kills the wolf. He is a hero because everyone knows wolves are evil. Everyone knows wolves are wild. Everyone knows only the child is worth saving in this story.

Child, wolf, death. It's that simple, that easy. Except…

I was born on the plains, not in the woodlands. I was born at sunset, and my first gaze found a million stars. I was hungry, yes, but for milk—not blood. And if there were children in the world, I hadn't met them.

That was years ago, years before I heard your call and came searching for another path to follow. Along the way I've met many men carrying axes and guns and death. One tried to kill me. One tried to save me.

Forget the legend; if indeed, you've heard it at all. This is where the true story begins.

I met him when I was young. He had firelight in his eyes. He smelled of putrefaction and sweat, his boots coated in ash. He was large—too large for me but I was hungry. And hunger makes wolves do stupid things.

The first night, I managed to steal some food without waking him. The second, I came too close.

Could he smell me, like I smelled him? He reeked like the clearing I'd found the week earlier; stained with blood, dusty with fear. I tried tracking beyond, but those stains were all I was to find of her.

There is just one grandmother in my story: my own. When my mother was shot and skinned before I could hunt for myself, she led me through tall grasses and under mountains too steep to climb. She told me to beware of men with their knives and guns. Men like the ones who made her vanish and left me alone. Men like the one I saw now, on the other side of a dying fire.

I wonder still if he killed her; if the darkened spots on his cuffs, half-visible in the night, were hers.

He quickly rolled to his feet, gun in hand. I knew then his slumber had been feigned.

"You won't get my grub again."

When he shot me, I was already in the air. My teeth found his neck. His bullet found my leg. We hit the ground together. Blood and skin and fur.

In this story, the big bad wolf doesn't die. She kills the man and she cries for her grandmother while she bleeds and bleeds onto ashy ground.

And that is where the child finds her.

He looked like a man. He did not wear red, but he carried something: not a basket but a bag. Filled not with cakes but seeds, he dropped it on the ground and knelt by me. He smelled of earth and grains. He smelled sweet, a kind of sweet I hadn't smelled before.

Apples, I would learn. He smelled of apples.

"Lord, have mercy."

When he came close I tried to bite him, but he was healthy and I had been lying on the stinking corpse of the man for two days and nights. He dodged my teeth and picked up my leg. Pain ran through me like water over stones. I howled.

Through a haze of exhaustion and agony I saw him: eyes dark, head down. He crushed leaves over my wound. The air turned sour.

"Lord, have mercy. Let life endure."

He tore cloth from his shirt and wrapped it around my leg. I howled and thrashed as much as I could, unable to breathe or think. He'd not yet tied the knot before I succumbed to darkness.

This is the story I bring with me, from a land not unlike this one. More threatened, less frozen. You have your own, inherited from other packs and encounters with men and guns. I hope you will forgive me for my divergence. I have not always run from them.

There was one I followed, for a time.

I lost those first three days to illness. I expected to die, but somehow, I endured. In the mist of what I remember, he was always there. Feeding me, giving me water in a tin pot. Checking my leg again and again.

You don't believe me. You don't see how a man could act like that.

But remember—he was really a child in the shape of a man. He spoke to me in soft tones and with my eyes closed I imagined my grandmother, her tongue on my fur. As my consciousness returned, she faded. Only he remained.

He read to me from a book he carried. Verses and songs that spoke of the world and seemed to bring him comfort. To me they brought confusion.

You know the story. The man kills the wolf. The man doesn't save it.

Over the days I learned he was trying to save me in many ways. He wanted my body to live, but he wanted also for me to change into something else. He spoke of belief and human civilization. He spoke of forgiveness—forgiving me for killing the other man; forgiving him for trying to kill me.

I realized then that he was not a man. He was not like the one with the gun and stench. His feet were bare, and he carried only food. I could have killed him as he slept, but as I healed I thought it would be better to let him live. He fed me still, and I doubted I was strong enough yet to hunt for myself.

After nearly two weeks, the moon waxing gibbous, he packed

up his meager things and turned west.

"Lord, I will turn these fields to forests in your name."

There were times I thought this was the name he'd given me, but from his book I learned he spoke to a ghost. He spoke to a father who was not there. A father who was dead and not dead, as he hoped to one day die and not die. I didn't understand, but it made me wonder about my mother and grandmother. It made me wonder about the paths of wolves.

"Farewell, friend. I do not ask you to follow me on my path." He nodded to me and turned his back, as he had so many times. He knew I could attack him. He knew I was strong enough now to end his life.

But I didn't. I watched him walk away, leaving only footprints.

When he was no more than a wisp in the distance, I set off after him.

I tracked him over the plains and into the hills, until I smelled more of his kind. I hung back then, my leg aching. I stayed on the outskirts, spending fitful hungry nights waiting for him to emerge. In daylight I saw him planting seeds in unnatural rows. After a week, he left the company of men and continued west.

How can I explain the bond I felt? Debt, perhaps. Or loss. I had no pack—not like this. You must understand I was alone, my world shrinking around me. I don't think what I did was wrong.

I followed him for miles.

When he stopped at a stream, I approached. My tongue was dry and he squatted by the shallows, washing his tin pot. He looked up as I drew near. In his dark eyes I saw no fear, only quiet recognition.

"You followed after all, friend. I'm afraid I've nothing to give you. I swore to Him I would not kill."

He opened his bag and I flinched back. But I should have remembered. Inside were seeds only, and some roots I knew men ate.

He saw my nervousness and showed me the contents more fully. "See? Nothing for a wild creature like yourself."

He ignored me then. I crept to the stream and drank for a long while, watching him eat his roots. If I'd had the ability, I would have asked him about his journey—the point of it. I wanted to know what it was he was looking for. Was he as lost as I?

After several minutes he got to his feet, shaking out his pot and putting it on his head. It reflected the afternoon sun. "May He keep you safe, friend."

He walked along the stream and out of my sight. Still, his scent was strong. I followed it into the evening.

When the sun rose, it rose behind him. Westward he continued. Westward I followed.

I followed him from settlement to settlement. He passed through his people like a creature of a different kind. Some treated him with admiration, others disdain. Once he was chased by younger men. I ran into the open and frightened them away.

This choice still confuses me. I doubt any of you have done the same—protected one man from another. But he was different. He carried no guns.

For a time, I considered him something like family. From the day I saved him, I ceased to keep my distance. I came close to him at night, hunted nearby his planting in the day. I didn't lose track of time—that's not it. It's more like…like rhythm. Seasons came faster in his company, and I didn't think to count them.

He continued his journey as if my presence was not unusual. He called me friend, and nothing else. He never did give me a name.

As the years passed, my world changed. The plains were not what they had been. Dust replaced grass. The landscape of my birth had never been empty, but the men I'd known from afar were gone, taken and chased and killed to make room for louder men. It grew loud everywhere.

He grew old. I did not.

Here I feel your interest waning. Yet we all have stories, don't we? I listened to yours. Mine may be foreign, maybe incomprehensible, but let me remind you of the story we all know:

Once there was a child walking alone. The child sees no woods, so he creates them seed by seed. He meets a wolf and, because he loves all life, he protects her. Because she is lost, she follows him.

But the wolf was not born in the woods. The wolf was not

always lost.

As she follows the child who looks like a man, she becomes less sure of what she is. She becomes less sure of where she walks.

The child knows he is doing something right. He knows he is not a huntsman with a gun and a treaty torn in two. He knows he is not a heathen because he carries a book he thinks will tell the truth. He knows many things, but he is only a child.

The wolf is older than the child. The wolf is always older than the child, and in most versions of this story, she is smarter, too.

The wolf sees the world is changing. She sees the child has a hand in it, a small hand, a gentle hand, but a hand nonetheless. Why does she follow him?

She follows him because she is afraid.

One day, in a town that was once beautiful wilderness, he died.

I didn't know it. I waited outside for days, weeks; until his scent had faded. At last I crept in under darkness and searched for him. I tracked the last wisps of his scent to a heap of dusty earth too dry for crops. Would a tree grow over his bones? I would never know.

What does the wolf do when child, man, and grandmother have all left the story?

She finds her way out of the woods.

I ran away from the town and went east, searching for the home I'd left so long ago. But the further I ran, the more men I found. It was not the landscape I remembered. I realized how much time had passed, how much the world had changed from what I knew. There was no more home for me there.

When I slept, I heard something. A song, a lament. A memory I never lived.

It came from you. It came from here, from generations of stories I never heard, and never forgot.

You know the rest: I turned north. I ran through plains and valleys, under alien trees into colder air. I ran until I found a scent I'd almost forgotten.

I howled, then. I howled for my lost lands and the life I'd wasted. I howled for a place as yet untouched by axes.

And you responded. I heard you howling in the hills, howling under the stars.

Twenty years after my grandmother's death, I found myself in the company of wolves again. You brought me further north, through woods that bore no foreign fruit. I followed you under the moon's cool glow and into a landscape I had never seen.

When we stopped at last, far from the nearest Frontier, we lay down together and told stories.

I learned at last the secret of my kind: we live as long as there is land to hold us.

And the legend? It lives in mouths other than ours, shared in songs without teeth. In some versions of the story, I don't exist at all. In some versions of the story, I am a footnote.

But you know the truth. You know how we really lived, all those years ago.

Once, there was a wolf who lost everything. Confused and weakened, she tried her best to live like a man.

The child-man she followed wasn't bad, she thought. He helped her and he helped others. He told stories, but he rarely heard them.

The wolf listened. And at night, in a distance no fingers could touch, she heard something else growing. A song and a memory.

When she decided at last to follow it, she carried with her a song of her own. A song of tin pots, bare feet, and apple seeds.

On the coldest nights, she still feels an ache in her leg, and licks a scar that's yet to fade.

~ * 🐺 * ~

Marisca Pichette is a queer author based in Massachusetts, where she has seen wolves. Find more of her work in *Strange Horizons, Clarkesworld, Vastarien, The Deadlands, Fantasy Magazine, Asimov's, Nightmare Magazine,* and others. Her poetry collection, *Rivers in Your Skin, Sirens in Your Hair,* was a finalist for the Bram Stoker and Elgin Awards. Her eco-horror novella, *Every Dark Cloud,* is out now from Ghost Orchid Press.

The Language of Leaves

Ville Meriläinen

In the light of a cold summer dawn, condensing mist dripped off pine needles to make a sound like rain, and a wolf caught a fawn by the lakeshore.

The fawn stumbled on rocks when it burst out of the thicket, and the wolf crushed its neck with a single bite. He had grown enormous the past winter, on grief, some said; he hunted alone, without a pack or his mate, and wasted half his kills due to an appetite too small for his size. The tall men had taken his cubs, tried to take him too, but the woods cared for him and warned him when they approached.

The wolf dragged his kill into hiding, away from the path the tall men used to bring their nets to the lake. Violets sang their laments for the fawn, but blueberries congratulated a successful hunt. The language of leaves was a symphony of whispers spanning the forest, one voice for every shared soul. Somewhere within the swelling choir his pack howled on an ethereal hunt, their voice gone from his throat and given to the trees on the night he betrayed them with a lie.

The tall men had lost the language like he had, but amidst them dwelled those who still remembered it. The wolf raised his blood-tinged muzzle from the fawn to sniff at the air, picking up a scent amidst the late summer blooms. Pulse quickening, he left his spoils to the foolhardy fox spying on him from behind a stump, and loped toward the path from where the scent came.

In the mist he saw a splash of scarlet, trailing down the shoulders of the one who'd first shown the colour to him. The girl was one of the tall men, yet as much of the woods as he: She sang with two tongues, one for the wilds, one for warding beasts, and the irony therein was their harmony had entranced the wolf.

The wolf had never stepped before her, for fear she would run or cry like others of her kin, but had listened to her singing for so long her melodies had encircled his heart like wisterias and captured it. Her songs weren't meant for him to hear, but were private confessions to the forest. Eavesdropping kindled shame in his chest, but the wolf sympathised with her feelings of being surrounded by those who feared her.

Whether there was magic or wisdom in her singing, she had taught him to feel as she did, to perceive as she did, until he had found the colour of fresh blood in the throats of his prey, on the wet, shiny cowberries around him, and in the hair of the young witch on the path. He moved with her as a shadow in the murk of pines, following her precious voice, and the leaves helped hide the rustling of his step. They knew he'd visit no harm upon her.

When the girl came to the lake, she paused by the bloodied rocks to inspect them with a frown. She looked around with caution, straight at the wolf for a while, but his black fur blended into the shroud the trees cast. The girl continued, circling the lake toward a house hidden in the distance.

She shivered in the chill of the air, and the wolf wished he could curl up around her and warm her, as he'd once done to his mate. The wolf didn't know whether the leaves told her she was there, if they told her not to fear him, or if they told her anything at all. He heard their voices, but could not ask, and so was privy only to what they chose to share. He knew the house she came to visit belonged to her mother's mother, that both were witches, and the woods were fond of them—mostly. He had come across the grandmother once, when she was harvesting lavenders and her lingering scent of rabbit stew had enticed him to follow. A gangly old birch nearby had forbidden him from attacking, and though it stood alone on the mountain slopes, its voice chorused with all its kind down the foothills. The crone had watched him warily, asked if he would eat her, and gone back to harvesting herbs when he'd merely sat staring.

The pines later told him she'd killed an eagle for its beak and feathers and the ash trees wanted her dead for it. He had ignored their plight, and the birches thanked him every day.

The girl ceased singing and vanished inside the house. The wolf returned to the fawn, growled at the fox who'd come for scraps to scare it away, and brooded over the longing she had unwittingly taught him.

That afternoon, when the mist receded and the tall men arrived with their nets, a huntsman came with them to the lake. The wolf had not learned anger from the girl, who—he was certain—was too sweet to know the vile feeling anyhow. He had learned it from this man, who did not speak the language of leaves, and made the woods cry with just his presence. Now and again the wolf did the same when he ate a creature to which one plant or another had taken a liking, but they knew he only killed to survive and forgave him in time.

The bitterness toward this man was different. It was sown deep in the soil and the grass and the roots, where the leaves who remembered his crimes had rotted. Sometimes he would fire his pistol at a squirrel or robin and laugh when his victim fell from its branch. He would set traps for rabbits and badgers, but never check them. Once, the wolf had shared his title as the crownless king of the woods with an old bear, but the huntsman had shot it dead because he thought its fur would look fine around his shoulders.

Tall men loved him for killing the beasts they feared, as did scavengers. The forest had pleaded with the wolf to hunt the man in turn, and he had answered.

A thousand voices had screamed in the tender dark of spring, when the huntsman murdered three princes and a queen and left them bleeding on melting snows. The wolf had taken his arm in revenge, and both of them still bore the scars of that encounter; one beast in his heart and hide, one underneath a sleeve stapled shut.

The wolf realised too late a growl seeped out of his throat while he watched the fishers and the huntsman, and the latter turned toward him with his pistol in hand. The wolf was gone before he approached, a swoosh the man mistook for wind hiding his leaving.

The wolf slept until the scent of beef aroused him, but fairy slippers warned him it was a trap, and told him instead of a rabbit who'd hurt herself and cried for rescue. The wolf padded away from the lake, until he found the rabbit at the edge of a wild field and gave her peace. When he lay down to feed, he caught an odd scent and noticed the tall grass moving.

From the grass emerged a she-wolf unfamiliar to him. Though he was mere steps away, the she-wolf did not notice him—until she faced him and jolted, as though she relied only on her eyes instead of her nose. Curiously, it was the copse of birches that first called out to him, telling him not to attack. Why should he have? She was the first of his kin he'd met in months, after loneliness had gnawed at him for so long he'd come to love one of the tall men.

And yet, she feared him. It was clear in her posture, even her eyes, peculiar as they were. He could not smell it from beneath her thick odour, and that disturbed him more than the lone ash on the far side of the field ordering him to tear open her throat. The trees fell into an argument when the wind picked up a whorl of leaves full of vitriol, and the wolf surmised there was something more wrong about the she-wolf than the miasma masking other scents.

She took off in a loping run and the wolf followed, unsurprised she veered toward the direction of the crone's house. He knew painfully well the tall men wore the furs of beasts, but not that they could *become* beasts. Yet, his suspicion only grew back in the deep woods, where the she-wolf lay crouched amidst the shrubs and listened to shouts coming from the house.

The shouts caught the wolf's attention as well, and elation and sympathy bristled through him at once when the girl came out. He'd been wrong earlier—she appeared intimately familiar with anger, face flushed as red as her hair when she sent the huntsman running out of her grandmother's house. He understood nothing of what she said, nor was there anything sweet about the sharp pitch and vicious tone of her voice. The language of leaves was absent from her tongue, as it was from around the wolf, as though the whole wood listened fearfully to their exchange.

The man responded in kind, pointing his pistol at her in a way that made the wolf want to charge him—the way he'd pointed it at his mate—but the girl retreated indoors and slammed the door shut so hard the windows rattled. The man shouted at her once more, then stormed off toward the path to the village. The fishermen had left for the day, and when the shore was deserted, the she-wolf arose and rushed for the house. She still hadn't noticed the wolf looming behind her.

She scraped the door of the house and the girl reappeared to let her in. The trees stayed silent, and more than ever, the wolf wanted to ask them what had happened, with the girl and the she-wolf and the hunter. Perhaps the pines heard the anguished pace of his heartbeat, for their voice laden with age and wisdom told him to run now, very fast and very far. They cared for him the deepest, and as it always was with favourite sons, the wolf ignored their advice. He had made a vow to his dying mate not to give up the hunt before the huntsman was dead, and he had already failed her once.

When the girl left that night, the wolf followed her bobbing lantern all the way to the village. There remained a simmering fury underneath the sweetness of her song, and it burned the wolf's thoughts like cinders. Never had he felt more kinship toward the girl, for he knew the hate was for the huntsman and it echoed within him. If only he could have told the leaves to beg for her to stay, to come find him in their shroud.

But he could not speak, and the girl could not hear, and so his yearning went unrequited as she climbed over the walls and her light disappeared behind them.

All the way back to his hunting grounds, the pines pleaded and pleaded for him to leave, and all the way the wolf ignored them in favour of brooding. When the huntsman returned under the cloak of night, the indignant pines did not warn him again.

The wolf awoke to a terrible silence. It was worse than when the witch and the huntsman had fought, as though all of the forest held its breath. He recognised the huntsman's presence from his smell of sweat and lamp oil and fermented grain, mixed with the primroses near the crone's house, but could not tell what caused the silence. It was only when he reached the house he understood.

The forest had gone mute with horror as it watched the one-handed huntsman hacking his axe into the crone outside her house.

What had prompted the attack, the wolf neither knew nor cared. In that moment, the opportunity of finding the huntsman alone in his domain seared the wolf's mind blank and he lunged out of the thicket.

Despite the smell in the man's breath, he dodged nimbly and swung his axe at the wolf. The forest roused as one, crying for the wolf to be careful—but so loud was their worry they disoriented him, and the huntsman buried his axe in the wolf's side. Fury redoubled, the wolf sank his teeth in the flesh of the huntsman's thigh and tore with all his might, but the axe rose and fell even as the huntsman screamed, until the wolf's maw parted and released the man.

The huntsman dropped his axe as he stumbled away from the wolf, both maimed and bleeding. The wolf tried to rise, but his legs shook and would not carry him. The axe had crushed more bone and parted more flesh than his fangs had, and though the wolf collapsed every time he pushed himself up, the huntsman managed to gain his feet. He gaped in turn at his side and the wolf, trouser torn and glistening in the moonlight like the surface of the lake. He studied the wolf's wounds, mouth hanging open, then fumbled for the pistol on his belt. His hand quivered as he aimed for the killing blow, but before he found the courage to pull the trigger, a voice spoke out from amidst the trees.

"Everyone will hear of your crime," it said, startling both the man and the wolf. "Everyone will know what you've done."

To the wolf, the voice was hushed and small, like that of berry bushes—but there was a force behind it, the way there was in the witch girl's song. The man stepped back, searching for the speaker in the thicket, then dove for the axe on the ground, threw it into the lake and limped down the path as fast as he could.

Moonlight faded in the wolf's eyes. The blood pooling around the crone and creeping toward him grew redder, redder, as if it absorbed all of the little light left in the night. A cold breeze chilled the warmth streaming out of his side, but as it carried leaves to float on the waters, it brought back the new voice.

"Feed on my flesh," it said, and now the wolf recognised the crone. She had spoken the language of leaves once before, in the mountains, when she had asked if he planned to eat her. "It is of no use to me now. I have no power to fulfil my threat to him, but at least I can heal you."

The wolf tried to rise again, but his hind legs had gone numb. He crawled to the body and took a feeble bite of the arm. There wasn't much of the tiny woman to eat, but then, he never ate much at all. After he had reduced the arm to bones, he felt strong enough to stand. His bleeding had stopped, and though he still felt drained, he knew he would not die abandoned like his pack had. He wished he could have thanked the woman, but it seemed his voice was beyond the crone's ability to heal, and now hers was gone too. It had weakened with each bite, until she'd bid farewell to the woods.

He noticed crows gathering on the branches reaching over the house. They looked disappointed enough at the loss of one meal, and on the wind he heard the distant plea of birches begging him to deny them the other as well. The house's door was ajar, and the wolf dragged the crone's body inside for shelter. With some effort, he managed to lift her onto the low bed and position her as though she were asleep, the way he'd seen the tall men do to their deceased out at the graveyard by the foothills. The room itself was a sepulchre of sorts: On the walls were mounted the head of a deer and a pike; on the table was an ornament of eagle talons, pinions and beak; and over the bed hung the skin the crone had used to transform herself, filling the room with its unnatural stench or absorbing it.

The wolf collapsed beside the corpse. His lids drooped shut, and though he feared the huntsman would return with allies, the forced mending of his flesh had left him terribly, terribly weary, so he could not bring himself even to leave the house. Sleep came for the wolf and took him without invitation, to a place halfway from where Death resided. So deep was his slumber the sunlight starting to filter in through the leaves and dusty windows did not awaken him, nor the cawing of the crows, nor even the warning cry of pines. Only when the witch girl screamed did he bound to his feet.

How great was her fury, how enormous her wrath! The redhaired girl covered her mouth with her palms, her muted keening flooding the room, but in her eyes blazed a fire set to consume the wolf. When she lowered her hands, her teeth were bared in a grimace and she lashed out with a knife for his throat. The confines of the cottage were too small for a creature of his size to evade with any nimbleness, and so the wolf crashed against a shelf of tinctures. Amidst the shower of falling vials and their shards, the girl cut into the muscles of his thigh. Her steel sent lightning through the wolf's bones, but he held against his instinct to bite the girl's outstretched arm, dashed past her to the open door, and broke for the thicket through morning mist.

The girl ran after him, shrieking with mad rage, ignoring or unable to hear the forest's pleas to stop and listen. The wolf fled over streams and under fallen trunks, but the reopened wound ensured he could not shake her. Every flower, every leaf, every blade of grass she ran over cried out that she'd been deceived, but her pursuit went on, down the slopes and mossy climbs toward the field.

The wolf hoped the tall grass would hide him, but as he laid still and watched the girl come out of the woods, his heart sank when they both noticed the trail of blood he'd left. His gambit had cost him distance, for the mist was too thin on the fields to give him shelter. The wound was wearing the wolf down, but he broke into a run again, intent upon losing her at the dry ravines farther from the forest.

Soon the grass underfoot gave way for loose rocks and the terrain turned steeper. The girl gained on him, and out in the barren foothills there were few places to hide. Further up, the hills grew craggy, and in their maze he might shake her off.

As he ran up the hill, from behind came a rumble and a yelp. He stopped to see the huntress tumbling down a scree. Her foot, so much less sure than the wolf's, had slipped on the uneven ground, and she'd caused a rockslide when she fell.

She rolled down into a pit, and when the dust and rocks settled, the wolf saw her lying still, buried under a pile. For a spell, his heart stopped, but the girl's meek whimper from beneath her cairn made him spring into motion and slide down the steep face of the cliff.

The wolf shoved rocks aside until he found an arm stretching out, palm up to the sky. The girl was beaten and bruised, but alive. Both her legs were crushed under a boulder, and the darkening skin under her torn clothes spoke of cracked ribs. Her eyes, though open, were unfocused and searched the sun beyond the veil of mist.

The wolf's heart ached for her fleeting life, one nail driven through it for every emotion she had taught. The coating of dirt and dust did nothing to hide the redness of her scattered tresses, wetted with blood at the roots. The wolf leaned closer to lick the wounds at her temple, and she reached up, closed feeble fingers around his muzzle. He yearned to thank her for everything she'd given, but his voice remained stolen from his throat, cast out somewhere on the winds ever since he had told his cubs he would keep them safe.

Then, a thought struck him. He turned from the girl, leaving her with the sun and the silent forget-me-nots to send her away— though if he was fast, they might yet mourn too soon.

His limp grew more pronounced the further he exerted himself, and only when he was back at the house he realised the shift in colouration of his crusted fur. He did not eat more of the crone, for fear of the uncanny lethargy taking him over again, but yanked the wolfskin off the wall and threw it over his back, then bit off a pound of flesh from the crone's side. Though he did not swallow his morsel, some of the power it contained seeped onto his tongue and hastened his flight back to the ravine.

The witch girl had cleared away what rocks she could, but still lay where the wolf had left her. She did not cry for help, but stared vacantly toward the sky, arms stretched at her sides, legs pinned beneath the boulder she hadn't the strength to move. She turned her head sideways when the wolf approached, then rolled away in disgust when he dropped the slab of saliva-coated meat beside her. He recognised the emptiness in her mien, the resignation to embrace the coming end. He had seen it in his mate when she watched their cubs slip away, one by one. When his promise had become a betrayal.

If he could have, he would've uttered those words again, earnestly, with certainty. The girl was inches away from salvation, yet when the wolf whined and prodded her, tried to get her to take the cloak, she pushed him away. Her face was ashen, breathing shallow, and unless she took the wolf's offering, her passing was but moments away.

He bowed his head, listened to the wind howling with beloved voices, sought from it the words long left unspoken, words he had forgotten. The howling grew louder in his ears, as though the pack spurred him on. His prior yearning had been selfish; now he needed them to save a life.

And so, with effort, he extracted the right words from amidst the calls. When he opened his mouth, the girl faced him with astonishment.

"Witch girl," he said, with the deep voice of a king. "Wear the skin. Eat the flesh. You will be made whole again."

She stared at him now, as though trying to see past his fur and skin into his very soul. "Why would you help me?" she asked, stained brows furrowing. "Don't you understand I'm wounded? I couldn't run if I tried. Better you bite into my throat and release me from this pain."

"Given no choice, I would." He nudged the piece of meat closer. "But I owe you too much to do so. Wear the skin. Eat the flesh."

She continued to study him, until her eyes welled with tears that flowed sideways down her cheek and over the dusty ridge of her nose when she asked, "Did you kill my grandmother?"

The wolf said, "No."

Finally, the girl accepted the skin and pulled it off his back. She wrapped it around herself, until it ceased being a cloak and knitted together to enclose her. The glass eyes came alive with the grey in her own, and the mouth parted to suck in a breath.

She remained trapped through the transformation, but as she chewed the meat, the wolf summoned all his strength, pressed his shoulder against stone, and pushed the boulder off her. The girl said nothing when she ate, nor after, but fell asleep as soon as she swallowed the last piece. Hesitant of leaving, lest the huntsman was brave enough to come out of his hut today and stumbled upon her, the wolf curled around her and whispered, "I will keep you safe."

The girl slept through the day and into the evening. The wolf left her only to hunt, and when he returned with a grouse, she was awake. She did not know how to shed the second skin—her grandmother hadn't taught her to wear one yet, though it was only a matter of time until she would find a way on her own. The wolf was glad for the company, however brief it would be.

She told him the huntsman had come to her house last night and told her he'd been out laying a trap for the wolf, when he'd found its tracks near her grandmother's house. She had not believed —the huntsman feared the crone too much to go anywhere near her house, especially alone at night. It was why they'd fought the day before: He wanted desperately to marry her, save her before she left the village and became a slave to the devil in full, and she had thrown him out for slandering her family. Why would she stay amongst people who were frightened of who she was any longer than she had to? The woods had always been kind, and she was determined to leave as soon as she had learned enough to survive on her own.

But, seeing the wolf in the bed had driven her mad with grief, and in that moment the huntsman's words of seeing the wolf rip apart her grandmother and then attack him became an infallible truth. In turn, the wolf told her what he'd seen, and had it not been for the lupine guise, she would've wept bitterly. Come nightfall, her sorrow had solidified into hatred mirroring the wolf's, and together they hatched a plan of revenge.

They travelled to the village, first running together, then with the girl riding on the wolf's back, the skin draped over her shoulders once she learned how to part it. The girl had healed his thigh with a touch, and he loped through the woods with newfound vigour owing both to the healing and the approaching retribution. The forest cheered them on, nettles urging them to torture the huntsman, spruces wishing them to be careful.

A wall of poles surrounded the village, but the girl scaled them with ease. They were made to keep wildlife out, and no one had minded when she had etched handholds on them for freedom of coming and going, given it kept her away from their children until they were safely tucked in. She lifted the bar shutting the gates off its holder and let the wolf creep into the settlement.

The tall men slept soundly in their tall houses, every window dark, save for a hut past the sheep pen and the chapel. The girl guided the wolf there, told him to wait for her signal, and knocked on the door. The huntsman appeared shortly, leaning on a cane, and gasped with shock when he laid eyes on her.

"You were right," she said, tongue parting to speak both the language of leaves and of men. "I found the wolf and slew it."

The huntsman stammered a response, but the wolf did not understand. The girl shook her head and said, "I'm fine. I simply needed time to grieve." She paused, hummed with a mockery of careful thought. "I also considered your offer. I will need someone to look after me, now that my grandmother is gone. And, I suppose …I suppose I could consider staying in the village, if you would still take me. Maybe I won't be looked at strangely anymore if people know I won't leave them for the woods one day."

The huntsman answered with excitement, and the girl stepped inside. In his glee, the huntsman didn't notice she left the lock unlatched, and that a thin strand of his lantern's light still escaped outside.

They sat at his table, the girl facing the door, and the wolf peered through the opening. The huntsman animated everything he said with his hand, but the gestures were as arcane to the wolf as the rolling of his tongue. The girl wore a placid smile, but under the table, she drew her knife from its sheath.

"I accept," she said, when he finally stopped talking. "But I want you to do it properly. If you want me to be your wife, kneel before me."

He laughed, but rose from his seat and searched his drawer for a brass ring. He brimmed with pride showing it to the girl, set his cane against the table, and knelt with grunts and winces in front of her. He spoke a verse, a rising lilt, as the daisies did with their endless questions.

Through a smile, the girl's tongues twined into one and brought the susurrus of falling leaves into the hut. "Come, wolf."

She slashed her knife across the huntsman's throat, and as he fell, the wolf barged in and sunk his teeth into the huntsman's belly. A flush of blood, viscera, and gastric fluids glistened with firelight on the floor as the girl tossed the lantern on the table onto the carpet. Coaxed by the girl's magic, the fire caught the huntsman's shirt, the blanket hanging off the edge of the bed, and climbed up the tablecloth like it were oiled. It filled the ceiling with smoke as black as the wolf's fur, and before the blaze swallowed him, the huntsman watched the girl he'd coveted whisk the skin on her shoulders over herself and become one of the beasts he feared and hated.

The witch and the wolf watched the huntsman's burial the morning after, hidden in the mist and the shadows of trees. The girl had donned the wolfskin, as much for warmth as for the comfort it offered. After the preacher had spoken and the villagers had interred the huntsman, the wolf asked how would they remember him. The girl said nothing; the birches told him it wasn't worth knowing, and that it said enough they hadn't buried the crone at all, but burned her bones together with her house.

The witch and the wolf ran far from the village and the woods and the lake, to another forest nesting between the mountains, where the pines welcomed their new king and queen with familiar voices. The girl never came to love the wolf the way he loved her, but grew to care for him, and their simple life was a happy one. With every season, the times she took off her cloak became fewer and fewer, until she enclosed it over her shoulders for the last time and forgot she was human at all, like her mother once had. On that night, when the snows were bright with starlight, the witch and the wolf climbed up to the jagged peaks and sang with the language of leaves. The forest answered, a thousand voices calling to the gentle night until it birthed aurorae in the shapes of a fallen queen and her princes. With their wild hunt over, the wolf gave his family to the great beyond, where they ran forever, free and avenged.

Originally published in Galaxy's Edge issue 49, March 2021
Reprinted by permission of the author

~ *  * ~

Ville Meriläinen is a Finnish author of fantasy and horror fiction.

The Wolf God's Path

Deby Fredericks

"Remember this," the wise woman said. "There are many gods. From here, you set foot on their path."

Gray dusk settled over the land, spreading great swaths of shadow across the hills. Lamps twinkled in the town of Losmoor, like a pond reflecting starlight. This was a between time, the wise woman had explained. After the sun set, yet before the moon rose. It was a time when the gods might speak.

"You may choose to step onto their path. Perhaps you will find an alter stone and change your future. But that is their boon to give or withhold," Mistress Henbane cautioned. "You cannot decide which of the gods you may meet."

Lily Madison listened nervously. Mistress Henbane wore a traditional dark dress with a stiff bodice and full skirt, a white blouse beneath it. Her body was plump, and her nose pointed like a pigeon's beak. Brown hair was pinned up under a white ruffled cap. The wise woman was younger than Lily had expected. Not even as old as Mama. Yet when she spoke, it was with the wisdom of ages.

However, there was a space in the stone circle behind Mistress Henbane. Lily could see the guardian stones that ringed Losmoor, standing tall and black against the fading day. Through another gap, the marble towers of a stately edifice gleamed from a higher hilltop. Mount Elizabeth College. Lily's throat tightened when she saw it. That was where she longed to be.

"Are you prepared to begin the ritual?" Mistress Henbane's words pulled Lucy back to the moment. Her dark eyes scanned the three young women before her.

Each of them wore a simple shift with a loose gray gown over it. They carried white candles. Lily didn't know them at all, except that they were doing the ritual together.

Her stomach fluttered with nervous tension. This ritual rejected her whole life before now. She squeezed Mama's hand, and felt her firm grip in return.

The oldest of women spoke softly, "I am ready." She stood alone. Black ribbons were plaited into her hair, marking her as a widow.

The girl on her other side muttered something. She was no more than five years older than Lily. The draping of her gown did little to conceal her swollen belly, and her face was puffy from tears. A stern-looking older woman had a firm grip on her shoulder.

"You must say yes or no, Leah," Mistress Henbane corrected. "This choice is for you to make." Her gaze rested a moment on the older woman, whose eyes narrowed. Lily could almost hear the clash of crossed swords between them.

"I said I'll do it," Leah blurted. She shrugged away from her companion's grasp.

Grandmama spoke gently from Lily's left. "Hold to your word and all will be well, my dear." The relative scowled at Grandmama. The girl, Leah, did not look up.

"I'm ready," Lily declared before Mistress Henbane could ask. Even with all her misgivings, she had been preparing for weeks. Grandmama told endless stories about the multitude of gods. Mama helped her sew the gray gown she now wore.

Unlike the other young women, Lily stood with family. Mama held her right hand, and Grandmama's hand curled into her left elbow. It was almost embarrassing, to have their open support when others walked alone.

Lily couldn't help them. Not yet. She snuck a glance at Mount Elizabeth's pristine summit. One day, maybe, she would be able to.

"Powers of the land, guardians of the circle!" Mistress Henbane began the ritual so abruptly, Lily jumped a little. "Our younger sisters come to you at this hour between. They seek the alter stones."

Lingering guilt coiled in Lily's stomach. Papa would not approve of this. He followed only Primus and refused to acknowledge the other gods. That was why they had waited until he went to Trusston on business before joining the wise woman's ritual.

"Guide them, according to the ancient pact," Mistress Henbane intoned. "Share your vision and your strength. Help them see the way more clearly."

As the wise woman spoke, mist filtered up around the stone circle. There didn't seem to be a particular source of it. Lily watched, fascinated, as pale tendrils crept between the standing stones. The circle where they stood was a full array of nine, the stones just above shoulder height. Three taller stones made a triangle at the center, directly behind Mistress Henbane. The landscape beyond the circle faded into a blur.

Lily muffled a nervous gasp as the stones themselves began to glow from within. The auras were emerald, gold and crimson, or midnight blue, or lavender pink. Hazy figures appeared within each stone. Some seemed almost human, but others resembled animal heads or more abstract symbols. Despite her worries, Lily was fascinated.

"To find your path, you must focus on what you desire," Mistress Henbane announced. "You may be drawn by the color, or the god's figure in the stone, or by some other sign. Go to the one that calls you."

A shiver went through Lily. Mama must have felt it, for she squeezed Lily's hand again briefly. She glanced over long enough to meet Grandmama's encouraging smile. No, Papa would definitely not approve of this! For the first time, that made it more exciting.

"No choice is right or wrong," Mistress Henbane continued. "Only remember that there are many gods. Not all of them are kind. If you feel danger or fear, you are permitted to turn back. Trust yourself, above all."

The wise woman murmured something more, and each of the candles ignited. Lily almost dropped hers, but then gripped it even tighter. Trust yourself! Papa did not trust her. That was why she had to come in secret. But Mama and Grandmama trusted her. As the candle's flame grew, hope glowed within her.

She squeezed Mama's hand and patted Grandmama's hand on her elbow before she slipped away from them. She drew in a deep breath and silently vowed, "*I can do this.*"

But how? Lily scanned the stone circle. What color called to her? What god would help her change her path? Some of the tints were different now. They looked duller, muddy. Only one was still vivid—a silvery gray stone, across from her and to the right.

Lily was hardly aware when the pregnant girl's relative shoved her forward. Then the young widow curtseyed to Mistress Henbane and moved off to the left. She held her candle confidently before her. Lily couldn't take her eyes off the silvery gray stone. The emblem inside was some kind of animal track. She barely remembered to curtsey toward the wise woman before her eager steps carried her to it.

The guardian stone was roughly hewn. In the flickering of her candle, Lily saw it wore a robe of its own, gray lichen mottled with muted orange.

"We match." Lily's interest quickened.

As she approached, rays of silvery light sprang up around it. Then pale yellow flecks appeared on the ground. Foxfire! A scattered line of tiny mushroom caps led to the left of the stone and into the fog.

"Help me find my way." Lily curtseyed to the stone.

Mist closed around her as she followed the foxfire trail. The area around the stone circle was open, covered in grass and wildflowers. Their scent was dry and sweet. Yet soon the fragrance changed to something like forest duff. Lily walked between trees with jagged leaves that hung down and tried to snag her neatly plaited hair. She held her candle close, cupping a hand to keep the mischievous twigs from igniting.

Somewhere in the mist, an animal raised its voice in a chilling howl. Was that a wolf? Lily halted and bit her lip.

All her life, Grandmama had told her about the gods who lived in the stones. There were some who watched over buildings, or the trades, or the seasons. But there were darker gods, too. Vultures, snakes and flooding rivers each had a god. What if she met one of those, instead of a helpful one?

Lily had always been a good girl, humble and obedient. But lately, Papa kept mentioning how his partner, Mr. Eaton from Trusston, had a fine son with bright prospects. In fact, he had gone off to see Mr. Eaton just yesterday. Lily didn't think it had to do with their furniture making business. She didn't like how this trip might end.

It wasn't that she was scared, exactly. It was just so soon. Lily was fifteen, too young for Papa to tie her to anyone. She had her own ideas, and Mount Elizabeth College was a vital part of them.

Then, yes, Lily was scared. She had to admit it. She was afraid of what Papa would say if he found out she did this ritual while he was away. But she was more scared of not doing it. She couldn't give up her dreams because of what Papa thought. Mama and Grandmama had agreed with her decision. She couldn't let them down.

That was why she had to follow the foxfire trail through this foggy wood that shouldn't be here, but was. She had to find an alter stone, whether Papa liked it or not!

Clinging to the excitement of her defiance, Lily pressed on. At times the foxfire seemed to vanish. After moments of anxiety, she spotted it again. The mushrooms' glow showed up between roots or on tree trunks, now high and now low, as if daring her to keep going.

The howl came again, maybe from more than one beast! Lily couldn't tell how close it was.

Didn't Grandmama say there was a god of wolves? Kirishac Redfang, maybe. Another howl pierced the fog. Her heart pounded, not just from walking. Her breath came short with nervous excitement. The howling felt like a call meant just for her. Could she really would find an alter stone?

She hurried on. Suddenly, the trees thinned out and the fog drifted away. Lily had come onto the crest of a low hill. Unchanging dusk revealed the land spread before out her. The hills were familiar, yet no town nestled among its farm fields and fences. No college towers, either. The grass grew much higher, and dark shapes prowled through it. She only caught glimpses of four-footed beasts skulking there. They had shaggy fur and triangular ears standing stiffly upright—she was right. Wolves!

Lily's heart chilled with fear as every story she had ever heard whispered in her mind. A wolf's head was a lawbreaker. A she-wolf used her charms to get what she wanted. The good girl inside her faltered. Was this really what she wanted?

But the newly rebellious daughter gripped her candle tighter. Nobody could *make* her be a lawbreaker. Those were just stories. Mount Elizabeth was real. Lily had to go there. She couldn't give up.

The sky above was neither darker nor lighter than when she left. The guardian stones loomed at the top of the rise. Lily seemed to have returned to the exact spot where she exited the stone circle. But there was one huge difference.

A large white wolf sat just where Mistress Henbane had been. Its eyes gleamed like yellow embers, and a silvery glow rippled around it. Beside it was a low, flat stone. The outline of a wolf's paw shone through the lichen. A circular hole had been cut above the emblem.

An alter stone! Lily couldn't breathe for a moment. She had really found one!

Silently, the white wolf stared at her. More wolves paced between the stones, but Lily could only stare at the white one. It shifted a bit, as if impatient. Gathering her nerve, Lily curtseyed and walked up to it. Her hand trembled as she pressed her candle into the hole. A light wind rustled in the grass. Or maybe it was the wolves trotting nearer.

"Are you Kirishac Redfang?" Her own voice sounded feeble to her.

The animal dipped its muzzle proudly. Words pressed into Lily's mind.

"Why have you come to me, Lily Madison?"

She wasn't surprised the wolf god knew her name. "I'm following the ritual. I need an alter stone."

"I know of the ritual," Kirishac answered. *"What do you seek from it?"*

"I don't know——" Those words were on her tongue as the habits of an obedient daughter suddenly clutched her heart. How could Lily think she deserved a god's attention? There were others, like the poor pregnant girl, who needed it so much more. But under those yellow eyes, something wild in her jumped up and fought back.

"I want to have a choice," she spoke out boldly. "My Papa is talking about marriage. He hasn't said it to me, but Mama thinks so, too."

Kirishac tilted its head to invite an explanation.

"Maybe it wouldn't be so bad. Mama says she's happy," Lily stammered, but then recovered her courage. "I'm only fifteen. There are things I want to do. To be collared and leashed…I can't breathe when I think of it."

"Freedom is important," Kirishac acknowledged. More wolves emerged from the grass, forming a loose ring around the stones, the girl, and their god. Their eyes shone with the reflection of Kirishac's light. *"How will the alter stone give you that?"*

Lily didn't know how to answer. Mama, Grandmama, Mistress Henbane all just said the alter stone would change her path. Nobody said how it was supposed to work.

"I want a different choice," she repeated when the wolf god kept staring at her. "I want to decide for myself!"

"Those are the words of a child." Kirishac was annoyed. *"You would put yourself first."*

Lily faltered. The good girl inside her said, *"See? You're just being selfish."* She shook her head.

"It's not childish," she burst out. "Once I'm married, my life will be all about other people. Pleasing my husband, running a household, and raising children… If I am not free now, there will be no other time."

"Hrrr," the wolf god growled, but in a thoughtful way. *"Suppose I did help you. I could gift you with my spirit and make you strong enough to speak up for yourself. But I hear that whelp whimpering inside you. What if you give up, and let your father decide after all. Why should my gift be wasted?"*

"It wouldn't." Even as she said it, Lily realized how empty those words might be. She wouldn't have foxfire and guardian stones every day of her life. "What can I offer, that wouldn't waste your gift?"

"No god likes to be forgotten." Kirishac slanted a burning glance toward her.

"Oh." Lily thought of something Mistress Henbane had said to Grandmama, that no one hearkened to the old gods anymore. "What if I was your voice? I could speak your wisdom among the people."

"You would become a wise woman, instead of what your father lays out for you? Or that misty dream I see in your mind," Kirishac sounded skeptical.

"The wise women speak for all the gods. I would speak for you alone," Lily told it.

A brief twitch of the wolf god's ears told her something was off. That wasn't what it wanted. Panic tumbled inside her. It couldn't be that she completed the ritual and found the alter stone, but still failed! Desperately, she summoned the strength to say what she hadn't even told her Mama.

"Over in Warrethy, there's a lady's school. They teach all sorts of things, accounting and nursing…but one of them is domestic law. I want to study that. Then I would speak up for the woman with a cruel husband, or the child who is neglected." That poor widow went through her mind again. She must have followed all the rules, but still ended up alone.

"*You wish to be their protector,*" Kirishac said, "*as I am to my kind.*"

"Yes. I would share your gift of freedom with them," Lily said.

"*You will be called mad. A she-wolf who fights for a lost cause.*" Kirishac scoffed, but Lily could tell it was pleased, too.

"I will speak up for them, no matter what people say." Or what Papa said? She pushed her guilt aside. "I will change my future, if you will it."

Lily held her breath. The white wolf dipped its muzzle. Golden eyes bored into Lily's.

"*That will do, Lily Madison. Touch the stone and alter your path.*"

Joy blazed inside her. Lily knelt and pressed both her hands within the outline of the wolf's track. Minerals grated against her skin, rough and hard. Then silvery light filled her vision. Wolves howled all around her as Kirishac's power flowed into her. Lily howled with them, her voice rising higher and higher in a song of freedom and hope for the future.

When the light faded, she straightened. All her limbs tingled. Her gray gown swirled as a soft wind made the grasses sway beneath the endless dusk. The alter stone was dull and blank now. Kirishac and the rest of the wolves were gone, yet their fierce will sang within her.

She breathed in, feeling the confidence and power burning in her chest. No longer was she a humble, obedient daughter who did what others wanted. She would not be collared and leashed. Yet, she was still a good person. Her heart for protecting the weak had not changed. It was her own will she carried into the world.

"It shall be done, Kirishac Redfang." Lily curtseyed again. Then she took up the candle, absently noting it hadn't melted down at all. She turned to follow the foxfire path, back to where her family waited.

She had a lot to tell them.

~ *  * ~

Deby Fredericks has been a writer all her life, but thought of it as just a fun hobby until the late Nineties. Since then she has published twenty fantasy novels, novellas and novelettes, either with small presses or independently. Her short fiction has appeared in

Andromeda Spaceways, selected anthologies, and small magazines.

In addition, Fredericks writes for children as Lucy D. Ford. Her children's stories and poems have appeared in magazines such as *Boys' Life*, *Babybug*, *Ladybug*, and *Spider*. Her latest project is Cleodora, a cozy fantasy duology for middle grades. A bold girl sets out to discover why the nature spirits have made it stop raining.

In the past, she served as Regional Advisor for the Inland Northwest Region of the Society of Children's Book Writers and Illustrators, International (SCBWI).

Mother's Love

Robert Allen Lupton

Saturday morning Sandra ate a light breakfast, dressed in warm clothing, and tramped through the light snow. She stopped, took off her backpack, and checked the last of the thirteen feeding stations she maintained in the Jemez Mountains.

She brushed the leaves away from the pressure plate and stepped on it. The food station opened. The plate required fifteen pounds of pressure. A wolf, even a young one, was heavy enough, but a coyote wasn't. The few bears in the area rarely figured out that they needed to stand on the pressure plate to keep the feeding area open, but if one did, well, good for her.

Like every time she checked, it was empty. She quickly unsealed three pounds of chopped mutton, stirred in a half dozen heartworm prevention chewables, and a fistful of multi-vitamins. Heartworms killed more of the pack than hunters and ranchers, or at least they had until Sandra had started her inoculation program.

She put the mutton inside the feeding compartment and operated the counterbalanced door several times to ensure it worked properly.

A chuff or a soft whine broke the silence. Sandra scanned the forest. A male wolf with one cub watched over the top of a fallen aspen tree. It looked like her mate, Kazar, and her daughter, Shera. Sandra inhaled. The scent was familiar. Shera and Kazar, sure enough.

Sandra barked a greeting and then moved away, smiling. Kazar and the cub would eat the mutton long before Sandra was out of sight. The cub was young. She'd need rabies and distemper vaccinations and Sandra would need boosters herself. Next month, Sandra thought. Next month she'd vaccinate the pack. Some years that was easy, but some years it was a battle for dominance. One thing wolves and people had in common was their inability to understand was good for them.

The two wolves gently nudged Sandra aside and ate the last of the mutton before Sandra could store it away. Kazar wiped his face with his forearms, licked them clean, and nuzzled Sandra. He whined gently and put his head in her lap. She petted him. The smaller wolf, Shera, circled Sandra warily before snuggling with her.

The shadows grew longer and Sandra noticed her breath was visible. The sun was setting and cold came quickly to the high country. She reluctantly pushed the wolves aside. "Kazar, I've got to go. You know I hate the cold. Walk with me."

The pack joined one by one until more than a dozen wolves walked with Sandra. They stopped near the edge of the small clearing surrounding a rustic cabin. The door stood ajar and no smoke came from the chimney. "Damn," Sandra muttered. "The fire went out. Dinner will be late tonight."

Neither she nor the pack cared about the open door. Sandra never locked it.

The fire wasn't completely out and Sandra managed to restart it from the embers. The cabin would be chilly when she went to bed. She shrugged. It was better than sleeping in a cave, although she remembered years of sleeping in caves.

She warmed a can of beef stew and made biscuits from a box. Delicious. She ate near the fire by the light of the full moon. She'd need to buy rabies and distemper medications tomorrow. The old vet was a kindred spirit, so that wouldn't be an issue unless her truck wouldn't start. It was always a bit temperamental after sitting idle for four weeks, but she parked it at the top of a hill. Let it coast for ten seconds, pop the clutch, and it would run fine.

The next morning, she reconnected the battery cables. It started on the first crank. Two hours later, she parked on a slight hill outside of *El Viejo Lobo*, a small veterinary clinic in Tesuque, New Mexico.

The Old Wolf, Mark Corrales, ran a one-man show. He specialized in farm animals, but he was willing to look at the occasional working dog. He did most of his work on the ranches and farms in the area, but he was always there when Sandra arrived for one of her regular visits. He gave her a quick hug. "Hope the pack's doing okay. I don't have much time today, got a mare in labor at the Robinson spread. She's in trouble. I've bagged the medication for you. Leave payment on the counter. See you next month."

"Spanish gold is still okay?"

"You bet. The coin dealer in Santa Fe can't get enough. The tourists pay stupid prices for those."

"My supply isn't endless, but I did watch Coronado hide his stash. I moved it."

"Sandra, you're hundreds of years older than I am, but you don't have to rub it in. I'm off, lock the door behind you. I marked the injections. Red tape is for the adults and blue is for the cubs. If you don't use them in the next couple of days, the vaccines will keep just fine in your cabin until next month. You look less than five years old."

"Must be my diet." She laughed and followed him out the door. *Five years old*, she thought. *More like five hundred*. She believed her body regenerated whenever she changed forms. All her injuries healed and any illnesses simply vanished. She'd been terrified pregnancies would be terminated by the change, but they weren't. She'd hoped her children might be like her, but none of them were.

Sandra took in a movie. She adored romance movies. She visited a local shopping mall and took the opportunity to charge her cell phone and her EReader, her solar chargers worked better in the summer. She ate three ice cream cones and drove to a nearby *carnicería*, a butcher shop, where she bought thirty pounds of frozen mutton and three cases of canned pork. Meat, it's what's for dinner.

Sandra stashed the food in an old root cellar and parked the truck on top of the entrance. She read all day Sunday, left her phone and EReader plugged into the solar chargers, placed a pound of dry dog food with three heartworm gummies in a plastic bag on the counter, and went to bed at sundown. She woke once around midnight. The last rays of the full moon were directly in her eyes. She went back to sleep.

She woke up on the floor. The world smelled differently than it had yesterday. It was sharper and clearer. The fire was out, but she wasn't cold. She stood on her four legs and shook her fur. Hungry, she paced into the kitchen, tore open the plastic bag, and ate the dog food.

A wolf howled from the woods, it was Kazar. She left the door open behind her when she ran to meet him.

She rarely remembered her time as a human when she was a wolf, but when she was human, she remembered being a wolf almost all the time. Her human memories were strong for the first couple of days. As she ran with the pack, she remembered who and what she was, at least for a little while. Her human memories came back to her as the change approached and whenever her wolf form was near a human. Self-preservation, she thought. Becoming aware when she was around humans helped protect her from them and knowing who she was before the full moon meant she wouldn't wake up naked in the snow. Waking up to clothes and coffee was a better plan.

Sandra had read several novels and watched several movies about werewolves, humans who turned into wolves, or into exaggerated wolf-like monsters whenever the moon was full. She'd never met one of those, but maybe they existed somewhere. Sandra didn't have a name for herself, for what she was, for what she did. She wasn't like the creatures in the werewolf stories. Some of them could change forms at will. She had never managed that, and not from lack of trying. She'd managed to sprout some fur and make her nose extend almost into a snout a few times, but the effort was too much and she'd never been able to maintain the necessary focus.

She wasn't a human who changed into a wolf, she was a wolf that changed into a human when the moon was full. She didn't know how old she was, but she remembered the time when the pack chased buffalo and humans hadn't learned to make fire.

The crisp air tickled her nostrils, the frost crunched under her feet, and she embraced the joy of the pack. A deer, a buck by the smell, fed in the mountains above her. She yipped eagerly at the scent. Kazar yipped back and ran uphill. She ran with him. Silently, the rest of the pack followed. The deer would sense them soon enough, but there was no reason to announce their coming.

The buck, hornless now that mating season was over, fled at their approach. Sandra was glad, she loved the hunt as much as she loved the kill. She and Kazar prolonged the chase to exhaust the cervine. He crippled the deer with a snap at one hamstring, and Sandra tore its throat out. Her human memories vanished before she swallowed the first bite.

Weeks later, the pack smelled smoke and investigated. They found six men camped in the forest. Hunters or men pretending to be hunters. The stench of liquor and marihuana overpowered the smell of unwashed bodies. Deerskins hung from branches and two coyote heads decorated the hood of a pickup. She was confused at first, but the longer she was around humans, the more she could remember about her human life, and the more she thought like a human. Her change was close and she always became more human mentally as the full moon approached. She understood right away the pack didn't have any use for these people.

Kazar, her mate, growled softly and she nipped him gently to quiet him. The underlying smell of cordite and gun oil was strong. The pack was brave, but bravery wasn't enough to confront men with guns. Sandra had been old when the Charge of the Light Brigade happened, but the death of those brave men reinforced the lesson. There's a difference between brave and stupid. Fight fire with fire.

She needed to lead her wolves to safety. It's never a good idea to be a four-legged animal anywhere around a bunch of drunken testosterone-driven idiots with guns. She nipped Kazar again and ran a dozen steps away from the camp. She bared her teeth and growled. He followed her and the rest of the pack followed him.

The next morning one of the hunters captured a pack member. Shera, her daughter, had ignored Sandra's warnings and let her curiosity get the best of her. She snuck back and was watching the camp when one of the hunters spotted her. He emptied his repeating rifle without hitting her, but when she ran, she stumbled into a snare trap. The steel cable tightened around her rear leg and held her.

Sandra could read the signs like she'd watched it happen. The only thing she couldn't tell was what the men had said to each other.

She ran to where she could watch. The men were breaking camp. Shera's paws were tied, but she didn't look injured. The men had wrapped her mouth with tape so she couldn't howl for help.

Motioning for the pack to stay back, she slipped close enough to hear. A man in a red hat grumbled, "Fred, it ain't right we all got to pack up and go just because you caught a baby wolf. Let's just skin her and stay the rest of the week."

Fred, who wore a bright orange vest and camo pants, shoved Red Hat. "Touch my wolf and I'll skin you. A young female like this, pure-blooded, she's worth fifty thousand. A breeding farm outside Taos has a standing offer. Wolf pups go for twenty, maybe twenty-five thousand. I'm taking her to Taos while she's alive and kicking. You got that, Charlie?"

Charlie pouted. "Fine for you to leave, but why do the rest of us have to go?"

"Because you ain't got the sense God gave a grasshopper. Without me to watch out for you, you'll probably shoot your damn foot off. And don't forget the wolves. They run in packs, you know. If I leave you behind, the wolves will be poopin' your carcass across the mountains by morning."

Charlie touched his sidearm. "Ain't afraid of no wolves."

"You should be. That's why I ain't leaving you here. I ain't telling your wife I let you get your dumb ass killed. Pack up."

Sandra watched the men load Shera into the rear seat of a silver pickup truck. She could see the license plate, but she didn't trust herself to remember it. It's hard to write without paper, a pen, or hands for that matter. The plate, emblazoned with chili peppers, read BDCH14. She watched the men drive away and made six piles of pebbles. Two in the first pile, four in the second, then three, then eight, one, and finally four. She'd need to remember which piles were for letters and which were for numbers, but after her change, she'd drive her pickup here. The license plate pattern would match her own.

Mark Corrales would help her find the breeding farm in Taos. Veterinarians talk to each other. The County Sheriff was one of his best customers and with enough gold on the table, finding out who owned the silver truck wouldn't be a problem. She'd have three days to get her daughter back, since the change only lasted three days. She repeated Big Dogs Can Howl Fourteen Times to herself and repeated it again. Need to remember the damn number.

She called Kazar and the rest of the pack. They were distraught. Sandra did her best to reassure them and ran to her cabin. Her change was only hours away and she didn't want to waste a second. Once changed, she'd have three days, seventy-two hours, to find her daughter, rescue her, and return to the Jemez Mountains. She had to find the wolf napper through his license plate while he still had Shera or, failing that, find the puppy mill near Taos in time to rescue her daughter. Frighteningly difficult tasks considering the short time available to her.

She usually slept through her changes. She'd go to sleep as a wolf and wake human or the other way around. Not this time. She whined and paced the floor. She kept going over what to do in her mind, but she never thought as clearly as a wolf, even this close to the change, as she did as a human. Get dressed, get in the truck, find Mark Corrales, and tell him the license plate number. *What was the damn number? Big dogs chase fifteen cats? No, that wasn't right. The first thing to do after starting the truck was verify the plate number. Rocks. I made piles of rocks. Why did I do that? License plate. Don't forget. Big dogs can dance? No, focus, focus.*

The muscles in her rear legs tightened, but it wasn't a cramp. The change came on her. Her nose tickled as it shrank. Her whole body itched as the fur was re-absorbed into her skin. It didn't really hurt, but it was uncomfortable. She remembered why she tried to sleep through the change. Muscle aches, head pain, and the maddening prickling tingle covering her body. Scratching didn't help. The nausea passed quickly, but the disorientation lingered for a while. She took several deep breaths, dressed, and grabbed a hidden bag containing three knives and a loaded double-action revolver. The truck keys were in her pocket.

Kazar stood by the truck. She nudged him aside. "I'll find her. You stay here. Take care of the pack."

She opened the door and her mate shoved his way past her, leaped into the car, and positioned himself in the passenger's seat. "Out! Get out!" Sandra ordered.

Kazar bared his teeth and growled deeply in his throat. He glared at her and shrugged his shoulders as much as a wolf could shrug, turned to face the passenger door, and curled up in the seat.

Sandra poked and pushed him, but it was like fighting water. He just ignored her. She slapped his hip. "Fine! Have it your way. I don't have time to argue with you." She tossed her weapon bag on the floorboard, crossed her fingers, and turned the key. It started.

She drove to the campsite and said, "You going to help me find the rock piles I made to help me remember the license plate?"

Kazar didn't quiver, but he shifted his body further down on the bench seat.

Sandra smiled. She hadn't thought for a second she could trick her mate into leaving the truck, but it was worth a try. She found a pencil stub and a grocery receipt and went directly to her rock piles. She counted and wrote them down, converting the first four counts to letters. BDCH14. She whispered, "Got you, asshole!"

Kazar jumped out of the truck at Corrales's office, visited a tree, and then waited impatiently at the vet's door. Sandra scratched his head. "Pleased with yourself, aren't you?"

A quick explanation to Mark and he was on the phone to the county sheriff. Sandra only heard one side of the conversation. "Yes, a puppy mill in Taos. The truck's owner captured a female wolf cub. Yes, I have a witness. BDCH14, that's right. You'll text me the owner's information? Great. How about the puppy mill? That too. Thanks."

Less than a minute later his phone beeped. He read the message. "Sandra, his name is Fred Harris. He's got a place just outside of Alcalde, it's on our way to Taos. It's outside of the sheriff's jurisdiction, but he'll try to get someone to meet us there. He's still working on finding the puppy mill. I think we should take two trucks. That rust bucket of yours might not make it five miles. Questions?"

"Only one. Why are we still here?"

No one was home in Alcalde. Sandra let Kazar out and her mate sniffed the air, the ground, and inside the outbuildings. She kicked down the front door of the house and Kazar was in and out in less than a minute. He whined and jumped back in the truck.

"She's not here, is she?" Sandra asked. She's never been here."

Kazar whined and nosed the ignition.

Sandra turned to Mark. "Kazar can't smell her. She hasn't been here. They must have gone straight to Taos. You got the address?"

"Entered in my phone. GPS will lead us right to them. You want to wait on the police?"

"Oh, hell no. Just text him that we're on our way. Ask him to meet us there."

The road to Taos winds along an area of the Rio Grande River called the Taos Box. In the spring the stretch is filled with class four rapids and a constant stream of rafts loaded with tourists parade downstream. As winter approaches the river isn't calm, but the rapids are smaller and the tourists have found other things to do. The last time Sandra came to Taos, she played tourist and rode the rapids with a guide called Spiros. She'd loved the slowly drifting water between the rapids, the rush of frenzied action and cold water, and the sudden quiet after the rapid. She remembered it as one of her best days as a human.

She let Mark take the lead. She'd have to learn how to use GPS. The human world changed so quickly it was hard to keep up, especially since she only had three days a month, and most of those were spent shepherding her pack.

Mark turned off the highway and followed a narrow trail away from the river. According to her odometer, he stopped three miles from the highway and got out of his car.

"Sandra, the puppy mill is on the left over the next rise and about a quarter mile off this road. The sheriff hopes to be here in about an hour. He didn't call the authorities in this county. Said he doesn't know who to trust. You want to wait?"

"No, Kazar and I are going after our daughter. You coming?"

"I'll wait on the sheriff. I've got an aerial view of the place on my phone. Take a look. You can see the kennel, the house, and a couple barns. The pictures are a couple months old, so it doesn't show what trucks are here."

Kazar growled, leaped from side to side on the front truck seat, and bit and clawed at the doors.

Sandra said, "Kazar knows she's here. He can smell her."

She checked her revolver one last time, patted herself to ensure she had all three knives, and opened the car door. She was barely able to step out of Kazar's way. "Mark, you and the sheriff best hurry. Kazar's pretty worked up, and to tell the truth, so am I."

She followed Kazar over the hill and the first thing she saw was the pickup. The license plate was clear—BDCH14. She didn't see any humans. Maybe they were in the house or an outbuilding. There had been two in the truck, Fred and Charlie, and there had to be somebody running this place. At least three people to deal with. Time to make a plan. Maybe go in quietly and catch them one at a time.

Kazar didn't wait for a plan. He could taste Shera's scent in the wind and he charged straight down the hill. *Need a new plan*, Sandra thought. *Keep up with Kazar and don't get killed. Good plan.*

Kazar howled as loudly as he could as he raced toward the cluster of buildings. Shera howled back and dozens of dogs chimed in. She didn't shout for her mate to stop. She couldn't possibly be heard over the canine chorus, but Sandra cut loose with a bone-chilling war whoop and charged.

Three men ran out of the main house, spotted them, and

ducked back inside. In seconds, gunfire erupted from the doorway and windows.

Kazar jumped to one side and ran out of the line of fire and toward the kennel. Sandra turned to follow him, overbalanced, fell, and rolled down the incline.

She stumbled to her feet and was shot in the shoulder. She dropped to her knees and was hit in her right arm and her stomach. She collapsed.

Kazar felt her distress and turned back to help her. He took a bullet in one haunch and another one in his shoulder.

Fred, Charlie, and another man slowly surrounded Sandra. They kept their rifles pointed at her. Charlie moaned, "My God, we've killed a woman. We're in trouble now."

Fred touched Sandra's face and she flinched. "She ain't dead. Leastwise, not yet."

The third man, Carlos, rolled her over. "She's got three bullets in her. Gut shot. She'll be dead soon enough."

Fred put his rifle to her head. "I'll kill her now."

Carlos pushed the barrel aside. "I got no problem defending myself, but I can't let you just shoot her. Without help, she'll die. Leave her. I'm more interested in that male wolf. If I can keep him alive, he'll be prime breeding stock. Let's get him in the barn. Even hurt, he'll fight like hell, so watch your ass."

Sandra groaned. The men threw a tarp over Kazar and wrapped him in it. They dragged him into a building while she watched helplessly. She was faint and felt herself bleeding out. If only she could change. The change heals all wounds, but she wouldn't change for two more days and she'd never live that long.

She needed to force a change, something she'd never mastered. *Change or die*, she thought. *Change, or doom your mate and child to a life as breeding slaves.*

She pressed one hand over the hole in her stomach, closed her eyes, and focused on her breathing. She pictured fur sprouting from her skin, her clothes tearing apart as her body changed shape, and claws extending from fingers and toes as they morphed into paws.

It hurt. It hurt more than the gunshots. She opened her eyes and stared at her right arm. It was thinner and fur-covered, but it was still bleeding. Her hand shriveled and her fingernails blackened. The bullet hole in her arm screamed at her, but she fought to maintain focus. The bleeding stopped and the bullet surfaced on her skin for a second before the flesh closed under it and the bullet fell to the ground.

She looked at her shoulder. The bleeding had stopped and the pain was gone. She felt a lump below the paw on her stomach. She brushed the third bullet away from the newly healed skin.

The agony of her bones changing shape was indescribable, but thankfully brief. The skull was the worst and the headache was piercing, but her mind was clear. Unlike the full moon change, she remembered everything.

The men and Kazar were in the barn. The scent of several dogs was ripe from the kennel, and the familiar smell of Shera was strong in the breeze. She used her teeth to rip away the remains of her clothing, ran down the hill, and nosed open the kennel door.

There were three, maybe four, dozen cages. She wasn't sure. Her mind was clear but when she was a wolf, she wasn't good with math. The cages were latched, but not locked. She pawed one and then nosed it, but was unsuccessful. She needed hands. She sat on the urine-stained concrete and focused on changing into her human form.

It was faster, but more painful than before. Barefoot, she ran from cage to cage and opened them. The dogs were loud and frenzied. Sandra knew the men would be here any second to check on them. She hugged Shera briefly and said, "We've gotta hurry. They've got Kazar. Stay with me."

Sandra found cattle prods hanging near the cages. *Bastards*. She stood beside the door and waited while the dogs clamored and pawed at it. Fred opened the door and the dogs knocked him over in their rush for freedom. Sanda stepped over him and he froze at the sight of her naked body. She sneered, "You wish," zapped him, took his rifle, and shot him.

In the barnyard, the breeder and Charlie scrambled after the dogs, but there were too many. A pit bull jumped on Charlie and took him down and a pack of a half dozen descended on the man. Sandra smiled and took aim at the breeder.

The breeder gawked at her body, but he shouldered his rifle. Sandra pulled the trigger, but nothing happened. The gun was jammed. She struggled to clear it.

The first shot missed her head by less than an inch and splinters flew from the kennel's door jam. There wasn't a second shot.

Kazar limped silently from the barn and jumped on the breeder's back. The man went down, arms and legs akimbo, and the rifle clattered on the hard dirt. A few seconds later, Kazar raised his head and howled. The breeder didn't get up.

Sandra went to Kazar's side. His eyes were wide with pain. Shera joined her and licked at one of Kazar's wounds. Sandra didn't think he'd live and thought if he did, he'd be crippled. She hugged his neck and cried.

Mark's truck roared over the hill and into the barnyard spraying dirt and scattering the dogs. He grabbed his veterinarian's bag and ran to Kazar. Shera put her ears back and growled. Sandra restrained her daughter. "Let him help your father."

Mark and Sandra carried Kazar to Mark's truck and put him in the back seat. "I'll take him to my office. You take your daughter home. Come for him on the next full moon. He'll be okay. I promise."

"What about this. Three men are dead."

"Sheriff's not coming today. Let the police figure it out if they ever show up. Put the rifles by the bodies. They have gunshot residue on their hands. Besides, the dogs are hungry and they'll likely destroy most of the evidence anyway."

"Mark, that's disgusting."

"Yeah, but I'm not waiting around for the cops. I've got to save your mate. Put your daughter in your truck and go home. I'll see you in a month. Any questions?"

"I could use some clothes."

"I've got spare jeans and a shirt in my truck. A vet never knows when a goat's gonna vomit. Get dressed and get out of here."

And she did.

Twenty-eight days later, she parked in front of *El Viejo Lobo*. Mark was as good as his word. Kazar wasn't completely healed, but he was much better. He whined when he saw Sandra and she whined back.

"I should keep him for another month," Mark said. "He's not ready for the wild. As far as I've heard, the cops have never checked the breeding farm, but I've treated a lot of found purebred dogs this month."

Sandra nodded. "Shera's in the truck. I left the Jemez wolf pack with one of my older daughters. She's eleven and has been aching to be an alpha for a while. They'll be fine. As for me, New Mexico's all right, but there are too many people. We're leaving for Montana right now. You want to join us?"

Mark smiled, "I believe I do. Give me a few minutes to load my truck."

~ * 🐺 * ~

Robert Allen Lupton is a retired commercial hot air balloon pilot. Robert runs and writes every day, but not necessarily in that order. Over 200 of his short stories have been published in various anthologies and magazines, both print and online. Over 2500 drabbles based on the worlds of Edgar Rice Burroughs and several related articles are available online at www.erbzine.com/lupton. He has four novels, seven short story collections, one cookbook, and four edited anthologies available from purveyors of the finest books available.

Visit his website at: https://www.minds.com/robertwriter/

Junebug's Secret

Jenna Hanan Moore

Junebug awoke from a dream of chasing Drakalupes across the universe and found herself nestled between her two sleeping humans. Their names were Daddy and Mommy, although they sometimes called each other Jeff and Paloma. Oh, how she loved them! She wagged her tail and stretched.

Also known as Junie-Moon, Peanut, and several other silly nicknames, Junebug was a sixteen-pound terrier with fluffy white fur and one brown ear. Being the size of a house cat didn't quell her desire to chase much larger animals. For although she was small, the blood of her fierce wolfy ancestors flowed through her veins. She would protect her humans with her life if necessary, just as her ancestors had protected theirs during the Drakalupe invasion.

But why think of that now? It was time to wake up her humans so they could take her for her morning walk. Oh, how Junebug loved her walks! She began licking Daddy's face.

"Silly girl," he said, petting her head.

Mommy began to stir too. "Good morning, Peanut!" Junebug turned to lick Mommy's face, then rolled over on her back so both humans could rub her belly.

After several glorious minutes of belly rubs and cuddles, Mommy and Daddy got out of bed. Junebug waited while they brushed their teeth and put on an extra layer of fur. At long last, Daddy said the magic words.

"Junie! Wanna go for a walkie?"

Oh boy! Did she ever! She ran to the bedroom door, wagging her tail. When Daddy opened the door, she raced downstairs, followed by both humans. Mommy put on Junebug's harness, and they headed out into the cool, spring morning.

Half a block from the house, they turned onto an earthen path that wound a short distance through the woods. The humans called this the nature trail; Junebug called it the best walk ever. She stopped to sniff the air. No sign of her nemesis. She trotted along next to

Mommy, turning her attention to the scents along the ground.

When they reached the end of the nature trail, they turned onto a paved path next to the road leading home. That's when Junebug spotted the large brown animal nibbling a shrub near the road. Mommy and Daddy called this animal a deer, but Junebug knew better. It was a descendent of the Drakalupes. She bared her teeth and growled.

Mommy tugged at the leash. "You are not going to chase that deer, Junebug! She could hurt you!"

Junebug let out a single bark. The deer looked up, then ran into the woods. Junebug trotted happily towards home, proud she had chased away the intruder.

"Come on, Junie-Moon," Daddy coaxed. "Let's go get breakfast." She picked up her pace. She loved breakfast!

After her meal, Junebug settled in on the sofa to nap while Mommy worked at her desk. As much as Junebug loved her family, she wished they could understand her language. She longed to tell them the story of the Drakalupe invasion. Maybe then they'd see the danger.

It was a bitterly cold night, but the wolves had to leave the warmth of their den to find food. Sometimes a nearby pack of humans left scraps of food near their fire, and other times they had to hunt. Leyira left the den with her mate, Janek, and two other wolves.

Soon, they reached the cluster of human dens, which sat along the border between the great plain and the forest. Tomasz, the friendliest human in the pack, was sitting on a large rock and holding his bow. The fire was out. Strange. Tomasz, wrapped in bear furs for warmth, was staring at the horizon. He did not react to the wolves as they approached. Also strange. The wolves sniffed the air. No food, but there was another scent. Fear.

Leyira approached Tomasz. He did not respond until she was nearly within reach.

"Oh hello, beautiful girl!" He reached out to stroke her fur. Leyira nuzzled his shoulder. She wanted to ask why he smelled of fear, but humans could not understand the language of wolves as wolves understood the language of humans.

Tomasz rose from his seat, slinging his bow over his shoulder. "I've got something for you." He walked toward a nearby tree, knelt, and brushed the snow aside. He lifted a wooden covering, reached into a hole where the humans stored food, and pulled out the roasted carcass of a small boar. Leyira licked her chops as the aroma reached her nostrils.

"You'd best take that to your den," Tomasz said. "That thing is coming closer." He looked toward the horizon. Leyira looked too, but no creature was approaching, only a faint, green light.

Leyira tilted her head inquisitively. Tomasz sighed. "I wish I could explain, but even the Elders don't know what it is." He dropped the carcass at her feet. "Go on. Take that back to your den." She nuzzled Tomasz's shoulder in thanks. He patted her head. "Go on home, girl."

She picked up the carcass as Tomasz rose and returned to the rock where he sat keeping watch through the night. Leyira turned and walked towards her companions, who were waiting on the perimeter of the humans' encampment. Their gazes, like Tomasz's, were fixed on the green light on the horizon.

When Leyira reached them, she, too, looked to the horizon. The light was growing larger and brighter, but the sky along the horizon remained dark. As the light approached, she saw there were three lights, not just one.

The air was filled with a gentle hum, which grew in volume until it was a loud buzz. A strange cylindrical shape took form in the sky behind the three lights. The shape gradually descended until it landed in the snow. The wolves sniffed the air, but the strange creature had no scent.

Tomasz readied his bow, and the wolves raised their hackles. They watched in silence as the creature opened its mouth and stuck out its tongue. Smaller creatures began to walk down the tongue towards the snow. Only then did the wolves begin to detect the faint scent of other animals, a scent they did not recognize.

Janek howled a warning, and Tomasz blew into a horn. "Take that back to the den," Janek whispered to Leyira, indicating the carcass. "We may have to fight." Instead, she ran to the top of a nearby bluff. She hid the carcass in the snow and waited silently, watching.

Several humans emerged from their dens, armed with bows, and six wolves arrived in response to Janek's call. The small group stood together in a single battle line, watching the strange creatures approach across the plain.

These four-legged creatures moved gracefully and swiftly. The closer they got, the larger they loomed. Although smaller than bears, the creatures were larger than all other known animals. They had brown fur, black hooves, and bulging muscles. Most had great racks of silver horns that branched out from their heads in elaborate patterns ending in sharp, spear-like tips.

When the creatures reached the encampment, they stopped running and formed a line of their own. They greatly outnumbered the humans and wolves. The largest creature stood at the center of the line, a full head taller than the creatures next to him. The sharp points of his massive antlers glistened in the moonlight. He did not open his mouth, yet a voice boomed forth, speaking a language that could be understood by both humans and wolves.

"We are the Drakalupes. We have come from a world far away to find food. If you step aside and allow us to take what we need, no harm will befall you. But if you do not heed this warning, we shall destroy you."

Perhaps the Drakalupe leader spoke the truth. Perhaps if there were enough food to share, the Drakalupes would leave them in peace. But this had been a harsh winter, and food was scarce. If the Drakalupes took what they wanted, the wolves and humans would not survive.

Tomasz broke the silence. "Our world has little food, just like yours. If we share what we can, will you leave us in peace?"

The Drakalupe leader showed no emotion. "Show me. Then we shall see."

Tomasz walked away from the encampment, motioning for the Drakalupe leader to follow. The other humans, wolves, and Drakalupes stood frozen, watching. From her perch atop the bluff, Leyira saw Tomasz was leading the Drakalupe towards the water.

In warmer months, the water was a place of abundant food. Berries grew on the plants that lined its shores. The grasses, now dormant under the snow, returned to life, and flowers bloomed. Caribou, rabbits, and marmots were drawn by the plants and berries. Birds were drawn by the insects that emerged in the spring and the fish that swam in the water itself. In winter, however, the flowers and berries did not grow, the water was covered by layers of ice, and most birds and animals stayed away. Surely, the Drakalupe would not be satisfied by what he found. Leyira raced down the back of the bluff, taking a different path to the water. She loved Tomasz almost as if he were a pack member; she could not allow him to face the Drakalupe alone.

When Leyira reached the water, she hid in the brush.

"Where is the food you promised?" the Drakalupe demanded.

"There is water under the ice, and fish swim in it. Follow me but be careful."

The Drakalupe followed Tomasz onto the ice. "You'd best stay here," Tomasz cautioned after they'd walked several paces. "The ice gets thinner." Tomasz got down and slid across the ice on his belly. He sat up, pulled an arrow from his quiver, and plunged it into a hole in the ice. When he pulled out the arrow, there was a fish on the end.

The Drakalupe started towards Tomasz. "Wait! The ice is too thin. Stay where you are." Tomasz slid across the ice towards the Drakalupe, then rose and walked the rest of the way. He removed the fish from the arrow and handed it to the Drakalupe, who swallowed it in one gulp.

"Is that all?" the Drakalupe asked, his voice booming.

"Food is scarce in winter, but if you camp here until spring, maybe we can help each other. You run faster than us, so you can hunt further out on the plains than we can go, but we know the secret places, like this one. We can find more food if we work together."

Leyira sniffed the air. The Drakalupe's anger was steadily growing. Silently, she crept through the brush until she was close enough to pounce on the Drakalupe with one leap.

Tomasz continued his plea. "When spring comes, food is plentiful. We can give you berries and fish and game to take back to— wherever you came from."

"Not good enough!" the Drakalupe bellowed. "We will take what is ours!" He began to stomp his front legs. Cracks appeared in the ice. Tomasz looked past the Drakalupe toward the shore. The Drakalupe lowered his head, pointing his great rack of horns in Tomasz's direction.

Leyira leapt from her hiding place. She tore at the flesh on the Drakalupe's rear leg with her teeth and her front paws. The Drakalupe cried out in pain and surprise. He turned to face Leyira, but she dashed to the side, out of his reach. With the Drakalupe distracted, Tomasz was able to reach the shore and ready his bow.

The Drakalupe tried to pounce on Leyira, but her agility gave her an advantage in the thick brush surrounding the water. The chase ended when Tomasz struck the Drakalupe with a well-placed arrow.

The huge beast fell to the forest floor. Tomasz knelt in the snow. Leyira ran to him, crouched at his side, and rubbed her head against his face.

"You okay, girl?" he asked, stroking her fur as she quietly nuzzled him and licked his face. "I wish I didn't have to do that. We could have helped each other."

They remained together only briefly. Soon, Tomasz trudged through the snow toward the humans' encampment, while Leyira ran through the woods to find more wolves. The wolves would need to take the Drakalupes by surprise if they were to prevail.

As daylight began to paint the eastern horizon, Leyira and fourteen other wolves approached the encampment. They came stealthily across the plain behind the line of Drakalupes that stood facing the defensive line of humans and wolves.

Meanwhile, Tomasz addressed the Drakalupes, describing the abundance of food they could expect to find if they waited for the warmer months that were just ahead.

A Drakalupe interrupted. "Where is our leader? Why has he not returned?" Several Drakalupes pawed the ground.

Just then, the approaching wolves broke into a run. The startled Drakalupes found themselves fending off attacks from both sides with no leader to guide them. Soon, they fled back to the strange cylindrical object from which they had emerged hours earlier. Once they were inside, the object rose through the sky until it disappeared.

The humans and wolves watched the spectacle in stunned silence. They did not notice until the following day the Drakalupes had left behind six of their smallest and weakest members.

Tomasz pleaded with the other humans to let the animals live. "These six pose no threat by themselves, and we have enough food to share with so few."

The other humans did not understand Tomasz's compassion for the remaining Drakalupes, but they could not have prevailed in the great battle without the help of the wolves he'd befriended. They agreed to let the six small Drakalupes live in peace.

Over the years and centuries that followed, the Drakalupes mated with caribou and produced offspring that were smaller and more docile than the Drakalupes. Their descendants—which came to be known as deer—learned to eat things humans and wolves could not—things like leaves, ivy, and tree bark. Meanwhile, the friendship between wolves and humans deepened. Over time, many of the wolves grew tamer with each generation, until they became dogs and moved into the soft, warm interiors of humans' homes. Humans forgot the story of the great battle when they stopped sitting around campfires telling tales of the heroes of yore. But wolves and dogs passed the story down from generation to generation.

And so it came to pass, one beautiful spring evening, thousands of years after the great battle, a feisty terrier named Junebug ate the bits of juicy steak that had been added to her kibble, licked her chops, and settled down on the sofa with her family for a nap. Her humans knew nothing of the Drakalupe invasion, but Junebug knew the story by heart. She'd heard it from her mother when she was a tiny puppy. When the Drakalupes returned, she would be ready to face them. As she drifted off to sleep, Junebug dreamed of chasing Drakalupes across the universe.

First published in Land Beyond the World Magazine (online, March 2022)
Reprinted by permission of the author

Jenna Hanan Moore loves to travel, take pictures, drink coffee, and immerse herself in nature or a good story. She lives with her husband in southern Illinois, but she left her heart in the Pacific Northwest. Her tales have appeared in places like *The Pink Hydra*, *Luna Station Quarterly*, *The Lorelei Signal*, *365 Tomorrows*, and *Friday Flash Fiction*, and in anthologies from JayHenge Publishing, Altitude Press, and B Cubed Publishing. She is the founder and editor of *Androids and Dragons*. "Junebug's Secret" was inspired by a little terrier named Juno, who was the best companion anyone could ever ask for.

Wolf Haven

Andrew M Seddon

The two moons were full, and under their light the wolves howled.

Impossible to tell if they were near or far away, the howls crescendoing and then fading away, while the shifting shadows made it equally impossible to discern if anything lurked in their depths.

Leina, standing at the entrance of the shelter next to Victrix and Rex in his habitual black-and-tan German Shepherd shape, shivered as she peered into the night.

Doc Hughes, Founder and Director of WOLF—Wellness for Other Life-Forms—gave his wife a questioning glance.

"Worried?" he asked.

"Not worried…unsettled might be a better word."

Hughes nodded. "With reason." He glanced down at Victrix, feeling the big German Shepherd's unease through the telepathic link they shared. He couldn't quite read Rex's response; the alien metamorph's emotions were still hard for him to access.

He laid a hand on Leina's arm. "But I don't think we have anything to fear. Not from the wolves at any rate."

She flashed him a quick smile. "You're a veterinary exobiologist, used to being around all sorts of animals. Most of them are new to me."

His expression was pensive. "Fear of wolves is almost primal. And yet it shouldn't be. Trust me on this."

"Oh, it's not the wolves, dear…it's whatever else might be here …whatever has got the wolves upset."

Hughes motioned towards the door of the shelter. "Let's get some rest. "We'll need it for tomorrow."

She preceded him, Victrix and Rex following, and he closed the flap behind them. Made of a nearly-impenetrable fabric, the shelter could resist any natural offensive armament wielded by animals. Able to sleep anywhere, he'd be fine, and he hoped Leina would sleep well too…or at least awaken reasonably refreshed.

But the wolves' howls affected him also, and he sensed Victrix was equally troubled—and not only troubled, but saddened, because that was in the wolves' howls as well. He was glad his schedule had allowed him to respond to this unexpected mission.

The call for assistance had come hard on the heels of a successful planet-call to the Extinct Species Recreation Project on Aafedt III involving dire wolves.

"Incoming message, Doctor," Sofi, the Starship Operations and Flight Intelligence, had announced while he was working out in *Wolf-1*'s gym, Victrix padding alongside on a treadmill, while Rex was amusing himself by contorting himself into a variety of seemingly impossible configurations.

"Play it," he said to Sofi, and a hologram materialized, that of a man wearing a gray jumpsuit with the logo of a stylized running wolf and the words "Wolf Haven" blazoned on the left breast. He appeared to be in his forties, with sandy hair, a short beard, and a worried expression.

"Doctor Hughes," he said, "my name is Foster Kelleher. I'm the Resident Manager on Wolf Haven. Perhaps you've heard of us. Something is killing the wolves and I'd be most grateful for your assistance. You can be assured we have eliminated common causes, so that is why I wish to enlist your expertise. Payment authorization is attached, which I hope meets with your approval. The wolves are very dear to me. Please come."

The hologram faded.

"Sofi," Hughes said, "How long to reach Wolf Haven?"

"Five days at Tach-six, Doctor."

That would work.

"Initiate."

"Confirmed."

Leina received the news with enthusiasm.

"Real wolves? I've always wanted to see a real live one. There's nothing quite like them on my homeworld."

"Then you're in luck," Hughes said. "We'll probably see plenty of them."

From orbit, Wolf Haven looked like many another inhabited world, blue ocean speckled with a variety of islands, but only one major continent, crowned by a range of mountains.

"So why haven't I heard of Wolf Haven before?" Leina asked as their shuttle entered the planet's atmosphere.

"It's what's known as a conservation world," Hughes replied, staring out the viewport, "which means no planetary association or government claims ownership of it. Most such worlds are Earth-registered and typically self-administered. Some are quite popular among eco-tourists, others are very restrictive. Wolf Haven is one of the latter. You'd have to wait years for a visitor's permit."

The shuttle banked through a cloud layer, skimmed low over a range of forested hills, on the other side of which appeared a sub-stantial cluster of buildings—a small town, really, Hughes thought.

Sofi brought the shuttle to a gentle landing next to another craft with "Wolf Haven Security" in large letters on the side.

"Power down, Sofi," Hughes said.

"Confirmed. Have a safe visit," Sofi replied.

Fresh air and sunshine greeted them as they descended the landing ramp, Victrix and Rex bounding ahead. Wolf Haven's sun was a pleasant orange K-type star, slightly cooler than Earth's sun.

A tall man whom Hughes easily identified as Foster Kelleher exited the nearest building and strode towards him.

"Dr. Hughes, welcome," he said, extending a hand. "I can't tell you how delighted I am that you could come."

Hughes returned the firm handshake. "My wife, Leina."

"Pleased to meet you," Kelleher said, giving her a handshake as well. "And this must be the famous Victrix," he added as the black shepherd gave him a sniff and a polite greeting. "I've heard about her."

Hughes wondered wryly if there was anyone who hadn't, thanks to stories on various news services across the civilized worlds.

"She's genetically modified, I understand?"

Hughes nodded." For enhanced intelligence and longevity."

"And telepathic to boot? Is that true?"

"Just with me," Hughes said. "We were independently subjects of failed experiments, but when I rescued her from a wrecked research facility, somehow our implanted neural nets meshed. I don't know how it works, but it does."

"It must be something else," Kelleher commented.

"And not always pleasant," Hughes said. "Dogs aren't people

…some of the things they do…"

Kelleher laughed, but it sounded forced.

Hughes tuned in to Victrix's impression.

<Tense. Very stressed> came her assessment over their link.

"But who is this?" Kelleher asked, indicating Rex.

"This is Rex," Hughes replied. "The newest member of my team." Since the skaggit was the last of his species, Hughes didn't like to disclose Rex's shapeshifting ability unless it became necessary. No sense in inadvertently risking undesirable attention from criminal elements or unscrupulous researchers who might want to steal the skaggit.

"This way," Kelleher said, sweeping an arm. "That's the hotel over there, but I've had to close it until the current crisis is resolved. You'll be the only guests. The Grand Howl Suite is all yours."

"We don't mean to put you to any trouble," Leina said.

"No trouble at all. We're paying the hotel staff to do nothing at the moment. Much though they enjoyed it at first, I think they'll be glad of some work. Do you want to settle in or learn the nature of the problem?"

"The problem, please," Hughes said.

Kelleher spoke into his commlink, then ushered them into another building and a well-appointed but functional office where two other people were waiting.

"Ramon Perez, head of security, and Dr. Sylvia Antoni, staff veterinarian," he performed introductions. Victrix gave them her usual quick scrutiny then plonked down to watch and listen while Rex curled up into a ball.

Kelleher sat behind a desk, motioning to the others to take seats.

He touched an inlaid screen, and one wall of the office illuminated to show a panorama…a scene of denuded hillsides, massive erosion, native vegetation stripped of its lower branches, saplings nothing but sticks.

"This is what the discoverers of Wolf Haven found when they landed here, some two hundred years ago," Kelleher said. "It was an ecological disaster, a totally unbalanced ecosystem."

"What happened?" Leina breathed, shocked.

"What we believe is a plague wiped out the dominant predator, a *Canid*-like animal, about the size of Victrix—totally exterminated the species. As a result, their major prey, a herbivorous species something like a small Earth deer, proliferated unchecked, and basically defoliated the continent."

"And the solution was wolves?" Hughes asked.

"Administration of the planet was acquired by the Wolf Preservation Society, which had long been fighting for the survival of *Canis lupus*. I don't need to tell you there were no remaining wild wolves on Earth."

"Still aren't."

"Breeding pairs from various captive programs—Gray wolves, red wolves, Mexican wolves, and others—were introduced. And you saw the results as you flew down. The herbivores were controlled, and ecological balance restored. The forests recovered, and Wolf Haven was born."

"A wolf paradise," Hughes said.

"Yes. Until something started killing them."

"Some *thing*, not some *one?*" Leina asked.

"Hunting is prohibited," Perez interjected. He was a stocky, well-muscled man with a square face and black hair. "And we would know of any unauthorized activity. While we can't afford top of the line monitoring, our systems can detect any unauthorized approach or landing…civilian, that is. Military would be a different matter. Besides, the findings are not consistent with hunting."

"Nor with illness," Dr. Antoni, a lithe brunette, said. "I haven't discovered any trace of disease." She glanced at Hughes. "You're welcome to review my test results, but I don't think you'll need to, especially after you see the photos." Her gaze shifted to Kelleher.

"This is graphic," the Resident Manager warned.

The image on the wall changed to show row upon row of wolves, torn, shredded, mangled, dismembered, some ripped in half.

Despite himself, Hughes shuddered.

Victrix whined and came to stand beside him, sensing his distress.

"Inter-pack fights?" Leina suggested.

"Not with this much damage," Hughes shook his head. "Some enormous predator."

"That was my impression," Dr. Antoni said. "Something big enough to rip up full-grown wolves."

"But that's where the problem lies," Kelleher said. "There

aren't any predators larger than a wolf. Certainly not in two hundred years. And based on what we glean from the fossil record—which is not extensive, and hasn't been exhaustively studied, I grant you— never were."

He folded his hands and leaned forward, the gaze from his green eyes intense. "That's why I called for you."

"When did the killings begin?" Hughes asked after a long silence.

"About six planetary months ago," Kelleher said. "The first carcasses were spotted by a team member doing a routine flyover. We try to interfere with the wolves as little as possible, but do conduct routine surveys to follow the movement of the packs. That also helps with planning itineraries for visitors."

"At first we ascribed the deaths to inter-pack rivalry as your wife suggested," Dr. Antoni said. "But it rapidly became clear that wasn't the case."

"Every month witnessed more deaths," Kelleher continued. "Some of the carcasses—or parts thereof—the ones you saw photos of—were brought back for Dr. Antoni to autopsy. But we stopped doing that when it seemed pointless."

Hughes pondered. "And there have been no sightings of this beast—if beast it is?"

Perez shook his head. "None. We've sent drones, done flyovers …nothing."

"But the deaths seem to occur around the same time each month," Antoni said. "At least the ones we know about. Of course, there may be more."

"All over the continent?" Hughes asked.

"Concentrated in this area," Kelleher said, bring up a map and circling a section. "Interestingly, several of the packs have shifted away from that locale."

"Have there been any staff injuries?" Leina asked.

"No," Perez replied. "As the scale of the problem became evident, I recommended to Manager Kelleher that all staff be confined to town, and a secure perimeter established. Tourists were evacuated, as well as any employees who wished to leave."

"Very prudent," Hughes said.

"So what do you think?" Kelleher queried.

"The answer is out there," Hughes said slowly rubbing his chin. "We just have to know who to ask."

Kelleher gaped and swept a startled gaze that included Perez and Antoni. "Who would that be?"

"The wolves," Hughes said. "They're the ones that know."

Morning brought sunshine and dew on groundcover that resembled a combination of grass and moss.

Hughes stretched as he exited the shelter, while Victrix and Rex headed off to do their business.

Ramon Perez emerged from another shelter nearby. The security chief had insisted on accompanying them, despite Hughes' insistence it wasn't necessary.

"Humor me," Manager Kelleher had said, siding with his security chief. "I don't want the eminent Doc Hughes to come to any mishap while I'm in charge."

Hughes had given in graciously.

Perez was slung about with various weaponry. He offered one to Hughes.

"Pulse laser rifle," he said. "Take down anything."

Hughes shook his head. "Thanks, but I don't carry lethal weapons. A neuraltranq is perfectly adequate."

Perez shrugged. "Suit yourself."

"Besides," Hughes said, "we're not going anywhere right at this moment."

Perez frowned. "I thought you wanted to meet up with some wolves."

"I do, but there's no point in us trying to track them—they'd probably try to avoid us...or watch us from a distance. Victrix and Rex will make initial contact, and then we'll follow."

Perez shook his head. "You're sending your dogs out after wolves?"

"In a sense. If there's an area the wolves are afraid of, I'm hoping Victrix and Rex can find out where it is. And that's where we'll search."

"I guess you know what you're doing," Perez said doubtfully.

<Come back> Hughes sent to Victrix.

<Work?!!>
<Yes.>
<On my way!>

Kelleher and Antoni had identified a wolf pack that might prove suitable, near what seemed to be the epicenter of the wolf killings. This pack had lost members but hadn't abandoned its territory. Hughes hoped the alphas might prove helpful.

Leina came out and handed him a breakfast bar. "Do you think your plan will work?"

"Victrix and Rex will do their part, I'm sure, but it all depends on what kind of connection they can make with the wolves. Wolves are intelligent, but I hope this isn't beyond their abilities."

"But won't the wolves see Victrix as an interloper?" Perez asked.

"That's where Rex comes in," Hughes said.

<Tell Rex look like wolf.> He told Victrix.

<Now?>

<Yes.>

A moment later, Victrix burst into the clearing, followed by a medium-sized wolf. They skidded, panting, to a halt in front of Hughes.

Startled, Perez raised his rifle then lowered it again.

"She found a wolf already?"

Hughes laughed. "That's Rex."

"But Rex is a German Shepherd—"

Hughes laughed. "Sometimes. Not always. He's a metamorph —a shapeshifter."

"What…? There's no such thing! Those are legends, myths…?"

"Not in his case."

Hughes bent down and locked eyes with Victrix who had dropped into a sitting position.

<Go with Rex. Find wolves. There is bad animal…dangerous animal …wolves know.>

<Victrix hunt bad animal?>

<No. I hunt. Wolves tell you where to find.>

<Victrix understand.>

"Good girl." Hughes patted her head, then Rex's. "Be off, then. Be careful."

Tails high, they ran off into the forest.

"Let's break camp," Hughes said, "have the flyer ready to go if the dogs make contact."

"And if they don't?" Perez asked.

"Then we camp somewhere else and try again." Hughes grinned. "In dealing with wild animals, patience is a necessary virtue. They don't always cooperate with human desires or plans."

The day passed with no news from Victrix. Hughes resisted the urge to contact her. There was no need to pester the big dog; he knew from past experience she would alert him when necessary. It was enough to sense she was pursuing her task with excitement and determination.

They camped in a new location that night.

"Aren't you concerned?" Perez asked as they sat around a crackling fire—one of those experiences Hughes always enjoyed, but which simply couldn't be done while on a starship.

"Hughes doesn't worry much," Leina interjected before Hughes could reply. "He says it's a waste of energy."

"You see," Hughes explained, "I always have an awareness of Victrix, even though we aren't directly communicating. I don't need to listen to her chatter any more than she needs to be distracted by mine. Right now, for instance, I detect a sense of well-being from her—I suspect she and Rex are curled up somewhere for the night. If she starts to dream, then I might experience that as well."

"Chasing squirrels?" Perez inquired.

"More than you might imagine," Hughes laughed. "But to be fair, she doesn't really appreciate human dreams, either."

Hughes was eating a breakfast bar the following morning when Victrix's thoughts came through.

<Found the wolves!>

<Excellent! Show me.>

Hughes laid down his meal, closed his eyes, and focused. Seeing through Victrix's eyes required concentrated effort, and was a skill that had taken him a considerable while to master. It wasn't something he tried often.

This time, though, the connection formed easily. He saw Rex, and a circle of wolves, lying down.

<Friends?>

<Yes. Rex talk to them. They know bad animal. Afraid.>

The skaggit's mental powers were something Hughes was still trying to understand. How the skaggit could communicate with other animal species remained a mystery.

<*Where are you?*>

<*Here.*>

He received a mental image of a conical mountain rising above a lake surrounded by what appeared to be moorland.

<*Stay there. We'll come.*>

<*Victrix stay. Good food here.*>

Hughes let the connection lapse. Eating raw meat wasn't his thing. He opened his eyes to see Leina and Perez watching him.

"They made contact," he said, then described the image Victrix had sent.

"Sounds like Crystal Lake," Perez said. "About fifty klicks from here."

"Let's go," Hughes said.

They packed up quickly, and were soon skimming above the trees.

"Rex could communicate with the wolves," Hughes said. "Is there anything special about them?"

"You'd have to ask Dr. Antoni," Perez replied, "but this planet has a lot of weird energies…electromagnetic radiation and God only knows what. Plays havoc with our drones and other systems. So I wouldn't be surprised if the wolves had evolved or developed mutations."

"It's happened on Earth and other worlds," Leina observed. "Nuclear accidents, for example."

"Do you think the predator could be a mutant?" Perez wondered. "A sudden evolutionary monster?"

"The thought had occurred to me," Hughes replied. "But I think it's unlikely."

On Hughes' instruction, Perez set the flyer down in a clearing a kilometer from the wolves.

"On foot from here," Hughes said, shrugging into a backpack. "Calm and confident."

Perez slung his laser rifle over his shoulder. "Sure you don't want one?"

"No thanks." Hughes picked up a pair of neuraltranqs, adjusted them to the highest setting, and handed one to Leina. "Just like any other weapon. Point and shoot."

Leina, he knew, from her previous work as an intelligence specialist for the Department of Justice of the Alliance, one of the larger planetary groupings, was perfectly capable of handling weapons.

Single file, Hughes leading, they set off.

<Tell wolves we are coming. Tell them friends.>

<I tell Rex. Rex tell wolves.>

<Perfect. Then come back and lead us.>

"Do you really think you can talk to the animals?" Perez asked, sounding scornful.

"Only to Victrix, and a little to Rex," Hughes said. "But animals can communicate very well with each other. And as far as wolves go, they are the ancestors of our dogs, don't forget. Humans and wolves go back a long ways together. In fact, it's thought they were allies before humans decided to label them as enemies and treat them as such."

"I'm not sure I'd trust them as much as you do."

"And yet you live here," Hughes said. "Has there even been an attack on a human on Wolf Haven?"

Perez shook his head. "No."

"The reason," Hughes explained, "is the wolves here have never been hunted, so they have no reason to fear humans. They've seen flyers overhead, have observed tourists. They have plenty of natural prey. To them we are merely a species of little interest. That's why I'm not worried about the wolves."

A game trail meandered away from the clearing and entered the forest.

They hadn't gone far when Victrix burst into sight, came to a screeching halt before Hughes, and gave a happy bark.

"Good girl!" he said, ruffling her head. "I knew you could do it!"

The trail crossed a couple of small streams.

"We're being watched," Hughes commented as they waded across.

"I haven't seen anything," Leina said, as Perez looked back over his shoulder.

"Neither have I, but Victrix can tell. A pair of younger wolves has been shadowing us."

And then the trail opened out into moorland, and there was the lake and the conical mountain on the far side. Ahead of them was the remainder of the pack. A big male and female—surely the alphas—stood shoulder to shoulder, regarding them with intense amber eyes and wary, though not threatening, posture. Three juveniles stood off to one side, while another pair of younger wolves stepped onto the trail behind them. There were no pups, Hughes noted—probably in the den being watched over by another adult. Rex was lying down, licking his paws.

Perez stiffened.

"Calm," Hughes reminded him quietly.

"Quite the assembly," Leina said.

"Wolves are social, family-oriented animals," Hughes replied. "These are all kin."

"Should we give them something?" Perez asked, a tremor in voice. "Some food, maybe, to show we mean no harm?"

"Absolutely not," Hughes said firmly. "The last thing you ever want to do with a wild animal is to feed it. You risk them becoming attracted to people—associated with food. We need to remain neutral in their minds."

He motioned to Rex. "Rex, come."

Obediently, Rex the wolf-look-alike rose and trotted over to him. Hughes bent over and stroked him, talking gently.

Then he straightened up again.

<Where bad animal?> he thought to Victrix.

<Not far. Rex and wolves show us.>

<Very good.>

She must have said something to Rex, because the skaggit, turned, made a bow before the alpha male, and faced the lake. Tail up, the alpha male cantered away, the female and one juvenile following, while the others stayed behind.

The trail skirted the lake before entering another forest of tree-like plants with bulbous trunks and leaves resembling ferns. For a while it paralleled a rocky outcropping dripping with water.

Then the trees parted to reveal the conical mountain straight ahead. The wolves halted, their hackles raised.

<Here.> Victrix said.

Perez raised a visual scanner and surveyed the scree and a series of cliffs.

"It looks like there's a cave entrance," he said, squinting. "But I can't be certain." He handed the instrument to Hughes.

"I think you're right."

Hughes knelt down and pointed. "Check it out, Victrix."

The black shepherd glanced at Rex, and the two loped off.

Hughes saw Leina's concerned look.

"I'm worried, too. But she'll be careful. Hopefully her nose will help warn her of any danger."

Hughes watched as they edged along a cliff face towards a darker patch. Suddenly a wave of vertigo swept over him and he swayed.

"Hon! What's wrong?" Leina clutched his arm.

He held onto her for a moment until the sensation passed.

"It was Victrix," he said. "She felt…something…"

"I saw her stagger for a second."

"They're coming back!" Perez exclaimed.

Hughes knelt down as Victrix and Rex came up to him. He put his hands on either side of her head. She was trembling.

<What happened?> he asked, fixing her brown eyes with his own.

<Bad place. Not right.>

<Was there a cave?>

<No cave. Feels strange. Victrix not like. Bad animal has been here. Many times.>

"There's something odd," Hughes said, standing up and relaying her report. "Rex seems edgy as well. I think the best thing we can do is remain here and see what happens."

"There's a flat area between those boulders," Perez pointed, "with line of sight to that dark area."

"Good idea," Hughes said.

"If you and Leina want to wait here, I'll go back to the flyer for supplies."

Hughes nodded assent. "The wolves—"

But the wolves had silently disappeared.

"If it's not a cave, then what is it, and why does the creature come here?" Leina wondered as they leaned against the boulders to wait.

"Hopefully we'll find out. In the meantime, I'm going to take a closer look at that dark patch."

"I'm coming too."

Victrix whined.

<Stay here, girl. I'll be right back.>

He felt nothing until he was almost at the dark patch. It seemed at first to be nothing more than black rock, but inlaid with sparkles of gold and silver—some sort of mineral.

He reached out to touch it, but paused.

Because as he did so, his vision grayed. It was as if he was simultaneously looking at a surface that was both solid and possessed depth. A flat surface and an opening. Something there and yet not there.

He drew back his hand.

Leina was pale, and he supposed he was also.

"That's weird," she said. "I can understand why Victrix was distressed. What do you make of it?"

He shook his head. "I don't know."

They turned at the whine of the flyer, and hurried over as Perez set it down on a patch of level ground—far enough from danger, but close enough they could reach it in a hurry if need be.

"Figured this was easier than lugging our stuff," he said.

"Good," Hughes said. "Let's set up camp."

It took only a short while to erect the shelters.

"Now we wait," Hughes said.

The remainder of the day passed slowly. Victrix and Rex shook off their discomfort and explored the area around the lake, frolicking in the water. Too edgy to concentrate on much of anything, Hughes and Leina made small talk with Perez who puttered around the flyer, and checked his weapon repeatedly.

As twilight arrived, Perez said, "We should divide up the night into three watches."

"Four," Hughes corrected. "Victrix and Rex can take one."

"You'd trust them to do that?"

"Absolutely."

"I can go first," Leina said.

"Then Ramon," Hughes suggested, "then I'll take third and make sure Victrix and Rex are ready for the fourth."

"Fine by me," Perez said.

Leina positioned a chair, and kept her neuraltranq close at hand. Perez gave her the visual scanner.

"Get some rest, boys," she said.

Hughes stretched out in the shelter. He hadn't expected much in the way of sleep, but all-too-soon Perez was shaking his shoulder to wake him, happy to change shifts.

"Nothing to report," he said, before heading to his own shelter.

Hughes took up his position outside. The twin moons cast a pallid light, and the night air was crisp. Victrix was dreaming of the woods and the lake, and that helped keep him alert. Every now and then a glimpse of an alien world intruded into his mind—that would be from Rex, possibly filtered through Victrix.

Eventually, his time was up, and he roused Victrix to take his place.

<Watch for bad animal. Wake me.>

<Victrix watch.>

She climbed onto one of the boulders and lay down, muzzle pointed towards the cliff. Rex joined her, having somehow developed larger eyes.

Hughes went back to bed. But he'd barely drifted off to sleep when a mental shout from Victrix jerked him fully awake.

<Something happening!>

He scrambled up, disturbing Leina in the process.

"Victrix is sensing something," he said, picking up the neuraltranqs.

Outside, the predawn sky had lightened. Victrix was standing on top of the boulder, like a black statue, Rex beside her. But it was the cliff towards which she pointed which seized his attention.

Whereas before it had glittered onyx-black, now it glowed with a faint luminescence.

A crunch of boots on stone signaled Perez joining them. "Couldn't sleep," he explained.

"Let's take a closer look," Hughes directed, and they made their way over to the cliff. As they drew near, the luminescence increased —now green, now orange, now blue, coruscating colors emerging and melting into each other.

Perez whistled. "It's unreal!"

<Bad animal comes!> Victrix shouted, breaking into frenzied barking. Rex leaped off the boulder.

The cliff face sizzled with a burst of energy.

And then something was upon them, something monstrous, roaring, all teeth and claws and fur and reeking of blood and death.

A huge paw sent Perez flying, his laser rifle firing a futile burst into the sky.

Hughes fumbled to get a shot as he staggered back, stumbling over a rock and pitching onto his back as a swing of its massive jaws just missed taking his head off.

Leina's neuraltrang whined, but the beast lunged for her anyway, moving insanely rapidly for all its bulk.

A pair of gray forms burst out of the half-light and tore into the creature's flanks, joined by Victrix who leaped and latched onto the creature's back. It whirled away from Leina and thrashed, sending one of the wolves flying. A large, bird-like creature—was it a raptor or something akin to a pterodactyl? —plummeted out of the sky scratching and poking at the beast's eyes with ferocious beak and claws.

The roars were deafening as the beast's fangs and talons slashed in every direction.

Still prone, Hughes loosed a shot from his neuraltranq. Leina's weapon whined again.

The beast staggered.

Hughes scrambled to get out of its way as its claws gouged furrows in the ground beside him.

He shot again, as did Leina.

Finally, the beast's front legs yielded, and it pitched onto its side and lay still.

"Hon! Are you all right?" Leina exclaimed, panting.

He clambered his feet. "Just dusty. You?"

"Fine. I thought that thing would never go down."

"Victrix?"

<Victrix ok. Wild ride!>

<Rex?>

<Rex good. Fun!>

The weird looking bird-like creature came to a landing.

"Nice, Rex," Hughes said to the shapeshifter.

"What happened?" the slurred voice belonged to Perez who was stirring from where he had landed.

Hughes hurried to help the man to his feet. "A team effort," he said. "But it's down."

Perez rubbed his jaw. "That bugger packs a mean punch."

They stared down at the creature. Some two meters high at the shoulder—equal to that of a tall man—and perhaps four meters long, it was covered with brownish fur with a mixture of black stripes and spots. Its muzzle was as long as Hughes' arm, its jaws lined with rows of vicious teeth. Its ears were small, but its paws outsized. Its flanks rose and fell with breathing, blood seeping from the wounds inflicted by the wolves.

"What is it?" Leina wondered.

"And where did it come from?" Perez added.

Hughes raised his shoulders. "It's obviously mammalian, in appearance like a wolf crossed with a thylacine—similar to various depictions of an Andrewsarchus from Earth's Middle Eocene epoch, some forty million years ago. But the sheer size of it...! As to where it came from..." he glanced at the shimmering cliff face. "Maybe from this planet's past, or from somewhere else entirely."

Perez picked up his laser rifle from where it had fallen. "Best I finish it off—something that kills for pleasure as well as for food."

Hughes laid a hand on his arm. "No. It's an unknown species."

"But it's dangerous! And how long will the neurotranqs keep an animal that size down?"

"Do you have a stasis field generator in the flyer?"

Perez nodded. "Yes, a small one, in case of emergency. But again—"

"Do you have a larger unit that you can lay your hands on?"

"I can have it flown here."

"Then let's set up the smaller unit until the larger unit arrives. We know the neuraltranqs will work if need be."

"Then what?"

"I think the folks on the Extinct Species Restoration Project would love to get their hands on it."

"It must weigh eight hundred or a thousand kilos." Perez pursed his lips. "It's doable."

"I'm sure they'd cover the cost of cargo transport. If need be, I could take it on Wolf-One."

"Darling!" Leina exclaimed. "You're not serious!"

"Probably not," Hughes said. "But while we're at it, it might be a good idea to rig a force screen over that cliff face to prevent anything else from coming through."

Perez nodded. "Can do." He touched his commlink and began to talk into it.

The mournful howl of a wolf broke into their deliberations.

<*Help wolf friend!*>

Hughes pivoted to see Victrix standing beside the alpha male. His muzzle pointed at the sky; the female lay on the ground, a red stain on her side. Rex, back in wolf form, had his muzzle resting on the female's forelegs.

"There's an emergency kit in the flitter—" Hughes began.

"On it," Leina said.

Hughes knelt by the injured female, relieved to see she was breathing. He laid a hand on her chest, feeling the fast heartbeat.

The alpha male lowered his head; Hughes was acutely aware of the intense stare from his amber eyes and thanked Victrix for projecting calm energy.

Leina returned with the medical kit. Hughes pulled out the medscanner and ran it over the female wolf.

"No internal bleeding," he said. "No broken bones. The laceration is superficial. Otherwise, just stunned."

<*Wolf friend live?*> Victrix asked.

<*She'll be fine.*>

He applied synthskin to the laceration, and administered an antibiotic and a restorative.

After a moment, the female's eyes fluttered, and Hughes stepped back to give her space. Rex also moved out of the way.

She shook herself and sat up. The male licked her face. Her gaze shifted from him to Hughes and back again. Then she stood, and caught sight of the beast. Her hackles rose.

<*Have Rex tell them the bad animal won't hurt anyone else.*>

<*Victrix tell Rex.*>

Gradually, the female's hackles went down.

The alpha male approached Hughes and gave his hand a quick sniff and the lightest of touches. Then he did the same to Leina.

"Thanks for your help, buddy," Hughes said to the wolf.

"Partners again," Leina observed.

"Just as we were millennia ago," Hughes agreed, "before human greed, pride, and stupidity disrupted everything."

"Maybe there's a chance we can coexist again."

"Let's hope so," Hughes said, as the two wolves walked stiffly away to rejoin their pack.

<*Victrix and Rex like new friends.*> Victrix leaned against Hughes' right leg while Rex took the left. He ruffled their heads.

"Reinforcements are on the way," Perez said, rejoining them.

"Excellent," Hughes said.

Then he gave Leina a quirky smile. "How did you enjoy your

wolf encounter?"

She smiled back. "Wouldn't have missed it."

"You should be especially pleased," Hughes said.

"How's that?"

"I think we're honorary pack members now."

Her smile widened into a grin. "An honor indeed. Perhaps Rex could teach me how to howl."

"Ask him at the next full moon," Hughes replied.

"Why wait? All together now!"

Leina tipped back her head and howled, joined by Hughes and Perez.

<Not bad for humans,> Victrix said. <But Victrix and Rex show you how it's done!>

Dog and skaggit enthusiastically joined the chorus. And from far away came the answering howls of the wolf pack.

An encounter with a wild wolf many years ago high in the Beartooth Mountains of Wyoming left **Andrew M. Seddon** with an abiding fascination for wolves. He is delighted to contribute to this anthology, and has himself edited an anthology of wolf stories, *Wolf Wanderings,* to benefit wolf conservation organizations. For further adventures of Doc Hughes and Victrix from the story *Wolf Haven* check out his book *The DeathCats of Asa'ican and Other Tales of a Space Vet.*

A native of England, he has lived most of his life in the USA, including thirty years in Montana. He enjoys writing non-fiction articles on diverse subjects, and short stories (including twenty anthology contributions). He has authored 15 books in the genres of science-, supernatural-, and historical fiction, as well as a book for writers—*Dr. Andrew's Curious and Quirky Compendium*. The proceeds from two volumes of short stories about German Shepherds —*Bonds of Affection* and *Ranger's First Call*—benefit rescues and K9 support organizations.

He is a member of SFWA and the Authors' Guild, and when not writing he can be found hiking, enjoying classical music, and running marathons. Now retired from the medical profession he lives in Florida with his wife Olivia and German Shepherd Baltasar, and has more books on the way!

You can find him online at: www.andrewmseddon.com and www.andrewmseddon.blogspot.com.

The Last Wolf

Oakley Beaumont

Hunting was the only option. Cities burned, electricity failed, and finally, crops turned to dust. Now, it was them against the endless. Every direction was bleak, fields yellowed by the sun, and trees bowed down in prayer for a drop of rain. Alas, no god was watching.

Reeva crouched down on the outcrop looking down at the valley beyond. A few deer still grazed there, as if the world hadn't ended. Lifting her gun, a vestige of a time almost lost to memory, she hoped the weapon would do her aim justice. The problem with age was that some things didn't work as well as they once did. Her gun had been a loyal companion for the last ten years, allowing her to serve her clan, but its failures were growing. One day soon, she would have to consign it to the ground and pick up a bow.

But today was not that day. Looking through, she made a single shot, the sound echoing for miles around. A herald to the animals who survived, a human still walked these lands. Her bullet flew straight, and the deer slumped to the ground without a sound. All around it, deer turned and ran, fear dogging their retreat. Slipping from her hiding spot, Reeva hurried across the barren plains to her fallen prey's side. Her aim had been true, splitting the deer through the skull, dead in an instant. Most importantly, no meat was harmed, though. The difficult part, however, was getting the animal back to the clan. Reeva was used to this part, though, and began sorting the sticks and material she carried for this purpose. Building a litter didn't take long, and dragging the deer onto it was no difficult feat either. Turning back to the way she had come, however, seemed daunting. It had taken hours to find the deer, and it would take her more to get back. If she didn't hurry, the meat would spoil, and it would all be for nought.

Tying the rope around her waist, she began slowly, working up to a marching pace. The gun remained on her back for the duration of the journey home. If something were out there that could hurt her, she would not be able to use it to defend herself.

The plains kept going, passing small copses of trees brave enough to still grow in the harsh environment. The first sign of home came as the sun dipped low in the sky, casting brilliant pink streaks through the gathering clouds; the hedgerows were the only crops they had managed to keep alive. Hardy berry bushes that provided blackberries and raspberries in large quantities. It was the closest thing her clan had to a farm, and it was still an hour away from the homestead. Part of her wanted to sneak a handful of berries but she couldn't; it was not her place. Instead, she soldiered on, her stomach growling at her.

But, it wasn't her stomach.

Turning quickly she saw a creature she had never seen before. Larger than the deer and covered in thick, grey fur, the creature glared at her with piercing, yellow eyes. Its muzzle and nose were scrunched and its sharp teeth bared for her to see. Reeva was at once awestruck by the fierce creature and terrified for it did not look friendly. But as she continued to watch it she saw the ribs sticking through the fur, and how gingerly it stood. Her heart shattered, and her knees almost gave way.

"I'm sorry," She said, knowing the creature wouldn't understand, "I have to keep going. You can't have it."

The animal growled and took a wobbling step forward. Its shoulders were heaving, it must have run to catch her.

"What are you?" she asked softly. So many animals darted through her mind, pictures from books they couldn't guarantee were accurate. Eventually, though, one stood out above the rest; wolf.

The wolf's growl faltered for a moment, a tiny whimper escaping in its place. Reeva knew she would regret this, but she took a small knife from her side, not meant for carving, but it would have to do. Bending over, she cut a strip of meat from the deer and held it out for the wolf.

Cautiously it approached, eyes never leaving her until it was close enough to snatch the meat from her hand. Though the meat didn't last long the wolf didn't follow, letting Reeva continue her journey.

The deer, even with the strip of meat missing, was still a prize to the clan. They didn't waste any time skinning it and setting it to roast. Before long, they were all enjoying the meat and berries as a hearty meal. The other hunters had found smaller animals that would be cooked and preserved as best they could. Reeva got clapped on the back and cheered for her success, but her mind was on the wolf. The creature looked so haggard and desperate yet still remained majestic in her eyes.

Her cabin was shared with other girls who had not married yet, and it was a small place for so many. Somehow it worked though. Reeva was restless that night, and long after sleep claimed the others and snores filled the cabin she was still staring at the ceiling. Eventually, she gave up on sleep and exited to look at the village. The cabins were wooden and unremarkable, with a large open fire usually burning in the middle. Only embers remained now. About fifty people lived in her clan; there were others nearby but desperation had not brought them together yet. There was no denying the harshness around them, it was a brutal world, one she sometimes wished she didn't have to be a part of.

Looking out across the plains she found the stillness peaceful, that at least she could savour. Then she spotted two yellow eyes in the fields watching her. The wolf had followed her. Reeva had no weapon on her but her feet carried her across the dirt to the wolf.

The wolf looked stronger and its muzzle was stained red. After her snack, it must have found a meal of its own. Its eyes didn't leave hers as it stepped forward. Instinct screamed at her to run but that instinct was held in check by fear: fear and curiosity. The wolf got closer and closer until its soft, damp nose touched her side.

Images flashed through her head, enormous trees and sparkling lagoons. They only lasted a second, but that was enough for Reeva. A single thought encompassed her: follow. Leaving without her gun felt foreign, but with the small knife in her belt, she followed. The wolf was happy to pad alongside her as they left. She wasn't exactly sure what she was going to find out in the beyond.

The answer at first was nothing. Running alongside the wolf took most of the night, and it was across familiar grounds. Fields and fields of dying grass, complete with an occasional whisper of an animal out there. Eventually, Reeva couldn't run anymore; her feet had grown sore, and her body was crying out for rest. Taking a perch on a ruin of some sort, she held her hand up to the wolf, trying to tell it to stop. The wolf looped around, pacing back and forth in front of her.

"I'm sorry," she panted, "I must rest, I have not slept and I have already done a great deal of work today."

It let out a small whimper but acquiesced, falling to the ground at her feet. Its fur was so thick Reeva wondered whether she would be warmer down next to the animal or not. More pressingly, it was becoming apparent her lack of forethought was going to cost her her life. Looking back, the way they'd come, it was still a distance she could cover. She could return to her tribe, and no one would be the wiser. But the wolf was still looking at her, its amber eyes unrelenting and pleading. The images it had sent into her mind came again, beautiful lands she could only have dreamed of before. They mustn't have to trail too far; the wolf didn't look aged, only hungry.

A noise came from not far away, and the wolf rose to its feet, hackles raised on the back of its neck. Turning to bark at her, the command clearly to stay put, it darted off into the thicket ahead. Reeva sat motionless, a statue in the moonlight, as her ears listened to the ensuing fight. Somewhere amongst the long, sad grass, the wolf scratched and bit at whatever it had heard. The howls filled the night along with a foreign sound; the guttural roar of a creature trying its best.

A singular howl filled the air and Reeva's breath caught in her throat, unsure if her guardian had left her with a vicious beast. Silence stretched, the wind falling still as if mourning the lost life.

Then slowly, the sound of paws padding through the grass until the familiar amber eyes and grey fur emerged with added crimson around the mouth. Slumping on the ground, the wolf let out a small growl and Reeva sank next to it. Running a hand through its fur she was struck by how warm it was, and thick. A coat of it would keep her warm in the coldest winters. The wolf made a noise that sounded almost like a purr and Reeva smiled. Together they looked up at the stars, letting the night tick past.

"I can't imagine not being able to see the stars," Reeva said, not sure if the wolf really understood. "They say before all of this happened, the world was so bright you couldn't see them like this. Now it's just fires and abandoned buildings. I bet it was special though; electricity, wildlife, shops. There are so many pictures in books, but I can't imagine it properly. So much was lost."

The wolf nodded and a flicker of images burst into Reeva's mind. Cities of enormous buildings rising on either side, plains lush and green, roaring engines overheard. She blinked and the images were gone. She shook her head. "How? You're not that old, are you?"

A single thought pressed upon her and she understood. Pack memory, all the wolves in this one's bloodline, they carried forward to him. He called himself Ash, his fur the colour of it after a great forest blaze. Ash was only two years old but he had not seen another wolf since his birth. Pack memory told him there weren't many wolves left. In fact he wasn't sure if there were any.

"I am sorry," Reeva whispered, "the world is still big, even if we are so tiny now. Maybe out there is a whole pack for you."

Ash let out a sound that sounded like a chortle before settling against the grass. Reeva's eyes stayed on the stars until they drifted shut.

Bump. Bump. Bump. Something was nudging Reeva, her eyes opened wide to take in her surroundings. Still next to the ruin, Ash was pacing next to her. The sun was already climbing the sky, high above the horizon line.

Water, Ash wanted water, and Reeva needed water. Every part of her ached as she pushed up to stand, aware grass and dirt were undoubtedly matting her raven hair but she didn't care at that moment. There was no one around. Ash jumped around though, desperately trying to get her moving. With a groan, she followed as he bounded across the grass towards the tree line. A wall of bark met her and soon swallowed her but Ash didn't stop. The wolf was on a mission, one that would hopefully bring them to water. These trees were not familiar, and they held no sign of anything other than leaves. And then she heard it.

Trickling, no gushing.

Ash's ears pricked up, and he ran the final distance, disappearing between a line of thick bushes. Reeva wasted no time following, pushing through the bushes and falling to her knees. The stream glistened in the sunlight as it filtered through the canopy. It ran freely over the riverbed, clear and clean. Ash was already diving into it, lapping up the water and washing his face clean after the previous night's battle. Reeva crouched down upstream from him to cup some water and drink it. More and more until she was sated. Unfortunately, that gave way to hunger. Her stomach growled as loud as Ash did but the river was a gift in multiple ways. Fish darted around her and Ash must have also been hungry as he caught one in his jaw.

Dropping it on the riverbank, he went back for more whilst Reeva set about starting a small fire. It wasn't much, but the makeshift spit from sticks would serve the purpose she needed. It didn't take long for the fish to cook and for her to be enjoying it. Ash took some of the cooked meat and wolfed it down. He looked pleased with himself but after eating he was keen to move on.

"We should stay by the river if we can," Reeva said, and she could have sworn Ash nodded. Leading on through the forest gave way to a gentle incline where the stream joined others to form a thick flowing river. Emerging from the trees Reeva gasped.

The forest had begun to climb a mountainside, where the river was flowing from. The sun was high above them now, the forest giving way to uneven rocks and tough grass that survived in the unwelcoming territory. Ash pointed up the river with his snout and Reeva sank to the ground.

"Rest first, just a short one," she said, "that is a steep climb."

Ash rolled his amber eyes and slumped by the river, enjoying the spray around him. Her tribe had tales of the mountains; allegedly, there was one to the west that had the faces of gods carved into it. Others believed they were climbing towards a higher place than this earth, a heaven above. Reeva never fell into religious superstition. Mountains always were and will always be. The rest of it was a leftover from the before. Facing the climb was a big one, but with Ash, she felt she could do it. Part of her now wished she had her gun and not just the hunting knife.

Rising once more she motioned for Ash to lead on.

At first, it wasn't treacherous, even though the uneven ground crumbled beneath her and had her skidding and grazing her hands. But ripping strips off her shirt to tie around them staunched the bleeding, even as Ash pressed them to continue on. When she had to start hauling herself up ledges, though, it began to tax on her. Her shoulders ached from the day before, and now they burned with a vengeance. Thankfully, the sun began to set as they reached a plateau, and Ash came to a halt. Sinking onto his haunches he looked out at the sunset and Reeva sat by him, her feet dangling over the steep edge.

Fire kissed the sky in shades of orange and red as the sun began its final descent. They watched for a long time as the deepest fires gave way to deep violets and mauve as the sun dipped below the horizon. Soon the stars would shine, a thought that gave Reeva comfort. Somewhere below her tribe would also see these stars. Some would wonder what happened to her, but most would accept her absence without a second thought. Part of her was not sure she'd ever return, a part that grew larger as she sat next to Ash.

Her wolf companion lay down, sorrow in his eyes.

When she touched his fur she saw the images in his head, of him alone staring at the sunset. No wolf with him. "I am here," Reeva whispered, "I may not be a wolf but I am here."

Ash bristled slightly away from her hand but not too far. There was a cool breeze in the air and Reeva wasn't sure how she was going to cope in the night air. Thankfully after some more fishing by Ash and cooking by her Ash allowed her to lay with him against the elements. His fur kept them both warm as they found sleep.

They awoke to an almighty roar. There, just above them, stood a cat of some kind, thick fur around its neck and sandy fur that showed off the ribs on the cat's sides. Like Ash, it was a predator going hungry. Reeva rolled and stood, pulling her knife out quickly, it was her turn to defend Ash. The creature jumped down and squared off in front of her. A word flickered in her head, lion.

Her heart was thudding in her ears, but she had no time to think. The lion was hungry, and it would kill. It leapt forward, and she had to move fast to avoid it. Ash stayed back but gave the occasional growl as the lion and Reeva circled. Soon, they were dancing, claws and knife flashing under the moonlight. A deep scratch ran across her arm before the dance ended, but her knife found a place to bury itself, and the lion stumbled. Struggling away from her, the lion teetered along the cliffside before the knife's toll was exacted. With a final whimper the lion fell, plummeting off the edge. Chest heaving Reeva looked over the edge at the majestic beast so far below and found tears forming in her eyes.

Ash padded over to her side and cuddled up next to her as tears began to flow freely. Reeva whispered, "It was just hungry. The poor thing was hungry."

No images passed into her head but Ash remained by her side until the tears subsided and her sobs fell quiet. With difficulty, she gathered dry materials and her flint and after a moment of trying was able to light a small fire. The fire danced through the night, smoke reminding her of home.

The next morning, they woke with the rising sun painting the sky fuchsia. Ash stretched and jumped down to the river. Reeva took that as her cue and began gathering scraps to form a fire. Fish was getting tiresome already, but it was sustenance, and though she was loath to do so, she clambered back down to drink her fill. Flies buzzed around the lion's corpse, keeping her away despite her desire for a different meat; if there were flies it was too late. Her entire body was already regretting the descent to re-ascend but there was no choice.

Thankfully, their path took a different direction as Ash pushed sideways, no longer interested in the vertical climb. They carried on until the sun was high above, then they began to steer down. There was a smaller stream on this side, enough to keep them hydrated, but no fish swam in it. Ash was angling between two mountains where, from her view, she could only see darkness. Reeva trusted Ash and as they got lower and lower and the sun set further they stopped. A large cave stretched out in front of them and Ash was pointing for them to go in.

"Do we have to?" Reeva whispered.

Ash nodded. Foraging around she found a large branch and tore more off her shirt to wrap around the tip. Normally she would coat it in fat of some kind but there was nothing around. With her flint once more she struck a fire to light the material at the end. It wouldn't burn for long but it would help.

"Let's go," she said, her torch aloft. Ash plodded ahead.

Inside, the cave was dry and quiet. Underfoot, the earth was firm and, apart from the infrequent stalagmite, pretty even. Ash kept pushing forward deeper into the darkness, her torch only doing enough to make sure she could follow him. Doubt crept in for the first time; perhaps she had misplaced her trust in Ash, and this was simply where he wanted to end her. Ahead, Ash had paused, and as she came up alongside him, he pressed into her leg, the image of the lagoon he had first shown her flickering in her mind. They were close.

Reeva's brows furrowed into a hard line and she followed deeper until they began to climb slightly. It was a slight incline but it was enough to be noticed.

She wasn't sure how long they had been walking when a small gust of wind came whipping through the cavern and the torch she was carrying blinked out. Thick, inky darkness surrounded her for the first time. Frozen to the spot she couldn't bring her feet to move. This was unlike nighttime or any other darkness she had experienced. This was the complete unknown.

Nudge. A soft touch on her leg. Ash. He nudged again, and she reached out until her hand touched his fur, and she could grab at it. Now completely at his mercy, they carried on until the gust came again, softer this time. Fresher. They picked up the pace and eventually Reeva could see. Just a little at first, shades of grey that allowed her to discern the stalagmites from the walls. Then she could see Ash and finally she could see an ending. A bright ending.

The lagoon stretched out in front of them, taking Reeva's breath for a long moment. The water was bright and blue, lit by the moonlight directly overhead. All around the lagoon, trees bearing fruit and berries in every colour she could imagine grew proudly. Ash bounded over to the waterside and stopped short of jumping in. Reeva treaded over carefully, taking in the exquisite beauty around her. Even the walls of the cavern-bound lagoon were gorgeous, crystal veins running through them, reflecting the moonlight above. Closer she could see, the water was startlingly clear, the blue coming from corals growing beneath the surface. Reeva dropped to her knees to inspect the water, catching sight of her reflection.

She was a state. Blood in her hair to compliment the mud and leaves. Her face was marred with dirt, and her leg was burning beneath her from the lion's wound. Around her eyes, dark circles hung, reminding her sleep was something she desperately needed. But it was her eyes that captured her attention, a slight amber light in them she had never noticed before.

Ash pressed up against her, an image of her in the water passing between them.

"Why?" Reeva asked, "What's special about the water?"

He pointed to the reflection. As she watched, the image swirled, revealing a white wolf looking back at her. Recoiling she looked at Ash and back at the water. "What was that?"

Ash looked at her mournfully and reached for her again pressing his muzzle to her hand as he had done back in the village. The image this time was him alone. Completely alone. The last wolf in the world. A pack memory burst through, an image of a white wolf they called Lupa. Powerful and unlike any other wolf. She was the mother-wolf and this lagoon could make her again.

At a cost.

Reeva looked at Ash and the tears beading in his yellow eyes.

"Can I turn back?" Reeva asked but she knew the answer already.

Ash shook his head, before letting it hang low.

Reeva rose up tall, looking up at the moon for the final time through human eyes. Though it felt strange to do so, she stripped her clothes off and stood at the lagoon's edge. Clearing her throat, she said, "Never in my life would I have predicted this would be where my humanity ended. But I suppose humanity ended a long time ago; all that's left are the remnants. But where the end of one comes may the start of another blossom."

With a final glance at Ash, she added, "Or should I say the saving of another."

Then she stepped into the water. It was cool against her skin, but she carried on until the water came up to her head. Taking a final breath, she submerged herself. Beneath the water, she didn't feel herself changing, but when she emerged from the water, she padded on paws and looked to Ash, her would-be mate, and glanced at the lagoon at her reflection. Reeva was gone, snow-white fur around bright amber eyes. She that remained was Lupa.

~ * 🐺 * ~

Oakley Beaumont is a self-published novelist who is bringing his love for writing to the shorter forms with 'The Last Wolf'. His first professional foray into short story writing comes at a point where he is studying Creative Writing (after many years of procrastinating), sparking an exploration of wider forms of writing. Alongside his studies, he works in education, trying to instill a love for reading into the younger generations. Debuting with this name in the Spirit of the Wolf anthology, Beaumont's previous works can be found under the name J.S. Young, his new identity marking a new chapter in his writing career.

Paradise,

Otherwise Known as Yellowstone

Missy Stephenson

Jan. 10
William A. Switzer Provincial Park, Alberta, Canada

By a lakeshore in Alberta, a large silver-coated wolf fed on a moose calf. It was a found carcass, probably drowned and washed ashore—he didn't have the heart to kill anyone's young himself. Others in his pack did, but he'd left them the day prior, off to start his own.

A she-raven dined with him, and the wolf didn't mind sharing the meal—it was her caws that'd led him to this poor calf, and she deserved a portion. She must've recognized a newly-dispersed wolf who hadn't yet gotten the hang of hunting for food by himself.

"Hello, Wolf Ten," the raven broke the silence to say.

Her caw passed through even his sensitive canine ears as background noise. He didn't have a name—names were not a custom for animals in harsher terrains. Death rates were too high, and mothers avoided getting terribly attached to their young.

He only paused his chewing and swiveled his ears to make sure a stranger hadn't approached.

No, he was alone. The raven must've been displaying just what birds were known for—meaningless, incessant chatter. They continued to peck and gnaw the carcass together as if nothing had been said.

After tearing one last chunk of meat from the calf's ribs, he'd had his fill. The cold would preserve the leftovers, and he'd feed again tomorrow to fuel his who-knows-how-far search for a mate.

Something distant crackled like a wildfire. His fur raised again. He glanced at the sky. The first faint swaths of green were beginning to streak from the northern horizon to the zenith.

As much comfort as the aurora's beauty brought, comfort much needed for a wolf with no pack, the snowless voids under the near-by cedars provided warmth that was just as essential. Their low, lush branches would block any view of the sky, but they'd just as much give him shelter.

He watched the lights for a moment as they whirled like playful pups and slowly wagged like tails, but a cold gust of wind made him quickly fix his eyes on the distant tree line and take a step towards it. Just as he did, the raven cawed again.

"I was speaking to you, Wolf Ten."

He stopped with three paws in the snow and one lifted. The raven hopped up beside him while he was still frozen in confusion.

"…What makes you call me that?" A strange name it was, too.

"I've heard whispers on the southerly wind, Wolf Ten. Us birds have been sent to let you wolves know of some matters we've heard regarding your kind. Very important, not just to you, but to all flora and fauna and river in paradise, too." She half-opened her wings for emphasis on her next words. "They're coming for you soon, very soon."

Another thing about birds was the only reason their chattering was considered disregardable is because they had a roundabout way of saying things that clashed with the straightforward ways of mammals. They held far more wisdom, and some believed they exceeded even man in intelligence—but undecipherable knowledge was worthless.

Still, the wolf tried. Planting all four paws on the ground and raising his tail to demand the respect an apex predator deserved, he asked, "*Who* is coming for me? And again—that name!"

"That is the name *they* will give you. Wolf Ten, you must listen to me. What is about to happen to you, I have witnessed play out before, and I do not wish for your experience to be as stressful as some I've seen."

"Answer me thoroughly, raven, or you'll end up like that calf." A growl began to rise in his throat, but he suppressed it. Warning her off too soon, before she gave an answer, would leave his curiosity festering.

"When they come on that machine which creates the very breeze it flies on, do not run. Close your eyes when they shoot, so your instincts do not take over and compel you to flee. When you wake up, dear Wolf Ten, you will be in paradise. A wolves' paradise. A place your kind belongs to, yet has not set paw in for generations —but the first pack to return there will be yours."

There it was again—her words faded out of his attention and blended with the soft crashing of waves. Curling his lips, he let out a snarl that told her, *leave me alone, you and your vague nonsense.*

She craned her neck first to peer somewhere towards the southeastern sky. Whatever she'd seen had made her feathers puff out and her eyes widen before she took off and soared across the lake.

Instinctively, he glanced in the same direction. A slow shooting star was travelling past Jupiter and Venus. A very, very, slow shooting star. But he ascribed its distorted speed to his own fatigue and quickened his trot towards the tree line.

The aurora flickered with extra liveliness this early morning. Not only did it bring a green hue to the sparkling snow and cast shadows as strong as those on a full-moon night, but its thin static escalated to a rumble. A deep flutter like a flock of a thousand geese beating their wings at once. A noise the wolf had never heard once in his short three years of life, nor heard rumored of in the tales and legends that spread among packs.

Before he was even halfway to the tree line, this rumble loudened enough to finally strike fear in him. It was not the aurora making that noise. Ears flattened, he looked to the part of the sky he'd been avoiding.

That shooting star was no shooting star. Between its strange movement and the raven's foreboding, he'd already feared that. A green-and-magenta reflection across its metallic body became visible as it approached, shining its own blinding spotlight right towards him.

His mind first went to the bush planes he'd seen pass low over the park. This wasn't quite that—though its tail was similar, stiff and split at the end like a fishbone, it had not the long, osprey-like wings. Whatever it was, it was in the same vein of man's incomprehensible creations.

Do not run. Birds always knew best, but what a ridiculous request —this thing was swooping right towards him. Its long, flat feet seemed poised to scoop him up like a raptor-bird.

Head low, he bounded to the tree line. His strides were strong, but the nearer the thing came, it let out such powerful gusts of wind and clouds of snow that he swayed sideways and nearly fell. Its rumble became too loud to bear. If he survived this, he'd come out with the hearing of a mole rat.

While the tree line was still far, the man-steered thing had slowed to a stop and now hovered a mere lynx's-leap away from him. Trembling, he tucked his tail and rolled onto his back in surrender. Perhaps it'd have mercy on him.

A weight hit his haunch, which instantly went numb. Exhaustion shot through his body.

The roaring blood in his ears ceded to a loud ringing. The cascades of aurora light above doubled. Vision blurred, he could only tell the flying beast had landed because those great wind gusts had ceased.

Still, an unnaturally-bright light basked him. The sound of several voices, as chatty and complex as birds, was muffled in his hearing.

A flat, furless face with white, expressive eyes was the last thing he glimpsed before drifting off and making peace with this terrible fate.

🐾 * 🐾

A full day later, the wolf awoke inside a metal box with a beeping collar around his neck. Such a jarring environment jolted him fully awake the second the tranquilizer and whatever else they'd drugged him with had worn off.

A barely-recognizable scent overwhelmed him. Based on several pairs of pink raccoon-like hands visible through the many little holes along the box's sides, he realized the part-clammy, part-sterile stench belonged to humans.

They conversed while carrying him. Their voices were breathy and exhausted, but excitement seemed to bubble under.

"Hope the Big Guy likes her," were the first words that made the wolf's ears perk.

"The Big Guy?" a woman questioned, followed by some more playful mocking from the others.

"Number Ten," the man corrected himself.

The raven was right. Ten finally accepted his name.

The group finally quieted, allowing him to try and observe—

through his nose and ears, for his eyes were of little use in a box.

The first question in his wondering mind was what kind of place this was; the second being who the *her* was.

He stood to raise his snout to the holes. Careful as he was, the humans staggered with his weight and laughed, but quickly adjusted and kept their steady marching. A moment later, they lowered him to the snow.

A breeze came, and Ten inhaled through the narrow opening.

The fur on his withers rose. Another wolf lurked nearby, but the air was too thick with various other scents—cedar, a cold river, sagebrush that'd gone dry with the winter, and a faint linger of something rotten—for him to discern any details past its species.

His ears had thankfully recovered from the flying beast's heavy fluttering. Just as he strained them to discover more, a hollow, drawn-out scream echoed in the distance.

"Bull elk!" one of the humans commented.

Elk, Ten had never heard of, but *bull* indicated some ungulate. At least there was food in this new place.

While he was still focusing, one of those pink hands reached around the front of the box. Its metal door swung open on squealing hinges and revealed a snowy, conifer-filled landscape not unlike that of his homeland. He wasted no time taking it all in and immediately burst out of the box.

The humans hooted and cheered like a flock of robins. He couldn't understand what their happiness was for—they weren't the ones that'd just survived whatever had swooped down on him the day before, nor had they been freed from a metal prison—but their species was too intimidating for him to lag behind and ask.

He darted into the thin copse of cedars until the group of humans was out of sight. As he slowed, his gaze wandered past the immediate forested foreground and to a mountain. He stopped in place at the sight of it, as he'd never seen one so close. And he nearly considered getting closer—that elk screech had come from the valley below it—but then realized a chain link fence stood only a few bounds away. It wasn't clear *what* was being fenced in. Wilderness lay on either side.

"They didn't give us much space in here, did they?"

Startled, he whirled to the voice and snarled. The stranger he'd scented earlier stood some distance off to the side. She took a few steps back at his growl, but kept her gaze on him, neck craning as she sniffed.

Her coat was as black as wildfire smoke, grizzled with amber and white like flames and dry ash. Her eyes were warm like his, though a fierier hue than his own honey-colored gaze.

"Space?" He looked up and down the fence. Behind him, it ran till it disappeared behind a cluster of trees. In front of him and behind the stranger, it bent at a sharp angle and ran vertical for a while, then bent again only to be concealed behind more trees. It would've taken no more than a couple of minutes to run the boundary of the entire squared-in area.

When he met her eyes again, she slowly wagged her tail and lifted a paw.

Ten was not quite as eager to be trapped in a cramped pocket of wilderness with a stranger. "Get!" Teeth flashing, he charged.

She did not run elsewhere as he'd hoped, only dipped her head and pinned her ears flat. Their wrinkled snouts ended up just inches away from each other.

"Calm *down*," she growled. "Where am I supposed to go?"

"I—" He huffed and composed himself, backing away some. She was right. She was just as trapped as him, and even wore the same occasionally-beeping collar.

Licking her lips in appeasement, she slowly stood back to her full height, but still avoided his stare.

"Did that metal beast get you, too?" he asked once the fur on his withers lowered.

Her wagging tail sped up, her fiery eyes seemed to brighten, and she nodded.

"I fell asleep when it approached," he continued, "and I don't know what happened after that. But I wish it'd scooped me up in its talons and eaten me." He whined—immediately ashamed, since he hadn't whined in such a sorry way since he was a pup. "I'd rather be dead than forever trapped."

"We're *not* forever trapped," she assured. "A flock of magpies came along and told me everything about what the humans are doing. Said they'd send me to paradise."

"The same thing happened to me, with a raven! But this is no para—"

"It is, it is!" she interrupted.

With each moment he spent in this pen, the chainlink fence seemed to creep in closer and closer. "*This* place?" He was snarling again, nose wrinkled in disgust. "If *this* is your idea of—"

"Listen!" She nipped him on the face as a warning, then quickly stepped back and held a calm expression to indicate she meant no real harm. "This pen isn't, no, not yet. But the land outside is. They're going to let us out in a moon-cycle or so."

"What's so special about it, besides the prey screams like eagles? It looks just like my old home."

"Just like it? Where do you come from?"

"…Man called it…" He struggled to recall at first, and then wasn't even sure where he'd ever heard the name. "Alberta."

"Me too."

"We've never crossed pawsteps."

"No surprise. It's a vast place. But if the magpies were right— and birds always are—we're now in Yellowstone. There are great mountains, like the ones *I* knew back in Alberta, but other than that, it's different. I promise, very different." She trotted to the fence and slowly paced along it, scanning the barely-anything visible through the trees. "The magpies chirped of a land dotted with little openings that are always puffing clouds into the air. Some of the lakes boil the color of northern lights and sunsets at the same time. There's thousands more elk for us to eat than there were in Alberta, and if you're skilled enough, great furry cows called bison that could feed a large pack with one carcass." She finally looked him in the eye when she said, "And no human can harvest us. The ones who put us here won't allow it."

His ears perked. Man was the only predator above wolves. "Really?"

"That's why you haven't heard many howls here. There were many packs, long ago, until man hunted us out. But enough of their kind has had a change of heart to return us." She sniffed the air, but the breeze was too still at the moment to pick up on anything distant. "There are a dozen or so more of us, in pens like these further away. When they let us out, we'll create the first packs to return."

Ten still couldn't figure out why man cared at all, but it was enough for him to warily forgive the metal beast and the ones who steered it.

"All the humans said I'm Wolf Nine," she continued, "but one of them called me Natasha, and I like that better."

"Ten. Wolf Ten." He didn't disclose the slightly-humiliating *big guy* nickname one human had given him. "Elk, what are they?"

"Deer, but stockier and nowhere near as agile." Her tail began to wag and her mouth began to drool a little before she even spoke these next words. "That's why they brought us."

"To feast?"

"To feast, because our prey went un-feasted on for too long and is now tearing up the earth."

"Did the birds tell you that, too?"

"No, not that part. I overheard the humans."

"But I...I just don't get it. What do they care? About us, or the land? They don't live in the wilderness. It's not their home."

Tilting her head, she softened her eyes as if she was looking at some poor abandoned pup. "You might only know them as predators, but some humans are kind. And some care deeply about things they have no need to. It's a kindness we cannot understand." She brushed past him, heading back in the direction of where they'd been dropped off. "They even left us food, since we can't hunt in here."

She trotted off and left him there by the fence, still trying to comprehend what'd been done to them. He sniffed the air—the humans and their box were gone, and it seemed a carcass had been left in their place.

Appetizing as it smelled, he couldn't trust it. He turned back to the fence and began digging. But after a foot of snow had been scraped up, he met impenetrable frozen ground.

This place was designed to keep them trapped. The humans had left, clearly not planning to let them out. Natasha's *in a moon-cycle or so* was a vain hope—and a terribly long time, even if true.

But he knew once the soil warmed, they'd be able to dig and escape. That was what determined him to keep going until spring.

It'd been about three moon-cycles, and every few days or so, the humans would come in lugging carcasses and big tubs of water while Ten and Natasha hid behind a thick-trunked ponderosa and watched.

For that entire first cycle, Ten would not dare put his jaws on anything with the smallest whiff of their clammy hands lingering on it. He'd rely on snow for water, and the only flesh he ate were leftovers Natasha brought to him after she'd already licked off any hints of human scent. And it wasn't just their smell that lingered. Behind a part of the fence mostly shielded by trees, a group of men with guns were stationed just outside. Natasha said the guards were there to protect them from other humans, bad ones, but Ten couldn't believe in such altruism. He knew man liked to gawk at things, and he was sure that was the real reason they put a couple wolves in a pen and stood by it day and night. But he woke up still-alive day after day, so he couldn't fathom what the guns were for.

As the next cycle turned along, he mustered the bravery to eat right from the fresh carcasses and drink right from the sterile-smelling tubs—after realizing Natasha had been doing just that and had not fallen ill or dropped dead. And when he did, he feared he'd face some teasing for being so cautious—his old packmates would've given it to him—but she only welcomed him. As they slept curled up next to each other for the first freezing-cold night, he realized he'd been letting his distrust of humans fall onto this other wolf for too long.

By the third cycle, Natasha herself had begun to lose hope, just as Ten had. But he assured her of his plan to dig out. The ground would be thawed in another cycle or so.

One morning, early enough into the spring the snow no longer reached up to their dew claws, Natasha woke Ten, splayed out under a tree after a meal. "I told you so," she said.

Blinking the exhaustion away, he raised his head off the root he'd been resting it on.

Natasha's tongue lolled like a dog, her tail wagging and her paws just about dancing as she paced around him.

"What?" he muttered.

"They opened the gate."

For a minute, Ten thought himself still asleep, having some too-good-to-be-true dream. He scanned the chain link fence. On the side facing a prairie blanketed in white, there was a bear-sized gap that had not been there before his nap.

They said no words to each other after that except yips of excitement as they raced—no, it wasn't a race, they ran together and beside each other—to the gap. On their way out, a group of humans stood some ways off. Cameras shuttered and the humans cheered, their noise only fading when Ten and Natasha had run far enough. They both glanced back up the hill the pen stood atop, then at each other with looks that said, *let's get far away from that prison.*

Ten sniffed a big gust of westerly wind—even the wind was bigger, out in the open—and scented something deer-like. *Elk.* Many of them. Another one of those hollow, echoing screeches came from the side of the valley where mountains didn't shield the rising sun's light.

A herd far bigger than any of the measly groups of deer he'd seen moved lazily in the distance, many nibbling bark off the willows and cottonwoods at the prairie's edge.

"That must be their territory," Natasha observed.

"We already ate today," Ten said. "But after being pent up for all those moon-cycles, I feel I have all the energy in the world. Shall we hunt right now? The cold will keep our catch good, so we can feed later."

Natasha was quiet for a moment. "Maybe we should look for a good place to dig a den. For when it is time."

Ten tilted his head. His eyes drew to her rounded belly, and he realized.

He remembered what the raven back in Alberta had told him. For the first time in generations, a pack would be formed in the place where wolves belonged.

Now out on a vast prairie—with a great herd of elk near the tree line that was large enough to feed a hundred packs, the rock-studded and close-up mountains, and those strange clouds of white smoke steaming up from random spots in the distance—he felt just as at home as he did in his boreal-forest territory in Alberta. Even *more* at home. He felt something that was rooted past just where he'd been born and ran with a pack before, something woven in with *being* a wolf, as if his birth-pack and all the packs before that he'd descended from had roamed here.

Natasha stood so still only her fur moved in the breeze. She must've had that same feeling in her bones. Then, she snapped out of it, and said, "We'll find one of those beautiful places the magpies told me about." By what could've only been instinct—they'd never set paw there until that moment, but somehow knew it as if they'd roamed it for a lifetime—they headed southwards.

The next moon-cycle was spent purely exploring, under the productive guise of den site-searching. Ten saw all the things Natasha had told him of while they were still in the pen—a golden-tan canyon that held a waterfall that roared like thunder, boiling lakes with centers deep-blue as the sky at dusk and edges orange as her eyes, spouts of steaming water that steadily rose into the air until they towered higher than the treetops. As if elk weren't enough of an upgrade from deer, they found herds of stocky, thick-coated bovines. *Bison.* The two wolves dreamed together of taking one of them down once their pups were born and grown, and they'd become a strong pack.

Natasha echoed that *I told you so* every time—though accompanied by a wagging tail and eyes admiring the landscape in front of them, it was only playful teasing.

On gusty days, the willows in the grasslands whistled, and they sat nearby and howled along. Songbirds nesting in them interrupted to inform the wolves the tree's whistling was actually their way of saying thank you; wolves would hunt the flora's main predator, so next year, far more sprouts would be able to grow into trees.

They did truly belong here. But by the end of that moon-cycle, as they lay one night in the sagebrush prairie below that old pen, Ten pointed something out while watching the Milky Way's core inch across the sky above.

"Natasha?"

On the edge of sleep, she only let out a short whine in response.

"Do you remember the northern lights?"

Still lying on her side, she stretched. "Hm?"

"Back in Alberta, I'd see them all the time."

She half-opened her eyes and nodded. "Yes, I saw them sometimes."

"Have you noticed there are none here? Never?" His words felt like a disservice to the shimmering lake of stars above, as they were breathtaking in their own right. But he'd loved those lights since he was a pup. Yellowstone was his true homeland, but one thing was missing.

"I do miss them a little."

"I miss them a lot."

She closed her eyes again. "Ten, we must dig our den soon. Really, this time. Tomorrow, we'll head north and find someplace."

"Why north? We've done plenty of searching south of here. Why not near that beautiful waterfall?"

"*Northern* lights," she emphasized. "Maybe if we go a little further north, we'll see them. And our pups will grow up seeing them, too. They'd like that, don't you think?"

"Oh, you're right." Even in that cold midnight, his heart warmed. "That sounds lovely. At dawn, we'll hunt and leave."

He curled up next to her, and his time asleep only felt like a moment. A bugling elk woke both of them while the eastern horizon was burning orange, and only the brightest stars and planets still shone.

Wind blowing towards them in their favor, they headed to the herd's territory and across the prairie. They went for a limping cow elk on the outskirts. Upon taking her down, they saw many wolf bites from a failed hunt marring her haunch.

With this, Ten and Natasha found another pack-to-be-formed had begun to make their territory in this prairie, and this only strengthened their need to head elsewhere.

They started at a quickened pace, then slowed to walking when the prairie rose up to mountains.

By sunset, they'd crossed the range and entered another valley that reeked of cougar-scent. Natasha was panting and dragging her paws by then, and the next line of mountains rose before them rose higher and rockier than the last.

Ten still strode with energy in his paws. Panting, Natasha caught up to him with a short sprint. "Go on and keep looking. I can't walk for much longer."

He stopped and twitched his ears, using this bout of silence to listen for any danger. "This valley doesn't smell safe."

"I know. We must look further for a place to dig the den."

"That's also exactly why I can't leave you by yourself here."

"It's only for a little while. I'll follow your scent and catch up once I'm rested."

"I'm staying with you." Before she could make any argument back, he located a nearby cedar with lush, low-sweeping branches and crawled under. "Come on. We'll both rest for the night. Cougars are lone—they wouldn't attack two wolves together."

With a long yawn, she trudged over to the tree and lay beside him.

Ten's sleep was, once again, just a blink. He'd been more worn-out than he'd thought.

The next morning, well after sunrise, it was the pure anxiety which had been festering in his heart that woke him. He'd been so concerned with Natasha he'd even forgotten to check for northern lights before drifting off. Thankfully, when he emerged from under the cedar and sniffed the air, the cougar-scent had gone stale. But still not a hint of prey-scent. The big cats must've spooked them all away.

He bowed down to gently nudge Natasha awake with his nose. "I'm going to look for something to hunt. There's nothing in this place."

She feebly nodded and stretched before closing her eyes again.

He stood and pawed the low branches, making sure she was concealed. Scanning the snow-mottled mountains, and deeming them not too difficult to cross, he set off.

Still no prey-scent, even as he travelled further. Ten resolved to move quickly to the next valley. In a wide-open, grassy place, surely there would be elk or deer.

Once the sun was a little over halfway down the western horizon, giving the surrounding mountains a golden tint, he caught his first glimpse of flat land through a break in the forest. A shallow creek rushed just past a two-lane road. He suddenly realized how thirsty he'd grown over the trek.

He ran downhill and halted just before a road. Gasoline fumes lingered, but he saw no car in either direction, so he sprinted across and leapt across a guardrail onto a riverbank of mossy stones. This time, he scented deer. They'd drank from this exact spot recently.

Not elk, but it would do.

Stepping only on the moss-covered spots of the slick rocks to avoid slipping, he crouched and lapped at the cold water.

As he drank, something else chattered under the burbling creek's noise. He'd assumed it to be some bird—it wasn't the singsong tone of passerines, so perhaps a grouse or duck—and paid it no mind. The hushed talk came from a deciduous forest across with trees so dense he couldn't see more than a lynx's-leap in, and the wind was only a fickle breeze blowing away from him—so the exact species was unclear for now.

The murmuring suddenly raised to a panicked shout. "What if that's somebody's dog? Lookit the collar!" No, this was a man's voice.

"You can't tell me that thing ain't a wolf!" a gruffer voice shot back.

Letting out a deep warning-growl, Ten raised his head and tail. If these men were here to take down deer, they were competition to be driven off.

"Well, even if it is," the first man persisted, "they don't want you t—"

Ten did not hear any more of their conversation.

Natasha barely remembered waking up. A cougar, its fur lit blood-red by the setting sun, chased her towards the mountains while its two cubs watched. Fueled only by adrenaline and the fact she'd been lying under that tree for over a day now, she managed to outrun that thing—or perhaps it'd let her escape upon realizing she was, too, a mother.

She stopped just at the edge of the valley, panting. As she glanced back, her lips curled into a snarl and her tail raised.

The cougar let out one more yowl, tail lashing, then joined her cubs in eating some starved-looking jackrabbit.

Natasha's paws seemed to want to drag her into the evergreen forest filling the dips between the mountains so she could lie back down under another tree. But Ten, gone since yesterday morning, hadn't returned with any catch. He hadn't even howled to let her know he was still out there. So, she put her nose to the ground and located his stale scent. Her amber eyes glossed over with tears as she breathed it in.

She raised her snout, forgetting about the danger on the opposite side of the valley for a moment, and howled as loud as she could, though even this left her breathless.

Nothing.

She made up, that while looking for somewhere with more prey, he must've caught the northern lights overnight, stayed in that place, and forgot to return. Perhaps he was too tired to howl back, as he'd walked so far.

And though she knew he'd never abandon her, but it was the only explanation she could think of.

Nose to the ground, she followed his scent between the mountains. Her breathing weakened to wheezes, and her legs felt thin and fragile as a fawn's, but that scent kept her going. Unable to hunt, she chomped every acorn on the ground along the way that'd dropped from sparse oaks in the mostly-conifer forest.

And at her slow pace, she zigzagged through those mountains until dawn. Finally, through a gap in the trees, she saw something red on the horizon, the land flat enough to reveal it. She'd finally reached the next valley, and Ten's scent was stronger here. Surely, this is where he'd be.

She trotted downhill and across a road—she was too tired to care about checking for cars, and humans typically weren't active this early anyway. Too weak to jump, she squeezed under the guardrail and came upon a creek, its shore made of moss-covered rocks. Ten was nearby. And she caught a faint whiff of deer, too—maybe he was hunting somewhere in that thick forest across the water.

Beep. Beep. Beep.

Her ears perked at a noise accompanying the sound of rushing water. It sounded exactly like her own collar, only more frantic, chirping at short intervals like a startled cricket.

"Ten?" she barked. That could've only been his collar. "Ten, I'm here, I'm here." Her words came out as gasps. She needed him soon. He'd best be near when the pups came. Birds of prey were sharp-eyed, and most other predators were unforgiving. She couldn't protect herself nor her young in such a state.

Beep. Beep. Beep. Beep.

Nearly slipping on the dark rocks, she stumbled towards the source. As the noise grew louder, a small, blinking red light caught her eye.

An unlatched collar laid half-submerged in the creek, hanging onto the sprawling root of a spruce tree planted in the soft soil next to the guardrail.

Her first thought was it wasn't his. Content with this conclusion, she was hesitant to sniff it and confirm. She took a step up towards the spruce where she'd lie under in wait for him, but curiosity turned her right back around. She bowed her head, nose nearly grazing the collar.

The first thing she picked up on was dried blood, invisible on the black nylon. The second was the very scent she'd followed here.

Her ears flattened. No, no, this was from another wolf. Maybe they'd fought, and he'd killed them.

Yet the only other scent remaining was not that of a wolf, but a human's hands.

Her legs finally gave out on her. She couldn't muster another howl, and only whined in grief, snout pressed against the collar, still breathing in what scent was left.

She was only allowed a minute of mourning before a sharp ache shot through her. Rolling over so her belly faced away from the creek, she closed her eyes. Her sides heaved, and the worsening pain gave her no breaks. She was certain she and the pups would join Ten soon.

🐾 * 🐾

Everything had grown blurry during that whole day, fumes from passing cars and 18-wheelers only further clouding Natasha's head, and she didn't slip back into full-consciousness until dusk when an osprey swooped down towards her. She feebly kicked it away, but it dodged her bad aim and flew off with one of the dark squealing bodies squirming against her belly. Seven left.

Beep. Beep. Beep. That collar next to her head tormented her all day, hurting worse than birth itself.

One of the pups quit its biting—the rest still hadn't figured out she had no milk—and clambered over her legs. It used only its nose to locate her snout and then stopped right next to the warm breath coming from her half-opened jaw. She feebly licked the pup. Mucus and blood came off on her tongue. She wished not to leave the others like that, but she couldn't lift her head to clean them.

Then, a vehicle pulled over. They'd come for her, too.

Human voices chattered.

"…wandered outside the park…" she heard one of them mention.

That's how Ten was killed. She and him had accidentally left paradise, the paradise where no human was allowed to hurt a wolf.

One of the humans entered her view. The woman took careful steps down the rocks to the creek, moving like a bighorn sheep would on a steep cliff. She cooed sympathetic words, but the gun in her hands said otherwise.

She crouched a short distance from Natasha and pointed the gun at her haunch. Suddenly, their eyes locked.

"Take me, please," the wolf whispered. "Just not the pups. Bring them to a mother who can go on."

As if she understood, the woman pulled the trigger.

But Natasha felt no pain—only a numbness. The same numbness she'd felt when they'd captured her back in Alberta.

Natasha awoke next sunset in a metal box with several patches of fur shaved off where they'd stuck needles in her. The spots were a little sore, but overall, she no longer felt on the edge of death.

She'd been here before. Those humans who found her were good humans. They were taking her back to Yellowstone.

She heard her pups still whining. Craning her neck to look through the holes in the box, all she saw in the noise's direction was a human cradling a smaller box. "I'm here," she yelped to them. In return, their whines grew louder.

This excited the humans, and they began chattering and laughing to each other.

"She'll find another," one of them said.

"But you're never gonna find one like Wolf Ten. Really."

A grief-laden quietness followed this comment. Before the silence grew awkward, the human changed the subject. "Big geomagnetic storm tonight, I heard."

"Solar flares? They'll show all the way down here, you think?"

"That's what they're saying."

Their conversation had dipped back into human matters Natasha didn't understand. She finally noticed the chunk of meat sitting at her paws. Crouching, she devoured it in mere seconds. Just as she finished and was still licking her chops, the metal box dropped to the ground.

She peered through the holes. The man carrying her pups kept walking.

She whined louder. Her paws lifted up and down. "You forgot me! *Where* are you taking them?"

The man disappeared behind a sweeping cedar at the base of a forested hill. A moment later, he returned with the box empty.

She snarled, pawing at the door and gnawing the holes.

A cautious hand reached towards the door. She tried to snap at it, only to bump her nose against the cold metal.

The door swung open. She raced to the tree, frantically pacing and sniffing until she located the pups under it. Their whimpers switched to elk-like screams when they sensed her.

She immediately lay down and curled around them. By some miracle the good humans must've done on her, the pups now had milk.

It was sunset again. Her mind wandered to Ten. She raised her head to gaze at the pups. All black, as newborn wolves always were, but some were bound to take on her mate's coat as they aged. She reached her snout inwards to nuzzle and lick them. They filled at least half of the hole in her heart Ten had left.

Night fell. The owls' hoots made her push her pups closer to the base of the tree and nudge them closer to her belly. She decided she'd dig a den under this tree after their needy mouths finally unlatched and gave her a break. And come dawn, she'd find food.

If she didn't have pups depending on her, she would've let the mourning drain her. She would starve without the will to hunt and dehydrate without the will to walk to a creek. She'd lay in the soil until it reclaimed her, and she returned to Ten.

No. She fought that sadness that threatened to kill her. *Ten would want me to keep going.*

After a moment staring at the pups, her spirits lifted ever so slightly.

An image flashed through her mind like a dream. A forest whose trees had been reduced to barren, charred, thin figures. An ashen ground. Tumbleweed-like jumbles of twigs that had once been bushes. Somewhere scarred by wildfire. But she'd lived long enough to know what happened to forests after such devastation. Winds blew the ashes away. Rain came and nourished the ground. The lushness and greenery returned, and one would've never known the fire had come through.

May that be me, she thought. *I don't know how long it'll take. But may that be me.*

Bullfrogs and crickets joined in on the chorus, lulling the litter to sleep. Carefully, Natasha wriggled out from under the cedar and stretched. The human hadn't chosen the safest tree. She'd venture a little deeper into the forest and dig a den there.

The air crackled. Static made the fur on her back rise. Head tilted, she turned towards the vast grassland that left a wide-open view of the sky.

Creeping from the northern horizon was a bright cascade of pale-green light crowned with magenta. It spread and formed a dancing ceiling over the prairie.

Eyes wide and heartbeat picking up, she watched.

The lights swirled like magpies in the air and whistled like the willows. They pranced like she and Ten did in their days exploring Yellowstone. They towered up like erupting geysers and sporadically brightened like fireflies.

Natasha raised her head and howled.

The northern lights flared—and another loud, echoing howl answered from their ripples.

~ *  * ~

Missy Stephenson is an aspiring author from Chesterfield, Virginia. She focuses on middle-grade fiction stories about animals grounded in meaningful lessons, similar to her favorite books she'd read as a child. With seven novels started, including three finished (though all are still prone to a billion more rounds of editing, as she believes "finished" is a near unheard-of thing in writing), she's received several Scholastic novel writing awards and has racked up a slightly concerning amount of hours spent in fictional worlds.

As fantastical as her works may be, each is primarily inspired by her real-world travels through America's diverse landscapes—from Maine's rocky shores, to California's giant forests, to the Southwest's red deserts, to Florida's Everglades, and to every mountain range she's found herself in. This has been the rule since she started her first novel at eleven, and every vacation spot is at risk of being turned into the backdrop for a furred (or feathered, or scaled) fictional adventure in her Google Docs.

When not writing, she's procrastinating over the rigorous coursework given at Maggie L. Walker Governor's School, listening to music while daydreaming about her characters, exploring the woods behind her house with her cat, Spade, or chatting with her poodle, Lady Diamond Jewel.

As of now, she's juggling two first drafts—one about a bear cub battling monsters made of sand from Colorado's dunes, and the other about elitist portal-travelling dogs in the cave systems near Nashville.

End or Beginning

Dana Bell

I lifted my muzzle to the sky and howled. My mournful cry filled the night as snow blew around me. Already our camp had been covered in a blanket of white. Leah's lifeless body lay curled in her sleeping bag. I had listened to her breathing slow until it stopped. Her heart falling into silence.

My human had been listless for days. I'd licked her face to wake her. Whined. She dragged her legs from one spot to another, dropping down, not even lighting a fire for warmth. Shivering in the cold. Supplies gone. No more bones for me to chew on.

"There was nothing I could do," she repeated time and again. "I'm so sorry." Her eyes looked skyward, moisture escaping and running down her face.

Whether it was to comfort herself or an apology to the unseen God she prayed to, I couldn't be sure. Maybe both.

She'd killed her captain after he'd shot the old ones. They'd used food needed for the breeders and the strong ones who defended their pack. His face had showed no remorse as they died. He'd ordered them tossed into the pit just outside the base. An insult to their own customs.

We'd checked on the base a few moons ago. No movement. No sound. No smells. I wondered if they'd fled, trying to escape the cold dark. As if they could escape what had engulfed the land. The world.

Since the night of spitting fire, the land had known no warmth. No plants grew. Only splintered shadowed trees and withered grass remained. Bones of many forest dwellers littered the ground. Some chewed. Others broken. Tufts of hair on a few.

I stood alone.

She'd called me Tanguy. It means Fighter. A good strong name. I felt unworthy of it.

Again, I howled, releasing my sorrow and loneliness. Wolves are not meant to be alone. We need the pack to survive and thrive.

Leaders to guide us. Pups to increase our numbers.

My ears listened for any reply. Any living thing to answer.

Only silence remained. Not even the whispering of the wind.

With reluctance I left the camp. Humans often buried their dead. As a wolf I knew their customs. I could not, however, honor the final respect. I apologized to my human releasing another howl. I hoped she understood and would not curse me from the place her spirit had gone.

Padding through the night I headed further south. Not that I expected much to change. The mountain had destroyed much. Little survived. Not even small animals on which I could fill my belly. My legs protested the use of what little energy I had left.

If I did not keep going, I would die and be buried under the freezing white. Forgotten. No pack to howl my loss.

How long I traveled, I could not be sure. I knew only that I had traveled a long distance from all that had once been familiar. Not that I noticed much difference. Blackish white snow covering the ground. Bare trees reaching to the sky. The dark which had not lifted for many moons.

Ruins tucked into the mountains, like empty tombs. The wind flapping rags. Objects whose purpose I could not fathom, scattered everywhere. More bones. Human I think.

My hunger grew. My limbs grew weak. I stumbled many times, forcing myself back on my paws. I must keep going. I must live.

Leah would want me to survive. I knew her desire to be true.

I heard a roaring sound. Following it I found myself staring across vast water. From the smell it was not good to drink. I watched as it attacked the shore again and again, like a constant battle and with no winner declared. Dead beaches covered in wood. Further down an old boat, skeletons littering the sand beside it.

Something wigged in a small pool. With caution I approached. I did not know what the creature could be and watched it struggle to escape. Long. Covered in shiny skin. Large eyes. I caught it in my mouth. It crunched and had nice tasting flesh. Wasn't enough to satisfy my belly, yet it proved to be food. I hunted for more, gobbling them up, not minding my wet muzzle. I sneezed. Shook my body. I could feel the damp cold drizzling down to my skin.

Sated, I moved to higher ground, finding a comfortable niche in the rocky side. I curled up and slept.

When next I woke, I felt strong. I'd earned my name. Tanguy. Fighter. For I fought to stay alive and had succeeded. I did not give in to the final cold sleep.

I rose, shook, and watched another like me hunting in the pools. It stopped, staring up at me.

Who? echoed in my mind.

Tanguy, I replied.

The one who traveled with a human. From the scent, I knew her to be female. Thick fur, the color blending into the sand, rare dark markings on her tail and near her paws.

My human died. I waited for her response. Feeling sad.

As many of them have. Come, she invited.

I hurried down the rocky incline and followed her. She led me to a small group of wolves, most younger than me. They'd made their home in a ruined shack, the boards grayed. Scattered on the ground were tuffs of grass.

We have no leader. The female sat down. *We have need of you.*

I had never thought to lead. Yet their eyes stared at me with expectation.

Could I lead and help us survive? Doubt filled me. My human had died. I could do nothing. Not even bury her as was the custom of her pack.

A flickering and I saw Leah, standing there. Her uniform clean, not dirty and torn. Her boots hugged her feet. She wore her hair short. She smiled and with her hand indicated the pack, as if to say, they are your future. Slowly she faded. Dark sky and falling snow were all I saw where her figure had stood.

For this season I had been born. To have my own pack, my own mate, and help us become what we were meant to be. A strong new species, in a world destroyed by fire, ash, snow and cold. A place where few humans survived. We would rise to take their place.

Briefly I saw others who would one day stand beside us in a future I would not live to see. Wepwawet the wolf god would bless us.

We are the new masters of this new cleansed world. I knew we'd prove worthy of it.

Dana Bell, a Colorado writer, enjoys composing tales set in places she has either lived or visited. She spoils her two resident cats, Taj and Esther, who are always close by to 'help'. Felines are often featured in her stories or books. She has six published books, more short stories than she can count and is an award winning poet. As an editor, she has launched many writing careers and has edited over ten anthologies.

Decorating dollhouses, making flower arrangements or candle holders are among her hobbies. Recently she also has begun creating her own recipes.

Bulwark

Rodney G Hatfield Jr.

Their town was nothing more than a tiny dot on the map, just a name scrawled next to the long road that sliced through the sprawling national forest. A traveler passing through might have dismissed it entirely, thinking it too small to matter, but for the people who lived there, it had everything they needed, and then some.

The grocery store was more than just a place to pick up milk and bread. It was where people caught up on the latest news. Mrs. Carter, the town's unofficial historian, was always stationed near the produce aisle, ready with stories about someone's third cousin twice removed.

"I heard Clara's boy got a scholarship," she'd whisper, leaning in close, her voice dripping with pride even though Clara wasn't anywhere near.

"Oh, you mean Sam? I always knew that boy was going places," another would reply, nodding sagely as they picked through the apples.

The hardware store down the street had a similar charm, though its chatter revolved around home repairs and DIY projects. Mr. Henson, the owner, was known for giving advice that started with, "Now, what you really want to do is…" and ending with a solution so detailed you'd leave with both the tools and the confidence to fix anything.

Main Street held a handful of other shops, each one a testament to the town's personality. There was a cozy bookstore where regulars lost themselves in paperbacks. Young Jenny, who worked the counter, always had her nose buried in some fantasy epic and would eagerly recommend titles.

"This one's my favorite!" she'd exclaim, holding up a well-worn book. "The hero reminds me of old Sheriff Doyle, back when he was spry."

Nearby, a flower shop added bursts of color to the street. Even in winter, its windows overflowed with poinsettias and wreaths, thanks to the owner's green thumb. Across the way, the café smelled of fresh coffee and cinnamon. Locals filled their tables every morning, sipping and chatting.

"This town's fuel isn't gasoline," old Mr. Grady liked to joke. "It's coffee and gossip!"

There was also the treasure trove that was the two-dollar store, packed with trinkets, oddities, and little treasures. Kids loved it, rummaging through bins for toys, while bargain-hunting adults looked for household deals.

Essential services kept the town ticking along. If your pipes were leaking, Joe the plumber was only a phone call away. The barber shop wasn't just a place to get a trim; it was where men swapped stories about fishing trips and shared laughs.

"Caught a fish this big," one regular would boast, spreading his arms wide while everyone rolled their eyes.

On Elm Street, the bakery lured people in with the smell of fresh bread. Mary Anne, the baker, greeted customers with a smile and always added an extra cookie for the kids. Next door, the little art gallery showcased the talents of local artists. Paintings of the forest hung alongside handmade pottery, making the space feel like a snapshot of the town's soul.

Traffic was light, just three stoplights and a handful of signs. Life moved at a slower pace. Come evening, the diner in the main square came to life, its neon sign casting a warm glow. The menu offered everything from burgers to home-cooked specials. "

Pie's on me if you beat me at checkers!" the owner, Hank, would holler to regulars as they filed in.

Despite its size, the town had a charm that drew people in. Travelers on the highway would stop for gas or food, bringing with them stories of far-off places. But even with the occasional bustle, the town was peaceful. Yet, one thing made it unlike any other: the wolves.

Their howls echoed through the valley at night, haunting and beautiful. Visitors often paused to listen, a mix of wonder and unease on their faces. "You'll get used to it," the locals would say. But not everyone did. Rumors swirled about people who'd wandered too far into the woods and never returned.

"Ain't nothing to fear if you mind your business," Sheriff Doyle would tell newcomers. "Wolves don't come into town. They know better."

Still, some farmers worried. "Lost three sheep last month," old man Barrett muttered once, shaking his head at the café. "You ask me, they're getting bolder."

Efforts to thin the population of wolves were blocked by regulations. Even hunters who tried their luck never made much of a dent. Yet, the locals had their ways of keeping peace. If a wolf got too close, someone would fire a shot into the air or set off fireworks to scare them off.

"Teaches 'em to stay back," Joe the plumber once explained. "Then they will avoid you their whole life."

For all the wolf tales, the town seemed unfazed. Most people saw the animals as part of the forest's rhythm, as natural as the changing seasons. Life went on, steady as ever, in their small corner of the world.

Occasionally, a young wolf would wander into town, drawn by the promise of smaller prey, maybe a stray cat or the scent of fresh garbage outside the diner. These curious pups, wide-eyed and unaware of boundaries, were always met with firm but humane deterrents. The townsfolk had long devised effective methods to handle such situations, ensuring a peaceful coexistence.

"Remember, wolves are smart," Sheriff Doyle would remind everyone during town meetings. "Scare 'em good once, and they'll steer clear next time."

Firecrackers were a favorite tool, as was the occasional warning shot fired into the air. Once, Joe the plumber even banged an old metal bucket so loudly a wandering wolf pup yelped and bolted straight back into the woods. The key, everyone agreed, was to instill fear of humans in the animals, keeping them wary of approaching again.

"That's how you keep peace," Mrs. Carter often said over coffee at the café. "You don't pick fights with nature, and nature won't pick fights with you."

For a long time, this approach worked. The town thrived alongside the wilderness, and life remained calm. But one quiet spring morning, something strange happened that no one could have anticipated.

The day began as usual, with bright sunshine casting a warm glow over the town. Birds chirped in the distance, and the scent of blooming flowers from the shop on Main Street filled the air. Everything seemed perfectly ordinary until people noticed the raccoons. They were everywhere.

"Oh, for Pete's sake!" Hank shouted from the diner doorway, waving a spatula in the air. "What in tarnation are they doing out here in broad daylight?"

Raccoons, typically shy and nocturnal, were frolicking boldly in the streets. They scampered across sidewalks, overturned trash cans, and even played in the park like mischievous children.

"Rabies, maybe?" old man Barrett muttered as he leaned on his cane near the café. "Ain't natural, that's for sure."

Despite the murmurs of concern, most townsfolk found the scene oddly charming. Jenny from the bookstore sat on the steps, giggling as a baby raccoon tried to climb her shoe. Over at the bakery, Mary Anne left out a small plate of scraps, watching with delight as the furry creatures ate with tiny, dexterous paws.

"They're just hungry, poor things," she said with a smile.

For the better part of the morning, the town seemed enchanted by the raccoons' antics. Children laughed, adults marveled, and even the skeptical Sheriff Doyle cracked a grin. "Well, this is a first," he said, leaning against his patrol car. "Hope they don't start thinking this is a permanent arrangement."

But the lighthearted atmosphere didn't last. Around midday, the raccoons abruptly scattered, darting back into alleys and climbing into trees. The laughter and chatter quieted as a low, mournful howl drifted from the outskirts of town.

"Wolves," someone whispered.

A pack, large and formidable, had appeared at the edge of the forest, just beyond the last row of houses. They stood still, their golden eyes fixed on the town like silent sentinels.

"Why aren't they moving?" Jenny asked nervously, clutching a book to her chest.

"They're too close," Sheriff Doyle said, his voice tense. "Too bold."

The townsfolk quickly armed themselves. Guns were pulled from closets, and makeshift weapons, like bats and shovels, were clutched in trembling hands. Fear rippled through the crowd as they gathered in the main square, watching the wolves.

"Why aren't they leaving?" Mary Anne whispered, her voice quivering.

"Don't know," Doyle replied. He stepped forward cautiously, his hand resting on the revolver at his hip. "But we can't let them come any closer."

A few brave souls joined the sheriff, moving slowly toward the wolves. The pack didn't retreat. Instead, they held their ground, their bodies tense but oddly calm, as if waiting for something.

"Shoot a warning," Doyle ordered.

The crack of a rifle echoed through the air. Normally, that sound would send the wolves scattering into the trees, but this time, they didn't flinch.

"Why ain't they runnin'?" Joe muttered, gripping his shotgun tightly.

The confrontation turned brutal. With no other choice, the townspeople opened fire. The wolves didn't fight back, not really. They snarled and growled but rarely lunged. Even as their numbers dwindled, they stood firm, their golden eyes unyielding.

"This ain't right," Barrett said, his voice shaking as he reloaded. "They're not even trying to defend themselves!"

It was over in minutes, leaving the ground littered with bodies. Blood stained the grass, and the once-proud pack lay broken. Yet even in death, there was something haunting about the wolves' silence, their refusal to flee, their reluctance to attack. When it was over, the townsfolk stood in stunned silence, staring at the carnage.

"They weren't here to hunt us," Doyle said softly, his voice heavy with realization. "They came for something else."

Days passed in tense reflection after the wolves' strange behavior and subsequent slaughter. People whispered about it in hushed tones at the diner and hardware store, their conversations filled with unanswered questions.

"I just don't understand it," Mary Anne murmured, wiping down the counter at the bakery. "Wolves don't just stand there like that. It's unnatural."

"They were protecting something," Sheriff Doyle speculated over his coffee one afternoon. "Or maybe someone. Animals don't act that way without a reason."

No one could agree on what the wolves were doing, but unease settled over the town like a heavy fog. The once-familiar woods surrounding the community now seemed darker, as though hiding some unseen threat. Then came the night when everything changed.

It began with a single, sharp cry that cut through the stillness like a knife. At first, people dismissed it as the distant wail of a coyote or maybe an owl. But then the sound grew, a chorus of shrill, guttural cries, eerie and otherworldly. It wasn't just one animal. It was many, blending human-like screams with primal growls.

"What in the hell is that?" Joe said, stepping out onto his porch with his rifle. His hand shook as he scanned the dark tree line at the edge of his property.

The noise grew louder, piercing and relentless. Lights flickered across town, casting eerie shadows before plunging the streets into complete darkness. Phones went dead, cutting off any hope of outside communication. The town, so small and tightly knit, suddenly felt vast and isolated.

"I can't see a damn thing!" someone shouted in the diner, where a few late-night customers huddled nervously.

"Stay calm, everyone," Doyle said, his voice steady but strained. He adjusted the flashlight in his hand, sweeping it across the room. "We don't know what's out there, but panicking won't help."

The cries continued, echoing through the night, carrying a strange rhythm that made the hairs on people's necks stand on end. Then, just as suddenly as they began, they stopped. Silence descended, but it was the kind of silence that felt alive—waiting.

A crash shattered the stillness. Then another.

"They're here!" someone screamed.

The source of the earlier cries became horrifyingly clear. The raccoons had returned. But these weren't the playful, curious creatures that had charmed the town only days before. These raccoons moved with purpose, calculating, cold, and terrifyingly efficient. They poured into the streets in a wave, their glowing eyes reflecting the moonlight like tiny flames.

"Oh my God," Mary Anne whispered, peering through the window of the bakery. "What...what are they doing?"

"They're hunting," Doyle said grimly, loading his revolver.

The first attacks were swift and brutal. A group of raccoons ambushed a man outside the general store, dragging him to the ground with shocking strength. His screams were quickly swallowed by the sound of growls and snapping jaws.

"Barricade the doors!" Doyle shouted, his voice cutting through the chaos. "Don't let them inside!"

Across town, people scrambled to fortify their homes and businesses. Chairs, tables, and shelves were shoved against doors and windows as the raccoons clawed and scratched, their war cries filling the night.

"They're too smart," Barrett muttered as he jammed a piece of wood into his doorframe. "They know what they're doing. How the hell do they know what they're doing?"

It quickly became clear the raccoons weren't acting randomly. They moved with unsettling coordination, setting traps and ambushing anyone who ventured outside. They climbed onto rooftops, dropped down chimneys, and used their small size to slip through gaps in defenses. At the café, Jenny and a small group of survivors huddled behind overturned tables.

"We have to get out of here," one man said, his voice trembling. "We're sitting ducks!"

"You want to go out there with them?" Jenny snapped, pointing toward the window where glowing eyes peered in from the darkness. "Be my guest!"

Meanwhile, Doyle led a group of townsfolk in a desperate effort to push the raccoons back. Guns roared, but for every raccoon that fell, two more seemed to take its place.

"They're everywhere!" Joe shouted, reloading his shotgun as fast as he could.

The night dragged on in a haze of blood and terror. The raccoons' small size and agility made them deadly opponents, capable of darting in and out of range before anyone could react. Despite their desperation, the townsfolk were no match for the overwhelming numbers and cunning of their attackers.

Amidst the relentless chaos and rising despair, a glimmer of hope flickered briefly as the surviving wolves, bruised, bloodied, and vastly outnumbered, emerged from the shadows of the forest to intervene. Their golden eyes glinted with a mix of determination and anguish as they hurled themselves into the fray. But their numbers were too few, their strength sapped from previous battles, and their efforts tragically futile.

Instead of the triumphant howls that had once echoed through the valleys, the wolves now let out mournful whimpers, cries of pain that resonated with the sorrow of their failed defense. One wolf, a grizzled gray alpha, stood defiantly between a group of raccoons and a barricaded building where several townsfolk hid. It bared its teeth in a final act of defiance, only to fall under the swarm of sharp claws and snapping jaws.

From inside the barricade, young Sam watched the scene through a crack in the boarded window.

"They're not fighting us," Sam whispered, his voice trembling. "They're fighting…for us."

Beside him, Mary Anne clasped her hands over her mouth, tears streaming down her face. "Oh, God… We killed them. We thought they were the danger, and now…now look what we've done."

The room fell silent as realization struck everyone. The wolves had not been the aggressors. Their haunting howls had been warnings, their presence an unspoken shield against the true enemy lurking in the woods. The raccoons, small and seemingly harmless, had concealed their malevolence behind an innocent facade.

Outside, the wolves' cries dwindled into silence, leaving a chilling void in their wake. The survivors emerged cautiously, their faces pale and streaked with tears. The town square, once lively with the sounds of community and laughter, was now a battlefield littered with bodies, human, wolf, and raccoon alike.

Sheriff Doyle knelt beside the fallen alpha wolf, his hat clutched tightly in his hands. "They were trying to protect us," he muttered, his voice hoarse. "And we…we turned on them."

"What do we do now?" Barrett asked, his voice shaking. "We're outnumbered. Outsmarted. How do we fight back against…those things?"

The answer came in the form of a revelation, one that shook the townsfolk to their core. The raccoons had orchestrated everything. They had exploited the long-standing tension between humans and wolves, sowing fear and confusion to ensure the wolves would be seen as the enemy. The townspeople, driven by panic and misunderstanding, had fallen into the trap.

Jenny, her face pale but resolute, stepped forward. "The wolves weren't our enemies," she said, her voice firm despite the quaver beneath it. "They were our protectors. And we failed them. But we can't let their sacrifice be in vain."

A murmur of agreement rippled through the group.

"We need a plan," Doyle said, standing. His expression was steely now, his grief channeled into determination. "We'll use what we have left, our weapons, our wits, and whatever resources we can scavenge. These raccoons may be clever, but we've got something they don't."

"What's that?" Joe asked, clutching his battered shotgun.

"Unity," Doyle replied. "They might outnumber us, but we can outthink them. Together."

The group nodded, resolve hardening their faces.

"We'll set traps," Jenny suggested. "Not like the ones they used —something bigger, smarter."

"And we can use fire," Barrett added. "Not enough to burn the town, but enough to smoke them out. Force them into the open where we can fight on our terms."

As the survivors huddled together, their whispered plans growing more intricate by the minute, the weight of their mistakes hung heavy in the air. But alongside it came a fierce determination to make things right, to honor the wolves' sacrifice and reclaim their home.

The raccoons' assault escalated with startling precision and aggression. They tested the townsfolk's defenses with coordinated strikes, probing for weaknesses with almost military-like strategy. In the streets, makeshift barricades were battered, doors clawed at, and traps cleverly circumvented. Every hour brought a new wave, and with each attack, the raccoons grew bolder, as if sensing their prey's growing exhaustion.

Inside the diner, a temporary stronghold for a group of survivors, Sam kept watch by a shattered window, his rifle clenched tightly in his trembling hands. "They're not stopping," he muttered, eyes darting at every shadow that moved.

"They're wearing us down," Doyle responded grimly, reloading his shotgun. "But we've got to hold on. They can't win."

Jenny, crouched behind the counter, added, "We need to outlast them. Use what we've got left to keep them at bay until..." She trailed off, unable to finish the thought. Until what? Reinforcements weren't coming. The power was out. The phones were dead. They were alone.

The raccoons launched another attack, this time lighting their war cries with eerie whistles and growls that sent chills through the survivors. Outside, traps were triggered, and bursts of fire momentarily lit up the darkness, driving back the invaders. The townsfolk retaliated with everything they had, each defense a desperate attempt to repel the relentless adversaries.

But as night deepened and hope wavered, an unnatural stillness fell over the town. The raccoons' cries faded into the eerie quiet, and even the air seemed to hold its breath.

"What's happening?" Mary Anne whispered.

Before anyone could answer, the mournful howls began. Low, haunting, and filled with sorrow, the sound seemed to come from everywhere at once, echoing through the shattered streets and battered buildings. Sam's breath hitched. "That's...wolves," he stammered, his voice barely audible. "But how?"

From the shadows emerged figures of ethereal light; spectral wolves with glowing blue eyes. Their translucent forms shimmered as they padded silently through the town, their presence sending a cold, ghostly breeze that raised goosebumps on every survivor.

"They're spirits," Jenny whispered, clutching Doyle's arm.

The wolves stopped in the center of the square, their ghostly eyes fixing on the humans. One of the larger spirits, its fur streaked with faint silver glimmers, tilted its head back and let out a long, mournful howl. The sound wasn't just heard, it was felt, resonating deep in the hearts of everyone present.

Sam stepped forward cautiously. "They're...they're not here to hurt us," he said, his voice trembling with awe. "They're here for the raccoons."

As if on cue, the raccoons began to emerge, their usual confidence replaced by visible fear. They hesitated at the edges of the square, their glowing eyes darting nervously toward the spectral wolves. For the first time, the cunning invaders seemed unsure of themselves.

The largest ghost wolf stepped forward, baring its teeth in a silent snarl. The raccoons responded with shrill war cries, but it was clear their resolve was crumbling. One by one, the ghostly wolves moved with eerie precision, lunging at the raccoons in coordinated strikes.

As the moon continued its watch over the town, the battle neared its fever pitch. The spectral wolves, now fully unleashed, moved with a terrifying elegance, their translucent forms flickering like ghostly flames. Their howls, mournful yet vengeful, reverberated through the cold air, a haunting requiem for the lives lost and the justice sought.

The raccoons, their facade of invincibility shattered, descended into chaos. Their once-coordinated strikes dissolved into frantic, panicked skirmishes. They scrambled over rooftops, darted into shadows, and tried in vain to regroup, but the ethereal wolves were everywhere. Silent and swift, the spectral protectors herded the cunning invaders into traps set by the townsfolk, forcing the raccoons to face their doom.

Mary Anne, wielding a flaming torch, led a group of survivors through the rubble-strewn streets. "Push them toward the square!" she shouted, her voice sharp with resolve. "We end this tonight!" Around her, others armed with pitchforks, shovels, and improvised weapons pressed on, emboldened by the spectral wolves' unwavering presence.

One of the ghostly wolves, its eyes blazing with unearthly blue fire, lunged at a raccoon attempting to climb a water tower. The raccoon froze mid-leap, letting out an ear-piercing shriek as the wolf's incorporeal jaws sank into it. Though the spirit left no visible wound, the raccoon writhed in torment before collapsing into a heap, its cunning intelligence seemingly snuffed out by the spectral assault.

In the square, Doyle and Sam had set up a final line of defense. They had constructed a massive bonfire, its roaring flames licking the night sky, casting grotesque shadows that danced with the chaos. "They're cornered!" Sam shouted, his rifle trained on a cluster of raccoons skittering toward them. He fired, the crack of the shot swallowed by the cacophony of battle.

But it wasn't just the flames or the gunshots that drove the raccoons into disarray, it was the wolves. With each passing moment, the spectral guardians became fiercer, their incorporeal forms more solid, more vengeful. The townsfolk couldn't decide which was more terrifying: the sight of the raccoons' disarray or the grim determination of the ghostly wolves who had come to claim retribution.

Finally, as the first light of dawn crept over the horizon, the tide broke. The remaining raccoons, fewer in number and driven mad with fear, scattered into the woods, their war cries now pitiful whimpers. Those who lingered were swiftly dispatched by the spectral wolves or trapped by the townsfolk's relentless pursuit. The battle was over.

The town lay in ruins. Streets were littered with shattered glass, overturned carts, and the remnants of barricades. Bodies of raccoons and humans alike were strewn across the battlefield, stark reminders of the brutal conflict.

The spectral wolves, their vengeance complete, gathered in the town square. Their once-fiery eyes now glowed softly, their forms less distinct, as if the weight of their mission had been lifted. One by one, they turned to the townspeople who had fought alongside them.

Mary Anne stepped forward, her torch lowered in a gesture of respect. "Thank you," she said, her voice trembling with emotion. "We…we were wrong about you. We didn't see you for what you were—our protectors. And we're so sorry."

As the sun crept higher into the sky, its golden rays revealed a town forever scarred by the events of the night. Shadows danced along the jagged edges of ruined buildings, and the cobblestone streets, slick with blood, gleamed faintly in the light. Survivors emerged from their barricades, hollow-eyed and weary, surveying the devastation with a mixture of disbelief and grief.

The spectral wolves, their blue fire dimmed, disappeared like whispers into the morning mist. The chill of their presence lingered, however, a subtle weight in the air that seemed to say, Remember us. Their mission was complete, but they left behind a town forever marked by the knowledge of their sacrifice and the grave cost of misplaced trust.

For days, the townsfolk worked to reclaim their lives. They gathered their dead, burying them with solemn ceremonies that honored both human and animal alike. The wolves were given special tributes, large stones etched with pawprints were placed in a circle at the edge of the forest where the pack had once roamed. This sacred space became a site of reflection, where townspeople would leave offerings to honor the memory of their protectors.

Among the ruins, Mary Anne took on a new role as the keeper of the tale. She gathered the children and told them of the spectral wolves who had fought alongside their ancestors. Her voice, steady but tinged with sorrow, carried the lesson of that fateful night. "It wasn't the wolves we needed to fear," she would say. "It was our inability to see clearly, to know friend from foe."

The tale became legend, passed from one generation to the next. Grandparents would sit with their grandchildren by the hearth, recounting the story of the cunning raccoons, the spectral wolves, and the human spirit that refused to yield. Some spoke of the battle as a warning against rash judgment, while others framed it as a testament to the unity that arose in the face of overwhelming odds.

Over time, the town rebuilt itself, but it was never quite the same. The scars of that night, both physical and emotional, remained etched into its character. The forests that bordered the town became a place of reverence and caution. Hunters, remembering the wolves' sacrifice, tread lightly, leaving offerings at the edge of the sacred circle. The town also bore a newfound awareness of the thin veil between the natural and the supernatural. They learned to question the intentions of creatures they once took for granted, and they honored the memory of the spectral wolves by remaining vigilant against complacency and deceit.

At the heart of the town square, a statue was erected: a ghostly wolf with its head lifted in a mournful howl, its eyes set toward the forest. The base bore an inscription:

"To the Silent Guardians: May We Never Forget."

~ * 🐾 * ~

Rodney Hatfield Jr. is an accomplished freelance writer with over two decades of experience, celebrated for his contributions to the horror & creepypasta genres. Rodney entertains 14,000 followers on his Facebook page, Horror Short Story Time, where he shares chilling tales and interacts with his audience.

Rodney's portfolio includes works in renowned anthologies & publications such as Running Wild Press, Horror Tree, Nat 1 Publishing, and CultureCult.co.in. Notable pieces include *Forbidden*

Hunger, The Retired Librarian, Crimson Moon, and *Dinky Noodle*.

Born in the rugged coal fields of southern WV, fighting autism and anxiety Rodney draws inspiration from storytelling traditions, family life, and a deep love for reading cultivated since childhood. His passion for preserving and innovating tales is evident in his writing. Still living in WV, weaving suspense in horror stories, experimenting with cozy mysteries, or crafting new poems.

Lyra

Laura Rodley

"I'm only human." I heard people say it inside the doorways of corner diners, outside the emergency room doors while they smoked their cigarettes. "I'm only human," while waiting to hear how their friend or relative is faring.

It's a phrase that is supposed to be helpful, I guess, but it does nothing for me. You see, I am a wolf. A wolf out of time, a wolf without a pack, a wolf in the inner city where I don't belong. Hunters killed my mother for her pelt and to stuff her head, and left me and my four other siblings. Only they didn't know we were there, or they might have stuffed us in a bag and taken us along. My mother had taught us to hide, to hide even our breath, to hold our noses under our paws to stop the steam from rising in the freezing cold, which is the weather in which we are born. Makes no sense to me, to be born when it is so cold, but it's one more thing that isn't up to me.

A wolf out of time, a wolf without a pack, a wolf in the inner city. After we heard the engine of the hunters' jeep roar, spin its tires on the snow, rock its tires back and forth as their jeep's hot wheels when they first parked had melted snow and become ice-locked, and then gunned it out of the woods, we all dispersed. I don't know how that happened. We were all so frightened. We didn't obey our mother's failsafe "rule of threes" —stay out of sight, stay together, stay where I can find you.

I ran too, no one's fault but my own. I didn't stay where she could find me because I knew she was gone. I saw the spirit rise from her breath and enter the frigid air as the hunters bent to sling her roughly over their backs. She had no time to say goodbye. I was under thick brush three yards from the hunters, hiding my nose under my paws, like my brothers beside me. The hunters made so much noise slapping each other on their backs, their boots scrunching on the icy snow they failed to hear our whimpers. Our whimpers which came uninvited. Which we bit our tongues to keep quiet.

Then we all ran in different directions. Only three months old, our fur was thick but not thick enough. I ran after the jeep, howling, as they took the turn towards the highway. Grief must have slowed me down, because I could not catch it. I wanted to bite the tires of the jeep. Bring her back, return my mother to the forest.

I followed the jeep's exhaust fumes to the gas station where they must have pumped gas to keep their vehicle running on the road, no pads on paws to become encrusted with ice, no need to stop and pick the ice that forms between the pads out. Which is what stopped me from catching up with them; I had to stop and gnaw the ice away from between the pads of my paws. And lick the icicles from my nose that formed from my breath. No hiding in the bushes to stealthily keep my breath warmer, stop it from freezing. The jeep's exhaust burned my nose, but I kept running. Until I stopped. I stopped in a city near a hospital where the men had parked and taken off again. I couldn't find their jeep.

But I found one of the men's scent wafting out the tall clear sheets of ice called windows that opened sideways as doors at the emergency room entrance. I heard his voice screeching for some-one to help him stop the bleeding, something about how he'd shot himself while changing shells in the rifle, how the she-wolf had moved and banged his arm, and that's how he shot himself. It wasn't his fault. The she-wolf was dead, but she had moved her head, banged his arm, then stared at him. I looked through the sheets-of-ice windows. They slid open sideways: my wish to enter must have opened them. I walked in as though I belonged there, and stared at this screaming man, by lowering my nose and looking at him sideways.

When he saw me, he started screeching, "She's alive, she's come back, she's after me! See her yellow eyes! Help!"

Two men dressed in white grabbed his arms, and eased him into a wheelchair, "Come with us, buddy, we'll fix you right up. Not the first time you've shot yourself, or had the DTs. Everyone knows there's no wolves around here. No mountain lions, either."

Then someone else turned and noticed me, eyes wide in sur-prise, too surprised to talk.

I turned, walked towards the door. The sliding door opened by itself and I walked out into the bitter biting wind.

Wolves aren't supposed to eat pizza but that's all I found the first night. Alberto's Pizzeria had thrown away slices of pizza into their metal dumpster and not closed the lid. It smelled like my mother's milk and a vegetable garden, not that I knew what a vegetable was then. The doughy crust was chewy, and filled my stomach. I lay down briefly in the dark near a fan that was blowing out and warmed me. My fur was still not thick enough to handle twenty-below-degree weather without my brothers and mother curled around me. Luckily it was only about ten degrees.

I smelled the girl before I heard her, the noise of the exhaust fan was so loud. I must have fallen asleep so deeply due to exhaustion, or the exhaust fan might been from a gas stove emitting some sleep-inducing vapors.

"You're so pretty," the girl said, leaning down near me. "You look like my old dog Raven."

I froze in place, hoping she'd forget she'd seen me, go on with her business. Remember, I'm only a young wolf, three months old, not so big. Yet.

But she kept walking forward. I slink up the way my mother taught us, encase myself in a cloak of invisibility, rise like the wind, a raven feather, and swallow the fear inside my mouth. It doesn't work. She still sees me. I jumped away, loping down the side street.

"You're so big! You could be my new dog. Don't go. Come back."

Believe me, it was tempting. I would have liked to stay and make that little girl happy, but wolves are not pets, and they are definitely not friends of humans.

I loped through long and short expanses of forests which I later learned were called lawns. I stopped on the snow-covered black asphalt, deciding on which direction to go, and the horns of cars beeped at me. I lunged across the road, horns still beeping, sliding on the ice, and leapt up the hill that had a brick tower like a castle. I cowered in the brush by the side of the tower where the winter's meager sun had warmed the bricks, and licked my paws. Yes, I cowered, I am ashamed to say. The horns had hurt my ears, similar to the earlier gunshots that killed my mother, but not so tinny. I was used to the breathing of my brothers and my mother, the sound of the wind, crashing branches of snow-weighted trees. My ears were still hurting from being so close when the guns went off.

I huddled, curled as tight as I could, soaking the heat out of the sun-warmed bricks. I should start moving but I was afraid, trying to hide, away from the horns, the guns. My paws were so cold, the pads so sore, my ears flat against me, it was hard to breath. It was a miracle when it started to snow. The snow saved me, its warm cover. Without it, I may have frozen to death. It covered me and warmed me. I let it lay on top of me, my nose stretched out one side as the snow formed a blanket.

It was dark, dark enough that fewer cars were driving on the snow-covered roads. Time to eat again. I had not seen one animal on my trek here. I shook the snow off, chomped some for water, licked my mouth, and headed for the pizzeria.

The lights were on in the building, and warmth flowed through the air from the vents as I scrounged in the dumpster. A spicy meat this time, from some unknown animal, and a wide green-leafed grass called lettuce. I swallowed it all, barely taking time to chew. I was used to fighting with my brothers to get my share, so I growled and tossed my head back and forth sideways but no one was hassling me. As a result, I ate more than I ever have in my entire life. Comfortable and warm, I did not forget the rules of three, but I admit I ignored them by promptly falling asleep, no mother nipping at my flanks to keep me moving, no siblings to jostle me.

Besides, the last two rules of the rules of three were obsolete now: there was no staying together as everyone had dispersed and my mother was not coming back to find me. There remained only one rule—stay out of sight—which I ignored when I decided to return to the hospital with the ice-window sliding doors of the emergency room, to see if the hunter came out. I'd follow him to have him take me to my mother. That could wait till dawn arose.

Meanwhile, I curled up, rested my head against my shoulder, and tried to forget.

The ground rumbles beneath me and water bubbles out. Inside, I hear a man yelling something that sounds like, "The pipes burst," then a large clank-clunk as something falls, and a hissing noise starts droning over my head, like a snake that smells bad, not like a copperhead that smells like cucumber but something else, like sulfur.

I remember I had eaten some cucumbers from the dumpster.

I try to stand but can't. I can't make my legs move and a bad taste envelops my tongue.

Then there is a roaring sound and a sheet of hardened snow falls off the roof, straight onto me and tumbles me upside down, crushing me in my newfound state of weakness.

I dig myself out from the crusty snow, while it seems to be raining as well as snowing.

I hear moaning, similar to the sound my mother made when the bullets first hit her. I dig my claws in the hard litter of ice-crusted snow, and slither to the door on my belly, still don't have enough energy to stand upright.

A man lies on the floor with what looks like blood on his legs but it doesn't smell right; it smells like the sauce in the pizza. The hissing sound is less here, but the smell of sulfur is stronger. I push on the door with my shoulder and it swings open easily, on a well-oiled hinge. The man is a funny color, turning pink and blue, mottled. I lick his face to wake him up, the way I would lick my mother or siblings. I lick his mouth, growl in his ear, shake his shoulder with my teeth.

"Hey, who are you?" he asks, opening his eyes. "Jeez, we better get out of here, smell that gas? Lucky I'm not dead. You saved me, boy, good dog." He pats my paws as I pull on his arm to get him up with my teeth.

"Whoa, my head's a freight train, can't stand. Okay, dog, you get the picture, get me out of here." The man crawls on his hands and knees as I pull on his shoulder, bracing my paws, walking backwards. Getting him out the door is hard as the door swings shut on me. "I got it," he holds it open with one hand, pulling himself along on the other hand, letting me help pull him.

"Great job, thanks." He promptly falls flat on his face in the snow. It isn't on gritty and hard pieces of ice like what had fallen on me on the side of the building or he would have slashed his face open.

I don't know what else to do as weariness overtakes me, so I curl up beside him for warmth, the sulfur smell still strong.

"Dad, there's dirty water coming through the pipes in the bathroom. I came down to see if you were alright." The girl is walking with her head down to keep the snow off her, then lifts her head. "Hey, what happened? What's wrong? It's you again, silver dog."

I can't move my legs again, the sulfur smell overpowering.

"I'm calling an ambulance. Oh no, that's gas, Dad, I gotta pull you further away." She tugs on his shirt and the apron. "You're too heavy, I can't do it.

"Here, silver dog, you're passed out too." She gently lifts me up and carries me about twenty feet towards the street.

She returns to her father and commences trying to pull him. "Hey, where you were laying is still warm, you must have helped keep my father warm. Thanks, silver dog." She struggles and gives up.

I feel energy returning to my limbs, and stand up. I edge over and pull his other arm. Together we move him about a foot, then another foot, and again, one more foot.

Then the blaring siren of an ambulance vibrates through the air and red lights flicker on the door. "Thank you silver dog."

I turn to race away from the sounds of the sirens but I collapse, semi-conscious.

Through a moving haze of sound that sparkles colors of blue, pink, and red, I can hear but am unable to move.

As the EMT approaches, he asks, "What's the problem, young lady?" Quickly, he completely changes gear. "Gas leak, move away, young lady, don't tap on your phone or it could ignite an explosion. Ernie, let's get him out of here. Roll him on that stretcher, one, two, three, move it."

The girl picks me up and carries me to the ambulance.

"We can't bring a dog."

"But he helped save my Dad. And he's unconscious too. Can't you help him?"

"We can't carry animals in an ambulance. Unless he is a service dog. Only then."

"Then he's a service dog."

"Good try. Ernie, call police to secure the building, gas company to switch off the gas main," the EMT said as he strings a nasal canula around her father's nose. "I can't turn the oxygen on until we are away from the source of the gas, so move it, put the dog down, get in here."

"He saved my Dad's life."

"We are leaving now for the emergency room, have to leave to be able to give your Dad oxygen. We're already severely at risk having the engine running but we can't turn it off and turn it on again without risking a spark and then explosion."

"I'm not leaving without the dog."

"Have to evacuate immediately. The gas leak could ignite—get in the ambulance."

I can feel the sky brighten through my closed eyelids as the girl carries me up the steep metal ambulance steps. A tornado of smells and sound, singing and harsh announcements crackling over a radio greets us.

She holds me in her arms, then lays me on a pillow filled with feathers, a bed of geese. I can smell their feathers but there are no hearts beating, no live geese. It feels like I am with my siblings again, the overall "fluffy-ness."

I want to tell her I have to find where they took my mother, and I'm never supposed to be inside a car, ever, I am supposed to hide from them. But I am still unable to move.

She lays her hand on my side, bends her head forward, holds back her long black hair as it begins to fall on my shoulders, and whispers, "Thank you for saving my Dad. I know you helped him get out. I saw the teeth marks and holes on his shirt and apron. Don't know how you didn't break his skin. You did a good job. I'm going to call you Lyra after the silver feathers on the lyrebird, silver dog. I've just been learning about them.

"I forgot to tell you, my name's Sylvia. I've been wanting a dog like you."

The shrill ambulance siren hurts my ears. I whimper. Sylvia gathers me up.

"We're almost there," the EMT said. "Even though it snowed, the earlier freezing temperatures created frost heaves, a freak occurrence, and burst water pipes and at your place, the gas main. You're both lucky to be alive."

"Like I said, this dog saved my Dad's life. His name is Lyra."

The brakes of the ambulance screech, there's more movement in front of me, the clanging of the gurney with Sylvia's father. They carry him out.

🐾 * 🐾

There are fireflies of light dancing over my head, and inside my head. "Gas exposure and carbon monoxide poisoning, just like your Dad, very dangerous, lethal combination. They are lucky they made it." the doctor informs Sylvia. "But we don't diagnose or treat dogs."

"Of course not," Sylvia said, holding me in her lap.

Through the fireflies' flittering, I smell one of the hunters and pick up my mother's scent. I ease myself off Sylvia's lap and scramble out the door, down the hall.

"Lyra, come back!"

Lying on a bed with tubes in his nose and an IV bag of intravenous blood draining into his veins, lays the first hunter I followed. Before him is the other hunter with red hair and dried blood on the shoulder of his jacket, and thick hobnailed boots.

Has he no shame?

I growl.

"She's come back, I told you," the man on the bed said. The other one jumps up, slings his foot back to kick me, then the door opens, blocking my view, as a nurse walks in.

"She's disappeared; told you I was haunted."

"We're both seeing things. I'm going home," the hunter with my mother's dried blood on his jacket said, rushing past the nurse, out the doorway, down the hall, and down the stairs towards the emergency room entrance door.

He starts running and he looks behind him as the ice-window doors slide open and cold air rushes in. He's still looking backwards as something slams into him—a black SUV, whose driver is also not looking where he is going, and flings him up into the air.

I step outside and stand beside him, lift my head and howl. I'll never find my mother now. I also will not ever bite a man, especially one who is down.

Emergency room personnel rush by on their way to pick up the man.

"Can't someone shut that dog up?"

Then the door swishes open again and running steps stop abruptly. "Lyra, you're helping someone again! My hero. My Dad is going to be alright and I can't keep you here. My brother's coming to pick us up. We can stay with him until the house is fixed. Come on, you're coming home with me."

~ *  * ~

Pushcart Prize winner **Laura Rodley's** latest books are Turn Left at Normal by Big Table Press, Counter Point by Prolific Press, 2025 American Legacy Award finalist for Narrative Poetry and Adventure/Historical, and Ribbons and Moths Poems for Children by Kelsay Books, winner of 2024 International Book Award for Children's Nonfiction, Moonbeam Books Award Bronze winner for Poetry, and winner in the Bookfest Outdoors Category and 2nd in Technical/Book Cover/Photography.

Guardians of the Grünwald

Henry Herz

In the mid-1800s, more than one monster roamed the shadowy Grünwald forest in the Grand Duchy of Baden.

A human fiend shivered in the evening chill, crouched in his hunting blind at the base of an ancient oak. Upwind in a clearing lay the skinned rabbit he placed to attract larger game, staring sightlessly at the stars. Moonlight filtered through the overhead foliage, offering ample illumination for shooting.

The hunter remained still with practiced patience. When a mated pair of red foxes tread cautiously into the clearing, the *jäger* didn't see beautiful creatures, but rather animals to be reaped for their fur. His grim, greedy smile didn't reach his eyes. He crossed his fingers that they wouldn't smell or hear him.

He drew his bow, the slow, smooth action silent from decades of practice. As the foxes sniffed at the rabbit, he loosed an arrow. *Thwack!* The shot struck a fox in the chest, the impact knocking it off its feet. The animal twitched briefly among the fallen leaves before its eyes glazed over.

The second fox bolted for cover. *Snap!* One of a half-dozen concealed steel traps clamped on its left rear leg. The animal screamed in anguish, twisting painfully in an attempt to escape. It snarled and offered a defiant *"ack-ack-ack-ackawoooo-ack-ack-ack"* when the *jäger* emerged.

He drew a large hunting knife and crushed the fox's skull with a pommel blow to avoid marring the animal's immaculate pelt with a stab wound. Another dead-eyed smile. *Two more carcasses for my wife to flay.*

Lukas Garrew and his fair wife, Grete, lived in a snug cottage atop an ancient fairy mound one kilometer from town and five from the edge of the Grünwald. Lukas worked as an apothecary, and Grete maintained their home, supplementing their larder by foraging mushrooms and berries.

The pair differed from other happy couples in but one way—both were *werwölfe*. Human superstition long held that every forest needed fae guardians to protect it. Unlike many superstitions, this one held true. Lukas was indeed the Grünwald's steward. He and Grete had long ago tamed their *werwolf* hunger for human flesh. For while they wore their enchanted leather bracelets, they remained in human form with human appetites. The village's inhabitants were none the wiser, even as they gave credence to other more pragmatic superstitions, like avoiding walking under ladders or breaking mirrors.

One evening, after a savory supper of *sauerbraten* beef roast and *spaetzle* noodles, Lukas enjoyed a generous slice of rhubarb trifle for dessert. "Delicious, dear. The only way this could be improved would be with fresh strawberries."

Grete nodded. "Indeed. But my favorite spot for gathering strawberries is where the stream flows out of the Grünwald. Lately, the berries look diseased, not fit for slugs to eat. When was the last time you patrolled the Grünwald, dear?"

Lukas cleared his throat. "It's been a while, my sweet."

She raised her eyebrows. "A while? A month of Sundays at the least, I'd say."

"*Ja*. But as the centuries pass, I find myself less and less willing to undergo the gut-wrenching pain of the Change."

Grete winced at her own agonizing memories. "Could you patrol as you now are?"

Lukas shook his head. "The Grünwald's far too vast for me to inspect without the speed, endurance, and heightened senses of a *werwolf*. Anyway, since the humans have declared most of the Grünwald a preserve, the animals are safe."

He pointed to their newly installed water closet. "I relish modern conveniences and the comforts of my human form." Lukas moved close to Grete. "As a man, I have no snout—the better to kiss you."

Grete grinned.

"I have hands—the better to embrace you. I have gainful employment—the better to pay for visits to the *bierhaus*."

"Ah, now we get to the heart of it," Grete replied with a laugh. Her smile faded. "But I tell you three times, something's amiss in the Grünwald."

Lukas leaned forward. "Whatever do you mean?"

"During my foraging, I've noticed changes in the wood. A foul-smelling brownish scum pollutes the stream. More and more, I find dead animals—quail along the stream banks, frogs floating past belly-up. Nor do I see as many foxes, martens, and rabbits as before."

Lukas frowned. "That does seem odd."

"Indeed," Grete agreed. "And there's another matter for you to consider. While shopping in the village yesterday, I observed a little blonde girl wearing a red cloak with a fox fur-lined hood."

Lukas glanced up from his dessert. "What about that concerns us?"

"I could smell those fox skins were recently tanned." Grete scowled. "And since there's no tannery in town…"

Lukas's fork halted halfway to his mouth. "You think someone's poaching in the Grünwald preserve?"

Grete shrugged. "Possibly. The girl's parents and grandparents, the Grimms, moved to town a few months back. Perhaps some of them have established a tannery within the Grünwald."

The following day, Lukas considered the Grünwald as he weighed herbs, mixed solutions, and doled out packets of medicine to customers. *What are a few dead animals in so large a forest? It is likely only an aberration that will soon pass without effort on my part. I'm more concerned about the logging beyond the preserve boundaries. Humans cut down large swaths of the Grünwald.*

Lukas sighed, staring through the shop window at passersby. *I'd rather stroll hand-in-hand with Grete along sunny streets than trudge under the shadows of gnarled trees. Each time I remove my magic bracelet, there's a chance someone could steal it and consign me to werwolf form forever.*

Still, Grete's news is disturbing. He stood straighter. *I am the warden of the wood. I must do something.*

A woodcutter with a weather-beaten face limped into the apothecary. He doffed his green felt cap. "*Guten tag,* Herr Garrew."

"Good day to you, Herr Holzhauer. How goes it?"

The man put a hand on his lower back. "Cutting wood is hard on these old bones."

"I've just the thing." Lukas reached for a small glass vial of anti-inflammatory powder. "Potent, but expensive—*zehn weißpfennige.*"

"Ten silver pennies!" Holzhauer gasped. He loosened his purse strings, glanced inside, and grimaced. "*Scheisse.* It seems I'll need to save up more before my back will feel relief. The greedy logging companies fell so many trees, it drives down the price of lumber. I hope they don't put me out of business." He rapped the wooden counter with gnarled knuckles.

Those human monsters will eventually cut down all my trees, Lukas thought. *The forest…That's it!* "Just a moment. I have a proposition for you. If you scout within the Grünwald and let me know if anything's amiss—people dumping trash, poachers, illegal homesteads —I'll give you enough medicine for a week. You start now and repeat every *Freitag.*"

Holzhauer's eyes widened at the odd request, but he soon concluded that strange or not, walking in the forest involved far less work than chopping wood to pay for the medicine. "I agree." They shook and Lukas handed him the vial.

The week passed quickly for Lukas. He locked the apothecary at day's end and strolled to the *bierhaus* with a bounce in his step, pleased with his solution to the Grünwald situation. *I'll be kept apprised if anything odd transpires in the wood without the bother of checking myself. Such cleverness deserves a beer. Or two.*

Lukas eased onto a stool at the worn wooden bar. Soon enough, he snacked on salty pretzels and tipped back a frothy mug of brown ale.

Holzhauer ambled through the doorway. "Ah, Herr Garrew!"

"Nice to see you, Herr Holzhauer." Lukas patted an empty stool. "Won't you join me?"

Holzhauer sat and waved at the *barmann*, a middle-aged fellow with salt in his beard and an arthritic elbow from years of pulling taps. Holzhauer ordered a lager and finished it in one long chug. "Ahhh. I expect you'll be pleased to hear I found nothing unusual in the Grünwald."

"Oh, is that so? Good." Lukas clapped the woodcutter's shoulder. "And how's your back?"

"Much better." Holzhauer smiled. "Your medicine worked like a *charme.*"

Lukas nodded. "By the way, did your walk happen to take you near the forest stream?"

Holzhauer shook his head. "*Nein*, I'm afraid not. Should I check it this week?"

"*Ja*. I would appreciate that."

The two enjoyed another round before Lukas excused himself and meandered home.

Lukas entered his cottage. "Hello, my love." He pulled her to his chest, brushing aside her luxurious auburn tresses. "Give us a kiss."

Grete's mouth formed an "o" in mock scandal. "What's gotten you in such an amorous mood?" She returned his kiss with passion. "Aha! There's the answer. Someone's been to the *bierhaus*." She wagged a finger at Lukas. "You better have left room for supper."

Lukas stared into Grete's sparkling green eyes, captivated. "I'm lucky to have you."

Grete giggled. "I've told you that for centuries."

Lukas turned his attention to a delicious dinner of beef *rouladen* and *kartoffelpuffer* potato pancakes. After eating his fill, he pushed back his plate and dabbed his lips with a napkin." You really outdid yourself."

"*Danke*. Are you ready for dessert?"

Lukas patted his stomach. "I couldn't eat another bite."

Grete tilted her head. "I made *apfelstreusel*."

Lukas rose and bowed. "Well, perhaps I spoke too hastily. It would be rude not to try your apple crumble, seeing as you went to so much effort."

Grete laughed. "How gallant! Now, I've held my tongue on the matter of the Grünwald. What news have you?"

Lukas coughed to cover his surprise at the unexpected change of topic. "The first patrol of the forest found nothing out of the ordinary."

"That's odd." Grete frowned. "Things seemed no better the last time I went berry gathering. Did you check the stream?"

"Sorry, dear. I was not near the stream." Lukas's stomach knotted at his lie of omission.

Grete's face brightened. "Well, since you said *first* patrol, that implies there will be more searching, right?"

"*Ja,* a weekly check."

That response satisfied Grete. Later, when the couple went to bed, Lukas further satisfied his beloved wife.

Lukas's secret employment of the woodcutter continued for another month. The woodcutter's tale remained unchanged—all was well in the forest.

However, after the first week, greed corrupted yet another human. Holzhauer realized he could earn more money by skipping his forest patrols, instead cutting wood to sell. His reports became pure fabrication, and Lukas unknowingly passed on these lies to Grete.

Grete was not only fetching but quick-witted. Though she sensed no lie in Lukas's eyes, doubt grew in her mind. Her foraging along the forest's edge revealed a Grünwald differing more and more from her husband's accounts. Nightmares of rotting plants and bloated animal carcasses robbed Grete of sleep. She vowed to search further upstream to discover what was fouling the water and killing the forest creatures in their charge.

One morn after Lukas departed for the apothecary, Grete dressed in walking clothes and a wide-brimmed hat to keep the sun off her face. She marched toward the Grünwald, fierce determination in her eyes.

An hour of brisk striding brought Grete to the point where the stream flowed out of the Grünwald, the brownish scum atop the water worse than before. A bloated hedgehog bobbed past like a morbid balloon. She scowled and strode upstream, seeking the source of the blight.

As Grete advanced deeper into the Grünwald, matters got worse. A dead fallow deer lay at the stream's edge, its head swaying with the current. A pheasant corpse stared open-eyed at the sun. Neither bore visible predator wounds nor exhibited the attention of scavengers.

Have they been poisoned drinking from the foul stream?

The stream grew more clotted and noisome with each step, the odor reminding Grete faintly of chemical salts and acids from a time Lukas showed her the storeroom at the apothecary. Even more eerie, though, was the silence of the wood—the utter absence of animal noises.

Around midday, Grete sat on a flat boulder to rest, wiping her brow. *The source of this foulness may still be a long way off. I can travel faster and with heightened senses in werwolf form.*

Grete sighed, steeling herself for the pain of the Change. She kicked off her shoes and disrobed, folding her clothes and setting them in a neat pile. Removing her braided leather bracelet, Grete dropped it atop her clothes.

Familiarity with the gut-wrenching agony of transforming into a *werwolf* did nothing to mitigate the awful experience. Grete screamed as bones broke and reformed. Her tendons and skin stretched. She howled as her skull elongated into a snout. Teeth, fingernails, and toenails thickened and tapered into sharp points. Eventually, the racking convulsions gave way to the lesser discomfort of stiff hairs bristling forth from every bit of skin. When the Change concluded and the itching subsided, she lay on the ground catching her breath; the only vestiges of Grete's human appearance her piercing green eyes and a thick auburn coat.

Grete scrambled to her paws, twice the size of a normal wolf. In the absence of typical animal noises, the sound of breeze-rustled branches took on a menacing timbre. She lifted her head and sniffed. Her snout wrinkled at the stench as she tracked the odor upstream. *I must find the source of this corruption.* Kilometers flew by under her untiring paws. She rounded a bend in the stream and pulled up short behind a tall privet bush.

Grete gagged at the horrific tableau. Oak trees had been crudely felled, the stumps like jagged teeth in a diseased crone's mouth. A large, freshly constructed cabin stood in the center of a wide clearing. A drain pipe oozed brown sludge into the stream with a series of repulsive plopping sounds. The chimney belched a volume of smoke more suggestive of a forge than a home. Grete's breath caught at the sight of a grotesque heap of skinned animal carcasses —foxes, hares, lynxes, martens, and badgers. The odor of draining chemicals mixed with malodorous gases emanating from the ghoulish pyramid of bloated bodies. The fetor made her stomach seize.

The fur along Grete's spine bristled. For the first time in her life, she knew fear. *What monsters are responsible for creating this hell?* Grete forced down her revulsion and crept toward the cabin. She peered in an unshuttered window.

An elderly woman wearing a cloak of badger pelts stood at a workbench, seemingly oblivious to the stench of death. She deftly flayed the skin from a rabbit, flinging the stripped corpse onto a bloody pile in the corner. Pelts of other animals soaked in chemical-filled trays. *This old woman's the furrier. She seems bent on killing every animal in the Grünwald!*

Thunk! An arrow embedded in the cabin wall, inches from Grete.

She turned and snarled.

An old man dressed in hunter's colors drew his bow for another shot, but Grete fled, her heart pounding. A second arrow lodged in a tree stump as she darted past.

I must warn Lukas! Grete sprinted for the safety of home. Her wolf's stride quickly outpaced the old *jäger's*. She raced along the stream until iron jaws clamped over her left forepaw with searing pain. Grete tumbled to the ground, gasping for breath. She tugged to break free, but the bear trap chained to a tree would not yield.

Grete nearly fainted from the agony of steel teeth embedded in her leg. Her heart raced when the distant sound of footsteps snapping brittle twigs and crunching fallen dead leaves reached her ears. The measured footsteps drew inexorably closer.

Grete struggled against the trap through the searing pain to no avail. Her pulse thundered through her veins. *Those monsters are going to murder and skin me. Should I gnaw off my foot to escape?* Her head turned at the sound of a mirthless chuckle.

"My, what a big pelt you have. That will fetch a pretty penny. And you know what they say. Find a penny pick it up…" The *jäger* advanced to within a few meters—close enough for an easy shot but out of Grete's reach. He nocked an arrow and drew his bow.

Grete snarled in defiance.

Lukas returned home after work to find his cottage empty. *Grete must be out late foraging in the woods for mushrooms.* His concern grew as the sun dropped below the horizon. He donned a heavy cloak, lit a lantern, and headed for the Grünwald.

Having searched without success through most of the night, Lukas collapsed under the trees, a heap of fatigue and worry. He woke with the rising sun. *I must get help! It will take too long for me to scour the entire forest.* He raced back to the village.

For three days, the villagers searched with Lukas, and for three nights he returned home in increasing despair. The town gave up Grete as lost, but Lukas would not relent. It was Friday the thirteenth, but Lukas gave the calendar no mind. Still, even a *werwolf* needs to eat. His pantry bare, Lukas headed to town to buy provisions. He rounded a corner and gasped.

A little blonde girl with the fox fur-trimmed red cloak handed a basket of foodstuffs to a wheezing elderly woman. Around the woman's shoulders hung a large wolf pelt…an auburn wolf pelt.

Lukas's mind went black and he knew no more.

He awoke in the road, surrounded by kneeling townsfolk, concern in their eyes.

The miller touched Lukas's shoulder. "Good, you're awake. You've been out for an hour. You've been pushing yourself with little food and less sleep. You're overwrought with worry."

Grete! Lukas thought. The image of the old woman in the wolf pelt flashed in his mind and he sobbed in inconsolable sorrow. *What have I done? Was Grete murdered in the Grünwald because I failed to discharge my duty as guardian?* Anger overpowered grief. Bereavement could wait. Lukas vowed to find the old woman and avenge his beloved wife.

He stood, brushing the road dust from his clothes. He scoured the town for the old woman but found no trace of her. His shoulders slumped. As he turned for home, a flash of red caught his eyes. Sprinting around a building, he discovered the little red-cloaked child alone.

"Excuse me," Lukas called to her. "You're the Grimm girl, are you not?"

She turned to face him. "Yes, sir."

"My name is Lukas Garrew. I'm the apothecary. Can you tell me, who was the woman to whom you gave the basket?"

"Oh, that was my *oma!*" the girl replied with a smile. "My mama told me to give her a custard and a little pot of butter."

Lukas nodded, balling his fists behind his back. "I haven't seen your grandmother before. Does she live here?"

"No, sir. She lives in the Grünwald with my *opa*." She raised a dainty hand to her mouth. "Oh, I wasn't supposed to tell anyone."

Lukas clenched his fists so tightly his fingernails drew blood. He crossed the fingers of one hand. "That's alright. It'll be our secret."

The girl curtsied and skipped away.

Turning, Lukas walked briskly to the edge of town. When the last building dropped out of sight, he broke into a run. *Grete mentioned dead animals along the stream. I'll start there.*

He reached the Grünwald sweating and breathing hard. Broad areas of tree stumps marked the latest predations of the greedy logging companies. Following the forest's scarred edge until reaching the stream, Lukas headed into the wood, halting after a furlong.

Lukas stripped, covered his belongings in a pile of fallen leaves, and endured the agony of the Change. Charging upstream, he bared his fangs in a silent snarl.

His fury grew with each dead animal he passed. *What have those human monsters done to my domain?* By the time he found the furrier's cabin, he was rabid with murderous wrath. At the sight of the pile of fly-encrusted, skinned carcasses, his last thread of restraint snapped, untethering Lukas from humanity.

The wooden shutters splintered as Lukas crashed through the window.

The old woman was caught by surprise in the midst of flaying another corpse. She had time only to turn in surprise before Lukas's fangs closed around her throat. She managed only a shallow stab with her knife before Lukas shook her like a rag doll, snapping her spine and tearing out her throat. Her blood painted the room, but failed to slake his rage.

With frenzied claw swipes, Lukas smashed furniture and shattered jugs of noxious chemicals. His wild eyes fell on a boiling vat. He pulled a burning log out of the fire, searing his snout, and tossed it into a chemical spill in the corner of the room. Flames attacked the walls. He turned and gently removed his wife's pelt from the bent form of the dead furrier and padded out of the burning cabin.

"Vile *werwolf!*" the hunter cried. "What have you done to my wife!" An arrow struck Lukas's shoulder.

Silver! Lukas realized from the pain of the burning wound. He released the auburn pelt and charged the *jäger*.

The man dropped his bow and reached for his knife. But Lukas's jaws clamped down on his forearm, shattering the bones. Screaming in agony, the *jäger* seized the arrow shaft with his other hand, driving it in deeper.

Lukas howled, releasing his bite. Before the *jäger* could back away, Lukas slashed his fangs across his neck. Crimson sprayed from the severed artery as the hunter collapsed. *My, what red blood you have.* Lukas grasped an ankle and dragged the writhing hunter into the burning house. *Burn in hell, jäger!*

The cabin went up in flames, the large clearing containing the fire.

Lukas returned to the pelt of his wife, tenderly draped it over his back, and staggered back toward his stash of clothing. *If I can put on my bracelet and change back to my human form, the silver won't be lethal.*

But grief and injuries hindered Lukas. The poison in his blood took its creeping, inexorable toll. The sun set.

With its human monsters eradicated, the forest's stream and air gradually cleared. Bushes and trees grew from the ashes in the clearing, eventually erasing all traces of the tannery. The fertile earth welcomed Lukas's body to its bosom, a part of the forest. A spruce sapling sprouted, nourished by his essence. Would new guardians arise to protect the Grünwald before it was destroyed by human avarice?

Originally published in Tales of Fear, Superstition, and Doom
(Redwood Press, 2023)
Reprinted by permission of the author

~ * 🐾 * ~

Henry Herz has written for *Daily Science Fiction*, *Weird Tales*, *Pseudopod*, *Metastellar*, *Titan Books*, *Highlights for Children*, *Ladybug Magazine*, and anthologies from Penguin-Random House, Albert Whitman, Blackstone Publishing, Third Flatiron, Brigids Gate Press, Air and Nothingness Press, Baen Books, elsewhere. He's edited ten anthologies and written fourteen picture books. Visit his website at: www.henryherz.com.

Touched by WolfSong

Carol Hightshoe

Selaynia leaned against the outcropping, stone cold at her back. Her cloak provided warmth and protection against the normal chill of Canthralas. However, tonight, something felt different. The air carried a strange edge, tension woven through the mountain chill. It curled beneath her skin, not quite fear, not quite warning, yet enough to make her shiver.

Above the peaks, sunset bled crimson and gold into the pale purple of dusk. Mist softened the ridges until the world seemed more memory than stone. It should have been peaceful. It wasn't. She closed her eyes and listened.

Wolves howled in the distance, their voices drifting with the wind, a part of the mountains as much as snow or stone. Their song had always comforted her; it was home. But tonight, it was off; it was thinner, hollow, as if voices were missing.

She felt the wolf song as much as she heard it, a second pulse beating beneath her heart. It usually brought peace. But tonight it tasted of blood, of cold metal on her tongue. Tonight, it brought fear and anger.

Eyes gleamed in the shadows. A dozen or more wolves watched, unmoving, silent.

"Why aren't you singing?" she whispered.

No answer. Only silence.

The fear wasn't hers, yet it seeped into her all the same. That was the price of hearing the wolf song, carrying both their joy and their fear.

Selaynia stood and looked again at the tree line. The wolves still watched silently. She turned toward the trail leading down to Grey Shadows. Behind her, a lone howl broke the silence. Long, mournful, and full of sorrow. It hung in the air even after the voice was gone, leaving an empty hollow where life had once been and she understood what the song was telling her.

"I hear you," she whispered. "I will not let them be taken." Her words rose into a howl, a vow carried on the wind. There was only one place she could go. The elders had to hear of this. Even if they turned away, she could not stay silent.

She hurried toward Grey Shadows, the windows of the council house glowing faintly ahead with a promise of warmth against the cold weight in her chest. She pushed through the doors. Smoke and pine resin wrapped around her as the elders' voices stilled. The central fire threw flickering shadows across the carved beams and the faces of the council members.

"They are taking the pups," she said without waiting to be acknowledged. "I heard it in the song. The wolves fear and anger. And the silence where voices no longer sing. Outsiders are stealing the pups."

The eldest, Rhalven, rapped his staff on the floor, and his gray eyes met hers. "You may be touched by wolf song, Selaynia. But the song is not a command."

"It may not be a command, but it cannot be ignored!" Her voice rose despite herself. "The wolves are our kin. Their children are being taken. Will you do nothing?"

Murmurs rippled through the circle. Some averted their gaze; others frowned in disapproval.

Another elder, Maelin, shook her head. "The clans have stood apart for centuries. We do not entangle ourselves in others' wars. To do so is to invite their wrath upon all of Canthralas. Would you risk the destruction of our clan, of the other clans and our world, for something that is only a feeling?"

"What good is my gift if we turn away?" Selaynia demanded. Her hands curled into fists at her sides. "I hear their grief and anger as if it were my own. I will not pretend I do not."

Another voice rose from the circle—hesitant at first, but firm. "We cannot ignore this," Jaharel said. His wolf, Smokeshadow, a silver-gray female, lifted her head at his words, her ears pricking forward. "Selaynia hears more than even those of us who are bonded do. If the wolves are grieving, if they are angry, it is because something has been taken from them. To do nothing dishonors who we are."

Murmurs rippled through the circle. The elders exchanged disapproving glances; some shifted under the weight of his words. Smokeshadow growled low, echoing the unease.

Rhalven struck his staff sharply on the floor. "Enough. You are young, Jaharel. Your heart is loyal, but you mistake loyalty for wisdom. This council does not act on shadows."

Maelin glanced from Selaynia to Jaharel. "For us to get involved, one of the pack alphas would have to come and ask for our assistance. That is the law."

Jaharel's jaw tightened and his gaze flicked to Selaynia. For a heartbeat she saw defiance in his eyes and she felt a surge of hope he might stand with her. But then his shoulders sagged and he bowed his head, the spark extinguished. Jaharel, who had just spoken for her, was now silent. She was alone.

Rhalven's voice was firm. "You know the law. We do not interfere with the packs. It has been this way since our ancestors came to this world."

"I know the history," Selaynia snapped. "Our people and the wolves fought until Talashia, who was also touched by wolf song, forged peace. Only then did the bonds between us begin. And now you would ignore that?"

"We cannot act unless the packs come to us," Maelin said. "We cannot risk doing something that would destroy that peace. They must ask for our help."

"Their pups, *their children*, are being stolen!" Selaynia's voice cracked. She paused and drew a breath. "Forgive my shout."

Rhalven's staff struck once more. "We guard our own and no more. That is the way of Grey Shadows. That is the law."

Selaynia looked from face to face, seeking one spark of agreement, one ally. She found only closed expressions, with lips pressed thin and eyes turned away. Even those who had once praised her gift would not meet her gaze. She bowed her head, not in respect but in bitter acknowledgment. "If the law demands silence, then the law does not have the song in it." Before they could answer, she turned and strode from the council chamber.

"Do not interfere, Selaynia," Rhalven's voice called after her. "Do not risk being exiled from your clan." The doors slammed shut behind her like a final judgment.

She lingered on the frost-dusted stones of the courtyard, staring at the mountains rising dark against the stars. The wind bit her cheeks, but the chill inside her was worse.

Sleep never arrived. The wolf song pulled at her thoughts with delicate threads of sorrow, fear, and anger. Every time she shut her eyes, she saw cages that her mind imagined, and heard the whimpers of frightened pups.

When the first gray light of dawn crept into the sky, she made her choice.

Selaynia pulled on her cloak, fastened her daggers to her belt, and slung a small satchel across her shoulder. She moved quietly through the clan holding, though the silence was not necessary. No one would stop her. No one would follow. At the outer gate, she hesitated, laying a hand on the rough wood. For the space of a breath, she almost turned back—to the hearth's warmth, to the comfort of belonging. Yet the soft whimpers of a frightened pup entered her thoughts, and she stepped through the gate.

The trail curved upward into the mountains. She followed it alone, her boots crunching on the frost-covered ground, her breath forming a pale cloud. The only sound was the cry of a distant raven.

Then, another sound. Soft and steady. The padding of paws.

She paused. From between the trees a large wolf emerged, his fur black and tipped with silver on his ruff and flanks. He moved as if he had been following her all along, his golden eyes fixed on her in an unsettling calm. Selaynia's breath caught. He came straight to her.

Then, a deep and resonant voice filled her mind. :*You walk alone. You should not.*

She stumbled back a step. "You...spoke."

The wolf sat, his tail curling around his paws. :*I reached. You heard. The song brought me to you. It has been many generations since one was chosen in this way.*

"The wolf song led you?"

:*Yes. You are touched by it, Selaynia. That is why I have come. You do not walk alone.*

Something shifted inside her then, sudden and absolute. The distant echo of the wolf song that had always danced at the edges of her mind surged within, becoming a true a second heartbeat. His heartbeat. Their heartbeat.

She knelt, hand trembling as she held it out. "Then we go

together."

He pressed his muzzle into her palm. The bond formed, as undeniable as breath.

:*We are joined. I am Shadowmist.*

She wrapped her fingers in his fur, feeling his warmth and power. "Selaynia," she whispered.

When she rose, Shadowmist walked at her side as if he had always been there. And for the first time since hearing that sorrowful howl, she did not feel alone.

The trail climbed beneath the pale light of dawn. Selaynia walked in silence, breath fogging, Shadowmist at her side.

After a time, his voice brushed her mind. :*You carry sorrow, but also resolve. Resolve sharpens the senses.* He stopped, nose to the wind, ears flicking. :*Come.*

She followed him off the trail, weaving through trees and stone. At first she saw nothing. Then the scent reached her. It was sharp and coppery. It was *blood.*

Shadowmist crested a low rise and stopped. Below, a clearing opened around a den dug into the hillside.

Selaynia froze at the sight. The ground was torn with boot prints and claw marks, and the smell of smoke and fear hung in the air. Scattered tufts of fur clung to the grass. No pups tumbled from the shadows of the den. It was empty.

:*They were taken in the night*, Shadowmist said, his voice grim. :*They fought bravely, but the outsiders carried fire-light. Too fast, too fierce.*

Selaynia felt a wave of anguish flow through the wolf song in her mind, carrying with it the echoes of the mothers' howls, the terror of the pups, and the silence that followed. She staggered, her breath coming in sharp gasps. "I hear you," she finally managed to whisper. "I will not let it end here."

Shadowmist pressed against her, steadying her. :*Breathe. Do not drown in their grief. Feel it, but do not become it.*

"They were here. Just hours ago."

:*Yes. If we follow, we may yet reach the little ones before their voices are lost.*

"Then we follow."

Shadowmist turned north, toward the peaks. :*Yes. We follow.*

Together.

Selaynia moved through the clearing, her eyes examining the torn earth. The raiders hadn't even tried to hide their passage. Broken branches and drag lines indicated where cages or nets had been hauled. She could almost see the pups struggling. She pushed the image aside. She had to stay sharp.

Shadowmist slipped ahead through the trees. :*They do not know these mountains. They mark the land as though it were nothing.*

"They'll regret that," Selaynia murmured, fingers brushing the hilt of a dagger.

They pressed north through ravines and ridges. The air sharp with the cold, but Selaynia hardly felt it.

Hours later Shadowmist vanished into the mist, then returned a few minutes later. :*Still ahead. They make no effort to hide. They believe no one follows.*

"Then we'll prove them wrong."

By midday the trail turned toward the high passes. Smoke drifted faintly on the wind. Selaynia crouched in the brush.

Across a ravine, a fire burned beneath a rock overhang. Figures hunched close to the warmth, their voices low and guarded.

:*Not the ones who stole the pups*, Shadowmist said. :*Different scent.*

"More off-worlders," she whispered. "Why are they here?"

:*Only one way to know.*

Selaynia drew a breath, steeling herself, and began to move forward through the undergrowth. Shadowmist followed, his dark form moving beside her like a living shadow.

The fire crackled louder as they neared. Words took shape: clipped tones, military in cadence, though roughened by travel. She made out at least four, maybe five voices.

One of the figures stiffened, turning toward the tree line. A hand went to a weapon at his hip. "Commander. We've got company."

Every head turned toward the shadows where Selaynia stood. In an instant, their weapons were out: sleek pistols glowing faintly along their barrels, humming with power.

Shadowmist growled, his hackles lifting as he stepped forward to stand between her and the strangers. :*They will fire if pressed. Do not give them cause.*

Selaynia's pulse thundered in her ears. Her hand tightened on her dagger. She could not match their weapons, not with steel, but she would not show fear. "You will lower those," she said, as she stepped forward, "or you'll learn what happens when wolves decide you are prey."

A wiry man with restless eyes barked a laugh. "Bold, for someone who is outnumbered and outgunned."

"Quiet!" The apparent leader raised a hand, and his people froze, though none lowered their weapons. His gaze lingered on Shadowmist, studying him, and Selaynia saw calculation, not fear, in his expression.

"Canthralian wolf," he murmured. "And bonded, by the look of it. Unexpected."

:*He knows what I am*, Shadowmist warned. :*That makes him dangerous.*

"Why are you here?" Selaynia demanded, her voice hard.

The group fanned out, nearly encircling Selaynia. She shifted subtly, putting her back to the ravine, Shadowmist at her side. If the men attacked, they'd fight on her terms.

Slowly, the leader lowered his hand. "Because we're hunting the same quarry you are," he said, his voice firm but not hostile. "The ones who took the pups."

The tension eased but did not vanish. Selaynia's grip relaxed slightly on her dagger. Shadowmist's growl faded to a low rumble, his eyes narrowing.

:*Truth*, he told her. :*But* not the whole of it.

The circle of weapons never wavered. Selaynia waited, one hand on a dagger, the other clenched at her side. Shadowmist's growl rumbled low and steady.

"Commander," one of the men muttered, his weapon twitching nervously, "say the word."

"Hold!" His eyes flicked between Selaynia and Shadowmist.

"You've no business here," Selaynia said sharply. "Our mountains are not yours to trespass."

The wiry man laughed. "Pretty words from a girl and her pet."

Shadowmist surged forward with a snarl, teeth flashing. The man stumbled back, his weapon on the ground.

:*Say that again and lose your throat*, Shadowmist's thought cut through Selaynia's mind. The fear on the man's face told her he had heard him as well.

"Enough!" the leader snapped. His glare cut sideways at his own soldier before settling back on her. After a long moment, he exhaled. "You want to know why we're here? That's fair. My name is Nolan. Commander, to them." He gestured to the tense figures behind him.

Selaynia inclined her head slightly. "Selaynia of Grey Shadows. This is Shadowmist."

The wiry soldier scoffed. "Figures she'd name it."

Shadowmist's growl deepened. The man paled further and edged back.

Nolan ignored him, his eyes steady on Selaynia. "Then we're no longer strangers. But that doesn't make us allies. Not yet."

"You still haven't answered. Why are you here?"

"We're hunting the ones who took the pups," he said.

Selaynia's pulse leapt, though her grip stayed firm on her dagger. "The raiders."

Nolan nodded once. "They're not just raiders or smugglers. If those pups leave this world, they'll be broken, bonded to other masters. Imagine it—wolf-bonded fighters, not loyal to Canthralas, but to whoever paid for them. That's not a risk the Alliance will ignore."

Her eyes narrowed. "And I'm to believe the Centauri Alliance suddenly cares about our wolves?"

Nolan's smile was humorless. "Not your wolves. About what happens if they turn up on other worlds. Your people keep to yourselves. Always have. That makes you predictable. But if wolf-bonded fighters start appearing on other planets, everything changes. And the Alliance doesn't like surprises."

Selaynia felt Shadowmist's agreement through their bond. :*Truth. He fears what others might do with us.*

She let out a slow breath, weighing his words. Whatever the motives, the goal was the same. The raiders had to be stopped. The pups had to be saved.

"Then we hunt the same quarry," she said at last, lifting her chin. "I know these mountains. You don't. I can help you find them."

Nolan's stare weighed on her. For a moment she thought he would refuse. Then his mouth tightened and he gestured to his people. "Break camp. We will follow your trail. But until we know you, you walk on probation. One false step, and you answer to me."

Selaynia nodded sharply. "Fair enough. But understand me,

Commander, if you falter, I won't let it cost the pups their lives."

She caught the flicker of approval in his eyes, but it was cool, distant. Nolan didn't trust her, and she didn't trust him. Their paths ran together for now, but only because of the stolen pups. Beyond that, she saw only calculation in him.

Shadowmist's growl rumbled like distant thunder. :*They'll see soon enough who slows who.*

Nolan's eyes flickered with the ghost of amusement before he masked it. He turned to his people. "You heard her. Move."

The fire was extinguished in silence, leaving only the lingering scent of smoke in the air. Weapons were slung, packs hoisted, boots scuffing against stone. Still tense. Still strangers.

In her mind, Selaynia could still hear sorrow in the wolf song as well as the fragile thread of lives not yet lost. She turned without waiting for Nolan's word and moved toward the ravine's edge, Shadowmist moving beside her.

"Confident, isn't she," the wiry soldier muttered, his voice low.

"Shut it, Jerrik," Nolan said. His tone carried the weight of command, but Selaynia didn't miss the flicker of irritation behind it. They didn't like her with them. Good. She didn't like them either.

The trail narrowed and climbed between stone teeth, treacherous to the untrained. Selaynia's boots found places to step without thought; Shadowmist nosed broken branches and paw-scraped earth. Behind them, the off-worlders clattered and cursed, armor scraping rock.

:*Loud*, Shadowmist observed dryly. :*Even the trees wince.*

Selaynia hid a smile. "They're working to keep up."

At a bend, she raised her hand, and the men froze. She crouched, brushing her fingers over chaotic patterns of overlapping boot prints on the trail. "They passed this way," she said. "Within the last day."

One of the men leaned over her shoulder, squinting. "All I see is dirt."

"Then look closer." She stood and tapped a bent reed with her boot. "Broken by a heavy cage. They're pushing hard, north and west."

Nolan stepped up beside her. "You're certain?"

Shadowmist answered for her, his voice like a low growl, and she could feel the force he was using to enter the off-worlders' minds. :*Certain. The stink of fear lingers here. The little ones still live.*

Two of the men flinched, staring at the wolf. One crossed himself, muttering under his breath.

Selaynia laid a hand on Shadowmist's shoulder. "You asked for proof, Commander. There it is."

Nolan's jaw tightened, and he gave a single sharp nod. "We keep moving."

Selaynia shook her head. "As much as I want to press on, it will be night soon. We all need rest and it will dangerous for those not familiar with these trails to try and continue."

Nolan took a deep breath and glanced over at his men then nodded. "You're right. Jerrik, you and Leyba set up camp."

The next morning the climb grew harsher as the trail continued into the high passes. Loose stone shifted underfoot, ridges broke like knife-blades against the sky, and the wind blew cold and sharp across the rocks. Selaynia pressed forward without hesitation, Shadowmist a steady presence at her flank. Behind them, the off-worlders muttered, their breath harsh, their boots dragging.

At a pass between two jagged spires, Shadowmist halted, ears pricked, nose lifted to the wind. :*Closer. The stink of fear drifts in the air.*

Selaynia dropped into a crouch, signaling the others with a sharp gesture. To their credit, they stilled quickly. She eased forward, belly low, and peered down the slope.

Smoke curled thinly in the sky. About a hundred yards below, half-hidden by a stand of stunted pines, lay a rough encampment. Crude canvas shelters clung to the hillside. At the heart of the camp, several heavy cages stood in a crooked row.

Selaynia could hear faint yelps and whimpers. Her breath caught. "The pups."

Shadowmist pressed against her shoulder, his low growl resonating through the bond. :*Alive. Afraid. But alive.*

Boots scraped behind her. "How many are down there?"

Selaynia counted quickly. Armored men moved between fires; a few stood guard near the cages, weapons slung casually but ready.

"Two hands, maybe more."

"They've dug in," another muttered.

Nolan leaned forward; his gaze cold as he studied the camp. His hand brushed the weapon at his side. "Doesn't matter. We're not letting them leave."

Selaynia's hand tightened on one of her daggers. She breathed slowly, steadying herself. "Then we strike."

Nolan's eyes swept the encampment, calculating. "Two guards on the cages. Three by the fire. The rest are scattered. I see two places near the camp we should be able to get to unobserved, where we can set up a crossfire." He pointed to a spur of rock to the right, about twenty yards from one of the shelters, and a large group of trees at the other end of the camp. "We can take them down before they scramble."

Selaynia stiffened. "And when the first shots send them into a panic? They'll kill the pups before you drop half of them."

One of his men hissed. "Better dead than carted off world to be slaves."

Selaynia spun on him, fury flashing in her eyes. "They are not expendable."

Shadowmist's growl rumbled, low and dangerous. The soldier flinched back, but Nolan's gaze held hers.

"Then what do you propose?" Nolan asked evenly. "Storm the camp with knife and fang? Do you really think that will save them?"

:You are part of the song. The packs will answer if you call. With them, we can overwhelm the raiders before they know the danger.

Her breath caught. The elders' warning echoed: *The wolf song is a blessing, not a summons.* To call the packs was to interfere, to ask the wolves to do her bidding. But Shadowmist was right. She could sense the wolves; they were not far, and they were waiting.

"There is another way."

Nolan's brows drew together. "I'm listening."

"I can call the packs," she said softly. "The wolves will come."

A ripple of unease ran through the off-worlders. "You mean unleash wild animals in the middle of a firefight? That's madness."

"They are not just animals." Selaynia's voice cut sharp as a blade. "They are kin. And they will fight to save their young."

Nolan studied her in silence. He didn't dismiss her, but neither did he yield. "And if they don't come?"

"They will."

For a long moment, the only sound was the wind.

Then Nolan exhaled. "Very well. Call them. But if this fails, we fall back to my plan."

Selaynia nodded once. "If this fails, the pups are lost."

:*Now, before the moment slips*, Shadowmist urged.

She nodded, then glanced at Nolan. "Go. Take your positions. When the wolves come, strike with them."

Uneasy glances passed among the soldiers, but they began creeping down the slope closer to the camp. Nolan stayed on the ridge, his gaze locked on her.

"Do it," he said.

Shadowmist pressed his muzzle against her hand, his eyes locking on hers. :*The packs are near. Open yourself. Let the song pass through you, not around you.*

Selaynia took a deep breath. She had heard the wolf song all her life; faint, distant, carried on the wind like a forgotten melody. To try to *answer* it, to call with her own voice? The elders had warned such things were not for humans. Yet Shadowmist's certainty steadied her.

She dropped to one knee; her hand buried in his thick fur, and closed her eyes.

The silence pressed in. Then Shadowmist's voice filled her mind, deeper than words. :*Breathe. Feel the rhythm. The song is already in you.*

Her breath came slow and even. The song welled up from within. A low hum in her chest, rising higher, weaving with Shadowmist's presence until it spilled from her throat as sound.

The howl tore into the air, rough at first, then stronger. Not just her voice, but something older carrying it; the echo of generations, the grief of stolen pups, the fire of defiance.

It rolled across the mountains, bouncing from ridge to ridge, scattering birds from the trees. For a heartbeat, the only answer was the wind.

Then another voice rose. A single wolf, distant but clear. Another joined it. Then a dozen. Then more.

The wolf song surged like a tide, flooding her mind, wrapping her in a strength so fierce it staggered her. She gasped, gripping Shadowmist's fur as the answering howls swelled into a chorus that shook the stones beneath her knees.

:*They are coming. The packs have heard.*

Selaynia rose, her breath shuddering, her voice raw from the call. She turned to Nolan, her silver hair whipping in the wind, her silver eyes alight with something fierce.

"The wolves are on their way," she said. "We should get to our positions."

Before Selaynia and Nolan made it to their position where they could reach the cages, the air filled with a chorus of howls. Closer now. Stronger. The sound rolled down the ridges like thunder, echoing through the stone, rattling the air in her lungs.

The packs had come.

Shadowmist's golden eyes gleamed. :*Now they will learn what it means to steal from wolves.*

From the shadows of the tree line, dark forms surged forward: wolves, dozens of them, pelts flashing silver and gray and black in the firelight as they poured into the camp.

The raiders' laughter turned to shouts of alarm. Weapons flared, beams of energy cutting through the night.

Nolan raised his arm, voice sharp as steel. "Now!"

The camp erupted in chaos. Raiders scrambled for their weapons as the first wave of wolves ran through the camp. One guard barely had time to shout before a silver-gray wolf bowled him into the fire, flames scattering as teeth closed on his throat.

"Cages!" Selaynia shouted, pointing with a dagger. "Get to the cages!"

Nolan's soldiers split into pairs, their weapons' fire disciplined and precise. Selaynia slipped through the chaos, her daggers flashing. She caught a raider's clumsy swing, turned it, and drove steel into the gap of his armor. He fell, and she was past him.

Shadowmist leapt onto another raider, his weight slamming the man into the dirt. The telepathic bond carried the savage joy of the kill into Selaynia's mind, fierce and steady, anchoring her to the rhythm of battle.

A shout rose from near the cages. Two raiders, panicked, were leveling their weapons at the barking pups inside.

Selaynia's cry split the air. "No!"

She hurled a dagger, the blade sinking into one raider's throat. Shadowmist crashed into the other before his weapon could fire, jaws snapping bone. The cages rattled as pups barked and lunged at the bars.

From the tree line, more wolves poured into the camp, striking in coordinated groups. The raiders fired wildly, beams carving brief arcs of light before wolves dragged them down.

Nolan's voice cut through the chaos, calm and sharp. "Keep the bastards away from the cages!" His soldiers shifted with precision, their fire controlled, driving the raiders back step by step. Selaynia felt their discipline, cold and focused; so unlike the raw, feral fury of the wolves.

A burst of energy scorched past her, close enough to singe hair. She spun, grabbing a fallen raider's weapon. It was heavier than she expected. She fired once, the energy beam cutting into the chest of a raider aiming at Nolan. The man dropped with a strangled cry.

Nolan met her eyes across the melee, gave the barest nod, then turned back to bark another order.

The wolves overwhelmed the raiders' defense. A last group tried to break for the ridge, but a half-dozen wolves pulled them down before they had gone ten strides.

Selaynia stood panting in the center of the camp. Shadowmist pressed close against her leg. Around them, wolves prowled the fallen, eyes still bright from the battle, ears pinned forward listening for any sign of danger.

Nolan's men lowered their weapons slowly, their faces pale as they took in the carnage. She caught fragments of their whispers carried on the wind: "...spirits, did you see them...wolves answering a human's call..." Another muttered, almost a prayer, "...*unnatural*..."

Nolan snapped a sharp order, silencing them, but their fear lingered in their eyes.

The pups whimpered in their cages.

Selaynia dropped to her knees, fumbling at the crude lock with her dagger until she was able to force it open. One by one, the cages clattered open, and the pups spilled out in a rush of fur and high-pitched yips. Small bodies pressed against her, claws catching at her sleeves, muzzles shoving into her hands. She stroked them one by one, murmuring, her words tumbling in a rhythm not unlike the wolf song itself.

"You're safe now...it's over...no one will take you again..."

Their voices rose in answer: a chorus of thin howls, fragile but unbroken. The sound made her throat ache. These were the voices missing from the song, the void that had driven her to defy the council. Now they sang again, their notes weaving clumsily with the deeper howls of the adult wolves who circled protectively around the camp.

Shadowmist pressed his muzzle against her shoulder. :*They will remember this. Not just the pups, but the packs. You gave their voices back to the song.*

She tightened her arms around the pup in her lap, burying her face in its soft fur. For a moment, the blood, the fire, even the fear of exile faded. All that remained was the sound of the pups.

One by one, the mothers emerged from the tree line, drawn by the chorus. The pups scrambled free of her arms, rushing to meet them. Selaynia watched as each mother lowered her head, nuzzling her young.

Shadowmist sat at her side. :*This is why we fought. This is why we will fight again.*

Selaynia bowed her head, voice raw. "Yes. For them. Always."

Selaynia sat where she was, cloak torn and blood spattered. Shadowmist lay close, his head resting across her knees, his eyes half-lidded but watchful.

For the first time since leaving Grey Shadows, the weight of what she had done settled over her. The council's voices returned, cold and certain: *We guard our own and no more. That is the law.* She had broken that law. She had fought beside off-worlders. She had called the packs. Her throat tightened. "They'll never take me back."

Shadowmist's thought came calm, steady as the mountain stone beneath them. :*You knew that when you left the clan holding.*

She brushed her fingers over his fur. "I told myself it was for the pups. That once they were safe, I might be able to find a way back." Her voice dropped, hoarse. "But there is no return. Not now. Not ever."

The wolf shifted, lifting his head until his gaze caught hers. :*The packs will remember. That matters more than the council's silence.*

Selaynia swallowed hard. "And what of me? What do I do now, Shadow? Where do I go?"

:*Forward,* he said simply. :*Whereever the song leads. You will not walk the path alone.*

She bowed her head against his, her eyes closing as the truth settled. She had chosen this path the moment she left Grey Shadows. Her actions here had only made it final.

The mountains still stood around her, vast and unyielding, but she no longer belonged to them. Her home was beside the wolf at her side; beyond that, she did not yet know.

The camp had grown quiet, broken only by the soft sounds of wolves settling near their pups. Selaynia sat with Shadowmist's head heavy across her lap, her fingers still tangled in his fur. The ache in her chest dulled, but it never vanished.

Behind her, the Alliance soldiers murmured, voices hushed but edged with unease. "…wolves answering her…never seen the like…" Another voice: "…if the packs ever left this world—" The words cut off as Nolan's voice cracked like a whip. "Enough."

She glanced over at Nolan then, catching the way he looked at her—steady, unreadable, weighing. He had silenced his men, but not out of loyalty to her. No, this was a commander thinking two moves ahead, calculating the risk she now represented. He wouldn't say it aloud, but she knew: in Nolan's eyes, she was as dangerous as the raiders they had just dealt with.

She lifted her head as Nolan approached. He stopped a pace away, then extended his hand. Not in command this time, but in offering.

"You've lost your place here," he said quietly. His tone was matter-of-fact. "I don't need to be Canthralian to know that. I've read enough reports, seen enough isolationist worlds to recognize the pattern: fight beside outsiders, break their taboos, and you are cast out. No matter the good you achieved…" He glanced at the wolf pups with their packs. "…your clan will never forgive it."

Selaynia froze. She had never spoken the words aloud, but he was right. He saw the truth without her having to tell him. She saw no triumph in his expression, only the certainty of a man who had measured costs before.

"You can't go back," Nolan continued, his eyes steady on hers. "But you can move forward. The Alliance will give you a new home. A new purpose. We could use someone like you. You and your partner." He glanced at Shadowmist.

Her heart twisted. A new home? Among those who feared her even now? She glanced at the soldiers, their whispers still echoing in the air. To them she would never be kin or comrade. She was a weapon they would want to use.

Her gaze fell to Shadowmist. He met her eyes with calm certainty. :*Not a weapon. A bond. The song chose you for more than Grey Shadows. Wherever we go, we go together.*

Her throat tightened. She wasn't leaving *everything*. Everything had already been stripped from her when the doors to the council chamber closed. What remained was the choice between drifting in exile or stepping into something new, carrying the song forward.

Slowly, she reached out and took Nolan's hand. His grip was firm, unyielding. She held his gaze, silver eyes hard with resolve. "Then it's settled. But remember this: I walk my own path."

For the first time, a flicker of respect touched Nolan's expression. "Fair enough. Welcome aboard."

Selaynia released his hand. Shadowmist pressed against her leg, steady as the mountain stone. Whatever lay ahead, she would not walk it alone.

Selaynia watched through the shuttle's porthole as Canthralas dwindled behind her, stars swallowing the peaks she had once called home. Her hand moved absently over Shadowmist's ears, where his head rested on her leg. "Exiles," she whispered.

:*You did the right thing*, Shadowmist told her, his voice wrapped in the echoes of wolf song.

She shook her head faintly. "That doesn't make it any easier."

Leaning back, she closed her eyes. The pain of exile, torn from her clan, from the mountains, from the song that had always been part of her soul. Yet beneath it pulsed the bond she shared with the wolf, and the memory of the pups' fragile voices rising. Yes...if given the same choice again, she would make it the same way.

The elders had said she was touched by wolf song. Now, at last, she understood what that truly meant.

~ * 🐺 * ~

Born in 1964, **Carol** grew up in San Antonio, Texas, spent 30 years in Colorado and now calls the tiny town of Brackettville, Texas home. An avid reader at a young age, her strong desire to write came from her love of (her husband calls it her obsession with) Star Trek. It was this early love of Trek that led her to the Science Fiction and

Fantasy genres.

She has been published in various anthologies and magazines and has published four books in her Chaos Reigns fantasy series, and is working on the fifth.

In addition to her own writing, she is the editor and publisher of the online magazine: The Lorelei Signal and the person behind WolfSinger Publications.

Visit her website at www.carolhightshoe.com.

Azure Wolf

Nicholas Samuel Stember

Coki lay on the smooth wet bottom of the canoe and felt the warm sun blazing overhead. He knew he should open his eyes, face the new day, but he was afraid he'd see the same thing he had over the countless days before…only open blue waters without land in sight. At least the ocean felt gentle today, unlike last night when the waves had become quite dangerous. In fact, as Coki lay there, he could feel he was in a few centimeters of water and knew he'd have to fix that. The mysterious current that had caught his canoe, ripping it away from his home island of Borikén, had torn him away from his best friend, Jejen, and everyone he knew. He had tried to call for help, yelling at the top of his lungs, but there was just no one to hear him. He had even tried to call for a spirit guide as he'd seen the village priestess do, but he had never tried before and was sure he had done it wrong for nothing happened. He knew the basics of the canoe and fishing but had never taken part in one of the trading vessels sent by his people to the neighboring islands, and he had foolishly picked a very large canoe…one that could easily hold over twenty of his tribe. It was large and sturdy, carved from a single trunk of a ceiba tree. So, it was coping with the waves of the open ocean, but it was also difficult to handle and clumsy. He knew roughly where the closest islands to his home were, but this current was carrying him away from them, and to the north and west. When he had first awoken from his fall, he had tried to paddle back towards where he thought his island was, but there was simply no getting out of this strangely powerful flow of water. Alone, in a large canoe meant for so many more oars, he realized it was hopeless.

But that was many days ago, so many he had lost count. At one point he was certain he spotted an island to the east of where he was. However, he was so far from home he couldn't be sure if it was an island of fellow Taíno, the tribes who lived peacefully on his island and a few of the neighboring ones, or the war like Carib tribes of some of the other nearby islands. In the end, courage failed him, and he had let the island pass by.

He had three large wooden bowls that were stored in the canoe, typically to carry the fish they caught; but now he had set them all out to capture any rain that fell and then covered them afterwards so the sea wouldn't get in. So far, he had been lucky; he had plenty of water, a lot of fish, and the skill to get more.

So why didn't he open his eyes to face the new day?

"That's a good question," a soft voice near him asked.

His eyes shot open, and he sat upright quickly. The canoe was empty in front of him, and there was barely a cloud to be seen as the sun rose high overhead into the clear blue sky. His boat was still speeding along this strange current at a seemingly unnatural speed, as it cut through the crystal turquoise waters.

"About time you got up," the voice said again, and he realized it was coming from behind him.

Coki jumped in his seat, and quickly pivoted to face the back of the canoe. The sudden action almost tipped the narrow craft over, and he had to swiftly grasp the sides to steady himself and the boat…as he stared and blinked at what he saw. There was an animal of some sort sitting behind him on its hind legs. He'd never seen anything like it before, it was big, graceful and covered with white and grey fur; with tall, pointed ears and a long snout and tail. Its eyes were large and yellow, but there was a gentleness in those eyes and despite the initial fear that gripped Coki's heart, he suddenly felt at ease.

The animal let out a soft chuckle. "I can see where you get your name, Coki. You jump like a little tree frog."

He let out a quiet grunt as he glanced around again to be sure there was no land nearby, nor any other canoes or craft. But, even though his boat was the only thing afloat on the water as far as he could see, this animal wasn't wet at all, leading him to the only explanation that made any sense.

"I must be asleep," he said as he shook his head and smiled.

The animal cocked her head to the side inquisitively as one of her tall ears went higher than the other, and Coki almost let out a laugh.

"That's an interesting theory."

He looked around the long canoe again for a bit and nothing seemed odd or out of place. He still had three large bowls of rainwater left, and enough fish for a day or two, if he paced himself.

"I've never met an animal that could speak," he finally said.

"All animals speak in their own ways," she said as her large eyes smiled, "but it takes a special gift and an open heart to hear it."

"Alright, then," he said as he sized up his strange new companion, "how did you get here? I'm in the middle of the ocean, far from any island that I can see. Did you swim here?"

She slowly shook her head.

"Did another canoe come along while I was asleep and put you here?"

Again, she shook her head. "Coki, you know why I'm here. You just haven't asked the right question yet."

Coki adjusted himself to sit on one of the few wooden seats that were in the canoe. Then he looked at the thin layer of water left on the bottom of the boat since the harsher weather of the last two days. Already the warm tropical sun was drying it out, but where this animal's paws and hind legs met the water, there was no ripple, almost as if the creature wasn't really there.

"You said that me wondering if I was asleep was an interesting theory, which makes me think that I am, but I don't feel like I am."

"You asked to see me, didn't you?"

Coki blinked a few times, trying to understand, then it hit him. "I asked for a spirit guide to help."

The animal nodded once, and her long snout seemed to smile.

"I'm on a vision quest?"

"Of a sort," the strange animal confirmed. "You've reached out to me in your sleep many times, and I've been watching over you, but now…"

"Now?"

"You're awake, Coki…and I'm here with you."

Coki's eyes narrowed with skepticism, and he reached out tentatively with his right hand, never taking his eyes off the long muzzle filled with sharp teeth and four fair sized fangs.

She made no move to avoid his touch, but when his fingers should have reached her soft fur…she vanished.

Coki let out a gasp and pulled his hand back…and instantly she reappeared.

"I'm your spirit guide, Coki…you can't touch me."

He sat back and a scowl formed on his tanned face. "How can

you be my spirit guide? The priestess told us when we went on a vision quest, the first animal we saw would be our guide, but I know all the animals on my island and none are like you, not even close to your size. Only the manatees that live in the water are bigger than you. How can I imagine something I've never seen?"

"You think your spirit guide is imaginary?" Her eyes twinkled with amusement.

"I...I...I don't know," he finally said, bewildered by what was happening. "I've been out in the sun for many days away from my people, maybe I'm hallucinating?" He lifted one of the water bowls, removed the lid and looked at the water for a moment, then drank a sip. It was warm, but still fresh. He opened one of the satchels he was keeping the fish in that he had dried himself and tasted some of it. It was still quite good.

"Satisfied you're not going crazy from lack of food and water?"

"You didn't answer my question...what kind of imaginary beast are you?"

"Hmm, well, I'm a bit larger than the actual animal I represent," she confessed, "but I assure you my kind is very real. No, we've never come to your islands, but there is a land that is not that far away now where we are as common as blades of grass."

"What are you called?" Coki asked, still trying to get a grip.

"We're known by many names; te-me, wa-ya, ba'cho, and so many more...even those I saved you from have names for us like loba, lupa or wolf.

"Why so many different names?"

"Many different peoples," she admitted. "Some of them are like you and your Taíno, the natives who live on those islands to the south, some are...different, but each have their own name for what I am."

"What should I call you?"

She shrugged. "You can call me Tala."

"That's not one of the names you listed."

"Those were names the various tribes and peoples call my kind ...Tala is my name, like Coki is yours."

Coki glanced at the piece of dried fish still in his hand and he offered it to Tala, but the large wolf shook her head. "I am spirit, I don't live like you do, but I do live."

For a few moments, he just quietly munched on a piece of

dried fish, then took another drink of water, as he tried to make sense of it all. Finally, he put the rest of the fish back into the satchel and covered up the water bowl again to keep it from evaporating.

"So…there are many animals on Borikén, why isn't my spirit guide one of them?"

"How do you think a vision quest finds your spirit guide?"

"Animals I like?" he offered with a shrug, but knew in his heart the answer was wrong.

"The spirits give you the guide you need, not necessarily the one you think you should have. You could have gotten a spider or a bat, your island has many of both. But what you needed was me, so I'm what you got."

Suddenly a thought struck him, and he folded his arms defiantly as a half-smile crossed his lips. "Wait a moment. You said I called for you, and I did when my canoe got caught in this strange current—"

"Stream."

"Stream? How is that possible? A stream runs through the land, not the water."

Tala let out a gentle laugh. "Yes, but in this case, this is a great stream that runs through the ocean not far from your islands and also along the ocean close to my home, then back out into the ocean again."

"And it's always this strong?" Then he shook his head, forgetting his question as he realized he had been sidetracked. "I was going to say you mentioned saving me, but I didn't call for you until I was in this…stream."

"I've been watching over you for far longer than since you set out on this canoe." She leaned forward and her long snout came up to only a few centimeters from Coki's nose, such that even though he couldn't touch her, he could still feel her warm breath on his face. It smelled of pine and maple, both scents that were totally foreign to him, yet filled his heart with enticement. "Spirits are drawn to people just like you can be drawn to us. We were meant to help each other."

"If you're helping me, why didn't you push my canoe back home?"

Tala's nose came even closer to his. "You don't remember how you got here, do you? So far from home?"

He shook his head, not sure why he couldn't remember how

he ended up in this large canoe out in the middle of the ocean.

"Well, regardless, I've been keeping you safe within the strongest current of this stream for many days. I've done my best to sway you from the storms, yet make sure enough rain fell to fill your bowls. I made sure your fish has not spoiled before drying out, nor have you failed to get more. I've even made sure the current kept you far from those islands that would do you harm."

"The Caribs…"

"Them, and others. You call yourselves Taíno, for it means good and noble in your language…but not all the tribes in that island chain feel and act as you do. There are dangers in these waters, and soon there will be much more."

"Island chain?"

"There are many more islands than you know of, but they are all far to the southeast of us now."

Coki made a face as he contemplated all Tala had said and he wondered how much of it was true. He rubbed his head where he imagined he had hit it to make him forget so much, as he thought of his village. He had no real family back there; his parents had died in a terrible storm that had winds so fierce the entire village was flattened as well as many trees. Coki had only been ten at the time, and his parents put him in a small shelter only large enough for him and his best friend, Jejen, as they had been playing together when the winds struck. Both his parents had held fast from the outside, protecting the two boys, and ended up sacrificing themselves. Many had died in the village from that storm, but Jejen's father had survived, and he took Coki under his protection and taught him to hunt and fish alongside his own son. He and Jejen were dear to Coki, but he hadn't felt like he had family since that day, seven years ago.

Yet he felt a sudden kinship with this spirit wolf he couldn't explain.

"Alright, so you've been helping me…how am I supposed to help you?"

"You will."

Coki frowned, feeling a little frustrated by this large spirit creature. "How can I know when to help you if I don't know what I'm supposed to do?"

Tala responded by flicking out her long tongue that seemed to pass over Coki's nose, sending a tickling tingling sensation along his face and he pulled back sharply, and despite his frustration, he laughed.

"What was that?" he asked, smiling despite himself.

"You may not be able to touch me, but that doesn't mean I can't touch you."

There were still so many questions that flooded Coki's mind, but for the time he concentrated on the essentials that were to keep him alive. He had set up two fishing lines that were always out and had to be monitored. Tala also helped by drawing fish up to the surface where he could spear them. Then at times her large yellow eyes would seem to almost glow, and a gentle rain would come and Coki would quickly uncover the three large rain bowls to catch as much of the fresh water as he could.

The day waned peacefully on, yet Tala seemed to be growing nervous.

"What is it?" he finally asked.

The wolf looked to the southeast and Coki followed her gaze. Far off in the horizon there was a huge amount of black clouds.

"I didn't see them before," he said, a sudden fear coming into his heart as his mind drifted back to the night he lost his parents.

"That's because a few moments ago it wasn't there. It's coming fast." Tala saw the fear in Coki's eyes and tried to smile. "It's not like that terrible night, but it's still going to be a bad storm, far more than this canoe can handle. We have almost left all the islands in your chain behind, but there is one last one we can reach…"

"What is it?" he asked, sensing the worry in her tone.

"This is not a friendly island and not one I'd have taken us to, but I'm afraid we must risk going there until the storm passes, which should be quick. When it's safe, we'll quickly get back onto the water…hopefully before we're noticed."

"But you can protect us, right?"

Tala took a deep breath, and her broad chest filled. "We'll see. But you have your fishing spear, right?"

He nodded, glancing at the long spear made from cane with the tip and barbs made of bone.

"You may need it."

Coki glanced back at the storm to see the black clouds were

much closer to them, but then he also noticed the canoe was out of the strange current and heading eastward against the growing winds.

"I still don't see land," he called out as he looked in the direction the narrow boat was speeding along now, but the sun was already starting to set, and it was harder to see far. He glanced behind him and watched the sun dipping down below the waters to the west, realizing it was the first time in days the sun hadn't set ahead and to the left of the boat.

"There," Tala said, pointing with a large paw.

He snapped back around and saw that indeed he could barely make out the dark silhouette of a large island ahead, it was much closer than he expected it to be. Still, he reached out over the side with his oar to try to urge the canoe on faster, though he wondered if he was making any difference with the mystical forces Tala seemed to be using to urge the craft.

He could feel the winds picking up, pushing against him as the black clouds now completely covered the sky to the east. They were just arriving on the darkened shores as the rain started to hit.

Coki jumped out of the canoe as they closed in and pulled it up onto the sands. At first, he was certain he wouldn't have been able to do this, as the large canoe was far too big to pull onto land by himself, but he knew that somehow the spirit wolf was making his task easier. Once it was up far enough, he pulled out the food satchels and rain bowls and put them to the side of the boat, then with Tala's help, flipped the canoe over so it was protecting his supplies, but there was no room for him to get under as well.

"What now?" he asked as he scanned the edge of the sands to the tree lines, watching the palm trees swaying violently with the winds as the tropical storm hit.

"The tribe here must certainly be taking shelter as well," Tala said, "so they will hopefully leave us alone. Let's get you under those trees over there until it's over."

Just then he noticed, now that it had grown dark, Tala was giving off a very soft blue glow. It didn't appear suddenly, he just hadn't noticed it before and it made him think she always had that shimmering aura around her and now that it was dark, he could finally see it.

"Follow me," the large wolf called to him, as she set off towards the tree line.

For a moment he watched her go, noticing she left no paw prints in the wet sand. It made him wish his own feet weren't leaving noticeable prints, but it was probably as she said and the natives here were also hopefully hunkered down tight.

Not that far into the deep tropical forest, Tala found a tiny cave Coki surely would have missed in this darkness. Soon they were safely in the small crevice and out of the torrential rains. Inside this small dark hole her glow was even brighter and took on a soft azure hue.

"Do I dare make a fire?" Coki asked, suddenly chilled by his damp skin and the fierce winds that still managed to creep into the small cave.

"I doubt you could in this wind," she said, but then noticed him shivering and came close to him. She saw he looked confused, but she smiled. "Remember, you can't touch me, but I can touch you." And with that, she curled her large body around his shivering form, and he felt that same tingling again. It started where her fur touched his skin, and then swept through him. It surrounded him with warmth and happy thoughts, and for a moment he found himself drifting back to memories of his mother's hugs when he was small.

And there they sat, young man and spirit wolf together, as the winds howled outside, and the torrential rains poured. It was hours later when almost as quickly as it had arrived, it started to break up, and soon the black clouds and harsh winds were gone, heading west.

Coki reluctantly pulled himself up out of the spirit wolf's embrace and walked out of the cave and headed back to the beach. Once out from under the thick palm canopy he could see the sky overhead was clear once more and was full of stars and a bright moon…which put plenty of light on the six tribal members who were surrounding their canoe. They were all armed with spears and seemed older and much stronger than Coki.

He felt a chill run along his frame as his muscles cramped in fear. Strangers were rarely accepted on these islands without invitation, and he had no idea what this tribe was like. He was fit and trim and had no problems with the games they played back in his village, and he certainly had beaten Jejen in wrestling more than once, but against six?

"Charge them," she whispered, her voice cutting into his fear.

"Wait...what?"

"Charge them...don't strike, just yell a lot and look threatening. When they break and run, quickly turn over the canoe and put the stuff back into it and push off."

"They aren't going to run from me," he protested quietly, his voice shaking.

"They won't be running from you," she said as she nudged him strongly from behind. "Go!"

His chest tightened and his breath quickened as he let out a cry and started charging forward. He held the spear in front of him as he yelled the best war whoop he could muster, his feet churning up sand as he sped towards the canoe.

For a moment the six warriors turned towards the yelling, and two started to laugh and the others chuckled as they readied their own spears and prepared to skewer the trespasser.

But as quickly as they formed into a line, their smiles faded and their laughter died. Coki could see an azure light reflected in their six sets of eyes.

Two of them stumbled back, and a third dropped his spear as his mouth fell agape in shock. It was then Coki felt a rush of wind as Tala ran up behind him and leaped over his head. In a flash of light much brighter than she had appeared before, she landed ahead of him and continued to run at the six until she stopped halfway between Coki and the warriors. She then let out a terrific howl, her fur now translucent and alight like an azure ghost blazing with mystical flames.

The other five warriors dropped their spears as well, and soon they were all running back along the beach away from the frightening sight.

Even Coki had been stopped dead in his tracks, his own yelling forgotten as he beheld Tala in all her majestic glory, as she put off more light than a bonfire.

"Stop gaping and turn over the canoe," she urged, "they won't be terrified long." Then she let out another deafening howl as she noticed the six of them hesitating as if unsure if they should keep running or come back.

Coki knew he had no more ability to turn over this large canoe on his own than he had before, but once again it seemed as light as balsa as it flipped over and he quickly put the water bowls and fish satchels back inside, as well as his fishing gear. Then for good measure, he glanced down at the six spears dropped by the natives and quickly picked one up. He was an excellent spear thrower back in his village and had been able to nail a tree from a long distance away. Even in moonlight, he was certain he'd have a fair chance of hitting one of the warriors. For a moment, he almost considered it, then he saw Tala was looking at him, and she cocked her head to the side questioningly and his resolve became clear. Pivoting towards the water, and with all his might, he hurled the spear far out into the ocean. Then he quickly picked up the other five spears and did the same, then tossed his own spear back into the canoe and began to push the long craft out into the water.

This seemed to spark the six of them into action and they began to run back towards them, but one more turn from the azure wolf, who barred her glowing teeth at them and growled angrily made them hesitate. Soon the canoe was in the water and Coki pulled himself up into it. Then with a last deafening howl, Tala leaped into the air and landed on the craft and this action pushed the canoe as if propelled by the energy of her light itself, racing away from the shore as the six warriors ran to the edge of the water, yelling angrily and waving their arms.

It was many hours later and the long canoe was back in the mystical current, same as before but moving faster than ever. Tala's glow had dimmed back to a softer azure hue as she gazed out into the water, the gentle night winds whipping through her fur as the moonlight reflected in the almost still waters.

Coki just stared at her with an almost boyish grin on his face as he couldn't help but feel exhilarated by the experience. He really wanted to give Tala a hug, but knew he couldn't touch her, yet he still got up and slowly approached her and sensing his desire, she backed into him just enough to allow the embrace.

"That's twice you've saved me."

"Three times actually," she said with a light laugh, then her face became serene, and her voice became a whisper. "It's time to remember, Coki."

He was still hugging her warm fur and reveling in the gentle tingles it gave. He was going to ask what she meant, but his question died in his throat as the fog blocking his memory of what had happened started to lift, and his lost day began to come back to him.

Suddenly in his mind he was back to that day, in shock at what he was seeing. For Coki had never seen anything like it, and he was both curious and terrified by what it could represent. He had no words to describe it, as his life among the peaceful Taíno natives of his island hadn't prepared him for something like this...

"They are far too big to be the canoes of the Carib," Jejen said, as the two of them stared at the many large vessels that had suddenly appeared in the waters off their island, with huge, tall masts that had drapes of strange cloth that billowed out with the wind.

"I count as many as on three hands," Coki said, as he steadied the large canoe he and Jejen had taken out that morning to fish.

"We must warn our leader, our cacique, these strangers may be raiders like the Carib."

"But we must also know more," Coki insisted. "We are close to shore, go warn our village and I will get a better look at who these people are."

Jejen studied him for a long time, knowing his closest friend was hard to dissuade once he made up his mind. With a nod he took a look at all the fish they had caught, though not nearly as much as they had hoped. "We took too large a canoe, and we are barely able to steer it with us both, how will you manage on your own?"

"I'll go slowly," Coki said with a confident grin. "I won't get too close. Just close enough to figure out which tribe they are, then I'll come back to shore and catch up with you so our village will know what's coming, and then they can warn the other villages."

Jejen put his hands on Coki's shoulders and smiled. "I should stay with you, but you're right, our village must be told. Don't get too close!" Then he jumped over the side of the boat into the crystal-clear waters around their home.

Once Coki had seen Jejen was safely on shore and running towards their village, he started to move the canoe towards the strange large vessels. It was very difficult to keep the canoe straight, but he was determined.

Closer and closer he got to them, and the closer he got the more staggered he was at their size. Their tall wooden hulls stretched up out of the water, and the ships were longer than many huts of his village combined. There were men on the decks that he could barely make out. They wore breastplates that gleamed like scales of a fish. Their faces were strangely pale and while some of them had similar armor on their heads, others wore nothing. He could see some had hair as black as the people of his village, while others had hair that was brown as the earth, or yellow as a flower's …and he was certain they were not any tribe he'd ever seen.

Several of the men on the ship closest to him were beginning to gather and point down at his canoe and they shouted in a strange language as the large ship began to turn towards him.

It was then the current seemed to capture his craft and yank it with such a sudden force the large canoe immediately reversed course, toppling him over to slam his head on the solid bottom of the boat.

He barely managed to open his eyes and tried to focus…something was with him in the canoe, looking down on him with soft yellow eyes…and he blacked out…

And he was back in the present, a strange feeling coming over him as he absorbed what he had remembered. He took a step back from the large wolf and rubbed his head where he had hit it.

"What were those large ships, those strange people?"

Tala looked straight at Coki and let out her breath. "They are just people, like you are. But…their ways are quite different from yours, and they seem to feel those they find should be like them… They will take over your island…peacefully at first…but whether by purpose or accident, I'm sorry to say that this is the end of your tribe as you know them."

Coki felt his chest tighten up again as he thought of Jejen and his father, and all his village. "I have to go back, to warn them."

But Tala just shook her head. "Nothing you can do will change what is to be there."

"Then why am I here?" he asked angrily, confused and upset by this memory and what it meant for the people of his home island of Borikén. "How do you know what will happen?"

"This is their first visit to *your* island, but they also appeared a year ago and visited other islands to the west of yours, and the result was the same…only this time many more ships have come…and they will keep coming, not just to your island but all the islands in that area. One day they will even come to the mainland we are heading to, where my kind live, but not for some years, and they won't be a concern for you until the time of your children's children."

Coki blinked a few times, unsure what this was really going to mean to him. "My children's children?"

"That is why you are here, how you will help me. For long before that time you will have prepared your new tribe to keep moving west when they see the signs."

"New tribe? I'm no leader."

"Not yet, but you will become one, and I'll be there to guide you, and my kind will help as well."

Coki's lips parted as he tried to absorb it all."

But Tala just moved her large face up to his and filled him with her warmth. "Look behind you."

Coki turned and gasped, for there was now land to the west, more land than he had ever seen in his life. The sun was just starting to come up behind him to the east, and the crimson rays of dawn were stretching out past him, sparkling on the waves as they crashed gently against the long white beaches of the shore.

And there, gathered on the sands, were wolves. Not as big as Tala or glowing, but they were many, a large pack, with little ones as well. They were all watching towards the canoe.

"They are waiting for you, Coki," Tala assured. "They are going to take you to the tribe you will one day lead, my special tribe…a tribe that lives as one with the wolf."

"Your tribe?" he asked as he stared at the wolves in amazement.

"They are good people," she assured. "Very much like your tribe you left back on your island. But they need you…and I've chosen you to help them for me."

"How will I even be able to talk with them?" he wondered, remembering the Carib didn't speak the same language as the Taíno, and he doubted the tribes in this strange place would either.

"You will learn…they will accept you when you come in with the wolves."

"And with you as well, right?"

Tala leaned her head gently on his shoulder. "They won't see me, but they know me. Only you will only be able to see me from time to time…but even when you can't see me, I'll always be there with you Coki."

"Always?"

"I'm *your* spirit guide, it's what I do."

He leaned his head into hers, though he realized she was the one leaning into him, and he gazed at the wolf pack patiently waiting for him on the shore of this mysterious new land…and he smiled.

Born in New York City, **Nicholas Samuel Stember** spent most of his life in the suburbs of Princeton, NJ. Growing up with a profound love of fantasy, science fiction and horror, the direction his writing took was firmly set. His love of those genres also found him a wife from across the sea, and he ended up marrying her and moving to the Faroe Islands, where he resides today. His works can be found in magazines, anthologies and upcoming novels. He also joined the Horror Writers Association in 2024.

You can find Nicholas online at https://nsstember.com or at www.facebook.com/nicholassamuelstember

Yāoláng

Mea Andrews

Yāoláng's teeth rendered flesh from bone, the screams of his enemies surrounding him and his pack. Once there had been a hundred or more of his kind. Together they would have stopped the Niántǔ Rén, clay-born, when they had first sprung from the yellow river at the hands of the creation goddess Nǚwā. But they had not come together.

Some packs had tried to work alongside them. The wolves teaching the two-legged creatures how to surround an enemy, to signal to another how far prey was. They passed spring and summer like this, working as a team.

It had been winter that ended their partnership.

Their spongey flesh had not been made for the cold. When the first wolf went missing no one suspected the newcomers, instead they thought the Hēixióng, black bears, with their long, yellowed claws and canines able to rip apart even logs, had taken down their brother.

A handful more went missing over the next few days, and it was only then the mangy beasts started proudly wearing fur. They fashioned leather from deer and small game into boots, belts, bags. These goods were deformed, any essence of their original form gone. It was not the same for the wolves.

They kept the heads attached to the pelt, protecting their heads and backs with the literal heads and backs of Yāoláng's brethren.

To add to the insult, Fúxī, Nǚwā's brother and lover, gave them fire.

Yāoláng remembered a time before gods and goddesses. When the world was a constant shifting of land and water while the moon settled into its place in the heavens.

A shattered whimper came from a wolf nearby as fire arrows pierced their hide. Yāoláng leaped and grabbed the nearest two-legged monstrosity by the throat in response, anguish feeding his ferocity.

He knew without looking that soon he would be the only one of his kind left on the battlefield. His family, the pack he had grown up with and spent the last few millennia hunting alongside, would be skinned and worn like decoration. Briefly, he allowed himself to wonder who among them would wear his own blue pelt gifted to him when the ocean lapped at his paw, the first being it had ever touched.

Still, he pushed forward. Nǚwā had only made a handful of the creatures, but the goddess's hands were large enough to fill holes in the sky.

Footsteps closed in behind him. Everyone at his flank must have already been brought down. Yáoláng twisted behind him, snapping his jaw at the incoming Niántǔ Rén. A spear drove at him, and he jumped, biting down on the gloved hand that held it.

How could they not have been happy with the prey animals? Why did they not stop when Fúxī gave them fire?

Something slammed into the back of his head and he was down, legs twitching.

Yáoláng supposed he should have been happy he hadn't felt the final blow, but he found himself more upset than anything. Why was he not dead?

Spring surrounded him. Trees fully leafed with birds, even the annoying koel with its wroo-wroo call, on branches and building nests. Grass tickled his nose and he sneezed, head swaying back and forth.

"What is this?" He called out, not surprised when there was no answer. This was not his world. Sniffing, he was confused to find he couldn't track the prey animals he relied on for strength or find the direction of his favorite Ginkgo tree. Weeks could pass without him visiting and he had never gotten lost making his way to it. Everything here smelled faintly metallic, like blood. It was as if every blade of grass and leaf above him was pollen coated iron and the birds, game that had already been snared.

His head spun. So much life swathed in death, His eyes and nose fought for dominance of his senses. Death was something to pick up your paws and run from, particularly if you hadn't caused it. Life was meant to sate hunger, find a mate, teach a litter how to properly apply teeth and claws to flesh.

This was not life.

He howled, a loud "Aroo." If any of his kind were here, they would respond.

Two heartbeats later, a response, low and long. Yāoláng couldn't smell this wolf, but from the pitch and length of the reply, he knew this wolf, whoever they were, was healthy.

Yāoláng ran in the direction of the sound. One of his kind, metallic scent or not, should be able to tell him where they were and why.

He ran for hours. Every few miles yowling with his head to the sky to gauge the distance. Only when he was on the edge of exhaustion did he find his compatriot. His tongue lolled out of his mouth, his breaths coming in short gasps. There hadn't been a whiff of a single clay-born on his journey. It had been a good run that he probably would have enjoyed in different circumstances.

The wolf in front of him was fatter than Yāoláng had expected, stomach bulging at the sides, with dull yellow fur that may have once been gold. Female, he noted, but likely too old for pups. Still, her eyes were sharp.

She stood in a clearing next to what Yāoláng knew as a clay-born's cooking pot but easily ten times larger. He growled.

"Why do you have *that*?" Yāoláng asked, gesturing at the pot with his head. He had half a mind to gut the bitch where she stood but restrained himself.

First, he needed answers.

"This is where I cook." The she-wolf answered, amused. "Creatures from all worlds come to eat what I make."

He growled, low and harsh, lips lifting to show teeth stained yellow with blood over centuries of hunts. Detestable. Creatures so wretched they couldn't stomach the raw flesh of their prey had no right to eat.

"Where are we?" It was better to get straight to the point.

"We are on Nàihé Qiáo, the Bridge of Forgetfulness."

At this, Yāoláng scoffed. This was no bridge he had ever seen. Trunks miles long over the widest rivers had existed for a brief time in his world, as had gaping canyons connected with the thinnest sliver of rock. But a whole forest as a bridge? Unlikely.

"Ah, yes. Of course. The famous she-wolf and the enormous

forest bridge," Yāoláng let his voice drip with cynicism. "I *had* been meaning to pay you a visit."

The she-wolf smiled, black lips raising to show glistening, sharp, white teeth.

"Many suspect they might find themselves here, or somewhere similar. But it is never like they thought it would be when they do."

She sat on her haunches, stomach bulging. She looked around and back to Yāoláng pointedly.

"The Bridge of Forgetfulness offers this forest to you as one final kindness," She pressed on, "Taking on the shape of the place you most love."

Yāoláng sighed, defeated for the first time in his life.

"I had heard rumors of death," He remembered when one of his kind had fallen into a ravine. There had been a splash of a reptilian tail and he was gone. This would happen every decade or so. Someone he knew disappearing from his or a neighboring pack forever.

"This is not what I expected."

It was true. Yāoláng did not remember being created, yet was sure he and his kin had, at some point, been some god or goddesses blessing to the Earth. He had thought death would be similar to being created: suddenly you were, suddenly you were not.

The she-wolf seemed to shrug her shoulders as though indifferent to what he thought might have been waiting for him in the afterlife.

"You lived a long life, Yāoláng, blessed by nature itself, created from stardust and moonlight. Later touched by the salty brine of life. Not all are so lucky."

If this was her attempt at placating him, it was a poor one.

"And what of the world I leave behind? Does it fall to those hairless, bipedal apes?"

"That's a hard question." The she-wolf sighed. "What if I said that in your case the world as you knew it died with you?"

Yāoláng wasn't sure he liked that answer.

"You lived through dynasties. Saw the rise and fall of trees, witnessed mountains rise from the ocean, felt the heat of lava singe your fur as land pushed to expand."

He remembered those years of growth, the very essence of the planet shifting under him and his pack's paws. There was a whole century the earth fought itself and his brethren had refused to sleep in caves for fear of being trapped inside if the shaking shook rocks free.

"That time of expansion has ended."

Yāoláng's eyes narrowed. The world as he knew it was ceaseless. Trees would grow until they choked out their competition and eventually fell to their deaths, root systems too large. Water would erode until it one day conquered the world. Volcanoes would push themselves up in defiance and burn everything around it until created new land to battle the ocean's rise.

"Who are you?" He finally asked.

"Mèng Pó," she said.

"Where are my brethren?" There was an edge to his voice. It had been a long day and even death did not seem to save him from feeling tired and annoyed. *Fine,* he thought, *Afterlife be damned. Give me my pack.*

"You will not meet them here. They have gone on ahead."

Mèng Pó studied Yāoláng, waiting for a response.

The male wolf looked around, puzzled. Was there more than this bridge-not-a-forest?

"Take me there. I would like to hunt with my pack." He shifted his weight from paw to paw. It wasn't that he was hungry, he wasn't, but inside him was this gnawing feeling of unease.

Since the dawn of his time he had not spent more than a night without at least one or two of his own kind. The weight of his bones and how his lids started to sag told him sleep would come soon, whether the sun ever set here or not.

He tried to stand up straighter. There was no reason for this strange Mèng Pó to know his weakness.

Mèng Pó lifted a front paw as if examining her nails.

"Do you know why you are here?" She asked, her tone bored. When he didn't respond, she continued. "You are the last Láng, the last true wolf that will roam your world. With your passing, an era comes to an end."

"Come here." She commanded and Yāoláng was surprised to find his body obeyed.

He stopped just beside the rim of the great pot. Looking in, he could see rose petals, grass, and strange herbs simmering in water.

"Are you forbidden from hunting?" He asked, twisting his face into one of disgust. What wolf, dead, immortal, or otherwise, would choose to *eat* plants?

The She-Wolf laughed.

"Has dying made you so ravenous you can't entertain the diets of others?"

He eyed Mèng Pó's midsection as if to say she didn't get plump on leaves and flowers.

Mèng Pó sighed, and with some effort got up to stand next to Yāoláng.

"Look in the pot again, carefully this time."

He did, at first noting the lack of meat, but then…a reflection in the water grabbed his attention. Clay-born marched on snow covered ground and with a shock Yāoláng noticed his own blue pelt and face wrapped around one of the creature's broad shoulders.

He snapped at the water, face centimeters from simmering broth, teeth bared with haunches raised. It was the way of the world, he knew, for the strong to pilfer the weak. For the strongest of animals to stand at the top of the world and howl its supremacy over others. When he had gone to war with the two-legged monsters, he had known it would be a losing battle. He and his pack had known they were likely to join the murdered kin and be used for warmth. But he had not expected to see himself being used in such way.

Death was supposed to be the end and in the resulting nothingness he would never know his fate.

"Why," he growled out, low and slow, "are you showing me this?"

"Your time has ended, and the age of humans has begun." A gust of wind wrapped around her, and Mèng Pó suddenly took on the form of a clay-born, larger in the middle than any he had seen before. She was wrapped in gold, the cloth unlike any leather he had seen before. It looked as though he could rip it to shreds with one swipe of a paw. The sleeves were impossibly long and around her mid-section a too large belt made from more of the strange cloth but in a darker shade of yellow seemed tied behind her back.

It looked restrictive. How was she going to hunt in that?

She smiled, showing teeth flat and ill-suited for tearing at raw flesh.

"Look again."

Yāoláng tried to fight her, but found his head turning on its own. In the water he saw what Mèng Pó called 'humans' cutting down trees to build homes, those too old to work manual labor cooking in pots similar to this one. All around was death. The cold took many of them, particularly the young. When spring melted the ice and groups went to hunt, hungry Hēixióng coming out of hibernation feasted on them instead, needing the meat to help them create milk to feed their cubs.

Shé, snakes, slithered on the ground and snuck through window and door openings to steal babies while their mothers cooked. Even more were doomed as they found some berries and fruits were poisonous.

Yāoláng huffed, the exhale distorting the image.

"They get what they deserve. The wolves had faced similar challenges in the beginning."

His words were half-hearted. In reality, his kind existed before the wrath of the Hēixióng or Shé. When they did eventually meet new creatures, they had merely observed them and shared information quickly. An unlucky few had lost their lives this way, but not in the numbers these humans were experiencing.

Mèng Pó seemed to know this as well.

"They are lacking," She gestured with her new hairless paw at the water, "They do not have the wolf's guile or leadership ability."

Even as she spoke, a group descended on a large antlered being and at the first sweep of it's too large head two of the men ran, dropping their spears. It was a problem Yāoláng had heard of from his peers. Clay-born were prone to leave one another if it meant they could save themselves. Even in his own battle with them, it had been the strongest and biggest who stayed on the battlefield.

"Leaders will emerge." Yāoláng watched as a spear holder moved forward in a crouching position, spear held ready. His compatriots who had not run watched, waiting for an opportunity.

"They would do better with you."

Yāoláng started, looking away from the images reflected in the soup and almost hissed.

"You want me to go back there while they—"

"You misunderstand," the woman cut him off, "They need what is inside of you, what the first creators gave your kind. As the first of the first, you Yāoláng, possess the initial spark."

The wolf turned his head to the side, confused. There was nothing inside him except entrails and blood. He had seen enough of his own kind perish to know.

"You possess authority. Cunning. A craftiness that only comes from the honing of pure survival instinct."

"They wear my family in winter. They have killed everyone I once cared for. Why should I deign to give them anything more?"

They can suffer and die, snuffed out by their own stupidity, he thought.

"Do you remember the great Lóng?," she asked, showing yet another image in the water. A long creature flying in clouds Yāoláng had only ever howled at emerged. Its body was gold scaled and as it burst through a cloud, others of various hues of red, blue, and black followed.

Yāoláng wracked his mind, body feeling weaker than it had just a few hours ago. All he wanted to do was lie down and take a long nap.

There had been, near the beginning, a race in the skies perhaps like these. He attempted to summon one to mind, but the memory was too far away. The memory eluded him, vanishing like a snow rabbit into its burrow; present, yet too deeply hidden to retrieve.

"They were powerful, maybe on par with the pantheon as it is now. They, who once ruled the skies and shaped the earth, saw the cycle. They knew their time was ending. They offered their wisdom, their prosperity, everything that made them great…" She trailed off, and seeing the realization dawning in Yāoláng's eyes, she finished, "to you."

Yāoláng worked to remember anything about the race, but the memory continued to elude him. There was no hint of a lie in her words, and though her current form as one of *them* was grotesque, she exhibited an aura of calm patience. It was as if he was a welp and she was a mother trying to lead him along, he realized.

He laid down, too weary to stand any longer. Taking his front paws under his head, he yawned.

"You would have me offer the same to men?" With an effort he kept his eyes open. He wanted to finish this never-ending conversation and rest.

"Your spirit is cooling even now. You will not stay tethered here much longer. The strength you possess will do nothing for you now."

Yāoláng felt in his bones she was right. He had once felt bound-less. In his prime he had organized hunts, leapt great chasms of darkness with only the backdrop of moonlight, cradled pups in his fur, learned the taste of the winter's bitter chill.

"Men…they are a plague. They destroy."

"Did you and your predatory kind not also destroy? Taking whatever you needed to survive?" Mèng Pó asked.

"Drink from my cauldron and rest. You will forget but not be forgotten, and your wisdom and survival instincts will pass to the new generation."

Yāoláng hesitated, his gaze flickering between Mèng Pó and the pot.

"They will squander it. They will turn it into weapons, into tools of destruction."

"And then the deities of that time will create something else. Perhaps something more peaceful." Mèng Pó reasoned.

"Perhaps Not." Yāoláng said.

The woman nodded in agreement, the folds under her chin doubling for a moment.

They both stared at each other for a moment in silence. The old wolf sat back up, knowing if he didn't move now he was likely to never move again.

"What's in the pot?"

The woman smiled.

"This is Mèng Pó Tāng, my own special creation," Her smile grew as she talked about it, eyes glowing bright with excitement. "Many call it The Soup of Forgetfulness. You drink this and you will forget everything about who you are and the pure essence of you will be distilled, scattered to the winds until it takes root in others."

Yāoláng's gaze fell back to the rose petals and herbs. No other visions brewed within.

He was dying, it was obvious. The blow in his world had placed him here and soon, much later than the deliverer of the blow had likely intended, he was going to breathe in his last scent.

A faint acceptance settled over him.

He looked at Mèng Pó and nodded.

"Drink, First Wolf of Creation. Drink, and be at peace."

~ *  * ~

Mea Andrews is a writer from Georgia, who currently resides in Shenzhen. She has her MFA from Lindenwood University and is still trying to learn how to make writing profitable. You can find her in *Gordon Square Review*, *Gutter*, *Orca*, *Oyster River*, *Potomac Review*, and others. She was a 2022 Pushcart prize nominee, and had a poem up for Best of the Net.

You can find her on Instagram @meawrites or on Blue Sky @meaandrews.bsky.social.

The Highland Wolf

Andrew M Seddon

My name is Jonathan Quick.

I am a composer. I work with notes and chords, melody and harmony, rhythm and structure. I hear it, and I can see it all in my mind. But I don't only see music.

I also see ghosts; to be more specific, I see one particular ghost, that of my fiancée, Meredith de'Ath, who passed away shortly before we were to be married.

This is not something I discuss in casual company, or any company for that matter, as past experience has taught me it inevitably leads either to a tiresome joke about our surnames or to a questioning of my sanity on the part of my listener. Sometimes both.

But it's true.

I asked my priest about it once, and after due consideration he pronounced if not his blessing, at least a qualified acceptance, since Meredith typically directs me towards the performance of a good deed of some sort. "I don't see anything diabolical here," he concluded.

And so it happened that one summer, my mind awhirl with scraps of melody and fragments of harmony jostling for attention, I tramped steadily over the Scottish Highlands north of Inverness, far from the binocular-toting tourists clogging the A82 hugging the shore of Loch Ness while seeking a glimpse of Nessie frolicking in the cold, dark waters of the loch. Other than a vanishingly few other hardy ramblers I had the heather-clad hills and wooded glens to myself.

At the time in question, I hadn't seen another human being for an hour or two.

But that was fine, because at the moment I didn't want human company—I wanted wild, unfettered nature. I'd accepted a commission to write the score for a documentary about rewilding in Britain, with a focus on apex predators, specifically the wolf.

Now, I knew little about wolves, except there weren't any in

Britain.

Nobody I'd spoken to associated with the production seemed to know how my name had come to their attention, since I typically composed scores for romcoms or science fiction movies, but no matter. A commission was a commission.

Besides, it was a new challenge for me, something different from my usual scope of work, and one I'd jumped at. But for some reason I found myself unable to create an acceptable score in the comfort of my studio. I'd crashed into a creative dead-end. Worse, it was as if I was struggling to free myself not only from creative bonds—but also from myself—almost as if there was another man trapped inside; a man bound by the trappings and constraints of civilization.

In short, inspiration just wouldn't come to me when surrounded by all the paraphernalia of modern life and society. I needed to get away from it all. Books and the internet weren't adequate—I needed to *feel* the wild, to experience something of it for myself before I could put it into music.

And so here I was, clad in newly-purchased, over-priced hiking gear, wending my way across rugged countryside, mulling over ideas and hoping they would take coherent shape. What key should this passage be in? What orchestration would best produce the effect I wanted? What mood did I wish to create?

I tried to absorb everything—the evanescent beauty of purple heather-clad hills and wooded glens as shifting sunlight played across them; the symphony of wind, bird song, and stream; the scent of pine and hazel; the feel of the earth underfoot, now firm and unyielding, now soft and spongy.

Thus occupied, it was with a shock the fragrance that inevitably indicated Meredith's presence suddenly intruded upon my reverie. I came to an abrupt halt.

Meredith, here, in the wilderness? Surely I was just smelling some flower or scented bush.

But there she was, reclining with her legs crossed on a rocky outcropping, the outline of which was visible through her. Her hair was splayed over her shoulders and her eyes twinkled. Being a ghost, of course she lacked colour and substance, but that was all right— I could visualize those easily enough.

As I stared in rapt amazement—seeing her always caused a

slew of emotions to course through me—she cupped a hand to her ear, as if listening intently.

I stilled the inchoate music in my mind, and tried to focus, hearing past the rustling of the breeze in the trees, the gentle trickle of a small burn, and the trill of some little bird, perhaps a crested tit.

And then I heard it.

At the edge of my perception, a distant howl that rose and fell in an unmistakable cadence.

The howl of a wolf!

I recognized it because I'd been listening to recordings as the next best thing to hearing real wolf song in the wild.

But it couldn't be—wild wolves hadn't roamed the British Isles in well over three hundred years…the last Scottish wolf was thought to have been killed around 1680, not that the date really mattered—the wolves were long-gone.

And so it couldn't be! I must be mistaking the sound of something else. Perhaps a distant siren of some sort?

But there was Meredith, indicating to me I should go and check out the source of the sound.

I shook my head.

I knew wolves posed a vanishingly small threat to humans, preferring to avoid contact with us. I knew tales of wolf depredations in Eastern Europe were likely due to times of famine or outbreaks of rabies. I knew *Homo sapiens* was a far crueler and more deadly species than *Canis lupus*. Intellectually I knew all these things, but I had no desire to find out for myself by encountering a wild wolf.

I shook my head again, and mouthed, "No way".

Meredith merely gave me one of her tolerant looks—a look with which I was well acquainted—and pointed.

It was abundantly clear to me from past experience she wasn't going to take 'no' for an answer. Meredith could be very strong-willed at times…and had the vexing habit of being right; characteristics that had accompanied her into this unusual post-mortem existence.

"Don't be a wobbly-bones," I could almost hear her say. "Where's my brave Jon?"

Happy writing music in his head, I thought. *Not interested in a close wildlife encounter.*

Her smile straightening, she pointed again, more firmly this time.

I sighed, shrugged, and made a resigned motion with my hands.

How can you argue with a ghost? Especially one who was presumably sent here with the tacit approval of the Almighty?

The howl came again. And was it tinged with sadness or pain?

I set off in what seemed to be the right direction, threading my way along a game trail winding through the wooded glen.

As I walked, I tried to calm my quivering nerves.

Surely Meredith wouldn't be instrumental in sending me into mortal danger. Throw me to the wolves? Never. Take me out of my comfort zone? Most definitely.

Meredith, who had a soft spot for animals, had a special attachment to St. Francis. And as everyone knew, St. Francis, that lover of all of God's creation, tamed the wild wolf of Gubbio. But I was no St. Francis. I wasn't even a saint at all. Not even close.

Perhaps it was a nice wolf, I tried to reassure myself, the kind that would dwell with a lamb.

I could almost hear Meredith snicker. "You, a lamb, Jon?"

As I trudged along, gradually the howls became louder, and did they resound with sorrow and frustration? Or was I simply imagining that?

Louder. I must be close.

I slowed my approach. Never surprise a wild animal. I knew little of animal biology, but I knew that.

I began to whistle…ironically, the theme from Prokofiev's *Peter and the Wolf.*

Dee, dee, de dee dee dee…

Great choice, Jon!

Transpose it into a minor key. Make it darker. *Jon and the Wolf.* Something I might not live to compose, even if I wanted to.

The howls stopped abruptly.

"Hello," I called, trying my best to sound calm and reassuring. "Don't be afraid."

How stupid was that? Doubts surged into my mind. I was the one who was afraid. What if the biggest, baddest wolf that ever prowled God's green earth was waiting for me out there? A monster wolf, all slavering jaws and fangs? The Fenris wolf, immense enough and mean enough to devour Odin?

St. Francis, I prayed silently, *tame this wolf.*

The trees thinned. I took a deep breath and called "Hello" again.

"Is someone there?" The voice that answered was hesitant, querulous.

"Yes!" I replied.

"Thank God! Please help me!"

A talking wolf? Now I was really losing it. Even the wolf of Gubbio didn't literally talk to St. Francis.

And even if somehow a wolf could talk, wolves' vocal apparatus couldn't mimic human speech that well.

Relieved, I pushed forward quickly, calling out, "Are you hurt? Have you been bitten?"

"My foot…"

I stepped out of the forest into a clearing. On the far side lay a man, half-raised, leaning on his elbows. He appeared to be middle-aged, his dark hair streaked with gray, his beard salt-and-pepper. He had a prominent nose, large jaw, and eyes of some indeterminate colour that tended towards amber.

"Am I glad to see you," he said.

Scanning the clearing, I hurried over to him. "What happened?"

He pointed. "This happened."

His right leg was caught in a steel leg-hold trap.

I dropped to my knees beside him. "These things should be illegal!"

"They are," he replied. "But someone put one here anyway. Probably after foxes." He exhaled. "I've tried for two days to get it off. I was beginning to think no one would ever find me. Not a pleasant way to die, eh?"

I shrugged off my daypack.

"What I need is a heavy stick," I said, standing up again. Fortunately the forest had an ample supply. Finding one suited to my purpose, I returned and began to pry the trap open.

"Why the wolf calls?" I asked as I worked, straining against the powerful spring.

"A man—or a wolf, for that matter—has to do what he can," he gritted. "I hoped it would attract attention."

"Like from other wolves?" I said, pushing harder, using the stick as a lever. "Unless you know something I don't, there aren't any. They couldn't open a trap anyway."

He grimaced as the jaws of the trap slowly opened, and with a relieved gasp he wriggled his leg free. I removed the stick and the trap snapped shut.

"You are truly a Godsend, mate," the man said, rubbing his leg where the trap had left deep indentations and red marks, then rotating his ankle.

"Do you think you can stand?" I asked, giving him an arm.

He nodded. "I don't believe there's anything broken." I hauled him up, and gingerly, he took a few unsteady steps. "I can manage."

He turned to me and held out his hand. "I can't thank you enough, Mr…"

"Quick. Jonathan Quick. A pleasure to be of assistance," I replied, shaking it.

"If you're ever in trouble out here," he said, his grin revealing a line of white teeth, "just howl like a wolf, and Uffe will hear." He patted his chest.

"I'll remember that," I said, smiling back. "And I'll be especially careful in case there are any more of these wretched traps lying around. Where are you staying?"

He motioned over the hill. "It's not far. I'll be fine."

I hadn't seen any dwellings, but that didn't mean there wasn't a small cottage or lodge tucked among the hills and woods.

"Are you sure? I can come with you."

He shook his head. "I wouldn't want to put you to the inconvenience. No, really, I'll be fine. Cheerio!"

And with that, he limped away, into the forest.

Pleasant fellow, I thought. *But maybe a tad odd.*

I watched him until he disappeared from sight, conscious of Meredith's approval—because there she stood, observing me with an approving expression on her lovely face.

I did it, Meredith, I thought. *I set him free.*

Bravo, darling! I knew you could! were the words implicit in the look and the kiss she blew me before fading away.

I picked up my daypack, feeling warm inside.

Nearly as an afterthought, I pulled out my cellphone to take a photo of the trap. If it was illegal, then I should report it to the relevant agency. Perhaps they could find the miscreant who had set it.

I took the photo.

Then something caught my attention.

I bent down and removed a tuft of fur from the jaws of the trap, and held it before my eyes. Black and gray fur.

The kind of fur that...

I shot a glance towards the forest, then strode in the direction Uffe had gone. A little ways into the woods was a patch of soggy ground where he couldn't have avoided treading. In it were prints.

Paw prints.

Large paw prints.

Canine paw prints.

I sucked in my breath, as a sudden sense of unreality made my head momentarily swim.

When it passed, I tucked the tuft of fur carefully in my pocket, feeling, as I did so, a new-found freedom and a connection to the world in a way I never had before.

Meredith, as usual, had been right.

"Thanks, Uffe," I said quietly, patting my pocket.

I picked up my pack to continue my wandering in the wild.

There were no wolves in Britain.

Or were there?

~ * 🐺 * ~

An encounter with a wild wolf many years ago high in the Beartooth Mountains of Wyoming left **Andrew M. Seddon** with an abiding fascination for wolves. He is delighted to contribute to this anthology, and has himself edited an anthology of wolf stories, *Wolf Wanderings,* to benefit wolf conservation organizations. For further adventures of Doc Hughes and Victrix from the story *Wolf Haven* check out his book *The Death Cats of Asa'ican and Other Tales of a Space Vet.*

A native of England, he has lived most of his life in the USA, including thirty years in Montana. He enjoys writing non-fiction articles on diverse subjects, and short stories (including twenty anthology contributions). He has authored 15 books in the genres of science-, supernatural-, and historical fiction, as well as a book for writers—*Dr. Andrew's Curious and Quirky Compendium.* The proceeds from two volumes of short stories about German Shepherds —*Bonds of Affection* and *Ranger's First Call*—benefit rescues and K9 support organizations.

He is a member of SFWA and the Authors' Guild, and when not writing he can be found hiking, enjoying classical music, and running marathons. Now retired from the medical profession he lives in Florida with his wife Olivia and German Shepherd Baltasar, and has more books on the way!

You can find him online at: www.andrewmseddon.com and www.andrewmseddon.blogspot.com.

Hana's Pack

Maria D'Antonio-Reich

Against her better judgment, Raven shut her eyes once the car finally skidded to a halt against the tree. Pounding rain on the roof of the car and her heart hammering over her own hyperventilating slowly filled Raven's awareness. Glass crunched to her left against the tree. She moaned before opening her eyes and climbing out the passenger side door into the storm.

She'd hit an animal.

She did try to swerve, but she still hit it with her car.

Clearing hair off of her face and out of her eyes, Raven walked to the middle of the road and spotted a large body. She inched closer. "Are you okay?" she yelled out over the rain, hoping the animal was just stunned.

Lightning flashed, illuminating a wolf lying unnaturally still.

Nausea settled in the pit of her stomach, especially when she spotted a ghost next to the body. It, too, was a wolf.

She'd killed it.

"I'm sorry," she said to the ghost. "I didn't mean it."

The wolf ghost simply sniffed its own body and looked at her. Raven wiped more hair off of her face as the rain soaked through her clothes.

"I can move the body out of road," she offered.

It approached her, and instinctively, Raven backed away until she remembered it was merely a spirit and couldn't actually touch her. Still, it looked at her expectantly, so she held out her hand. The ghost gave it a sniff before sitting down next to its body. Raven took a few tentative steps, but when the wolf just sat there, she grew confident enough to grab the body by the hind legs and drag it out from the middle of the road. As she did so, she kept an eye on the ghost.

She'd seen ghosts and spirits all her life. Most of them had been at funerals or graveyards, and up until today, all of them had been human. She didn't know animals could become ghosts and figured she would ask some of her dead friends or even that eccentric angel of death who stopped by the cemeteries on occasion.

Once the wolf's body was out of the road, she walked back to the car, climbing in the passenger side again. She settled in the driver's seat and squeezed her eyes shut as she started the engine. Thank god it started. She shifted the car into gear, and it sputtered as it made its way off the grass and back on the road.

The ghost of the wolf watched from its post next to its body.

Raven sighed as the rain fell in from the driver's window. "I'm sorry," she said again, "but you can move along now. Nothing's going to hurt you anymore."

Shivering in the rain inside of her car, Raven drove much slower and much more carefully back home.

The next morning, she inspected the damage to the car while her coffee brewed. Just as she figured from her inability to exit via the driver's side, the driver's door was smashed in. She sighed. To be fair, she did kill the wolf last night, she probably deserved some type of punishment.

The aroma of the coffee beckoned her back inside.

She lived by herself in a one-bedroom cabin on a small plot of land in the mountains. She maintained a small garden in the front and grew herbs on the windowsill. Sitting in one of the mismatched chairs at her small table, she sipped her coffee, dreading going into work.

It was why she probably hit that wolf, worrying about going to work.

Four days a week, she worked from home, but she had to physically go to the office on Wednesday. Every Wednesday, she got to hear interesting stories about her coworkers' lives or families, listen to antics and pranks played on each other, yet all from the outside. She just wasn't part of their life. She did her job and went home without anyone taking notice, much like the ghosts.

At least the dead were interested in her. She'd tell them about the gardens, play her flute for them, and tell them of her struggle to possibly, maybe join a book club.

They wanted her to join with much more enthusiasm than she did, but she suspected that had to do with the fact the book club would give her something new to talk about.

Well, at least today she had a new story.

Once she finished her coffee and made herself presentable for work, she got in her car via the passenger door, started the engine, and screamed.

The wolf ghost sat in the back seat and stared at her from the rearview mirror. Raven took a deep breath and turned around. The wolf ghost was still there.

"What are you doing here?"

The ghost continued staring. Raven gulped. Oh god, was it going to haunt her? She'd heard stories about it from the angel of death, but she'd never seen it. Was it finally happening to her? She did kill it, albeit on accident, but to the wolf, that didn't make a difference.

Oh well. It couldn't hurt her. She turned around and put the car into drive with one last look in the mirror. Yep. It was still there.

It stayed the entire forty-five minute commute. Watching her. Like it had nothing better to do. Well, thanks to Raven, it didn't.

It followed her out of the car. It followed her into the building. It followed her to her cubicle. When she sat down and turned on her computer, it sat underneath the desk and curled up.

No one else saw it.

On normal Wednesdays, Raven found it difficult to function at the work office. So much laughter and conversations she wasn't part of buzzed around the building. The newer scientists who carried out her simulations would occasionally come up to her, but only to repeat the negative reports she'd already received an email about. Mostly coworkers just said their hellos before ignoring her completely.

Today, she had a wolf ghost with her, and while she noticed it, no one else did. It even followed her to her mandatory meeting where she gave a report on her computer simulations to a group of bored coworkers. The wolf ghost watched her presentation with interest.

Maybe she should be nervous. No one ever paid that much attention before.

When it ate some crumbs from her sandwich and stole a cookie from her lunch, she resolved to go to the graveyard right after work. She even sent a little prayer, more of a message really, to the angel of death to meet her there. That angel was the oldest creature Raven knew, and if it didn't have the answers, no one would.

After all, why would a ghost need to eat and follow a living person around? If it could eat, could it interact with her physically?

The afternoon passed in a blur. She occasionally checked the wolf at her feet, but it seemed content to just sit there. When she left work half an hour early, the wolf ghost followed her out of the building and back to her car. It waited for her to open the passenger door and hopped in ahead of her. Raven followed numbly and climbed into the driver's seat. Then she realized no one had commented on a banged up car in the parking lot.

Blinking back tears, she drove to the cemetery.

The wolf ghost's reception at the cemetery was very different than the office. Once they crossed the gate, ghosts pointed and screamed, before disappearing and flying away. The wolf ghost tilted its head before giving chase with huffs and grunts like dogs playing.

At least someone was having fun.

The angel of death waited underneath the maple tree, her ruffled wings relaxed at her back. She gave a half smile at the ruckus in the cemetery before turning one eye in Raven's direction. The other eye remained fixed on the wolf.

"This is unusual, isn't it?" the angel said with her airy voice. Pastel light shimmered around her, blurring the edges of her clothes and the ends of her honey-colored hair, which also shimmered as if under water.

"I sort of hit it with my car last night, and it turned up at my house this morning." Raven gestured to the wolf happily galloping after the residents of the graveyard. "Is it going to hurt them?"

"No." The angel of death held out her hand, holding a small pastel light in her palm. After a moment, it brightened, bathing the cemetery in a blinding brilliance. Once the light faded, everyone still stood, even the wolf.

The angel walked up to it and patted it on the head. "There, there," she cooed. "It's not nice chasing people around. Be still now."

Raven found herself calming down as well. She inched closer to them, watching the pair in silence. It was hard to ignore the angel of death's commands, especially in a graveyard.

Eventually, the angel straightened up. "It lost its pack the night you killed it," she said as she turned around. "There was a disease, the pups and her mate succumbed to it. The yearlings died two nights ago."

"Did she have it, too?" Raven asked.

The angel of death shrugged. "I don't know. That is for the living. She is dead now." She smiled. "Oh, to answer your question about the food. Animals exist in the moment. In that moment, she saw your food and wanted some. She did not think, because she is dead, she should not eat like a human spirit. All that matters to her is what is."

"Is she going to follow me around everywhere?" Raven eyed the wolf ghost.

"I don't know, but I have other dead to tend to. The ghost cannot come with me. Goodbye, Raven." With that, the angel of death melted into a pastel wisp of light and floated away.

The flighty angel tended to leave suddenly, and apparently, the appearance of a wolf ghost wasn't interesting enough for her to stick around.

Raven frowned at the wolf ghost and walked back to her car. When she opened the passenger door, the wolf jumped in before her. This time, Raven was not surprised.

When she woke up the next day and the wolf ghost was still there, Raven accepted it as a penance for killing it. She made herself breakfast and fed some to her new houseguest before opening her computer and starting her work.

The wolf ghost snoozed in the sun before wandering around the small cabin. It pawed at the window whenever birds landed on the bird feeder. It grabbed a box of fig cookies off the table and ate some before Raven rushed into the kitchen and put the box on a higher shelf.

She figured she'd have to check out some books at the library to see what she was dealing with. So after work, she drove to the library with the wolf ghost in the back seat. She meandered around the shelves, watching the ghost follow her out of the corner of her eye. It took some food out of a student's backpack.

Thoroughly embarrassed, Raven checked out an armful of books as quickly as she could and left. The wolf ghost followed, licking its lips.

For the next few days, Raven poured through all the books, learning about wolves, packs, how they ate, how they communicated, how they were skittish of humans… She glared at the wolf ghost. "I think you missed the memo here," she said. "This book says you're supposed to be shy around people."

The wolf ghost huffed at her before devouring her banana, skin and all.

Raven played movies depicting wolves in the background while she worked. So far, her favorites were entirely unrealistic, 'Teen Wolf' with Michael J. Fox and 'Wolf Children,' a cartoon.

She started calling the wolf ghost Hana after the main character of the cartoon.

Hana seemed to like her name and continued following Raven wherever she went. A week went by, and Hana's presence now felt familiar and reassuring, as if she'd been there the whole time.

Raven bought a bed and some toys for Hana. Like the angel of death said, Hana did not care that she was dead and that dead things could not affect the world of the living. She chewed up her toys and curled up in her bed in the sun.

In the afternoons, the pair would walk the nearby trails after work to a small river about a mile away. Raven would sit down and play her flute at the water's edge while Hana ran amuck in the woods. She always returned whenever Raven called out to her. They would make it back to the house just in time for dinner.

She watched Hana gnaw on a chicken leg as an idea formed. She threw back her head and howled.

Hana looked up and stared at her. Raven grinned and howled again. The third time, Hana joined in, howling in a slow, happy song. They howled together before Hana remembered her chicken leg and finished eating it.

It became part of daily life for Raven. Work, walk on a trail, eat dinner, and howl with Hana. The car was eventually repaired, and the commute got easier. She still visited the ghosts of the graveyard, though the angel of death hadn't made an appearance since the day she brought the wolf to the cemetery. The ghosts eventually got used to Hana and things continued as before.

The loneliness she felt on Wednesdays was softened by Hana snoozing under her desk. She'd lean down and pet the wolf ghost whenever it got particularly bad. Hana kept following her.

Three weeks after she'd killed Hana and unwittingly became the wolf ghost's family, Raven went outside for their afternoon trek and into a mist. Hana nudged her. "We can't stay at the river for long," Raven said. "The weatherman said it's going to storm again." It'd been storming for the past few days, and she could tell Hana was missing her afternoon hikes.

The wolf ghost huffed and grabbed her sleeve, pulling her outside.

They set off. Raven took her flute anyway, just in case the weatherman was wrong.

The clouds rolled in, darkening the sky, just as they reached their usual spot. She didn't want to turn back after just arriving, so she took out her instrument. One song, maybe two, and then she'd head back. She stood farther back than usual, as the water had risen with the past thunderstorms and splashed over the banks. Hana ran upstream today with more purpose than normal, but Raven just figured she had a lot of catching up to do from their missing walks earlier this week.

As she played, she lost herself in the music and her mind meandered from there. Once again, she wondered if Hana could get wet. And if she could get wet, could she track muddy pawprints in the house?

A sharp, familiar howl jolted Raven as she stopped blowing mid note and looked up ahead where Hana had run.

"Hana?"

The howl again.

Raven ran upstream, her concern for Hana's safety overriding her deep confusion of how a ghost could manage to hurt themselves. Drizzle fell gently from trees above and on the top of her hair. Once she spotted Hana, she breathed out a sigh of relief. Then she was immediately confused.

Another ghost stood with her, crying. The boy couldn't have been any older than fourteen. Hana huffed when Raven approached. "Um hello?"

"I fell in the river!" he cried turning to her. "I was running, because he got really mad at me. I heard some music, and I thought someone could help me, because he was chasing me, and he was going to get me. Then he tried to grab my shirt, but I slipped and fell."

"It'll be okay," Raven said, not at all sure if that was the case. "I have some friends who can help."

Hana growled at something upstream.

"What were you running for?" Raven asked as something stirred in her gut.

The boy pointed upstream. "He was that way. He killed two wolves, and I was going to tell my mom. And then I found this wolf and you came. Can we go to my mom please?"

Oh god. The boy didn't even know he was dead. Raven gulped and then jumped when Hana's growl took on a particularly vicious tune.

A camouflaged hunter emerged from the tree line, rifle in hand. He stared at Raven who stared back. "Are you talking to yourself?"

Raven considered her answer. "Uh, yeah."

"Have you seen a boy about twelve years old? He was running alone in the forest, and I wanted to check on him."

"I'm thirteen!" the boy cried. "And can't he see me?"

"No," Raven said as Hana growled again. She thought she saw something creeping up behind him. Then her eyes widened.

Two wolf ghosts stalked him, growling. Hana stood in front of Raven. The boy pointed at them. "Those are the wolves he got!"

Lightning cracked in the sky, reflecting the wolves' ghostly eyes before they howled. Hana joined in, and even Raven had to admit, in the dark forest with the smell of rain in the air, it was creepy.

The man apparently heard it. He jumped and spun around, but his foot slipped, and he tumbled into the river.

Raven and the boy gasped before following the man downstream. "Hang on!" she cried out.

"Help!" He went under. For eight seconds, Raven couldn't see him. It began to rain.

"Try to get to shore!" she screamed when she saw him bob up again. "Swim to shore!"

"I can't swim!" he shouted.

Seriously? He couldn't swim? Raven looked back at all four incorporeal beings following her who would be of exactly zero help. Though she could swim, she wasn't strong enough to jump in and pull him out.

All three wolves howled behind her.

Raven kept running, but the rain picked up and the sky darkened more. He went under again. She coughed as she forced her legs to run faster. She really didn't want anyone else to die in the storm.

"Ah, hello Raven," the angel of death said without any preamble. She simply appeared beside her from thin air. "There are three wolves now." The angel flew alongside her.

"Can't you help with him?" She pointed out the hunter's head that just came to surface for a moment before getting sucked down again.

"I am an angel of death, not life." She paused in her flight, but Raven didn't stop.

Not until the angel spoke again about thirty seconds later. "Well, maybe now I can help him."

"He's dead?" Raven fell to her knees. Hana trotted up beside her. The boy and the two wolves took their places behind Hana.

"Uh, lady? Who's that person with the wings?" the boy asked.

"Angel of death."

"I should see why these two animals are still here," the angel said. She landed and walked on the ground. She glanced at the boy when she passed. "Hmm, it's not your time yet, Colm. You still have things to do."

With that, she settled in front of the new wolves and rested a hand on each of their heads.

"I made it!" a masculine voice shouted.

Raven shivered as she turned and saw the ghost of the man climb out of the river. Hana growled again, but it lacked menace.

Raven shook her head and pointed at the angel still with the wolves. "That's the angel of death, so…I'm actually the only living person here."

The boy and the man stared at her in shock before opening their mouths, but the angel's blinding light cut through everyone. This time, it had a little heat to it. Raven welcomed it.

"The wolves didn't realize they were dead," the angel said. "They were merely protecting their den. They've gone now." She glanced at the man. "Henry, I'm afraid you won't be coming with me. I'll send a message to my demonic counterpart, and she'll be on her way to collect you. Please don't wander far."

"But I didn't do anything!" Henry shouted. "It wasn't my fault. That boy slipped!"

"I know," the angel said brightly. "That's why my comrade is coming to collect you. Raven, you may stay if you want to meet her. She won't hurt you, Colm or Hana. Until we meet again." The angel of death disappeared.

Raven sighed and shivered in the cold rain. "Let's go," she muttered to Hana.

"Wait! What about the pups?" Colm tried to tug at her sleeve, but his hand went straight through.

Hana pawed at her and whined. The rain fell even harder. With a groan, Raven stomped back upstream. "Well, where's the den?"

It turned out Colm's mother ran a nearby wolf sanctuary, which explained why he was so passionate about going back to the den. They found the two pups and dropped them off at the sanctuary. Raven knocked and ran before anyone answered. Colm stayed with the pups while Hana followed her home.

Hana stood sentinel as Raven tried to process what had happened. The wolf ghost let Raven hug her and cry on her after she called the park rangers to alert them the river had claimed two lives. She was to go in tomorrow for a statement, but for now, they treated themselves to a quiet evening of wine and snacks under a cozy blanket, listening to the rain.

For once, Hana took herself for a walk the next morning instead of accompanying Raven to the police. Raven couldn't help the stab of loneliness when the wolf ghost didn't jump in the car with her. So, she braved the station alone. She bit the inside of her cheek while she answered their questions, all the while wishing Hana was there.

When she came back, Hana and Colm waited for her. She really shouldn't have been so surprised to see both of them.

"Why don't you want to go home?" Raven asked after she settled. "The police are looking for your body now. They'll probably find it soon."

Colm just shrugged as he petted Hana. After a while, it was time for Raven to turn on her computer and begin the workday. She turned on the TV for her new guest, set a new bone down for Hana, and started to work.

They spent the day in companionable silence, but Colm inched closer to her throughout the day. By lunchtime, he stood behind her.

"Um, Raven?" He wrung his hands. "My mom can't see me."

She bit her lip. "I haven't met anyone else who could. I'm sorry." She tried to smile and hoped she didn't look sick. "Stay here as long as you need."

Hana huffed in agreement from her bed.

Colm just looked away and nodded.

The days passed in comfort. Colm was always next to Hana, petting her. Hana kept following Raven around, and for the first time in years, Raven didn't feel lonely. Every once in a while, Colm would grow melancholy and disappear for a time, but he always showed up in time for the afternoon hike. Raven altered their path so they wouldn't go by the river. The trio typically spent at least three hours outside, letting Hana lead them to different parts of the mountain. They trekked through the tall trees, coming upon different dens and nests.

Eventually, Raven bought a book so she and Colm could track the different animals and plants in the mountain. It gave him something to focus on other than his own death.

She knew she should talk to him about it, but every time she tried to bring it up, he disappeared. He would only reappear when it was time for Hana's hike.

Wednesdays became less nerve wracking. Hana always took a ride with her and snoozed under her desk. Sometimes Colm came, but he usually grew bored or depressed and disappeared.

Meanwhile, Raven stopped wondering about her coworkers' lives outside of work. She let herself listen to their stories and enjoy them for what they were. Hana enjoyed sniffing every single person she interacted with. It was cringy to watch, but at least the wolf ghost had something new to do on office days.

As time passed, Colm spent more and more time with them. He started running with Hana and having conversations with Raven that lasted longer than three sentences. He asked her for comics and requested specific shows on television.

"I think I'm not going to think about being dead too much," he announced randomly. He'd been gone most of the morning and returned just as Raven and Hana settled in for lunch.

"That sounds healthy," Raven offered.

"Well, it's not like I'm going to stop being dead," he said, sitting next to the wolf ghost. "Besides when I'm with you and Hana, it doesn't feel like I died, just like I moved or something."

"I'm glad you like it here," she said, staring at her lunch. "It's nice having company. Not so lonely."

Colm folded his arms. "I've been thinking about that, too. Raven. You're all by yourself. I never see you with any friends or anything. What did you do before me and Hana?"

Raven sighed, suddenly not hungry. She'd been focusing on making her home more comfortable for him and Hana. Of course, Colm would speak his mind directly. "Since I've moved here, it's just been me."

Maybe she'd get into the reason for moving and why she couldn't keep any friends, but today wasn't the day.

Hana rested her head on Raven's lap. After a few moments, her stomach relaxed enough to eat. Once she returned to her meal, Hana huffed and went back to chewing her toy. Colm scratched behind her ear.

"Do you ever feel like she's the one who chose us?" he asked.

"All the time." Raven grinned at him. He grinned back.

One day, weeks later, lying underneath the sun in a small meadow, Raven looked over at Hana and Colm playing in the tall grass. He smiled more often now, and she had a feeling Hana played a huge part in his recovery. While he never ate or slept like Hana did, he experienced the world as it was, just like the wolf ghost.

Raven prayed to the angel of death later that night.

The angel woke her up just before dawn. Raven wiped the sleep from her eyes and led her guest outside.

"This is unexpected," the angel said. "Colm isn't ready yet. And Hana doesn't need me to move on. She simply will when she's ready."

"It's not about that. I have a favor to ask you." Raven wrung her hands. "You know how you said there's a bunch of ghosts who got separated from their bodies and now they're just aimlessly wandering around?"

The angel tilted her head. "What did you have in mind?"

Raven smiled as she shared the details of her new idea.

The next week, while Colm visited his mother, Raven painted the finishing touches on her sign. Tomorrow, "Hana's Healing Hikes" would open. She put the sign out in the yard to dry. Hana trotted alongside her and huffed.

"We're going to start having a lot of company for our walks now. Maybe we'll even do group howls." Raven smirked at Hana before howling.

Hana only stared in judgment for a few seconds before joining.

The angel was bringing some wayward souls tomorrow. Raven had hung up a poster in the office last Wednesday and received two emails inquiring about nature walks after work. Something about those walks helped her and Colm focus on the here and now, and she figured the other dead and living might need a little dose of that every once in a while.

"You've started a whole thing here, the dead and living going on hikes in the mountains." Raven smiled. "I'd be smug if I were you."

Hana huffed once before starting another howl. Raven threw back her head and howled with her.

Maria D'Antonio-Reich wrote for local magazines after college before beginning a career of ultrasonography. Now working at a high-risk pregnancy clinic, she still spends her free time escaping into fictional worlds and making herself holiday skirts. She lives in New Orleans with her husband and two rescue dogs.

And Still He Runs

Robert MacWolf

"A Wolf met with a Dog, and, seeing that he was both well-fed and healthy, came to ask how. 'The Master feedeth me,' answered the Dog, 'come, and thou too shall eat thy fill.' So the Wolf went along with the Dog for a way. Presently the Wolf happened to ask, 'And what is it that maketh that bare mark upon thy neck?' The Dog answered, saying 'It is only where the collar weareth away at my fur.' Hearing this, the Wolf departed at once, saying," "BETTER TO STARVE IN FREEDOM, THAN TO LIVE IN CHAINS."

—Fables of Aesop, Perry Index 346.

It was cold, upon the steppes. It always had been, and always would be.

"How goes it with you, then?" Wolf asked.

"It goes well, I think," Dog said. It was less than two thousand years since he had taken this new name, and he was still getting used to it. "I help them hunt, and they feed me."

"That is no different," Wolf scoffed, "from having a pack."

"A pack that has fire? That can make any place they choose to den become, as long as they remain there, its own little summer?" Dog growled.

Wolf pawed the ground before he answered. "Summer always comes, in his own time." But he could not say it with great vehemence. The wind that blew down from the glaciers was very bitter, this evening.

"It is not..." Dog hesitated, "...it's not too late, you know. You can still come with me."

"You," Wolf's voice was as cold as the plains, "were never supposed to stay with them. You were supposed to get their attention, lead them to a mammoth like leading a badger to a burrowful of marmots, and then go hide yourself, with me, until they left. And then we scavenge the scraps! *That* was the plan, not this..." Wolf trailed off, lost for words. Words were a human matter, after all, and he was no expert in human things.

"Can you really not believe," Dog sounded hurt, which he had of late learned was a very useful skill, "that I found a better way?"

"And when they get hungry, and see how fat they've made you?" Wolf snarled, "Or cold, and envy how thick your coat has become?"

Dog shook his head. "They love me."

"They don't love," Wolf spat, "they're only human."

"Then why," Dog spat back, and there was a strange quality to his voice, Wolf had never before heard, "when I broke my leg, did they take me to the shaman, and he bound it with wood and sinews and holy herbs, and prayed over me, the same as he had his own pups?" It sounded as if a howl were chopped short. "Why when my son was born small and weak, did they not leave him to die but laid him in their own pups' arms, and fed him milk and fat, and kept him warm at night beside them in bed for weeks until he at last he opened his eyes and walked, long after the age our own poor brother starved in the cold because he couldn't keep up?" No, not chopped short, rather it was as if all the power of a howl were compressed down, as snow is hardened and solidified at the bottom of a footprint. "Why, when my mate died, did they lay her bones beside those of their own parents under the heaped stones," it was like being struck, but with a voice, and Wolf did not like it, "where they still lay flowers every year when we follow the herds southwest through the valleys?"

"You said," Wolf took a cautious step back, circling, as if it were not his brother he spoke to, but a lynx or a wolverine, "when '*we*' follow the herds?"

Dog stopped short. His ears went back, and his tail lowered. "I mean, well, you know I live with them. They follow the herds, so I go with, so…that's all I meant!"

Wolf took two more steps away. The snow crunched under his feet, and his breath steamed. "Someday," he said, "you will grow tired of this nonsense. You will find the wild still here, waiting, where it always has been and always will be. And I will be waiting there too, to say I told you so."

Wolf turned, without another word, and trotted away across the plains. Dog shook his head, and went the other way, toward the light of the human village.

"What nonsense," Wolf tossed a bone to Dog as he approached, "are they up to now?"

"It's a city, of course," Dog caught the bone, chewed once or twice to be polite, but was too excited with explanation to crack it yet. "Now that they're staying between the rivers, anyway, to grow the grain, they can make bigger, solider houses, that don't have to be carried about. Oh, you should see it: they can stand up to any storm, and the fires within never go out or have to be relit, they can just keep feeding them and they stay warm forever."

Wolf rolled his own bone between two back molars. "What is any of that to you or I?"

"Well, it means I have a new job!"

"Is that supposed to be a good thing?"

"I guard the herds!"

"I thought you were supposed to follow the herds." Wolf flicked an ear. "That was part of the nonsense you said last time."

"Well obviously we can't follow the herds now that there's the city, the city remains in one place, so the herds have to be kept there too. And that means they need to be guarded!" Dog puffed up his chest, proudly and puppyishly, and his tail wagged.

"Guard them from what?" Wolf looked serious.

"Why, from thieves and predators." Dog tilted his head.

"Oh," Wolf said.

"What does that mean?"

"It means," Wolf huffed, "Oh. And it means maybe don't go telling them about the snack I just shared with you."

Dog looked down at the bone between his paws. If it occurred to him how much it had tasted like the mutton scraps he'd had for breakfast, he gave no sign. "And how have you been?"

"Why, better than ever." Wolf grinned, for he'd noticed Dog suddenly change the subject. "The glaciers are going, the forests are spreading, there is more room than ever in the wild. If it weren't for having to keep an eye on you, why, I'd never need to come anywhere near a human."

Waraba was only a pup, and not yet expected to understand

things.

He didn't understand why Mother and Father had insisted he stop playing with his friend Wulu, who lived with the big loud humans. He didn't understand what they meant about "the rainy season" or "not as often as it used to," or their worry over the savannah turning to sand. He didn't understand why Mother and Father were so awestricken with the Stranger who had shown up at the beginning of the season.

But they were about to move south, toward someplace the Stranger called the river of gold. And Wulu's humans would be moving east, and one thing he did understand was that meant he had only one chance to say goodbye to his friend.

He was very surprised when the Stranger volunteered to escort him.

Wulu, and his parents, and their Humans had gathered under a Baobab. The humans startled when Waraba approached, but another Dog barked something at them—could Wulu and his family speak Human?—and they calmed, though they still looked uneasy.

The Stranger and this Other Dog did not speak, but they seemed to Waraba to know one another.

But Waraba didn't need to understand about that. He and Wulu said their farewells, and yipped excitedly about their journeys. Wulu said they were headed for another river, even mightier, at the other end of the sand-savannah, where floods meant there was no need of a rainy season, and Waraba suspected Wulu didn't understand what he was talking about.

But they were both only pups.

Tschitranga did not think much of wolves. They were good-for-nothing, untrustworthy blaggards, always looking to steal one of Master's sheep or break into Mistress's larder. They lurked in the ruins of Old Harappa, and nobody honest would live there. It made one wonder if they might know more than they should about the downfall of that illustrious city.

But this Wolf was travelling with Lord Kukkura, first among their kind, so she merely watched vigilantly, ready to raise the alarm at a moment's notice. The two of them proceeded along the road by moonlight, and talked of who-knew-what, before Wolf went northeast, into the hills and toward the abode of snow, and Lord Kukkura trotted back past her guard post.

Tschitranga greeted him politely, as was only proper, but not with great warmth. He'd been in the company of wolves, after all.

"Oh thank the gods you're alive!" Dog said.

"Of course I'm alive." Wolf shook his ears. "Why wouldn't I be alive? I'm not the one who's been forgetting everything he used to know about fending for himself."

"Why? The flood of course!" Dog insisted. "You were nowhere on the boat!"

"What are you talking about?" Wolf said.

"The flood came, and the Human built a boat and put all the animals aboard. I spent the whole time looking, and we were afloat seven days so I had plenty of time, and you were nowhere to be found." Dog sounded baffled that he needed to explain this. "Where were you? The place stank pretty badly, by the end, but I would've been able to find your scent."

"I've been on no boats."

"You must have, the flood washed the entire world away!" Dog insisted. "Only those aboard were spared."

"I've been in no floods, either." Wolf shrugged. "I don't know what to tell you. Do you mean when the sea broke though the Bosphorus? Or are you talking about Doggerland?"

"No, I mean the one that washed away the whole world."

"There's still a world. Obviously."

"Look, I don't pretend to understand it, but we can settle this: the gods—well, the ones that were grateful, at least—they made the Human immortal as thanks for saving all the animals, well except Raven of course, he didn't get aboard, he just flew away and brought back a stone that he dropped in the water, it turned into an island so the boat could land and…" Dog trailed off. "Anyway, the point is, we can go to the Human and you can ask him yourself! He'll explain it!"

"Absolutely not!" Wolf said. "You're just trying to talk me into getting domesticated. *And* your whole flood story is absurd. *And* who'd be stupid enough to let a human be immortal?"

"Of course you wouldn't understand," Dog rolled his eyes,

"about the gods."

"I know the gods," Wolf insisted. "I have nothing against the gods. It's the humans that can't be trusted."

"Well," Dog didn't know what to make of that, so he didn't try, "I'm glad you're safe, I was worried sick about you!"

Wolf decided to accept that for what it was worth.

The funeral procession of the noble Abutiu took an hour to pass, on its way to the Nile barges to the funerary temple up the river. The Pharaoh himself walked alongside. He could be observed to weep, though it would've been unwise for any of the humans to notice such tears.

Only Dog, settled in among the crowd, marked how the most powerful human in the world, held by all to be a living god himself, wept over the death of his dog.

He had no idea how to explain it to Wolf, though.

"It's funny," Dog pawed at the dirt on the side of the road, "they love me, they work with me, they see me every day. But it's you they put in all the stories."

Wolf looked back over his shoulder. "What do you mean?"

Dog had started the conversation by showing off his new collar. Polished leather, with brass studs and dyed-wool stitching. Wolf had done his best to try to find something about it to admire, since obviously Dog was very proud of it, but had largely failed to see the point of the thing. "Doesn't it chafe?" he'd asked

So Dog had found something else to talk about. "Well, there's all the humans over on Turtle Island, who've got I don't know how many accounts of how you taught them to hunt."

"Well…someone had to," Wolf grumbled. "And anyway that only counts as one."

"There's Fenris! And Hati and Skoll, and Freki and Geri, and—"

"Very well, I'm popular up north. So what?"

"Then there's whatever you were doing down by the Nile," Dog carried on, determined to have his say, "with the heart-weighing, and the gates to the Duat?"

"That wasn't me," Wolf protested. "That was Jackal."

"Really? I could've sworn…well, what about the Lycaons? Or Autolycus? Or what's this new one I hear about whatever a Vukodlak is?"

"I didn't do those. Those're just jealous humans wishing they could be me," Wolf insisted.

"That's what I'm saying." Dog was doing his best to talk very seriously but he couldn't help whining a little—who can help, when talking to his older brother, slipping into an old pup-like habit or two? "I'm the one who's faithful and loyal. I'm the one who lives with them, who protects them. But you're the one they can't get enough stories about."

"If you're looking to be told the humans are good and trust-worthy then you're talking to the wrong canine." Wolf scratched an ear, thoughtfully. "You didn't really think Anubis was me, did you?"

"You and Jackal always looked alike, and it'd been so long since I'd seen either of you," was the best Dog could come up with.

"Look, they're not stupid, and they're not oblivious." Wolf grudgingly decided to spare his brother's feelings. "Well, not com-pletely oblivious. They just…when they need a god, it's because they can't handle the wild and the world. They need to put a face on whatever part of it they're dealing with: on winter, or the forest, or on some river, or whatever. That means when they're going to their gods, they go to the wild, and that means going to my side of things. That's all. They've put you in the stories too."

"Like where?"

"There's Xolotl, for one. Just like you to be first in line for a ball game."

"Wait, hold on." Dog wasn't listening. "Someone watching us."

On the other side of the crossroads, beyond a field of wheat stubble, an old man was leaning on the wall of an olive grove, peering at the two of them.

"Huh." Wolf seemed unimpressed. "Well, so what if he is?"

"He might be planning," Dog's eyes narrowed, "a theft or a murder or something. What if he realizes I'm away from my post?"

"Aren't you supposed to be the one arguing the humans are good and trustworthy?"

"I'm just concerned." Dog's ears were up, his tail stiff, his eyes fixed on the old man. "If he recognizes my collar, he might know which house to rob—"

"He doesn't care about your collar any—" Wolf caught himself just in time to avoid saying 'any more than I do.' "He's probably just gonna go put us in a story. Ugly wastrel, isn't he?"

"As if you could tell humans apart." But Dog at least calmed himself. "Anyway, if he puts us both in a story, then we're even still. Oh, I almost forgot Romulus and Remus!"

"Ugh, I wish you had," Wolf sighed. "We'd all be better off if everyone forgot *those* two." He spat, disgusted, into the gravel at the roadside. "At least you've always got Cerberus."

Dog had to admit getting to be Cerberus was pretty good.

"There you are!" Dog jogged up around the bend in the road.

Wolf halted, further down the rough hillside, menacing and liminal like the bandits who preyed upon the silk merchants. Above and behind him were the mountains, the abode of snow, a mere remnant of the continent-dwarfing glaciers his youth had known. Ahead and below were the desert wastes. Neither was any more a place for a Wolf than it was for a Dog.

"What have you done?" Dog was already asking before he skidded to a stop. "They say you threatened to eat a man in Zhongshan!"

"And you followed me all the way from there?" Wolf scoffed. "Through the wars of gods-know-how-many kings chopping off gods-know-how-many bits of each other's kingdoms? For nothing but pride! You'd never catch wolves caring about something like that."

Dog decided not to speak of a Wolf who had refused to come in from the cold for twenty-seven thousand years out of pride.

"This man I supposedly threatened to eat," Wolf continued as he resumed walking west, "must have been important."

"He was just an itinerant scholar." Dog hastened to catch up.

"Well, whatever he was I didn't eat him!"

"His job doesn't matter," Dog insisted. "What matters is that you can't go around eating humans!"

"Ha! That's what he said." Wolf was fuming now. "We had a little debate on the topic, which I very thoroughly won. I would've been well within my rights to have eaten him: that's just as animals do, why should the humans think themselves an exception? And it's just as they do to the animals: ask any passing water buffalo how they treat him. Ask any fruit tree how much it gives them."

"I don't care," Dog growled, "who wins debates, I won't allow you to eat humans!"

"I crossed Zhou and Qin before you caught up with me," Wolf shook his head, "and I'll be further by dawn. If you mean to stop me from doing anything at all, why, you'll have to come with me." And for a moment there was, unmistakable, a whine in his voice, plaintive and lamentory as a howl at sunset on the other end of the tundra. "You…could. Come with me, you know."

Neither of them said that they were not so far, along the roads between the mountains and the desert, from the steppes where they had separated. Not what any species whose distribution spanned the globe would call 'far,' at least.

"I only came to warn you." Dog hung back while Wolf trotted on a few more paces. "The King of Qin—well, he's not just a King anymore, but anyway—he's banished you. All your descendants, he's decreed, from the all he lands of the Yellow River, between the ocean and the plateau."

"My children," Wolf snorted, "know how to take care of themselves. They don't heed human laws, and they don't need humans to look after them, unlike some. But fine! They want the place, they can have it! There's all the rest of the world that still belongs to the wild."

But he didn't storm off, just yet.

"I suppose I'll find you out there somewhere, then," Dog finally turned back east, "to see if you've changed your mind."

"Or when you're ready," Wolf continued west, into the desert like a bandit, "to change yours."

"You haven't even considered it?" Dog sounded frustrated, because he was, and annoyed, which he was also.

"Why would I?"

"The story I heard," Dog's tone was aggrieved, "was that you'd met the Saint of Assisi, and promised to stop attacking people if the town would feed you. And I thought, why, I've heard that proposal before!" He took another step toward Wolf, as if in hope all the misunderstandings would prove to be a matter of not being near enough. "I thought someone had got through to you."

"There was a dirty, scrawny beggar who ranted at me," Wolf sniffed, "while the whole town watched, if that's who you mean. Going on about 'thou hast even dared to devour man, for which thou deservest to be hanged,' usual human nonsense."

Dog wasn't sure what to say. All the congratulations, the grateful welcome, the long longed-for reconciliation he'd come looking for, and been ready to give in turn, had proved phantasmal. "Well then," he reached for the first thing that occurred to him to say instead, "what were you doing in Umbria, if not meeting the Saint?" Unfortunately, that just made him sound suspicious and accusatory.

Wolf grinned. "I had some work to do. I'm not about to let what happened in Qin happen again. And I'm not the only one who's been crowded out by your oh-so-clever humans."

Dog wondered if he'd been right to sound suspicious and accusatory.

"There's talks of an alliance." Wolf explained, "Keep the wild among us wild, give the tame ones a little more leverage, and make everything a little less under human control. It was Fox's idea. He talked to Chicken, Lion, and Badger, and came to me next. I was in the Umbrian highlands to meet with Donkey, who was stuck doing some kind of holiday theatrics for your Saint of Assisi fellow. Putting the 'ass' in 'Assisi,' I suppose."

"Please tell me you didn't make that joke in front of Donkey," Dog sighed.

"Well, we didn't actually meet," Wolf admitted. "She wasn't eager to be alone with a wolf. Apparently some animals, even after going domesticated," he looked hard at Dog, "remember how things worked in the wild."

"There's no need to be so grim."

"It isn't grim! It's honest!" Wolf insisted. "Anyway, I'll tell them to send a less frightening envoy, Hare maybe, and then I'm heading north to talk to Bear."

Wolf trotted away, up the road toward the mountains, before Dog could work out how to ask how this alliance was any different from his arrangement with the humans.

Dog lay on a sandbar piled against the northeast bank of the Dniester.

"Is that you?" Wolf stood on the other side, just beyond the dense pines.

Dog flailed, scrambled to his feet, gouged the dense sand into the water. "Stay away!" he yelped.

"I…" Whatever Wolf might have been expecting, this wasn't it. "I'm not going to hurt you, I'm all the way across the—"

"No, I might hurt you!" Dog whimpered. "I might have it!"

Wolf tilted his head. "What on earth are you talking about?"

"The scourge!" Dog cowered among the reeds, back bent, head low, ears flat. "If you come anywhere near me you might get it!"

"Is this like when you thought the world had been washed away in a flood that didn't happen?"

"For god's sake you have to listen!" Dog yelped. "It's horrible! They're all dying!" His yelps turned to outright weeping. "They're all dying and I can't help and I can't stop it!"

Wolf slowly sank to his haunches. "Alright, I won't cross the river if you don't want. Just tell me what you're talking about."

"There's a sickness." Dog panted, fast and frantic, eyes wide. "I…I was down by the coast, by Theodoria and Gazaria, and there was an invasion, and I was just trying to stay out of the way! But…" he trailed off and stared into the water.

"There have been plagues before," Wolf began.

"You don't understand." Dog leapt to his feet. "There are towns and villages entirely empty, no one left alive! Not just humans, cats and rats and dogs, my own children, and…I watched them die! I loved them and they died and I couldn't help!"

"Alright, alright, I believe you!" Even at the worst times, Wolf had never seen Dog like this. "What would you have me do?"

"Warn them, somehow," Dog wailed. "It may be too late for the humans but if your descendants can get word to mine…what about your alliance? With Lion and Fox…and Badger, wasn't it?"

"That, well, that didn't last." Wolf frowned. "Shouldn't have trusted Fox: all just one of his schemes, from the start. But…I'll send what warning I can, maybe some will believe me. What do I say?"

Dog pulled himself back to his feet and calmed himself. "Well. Say…it's travelling west. About Horse's walking pace, faster along the seashore. Say it's not safe near anywhere it is. Tell them to take to the wild! Don't try reclaiming human places, I don't know if it might be lying in wait, after everyone in a town dies, for anyone who tries to move in. And…I know you don't care about them, but…if anyone, *anyone*, can warn the humans somehow?"

"I understand." Wolf's voice was grim. "I'll tell mine to take your descendants into their packs, if they decide to flee."

"That…" Dog almost began to wail again. "God of grief, that might be for the best. But don't let them get infected!"

"And what about you?"

"I'll…stay here. Wait to see if it comes for me. If I already have it, then it's already too late."

"You'll survive." Wolf's grim voice grew grimmer. "You've survived near thirty thousand years under the hands of the most ungrateful bastards ever to set foot on this world, you will survive this." But then it softened. "And I don't smell any sickness on you. Except fear."

"I don't know," Dog said, though he sounded somewhat comforted. "I don't smell it either, but I don't know if I trust my nose anymore."

"That's the most frightening thing you've said!" Wolf said, and he took the warning and ran.

Dog remained by the river alone, and tried not to wonder if he would ever see Wolf again.

It was after sunset, in the woods, in what some were determined to call 'New England.' The outlines of the bare branches were black against the darkening crimson sky.

Dog stopped short, at the crossroads. He'd seen a pair of yellow eyes shine, for a just moment, at the edge of the forest. "Is that you?"

Wolf slunk from the shadows. In front of the evening light he was like a patch of midnight cut into the shape of a wolf.

"It is you!" Dog wagged and bowed. "I feared I'd never see you again."

But Wolf was not so excited. "Are you with them?"

Dog stopped wagging. "What?"

"Are you," Wolf repeated, and he was growling in earnest now, "here with the humans?"

"I've always been with the humans." Dog answered tentatively.

"You know that."

"You have *not* always been with the humans," Wolf howled. "You used to be with *me!*"

"Why does that suddenly matter?" Dog barked. "You never had this grievance before!"

"Don't you tell me what grievances I didn't have." Wolf bared his teeth.

"I thought you'd be happy to see me."

"You thought I'd be happy to—" Wolf was lost for words, which remained a human thing at which he was inexpert. "They're trying to drive me to extinction."

"Oh, there've always been hunters—"

"I didn't say hunters," Wolf snapped. "I heard them say it myself, when they didn't know I was listening from the undergrowth. They want every wolf on the continent dead."

Now Dog was lost for words.

"I've said it for ages." Wolf paced a slow, furious circle, clockwise, around Dog. "The humans don't love you. They don't love each other. And they'll never stop hating me! Well here's some that've gone and proved me right. Good for me!" He spat.

"You can't expect them to love you when you prey on their livestock,"

"I don't expect them to love me. I expect them to love *you!* I expect them to love each other! Loving their own kind ought to be an easy test to pass, right? But *these* humans," Wolf's snarl was all the angrier for its incredulity, how dare Dog need this explained? "are trying to fully wipe out the *other* humans. Why the hell would I trust them, welcome them, when they won't spare their own kind. Their own pack! Or, hell, maybe they aren't their own kind anymore, maybe they've split into being something else! *Just like you did!*"

They remained staring at one another for just long enough that they might have been about to fall to fangs and claws.

But instead Wolf slipped into the darkness and was gone.

Dog followed a party of humans with clubs. They would've preferred guns, of course, but it wasn't legal for anyone of their estate to carry anything more warlike than a kitchen knife, so these would have to do.

If Dog had a preference it had not been consulted.

For a year now these farmers and cowherds had been terrorized by what they called La Bête du Gévaudan. They could not agree on what it was. They could not agree on whether there were more than one. They had no idea why it killed.

Dog feared he knew the what, and the why. He prayed he was wrong.

When dawn approached and they turned back toward town, empty handed, Dog breathed a sigh of relief.

He wasn't here.

It wasn't him. He had killed, and been killed by, no one.

But once all the poor frightened humans were guided back to their individual dens, and Dog set off across the fields toward the next village, he saw a familiar pair of ears atop a lanky silhouette in which yellow eyes burned.

Wolf turned and vanished into the forest before they were close enough to speak.

The sled was crashed and abandoned not far from the frozen lake. The humans called this place Destruction Bay, but that no longer mattered. The pack had been here first.

Väŋiv and his brothers, sisters, siblings and cousins surrounded the wreckage without hurry. There was no whiff of danger here. And the Ancient One was unconcerned.

The pack needed no permission, no advice, to know what the Ancient One who walked with them would have them do. Väŋiv had been in awe of Him, at first, but He'd taught them much, in the season He had spent with them, and they had gone from shivering and starving to fat and healthy. Two of Väŋiv's sisters, and one cousin, bore His litters, proudly, were busily gossiping to one another about where and when to den. Väŋiv himself had been suffered to sleep curled up beside the Ancient One, more than once.

The humans feared them more, now, but saw them less.

And they had finally stopped scavenging in the trash piles around Silver City or Hane's Junction. The Ancient One had seemed relieved at that.

The wreckage of the sled was swiftly torn to pieces. What few edibles were on it—dried fruit, salted meat, tallow, hides—were devoured. What was not edible—a couple cloth bags of strange glittering sand, a smaller one of dark grey powder which made Väŋiv sneeze, a gunstock, a great mass of papers—was torn and tug-of-warred to scraps.

The remains of the human trapped and frozen beneath the sled were also devoured. Perhaps this had been his sled, or perhaps he'd been abandoned here by those whose sled it was. In either case he didn't need it anymore.

The pack looked up when they heard the crunch of snow.

A single husky was peering tentatively around a red cedar. She was thin and bedraggled. The remnants of a harness trailed from her back, in some places broken, in some plainly chewed through. Her eyes were terrified, but also hopeful.

The pack forgot the sled. Their hackles raised, their lips curled. But before anyone attacked, Väŋiv saw Grandmother look to the Ancient One for wordless advice.

He seemed to spend a long time considering this dog.

At length Wolf let this husky approach, sniff his nose, lick his jowls.

Väŋiv made it his charge to make this new wolf welcome. By the time the Ancient One left the pack to move on, with his blessing, she, now properly named Nataw, had become a great favorite with the newborn pups, and had privately hinted to Väŋiv that she ought to have a litter of her own.

Väŋiv blessed the memory of the scent of the Ancient One all his days.

Duquessa lay in the shade beside the bench at the bus stop in Surquillo. It was her duty to wait for Father to appear here, in the evening, and walk home with him. But it had now been a year since he had begun failing to do that.

Duquessa was not a fool. She knew the strangers, other humans who were nothing to her, thought she did not understand that Father was not coming back, that he had died. But that made no difference. This was where she waited for him, and that is what she meant to do, thank you. Now if you were not going to give her a treat, then kindly be about your business. She was waiting.

Duquessa was no longer young: she had no doubt she was no

longer waiting for Father to come to her, she was waiting to go to him. That made no difference. And there was always the possibility that he would somehow come back, after all.

Soon it would get dark, and she would rise, huffily, and walk home along the route she'd taken with Father for many years, and sleep beside the oven where Mother had used to hold court, though now Mother's second-oldest's mate had taken that place. Well, she was welcome to it. If there was one thing Duquessa understood it was doing as one had always done in memory of those who had gone before you.

But this evening she had a visitor.

Duquessa sought no advice from el Perrísimo, and he professed none to offer her. This was merely an honorary visit, ceremonial, in recognition of her great loyalty and faithfulness. He spoke politely of others of their kind whose loyalty and dedication had merited such honors: Waghya, Greyfriars Bobby, Hachi. "It was gratifying to know," she had told el Perrísimo, "such deeds were not forgotten. The humans, much as one loves them individually, are not good at remembering the things that really matter. You can't rely on them to be loyal and faithful to an absent loved one, alas, even after that absence grew into years."

El Perrísimo, Duquessa thought, had seemed pensive when he took his leave and vanished toward the Andes foothills.

Dog followed rumors, of course. He sought out places he thought Wolf might go. He asked, when he saw them, Boar, Hare, Crow, and even Fox.

But most things one finds are found by chance.

The vacant lot behind the gas station was weed-grown and trash-strewn. The air was nearly as dusty as the ground. Dog had only meant to take a walk while the travelers he was with, somewhere between Missouri and California, took their turns with the untrustworthy restroom and considered buying Hershey bars, but there he was.

Wolf got to his feet. His coat was thin and dusty, and his ribs were showing. The three coyotes who had been lounging beside him turned wary ears toward Dog, but a muttered word from Wolf and they slunk away into the sagebrush.

"You don't look so good." Dog had never been much for holding in his feelings.

"Well," Wolf huffed, "it's been lean times."

"Where have you been?" Dog tried to open gently, because Wolf didn't seem to be angry anymore. Maybe things could be worked out.

"It doesn't matter where I've been," Wolf said, heavily, listlessly, and it was worse than anger. "The story's the same everywhere. There's no space left, they're filling it all with suburbs. There's no deer left, they're driving them all out for pastures. There's no forests, just asphalt and interstates and powerlines."

"They can do amazing things with the powerlines," Dog offered. There was no need to ask who 'they' were.

"Just like they used to do with fire, and now the world is a furnace and air itself is smoke." Wolf shook his head. "How long before they do so many amazing things with the powerlines that the night sky can't be seen?"

Dog nosed toward Wolf, who did not bother to react. "Are you hungry?"

Wolf turned an expressionless face to him. "I suppose."

"The humans I'm travelling with, they're, well, they're…" Dog had to stretch his vocabulary, which was unfair, since these humans themselves hadn't yet settled on a word for what they were. "They're unconventional. I think they'd be willing to have a wolf travel with them, a ways, and they've been very generous with the food so far."

"That's your answer still?" Wolf asked. "Domestication? The Master feedeth me, come, and thou too shall eat thy fill?"

"That's not what I said," Dog said. "But if it was, would I be wrong? Look at you, you're starving!"

Wolf closed his eyes. "There's those who would say it's better to starve in freedom than to live in chains."

"And is it?" Dog asked.

Wolf didn't answer.

"A long time ago," Dog said, quietly, "my brother told me the day would come when I was tired of my nonsense, and when it did the wild would still be there, and he'd be there, to tell me he told me so. Well, where is it?" Dog looked pointedly about, from chain link fence to sun-bleached asphalt to discarded truck tire. "Where's the wild, brother? Staying out in the cold will not keep you in the wild, it will only keep you cold."

"As long as I refuse," Wolf's voice, was like thunder so distant it was all but inaudible, "then I'm still wild. And that's enough wild for me."

"And if you die?"

"Then at least," Wolf followed the coyotes into the sagebrush, "I die wild."

Only a week or two ago, they met in a place whose name had once meant 'village' but had expanded from coast to coast, as human things tended to do. It was cold, there, but it always had been, and hopefully always would be.

"How goes it with you, then?" Wolf asked.

"I don't know, honestly," Dog replied. "I suppose things have been worse. But I'm worried."

"You look worried," Wolf said. He was doing better, looking stronger, than last Dog had seen him. National Parks and Species At Risk Acts suited him. Dog would have, in earlier days, thrown that in Wolf's face, said it was proof that yes, humans could feel love, but it had been less than a hundred since his brother had been speaking to him again, so he kept his peace.

"I don't think the humans," Dog said instead, "are doing well. I used to think they would last forever, but we thought the glaciers would last forever, and look what the humans did to them. Maybe the humans are like flowers, everywhere in their season, and then gone."

"It's been," Wolf huffed, "a mightily long season, then."

"The end of a season comes in its own time, though," Dog carried on. "The strongest ones don't seem to think they're the same kind as the rest of them, resent having to be in the same world as them. I don't understand why." He braced for Wolf to say he'd told him so.

"Have they hurt you?"

"No!" Well, no more than they always had. "They just…it feels like… It's like in the days of the disease, or just before the flood, or in old Harappa. As if everything is going to fall apart at any moment."

"Or like how it ended with Romulus and Remus." Wolf was

disappointed and unsurprised in advance. "But you're not going to leave them,"

"I can't," Dog said. "What would they do without me?"

Wolf turned to look down over the forest to the shining city on the coast, the islands beyond, and the sun setting behind them. "Find some way to survive, I suppose. Like any other animal does in the wild."

"But they aren't in the wild." Dog was confused. "Haven't you always said they're, by definition, the opposite of the wild?"

"Aye. As long as I refuse to go to them, I am the wild, and the wild has me, at least, to be. But if they do tear down all they've built, if it does all fall apart, then there'd be no more *them* for me to go to. All the world would be the wild." He did not add 'as it ought to have stayed' but he clearly thought it. "Where does that leave them? What then do they become? Just another animal in the wild." He should've been gloating, shouldn't he? But he was not. "So if they must face the wild...they'll need someone to show them how to live there. They'll need someone there to say he told them so."

"You've never told them so," Dog said, "you've just told me."

"True," Wolf said. "Just you."

Dog understood.

They sat beside one another, in silence, for some time. The wind through the trees was cold, but not cruelly so. Eventually the sun set and the night began. The city below was a beacon, like a bonfire on a long-ago steppe.

"Till next we meet, take care of yourself." Dog trotted back down toward the light of the human city.

"And you take care of them," Wolf answered, who ran off his separate way.

~ * 🐾 * ~

Rob MacWolf lives somewhere in North America, waiting for the world to end. His other works include *You Look Lost, Pup* and *Of Late Belonging*, available from Fenris Publishing, short stories in anthologies from the Furry Historical Fiction Society, and numerous stories on *The Voice of Dog* podcast.

More Books from
WolfSinger Publications

The Enclave – Mark Thomas

"It's a lovely wall, we've got no complaints there."

Allan Ripke wakes on the bank of a tranquil river, surrounded by cheerful strangers, quaint shops, and a towering wall that encloses everything.

He doesn't know who he is. He doesn't know how he got there. But no one seems to think that's strange—not even when names change overnight, newspapers print impossibilities, and fog rolls in thick and unnatural. The residents smile, nod, and tell him what a lovely wall it is.

As Allan stumbles through the pleasant absurdity of The Enclave, memories slip and identities morph. Is it sanctuary, experiment, or prison?

Step inside. But be warned: once you enter the Enclave, you may not leave the same.

Blue Grass Dreams Aren't for Free – Gerri Leen

These racehorses can talk, race riderless, and manage their own careers thanks to genetic manipulation in the past intended to make Thoroughbreds hardier. But living free doesn't mean living without problems of the career and family (both blood and found) kind. Nor does it mean they are free from having to interact with humans.

In this mosaic novel, stories of two very different stallions and their friends and families (both four legged and two) interconnect to explore how these horses deal with career decisions, love, family, retirement, illness, and having to find alternate paths when flat racing does not prove a profitable or fulfilling life choice.

Not all roads lead to the winner's circle, and even when they do, winning doesn't always equal happiness without someone to share it with.

Midnight Menagerie — edited by Carol Hightshoe

Step right up, dear traveler—your ticket to the extraordinary awaits.

Beneath the striped canopies of the *Midnight Menagerie*, wonders stir and nightmares awaken. Strongmen flex their might, fortune tellers spin futures, and acrobats defy the stars. But if it is shadows you seek—if you are drawn to the hush of velvet-draped corners where the line between spectacle and sorcery blurs—then step closer.

Here, within these pages, beasts from beyond the veil prowl in cages not quite strong enough. Carnival performers barter in secrets instead of silver. Mystics weave illusions that refuse to fade, and every whispered promise carries a cost. From the neon glow of alien menageries to the flickering lantern light of haunted carnivals, *Midnight Menagerie* is a collection of the eerie, the wondrous, and the strange.

So take your seat, dear reader. The lights are dimming, the curtains are rising…and the show is about to begin.

The World of the Moho — Tyree Campbell

Aldon (Allie) McIntyre, a white American geologist with a thirst for adventure, and Thadie Mayane, a Black South African mining supervisor with a commanding presence, are exploring the depths of an abandoned mine when the floor collapses, hurling them into an extraordinary realm known as Below. Nestled between the Earth's crust and mantle, this vast world is home to breathtaking landscapes, intelligent species—some friendly, others predatory—and dangers unlike anything they've ever imagined.

Forced to rely on each other for survival, Allie and Thadie must navigate treacherous terrain, fend off alien predators, and face the looming threat of capture by those who see them as little more than slaves. As they search for the legendary passage back to Above, their uneasy alliance will be tested by the perilous environment—and the prejudices and mistrust they each carry.

Will they overcome the trials of Below and find their way back Above? Or will this stunning and dangerous world consume them entirely—if they don't destroy each other first?

Mars in Carnage — William Paul Lazarus

Humanity's dream of colonizing Mars quickly becomes a fight for survival. Mission director Lt Col. John Hathaway sends astronauts Aadya "Kate" Khatun and Hamza "Arti" Artsruni to explore and establish a foothold on the Red Planet. One astronaut is killed, during what appears to be an alien attack; the other makes a solo, dangerous return to a hero's welcome on Earth.

Over a century later a Martian colony has firmly established—the underground city of Katarti, Cecil Townley, a tour guide for visitors to Mars is captured by a band of terrorists trying to end what they believe are horrible governmental actions on Mars. Hiding in underground tunnels, they begin their attack with Townley forced to be their guide. Their actions introduce him to a world he never knew existed, far from the innocent tale he had been telling newcomers for years.

Cowboy Up — edited by Carol Hightshoe

Cowboy Up gathers stories that celebrate the timeless tradition of rodeo. The dust, the grit, the glory—it's all here.

From the echoes of the past to the rodeo arenas of today, these stories will take you on a wild ride through the highs and lows of rodeo life. You'll share in their triumphs and their heartbreaks. From the unbreakable bond between rider and horse to the courage it takes to get back in the saddle after a fall, this anthology is a tribute to the spirit that keeps rodeo alive.

But this book isn't just about telling stories. It's about giving back. Eighty-Five percent of proceeds from Cowboy Up will be donated to the Justin Cowboy Crisis Fund, a non-profit organization dedicated to helping injured rodeo athletes get back on their feet. Your purchase helps support those who risk it all in the arena, offering them a lifeline when they need it most.

So saddle up. Dive into these tales of resilience, heart, and the cowboy way. With every story, you're not just reading about rodeo —you're helping to keep its spirit alive.

Homefall Search — Dana Bell

Charged with finding the best place for a new Homefall, Jehna

Talon searched on Saris, a world located in the Tashiti Nebula. Along with her Arial shapeshifter companions, she goes into the Ghost Mountains to find a specific valley, only to become trapped during a storm and encounters a native dragon.

With local rancher Harrison Talbot she negotiates the price for the land. Brides, for him and his hands. As her uncle taught her, there's always a need to be filled. Traveling to Aris and with the help of a local contact, she finds women willing to brave the frontiers of space.

Returning to Ronia, home of the Talons, she learns opposition from the other clan leaders may stop the dream she had of becoming a clan leader. They argue there are too few Rovers, and she'll never succeed.

Could they be right, despite her already finding the ideal location?

The Dragon's Hoard 3 — edited by Carol Hightshoe

In this anthology, twenty-six authors weave enchanting stories of dragons—from the fierce and fire-breathing to the wise and benevolent. Enter a treasure trove of tales where dragons reign supreme, and hoards are more than mere gold.

Discover hidden gems of wisdom and magic within these lairs. Feast on tales that shimmer with magic, adventure, and the timeless allure of dragons. Explore the myriad treasures dragons hold dear and the legends that surround them.

From heartwarming tales of friendship and loyalty to thrilling adventures filled with danger and magic, these tales offer something for every dragon lover. Whether they are guardians of treasure, seekers of knowledge, or forces of nature: the dragons in this collection will ignite your imagination.

The Dragon's Hoard 2 — edited by Carol Hightshoe

Welcome to realms where dragons reign, treasures abound, and every adventure leads to magic. Explore stories that spark the imagination and might just awaken the dragon within. Are you brave enough to face the dragon and claim your prize?

From the unyielding grip of ancient magics to the cunning of those who seek dragons, their treasure or both—each story weaves a rich tapestry of magic and lore.

Whether it's a battle for survival, the forging of an unlikely alliance, or a humorous twist on hoarding habits, our authors invite you to delve into realms where dragons not only hoard gold but also secrets, spells, and sometimes, even friendships. After all, in the world of dragons, not all treasures are silver and gold—some are stories waiting to be told.

The Hounds of Ardagh – Laura J Underwood

Ginny Ni Cooley never desired more than the simple life she had, living in Tamhasg Wood and using her magic to occasionally assist the folk of Conorscroft while putting up with the machinations of the ghost of her former mentor Manus MacGreeley. But her peace is shattered one night with the arrival of a lad who is fleeing a pack of red-gold hounds led by a hound-shaped demon known as Nidubh.

So much for peace and solitude. By rescuing Fafne MacArdagh, Ginny becomes wrapped in the fabric of an intrigue involving a family feud, a traitorous son, and a blood mage named Edain who is determined to keep her soul. It is she who cast a spell on Fafne's family and household and transformed the MacArdaghs into hounds.

Ginny gives Fafne her word to take him to Caer Keltora so they can report the matter to the Council of Mageborn. But Edain is determined to keep her secret and her soul intact and moves to thwart Ginny at every turn.

For Ginny Ni Cooley who has faced many bogies, dealing with a demon, a bloodmage and the Dark Lord of Annwn will be no easy task. But she will do what she must to undo Edain's spells. If not, Manus' soul will become part of Arawn's Cauldron of Doom. Ginny will become a demon's feast, and poor Fafne will join the Hounds of Ardagh.

Wee Folk and Wise: A Fairies Anthology
– edited by Deby Fredericks

All over the world, fairy tales are told.
There are big fairies and little fairies.
Ugly fairies and pretty fairies.

Wise fairies and silly fairies.

Sweet fairies and scary fairies.

Seventeen authors share their own fantastic fairy tales in this magical collection. What kind of fairy will you meet here?

Infinity – Ted Pennella

In the distant future, when peace between humanity and the artificial intelligences their ancestors created has been settled, Conrad Conner tries to live a quiet and unassuming life in orbit about Jupiter on the city-station Socrates' Odyssey. When Conner's attempt to create a prototypical communication artificial for use by the Sol-Humana Confederation's Stellar Fleet gets derailed by the attempted murder of the very artificial he's created, his life spirals into a mad flight back to Earth to try and save at least his sister's children, if not his sister herself. Past failures and heartaches resurface as seemingly unconnected dots become a plot by the First Admiral to steal not just power over the Confederation, but a secret Conner holds within himself.

A secret not even Conner knows about.

And more – check out our books at

www.wolfsingerpubs.com

www.ingramcontent.com/pod-product-compliance
Lightning Source LLC
Chambersburg PA
CBHW071426260626
47170CB00008B/2607